# the Spider Catcher

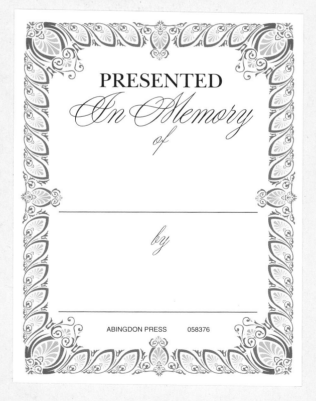

**PRESENTED**

*In Memory*

*of*

_____

*by*

_____

ABINGDON PRESS          058376

## Other Books by Gilbert Morris

# GILBERT MORRIS

## the Spider Catcher

**ZONDERVAN**®

**ZONDERVAN**.com/
**AUTHORTRACKER**
*follow your favorite authors*

*The Spider Catcher*
Copyright © 2003 by Gilbert Morris

Value Edition 978-0-310-28798-8

Requests for information should be addressed to:
Zondervan, *Grand Rapids, Michigan 49530*

---

**Library of Congress Cataloging-in-Publication Data**

Morris, Gilbert.
    The spider catcher / Gilbert Morris.
       p.   cm.
    ISBN-10:  0-310-24698-9
    ISBN-13:  978-0-310-24698-5
    1. United States—History—Revolution, 1775–1783—Naval operations—Fiction. 2.
Shipbuilding industry—Fiction. 3. Welsh Americans—Fiction.
4. Physicians—Fiction. I. Title.
PS3563.O8742S69   2003
813'.54—dc21

                                         2003002521

---

Published in association with the literary agency of Alive Communications, Inc., 7680 Goddard Street, Suite 200, Colorado Springs, CO 80920.

*Interior design by Beth Shagene*

*Printed in the United States of America*

---

08  09  10  11  12  13  14  •  21  20  19  18  17  16  15  14  13  12  11  10  9  8  7  6  5  4  3  2  1

To Helen Cook
A charming, beautiful, witty, and wonderful lady.
I wish I'd met you fifty years or so ago
so that I could have had the pleasure of your company
for a long time! Better late than never!
And thanks to you, Pat and Clint, for your warmth
and hospitality.

# THE Spider Catcher

# Part
## -1-

# Chapter One

"YOU MARK MY WORDS, REES KENYON, THESE RESURRECTION MEN will be the death of science!"

"Resurrection men?" The speaker was a lanky young man with coal black hair and blue eyes so dark that they seemed black as well. He put down the book he was holding and looked up at the older man with a quizzical expression. "What's a resurrection man, Dr. Crawther?"

"Well, devil fly off!" Dr. Howell Crawther paused long enough to wheel around and stare at his companion. The physician was seventy-two now, and the snow of these many years was in his hair. He was almost fragile, though in his youth he had been an athlete of some renown. The pipe clamped in his teeth jutted out at an acute angle and glowed like a miniature furnace as he puffed at it vigorously. "You mean to sit there and tell me you don't know what a resurrection man is?"

"No sir. I don't believe I've ever heard the term."

"Well, there is dull you are!" Crawther threw himself down almost violently in the chair across from young Kenyon and shoved the books away from the cluttered desk, making a place for him to plant his elbows. Taking the pipe from his mouth with one hand, he jabbed it toward Rees as if it were a weapon. "Resurrection men," he said sternly, "are men who sell corpses."

"Sell dead bodies? To whom do they sell them?"

"Why, to doctors like me, of course!" Dr. Crawther's face expressed disgust. "How do ye think I could know what's on the inside of a person if I had never looked?"

"You mean, Doctor, you're going to buy a corpse, is it?"

"I scarce can afford to buy one by myself these days, and I was counting on this one. It was a young woman, only twenty-two. She died of liver disease." Dr. Crawther jammed his pipe back into his mouth and, reaching up with both hands, grabbed his thatch of white hair. He had an odd habit of seeming to lift himself off the earth with both hands in this manner, which was both comical and alarming. Lowering himself back into the chair, he said, "I'll have to let Dr. Preslow and Dr. Donner share that lovely corpse — but they do hack away so frightfully!"

"But . . . where would these resurrection men be getting bodies?"

"Where would you go to get a dead body, boy?"

"To the cemetery, I suppose."

"Well, it's a bit of sense you have left! You're right, that's where they get most of them."

"You mean they just go . . . dig them up?"

"There's no other way to get them out of the ground, boy! But you have to be careful with these resurrection men. Sometimes they bring a corpse so old and stringy, it's of little worth. I've been cheated more than once by those scoundrels!" Dr. Crawther could not keep still, for even at his age he was compelled by nervous energy. He paced the floor, leaving a trail of smoke from his pipe and jabbing the air as he continued to speak of the necessity of dissection. "Ah, give me a nice, fresh corpse; still warm would be best of all. A fine pauper from the workhouse, with little fat on him — there's your gem of a corpse!"

Rees Kenyon had been sitting at the table, a book open in front of him, but now he gave his full attention to his mentor. The room he sat in, Dr. Crawther's office, was cluttered almost to a terminal condition. The four walls were hidden by painted shelves built all the way to the ceiling and were stuffed with the tools of the physician's profession. Books of every size and shape bulged from many of the shelves, along with manuscripts, newspapers, and periodicals, all apparently in no order. Other shelves held boxes, packages, and tubes large and small. Some had labels on the outside, and others displayed merely a blank face to the world. Two long tables flanked the shelves on the north and east side of the room, covered with flasks, knives, several saws, some still showing traces of blood. Forceps, probes, retractors, and dressings of all sorts were thrown haphazardly across the surfaces, mixed with a variety of other instruments used by physicians. "But Doctor, breaking the law are you? Isn't it against the law to sell bodies?"

"Against the law? Of course it's against the law! And worse than that — it's expensive." Dr. Crawther spoke so rapidly that only long practice had enabled Rees to understand him at times. "Oh, it's dear, these corpses, but a man's got to learn the body, boy." Once again he came to a halt. Using his pipe as a pointer, he jabbed it emphatically toward his young friend. "Some so-called physicians do all their practicing on live patients. Why, every man makes a mistake, doctors no less than others. If you make a mistake on a corpse, it's no matter. But when you're cutting into a living human being, there's careful you must be!"

Dr. Crawther continued his diatribe, which was his manner of teaching. At times he was like a butterfly, fluttering from idea to idea with confusing rapidity. At other times he was more like a bull, charging straight forward as if he would implant the principles of medicine in his young pupil by brute force. Sometimes he would even catch Rees by the hair and shake the young man's head back and forth as if that somehow assisted the importation of knowledge.

Finally he picked up the bottle on the table, poured himself a tumbler full of pale, amber ale, and sitting down, gulped at it thirstily as he looked at young Kenyon with a steady gaze. "Maybe I'll let you watch while I dissect this one, if I decide to buy it." The idea of the high price of corpses seemed to overwhelm him. "It's shocking how corpses have risen — shocking indeed! The villain had the face to ask me four guineas. I told him in no uncertain terms that his greed was going to stifle science. But I'll pay it, I suppose. I need a good, fresh liver to show you, Rees."

Dr. Crawther gulped down several swallows of ale, then studied the young man who sat across from him. They had become good friends over the years, and Dr. Crawther had literally watched young

Kenyon from the time he was born, for he had brought him into the world. He lived only a short distance away from the Kenyon family and had been their family physician for years. There was satisfaction in the old man's eyes as he took in the lean figure of Rees Kenyon. Rees was twenty now and his looks were deceptive. He was slightly over six feet three and was so lanky that he looked weak. His hands were marvelous — long fingers, tendons standing out like steel cords, calluses from his work in the shipbuilding trade. In that long, lean body, Crawther knew, there was a strength that was surprising.

The face of Rees Kenyon was homely, not handsome in the least. His eyes were deep-set, and his cheeks slightly sunken, giving him a craggy look older than his years. His mouth was wide and mobile, with a vertical line at each corner. High cheekbones and a high-domed forehead lent a look of strength, and his hair was coarse and coal black, as were his eyebrows — and his beard, if he had ever decided to grow one. His hair was thick and roughly cut, but his eyes were the only features that could have been called strictly attractive. They were dark blue, so dark that they seemed almost black, especially when he grew angry. They were shaded by long, black eyelashes that were the envy of many a young woman. Right now there was a gentleness in those dark eyes, as there usually was, but on several occasions Dr. Crawther had seen anger turn them to a shade as black as the coal that came out of the Welsh mountains, but with a glow that seemed to burn from somewhere deep within the young man's spirit.

Dr. Crawther poured himself another tumbler of ale, then in an afterthought shoved the bottle toward Rees. "Have yourself a drink, my boy."

"There is kind you are," Rees murmured. He had a pleasant speaking voice and was the best tenor in the area. The men of the village had formed a large choir, and Rees's voice could always be heard soaring above the rest of them.

As Rees poured the glass full and sipped the ale, Dr. Crawther refilled his pipe, which he seldom allowed to go out. The ashes decorated the front of his snuff brown vest, and he never bothered to brush them away. Taking a straw from the slender slivers of wood on a tray, he touched the candle flame and waited until it caught, then lit the tobacco in his pipe. He blew the light out, then puffed away, saying, "Never become a smoker, boy, you hear me? It'll cut your life short. Man's a fool to put such stuff in his lungs!"

Rees smiled. "It hasn't cut your life short, Doctor."

"Never mind that! You do as I tell you, is it?"

"I think I can promise that I won't be smoking."

Silence settled over the room then as the two sat there. Finally Dr. Crawther said in a softer tone, "I remember how I took you with me on calls when you were barely out of nappers."

"I remember, too," Rees said, nodding. "I must have been a terrible pest."

"All boys are terrible pests, but you were not as bad as the others. Other boys wanted to take part in sports, but not you. I remember you followed me around until I got to where I could bear you."

Rees smiled slightly. The irregularity of his features was thoroughly masculine, and the small smile was a signal of his character. It showed the world a serene indifference, and yet there was a sadness somehow that moved Dr. Crawther to ask, "How are things at home?"

"Just the same."

The single sentence told Crawther much. He knew that Bran Kenyon had no patience with his youngest son's burning desire to become a physician. The older Kenyon was a builder of small ships, and he drove his four sons like slaves. Crawther had known instances when Rees had come for his lessons with his back striped by his father.

Rees Kenyon, Dr. Crawther knew, had become a good carpenter and shipbuilder. He spent much of his time out searching for the oak used to build the ships. He also knew that Rees was not overpaid, for Bran Kenyon was a miser where money was concerned.

Suddenly Crawther rose and walked over to the bookcases, muttering under his breath, "Where is it now? Come on, you old book, don't hide from me!" He had the odd habit of speaking to inanimate objects, which amused Rees greatly. Finally he gave a snort of triumph accompanied by a series of big puffs on his pipe, which remained clenched between his teeth. "There you are!" Yanking a book out of the bookcase, he came over and slapped it down so it made a loud thump as it struck the table. "There you are. Happy birthday, boy."

"It's not my birthday."

"Stubborn like an old mule you are! You'll have a birthday someday, I suppose. So there it is."

Rees ran his fingers over the cover of the book. He looked at the spine, holding it up carefully and with reverence. He had an almost superstitious reverence for books. *"Anatomy."* He spoke the title aloud. Then he looked up and swallowed hard. He had known little kindness in his home except from his mother and sister, but this man, with all his rough ways and explosive speech, had been the one bright shining light in his life. He had indeed followed the doctor with such persistence that finally Crawther had said one day, "Right, you! Come along. A lesson we'll have." He had taken the young man inside and started the first lesson of what would become the best part of Rees Kenyon's life — the study of medicine.

"I thank you, Doctor," Rees said. "You've always been so good to me. My life would have been so empty if you hadn't helped me."

"Well, well, there is soft you are! It's only a book."

But to Rees it was more than that. He opened it and knew that this book would be his if he lived to be as old a man as Dr. Howell Crawther. He caressed it almost as if it were a woman.

Crawther felt a keen sense of satisfaction but concealed it by saying gruffly, "Mind you memorize it, now! A book's no good unless it's in your head."

"I will," Rees said in a voice that was gentle but at the same time held a resolution as hard as steel.

"I'll be retiring soon."

"A sad day for me and for the people of the village."

The distress in Rees's face was very real, and Dr. Crawther felt the love he never spoke of for this young man seem to swell. He had no sons of his own, only one daughter, but this one had become his son in all but blood. "You've heard me mention my brother-in-law."

"Dr. Freeman?"

"Right, you. Dr. Howard Freeman in London. He's a good man. He had to be to marry my dear sister Elizabeth, or I would have pounded his head."

"I remember him, sir, when he came to see you four years ago."

"Right, you. He's a good man," Dr. Crawther repeated. "They have three children, two sons and a daughter. I've been writing to him for years now about you. Rees, I think you should go study with him. I've asked him if he would take you on and he's agreed to do it."

Rees's eyes burned suddenly and then he seemed to slump. "My father would never hear to it."

"Is he a rat with green teeth, then?" Dr. Crawther thundered. "What's in a man that wouldn't give his son a profession instead of building silly boats?"

"You know my father, sir."

"Well, you're twenty years old now, Rees Kenyon. A man you are." Dr. Crawther suddenly reached forward and put his hand on Rees's. He felt the strength of that hand as he squeezed it, and his voice became unusually persuasive. "I'll be leaving here to go live with my daughter in Edinborough. I want you to go study medicine with my brother-in-law. It's what you were born for, Rees."

Rees was conscious of the pressure of the doctor's hand. He always treasured those rare times when Dr. Crawther touched him with a show of affection.

"It's home I'd better be going, Doctor." Rising to his feet, he ducked to avoid the low beams. He had learned by hard experience that most houses were not large enough for him. Now he held the book in one hand and ran his other hand across the face of it. "Thank you, sir, for the book."

"Go you now, Rees, but remember, you were born to be a doctor. Go you to it!"

"I will think on it."

Rees left the doctor's cottage and moved slowly through the village. He had lived in this place all his life, so he knew every house in Llandudno. The fishing village was perched on a small peninsula protruding into the Irish Sea. On clear days Ireland was barely visible on the horizon as a long, horizontal line. Rees had sailed the sea, touching a few times in Ireland itself, which looked much like Wales to him.

Not far northeast of the village lay Liverpool. It was the largest city Rees Kenyon had ever seen. He had been there only twice in his life, but he still remembered how different was the hustle and bustle of the crowds — such a strong contrast from his own tiny village.

The sunlight's last hazy glow turned the narrow valley that contained the village amber and blue. Low ridges hemmed the valley on either side, and a river made a glittering, willow-fringed lane down its middle. Far away to his left a line of bluffs rose to box in the valley and the river alike. The afternoon was warm, all of summer scorch gone out of it. The deep haze of summer had lightened, and the land was touched with the tan and ashy colors of fresh sunlight. As he moved out of the village into the farmlands that surrounded it, clouds of blackbirds wheeled and disappeared into the fading darkness. He passed a young woman, who greeted him with a smile, calling his name, and he smiled back, a deep line breaking out at the corner of each eye.

It gave him pleasure to watch the colors of the land run and change along the horizon and far off in the distance. He loved the evening time, and as pearl shadows came upon the eaves of the houses and the dusty roads took on soft, silver shadings, he was struck as evening's peace magnified the distant sounds. And he felt for one instant the closeness of the town and the closeness of the people. He stopped, as he nearly always did, at the cemetery where his ancestors slept a quiet sleep. This place had something in it that drew him, and now he stood for a time thinking of those who lay there. They had once been alive and beautiful. They had known hunger. Their lips had been red and warm. They had all had dreams. They were gone now, but once they had lived — had left their mark upon the earth. They had hated and loved. But now the time had passed over them. The space that they had occupied was now empty. Perhaps someone remembered the more recent occupants of the cemetery, but some graves were so old that no living being could have a vital memory of the one who lay beneath the sod.

Rees stood looking down at one grave that had a stone so weathered that the name was now gone and every record was erased by the wind and the water that had washed over it. He was suddenly struck by the loss that was here, by the thought that now whoever lay under this sod was forgotten, with no one to come and bring a flower to place on the grave. In a gesture of rebellion, he picked up a stick and began to trace the outline of the grave, to sharpen the borders and for at least a time to put away the oblivion that had already begun. The thought troubled him, and with a sudden anger he threw the stick down, his face craggy and harsh for that one moment, and continued on his way toward home.

He heard the sound of laughter and voices and turned to see the miners who had left their holes in the ground after a hard day's work. They came as if in a parade, all their faces ebony with coal dust. For the moment they seemed happy enough, but Rees Kenyon felt a shiver. He had a fear of being underground, and the thought of going down into the bowels of the earth and groping about like a blind mole sent terrors through him. He knew he would die before doing such a thing.

"Rees, walk with me!"

Turning, Rees smiled at the woman who had joined herself to him by taking his arm. Marged Prosser was not a beautiful young woman but somehow made you think she was. She had eyes as dark as Rees's and a firm, curved body that she now pressed against him. She had come from a day's work in the mine, for women went down to haul the coal carts out from the depths of the mine to the elevator shaft. "I'll be having a bath," Marged said, looking up at him, her eyes dancing. "You can come and wash my back."

Rees laughed and shook his head. "I have no wish to have my back broken by Dai Gilbert."

"I wouldn't let him do that."

"He's so jealous of you, he would ruin me before you could stop him."

"Come now. Let's make him jealous." She pressed herself more closely against him, and as she had hoped, a tall miner, sturdy in the shoulders and with a scowl on his face, came over to join them.

At once Rees said, "I was just telling Marged, Dai, how fortunate she is to have a good man like you."

Marged laughed and shoved Rees. She took Dai's arm and winked at Rees. "Beat him up, Dai. Break his bones. He asked me to meet him tonight in the woods."

Anger flared in Dai Gilbert's eyes, but then he saw the smile on the tall young man's face and, turning, caught Marged winking and smiling.

He laughed, grabbed her by the back of the neck, and shook his head at Rees. "Stay away from my woman, boy. As a matter of fact, stay away from all women. That's the best I can tell you."

Rees laughed, for he and Dai Gilbert were good friends. He waved, saying, "Home, me," and left the parade. He made his way down to the wharf and the shipyard where he had spent so many days and hours of his life working on the wooden ships that now sailed in many parts of the Irish Sea. He gave the shipyard itself little attention but turned into a clapboard house sadly in need of a painting. He had once urged his father to paint it to make his mother happy, but his father's only reply had been, "No money in painting a house there is, boy."

As he entered the room, the odor of cooked meat and tea came to him, and the bubbling of a kettle on the stove. He took off his hat, hung it on a peg, and then went into the kitchen, where his father and his three brothers sat at the table. He went over to his mother, gave her a hug and a kiss, saying, "Good evening to you, Mum."

"Sit down. You're late."

Gwen Kenyon was thirty-eight, twelve years younger than her husband. She was his second wife and had borne him two children, Rees and a daughter, Seren, now married. The other three sons had been borne by a sturdy woman named Elizabeth, Bran Kenyon's first wife. She had died giving birth to Dafydd, who sat now at the table, eating steadily with his brothers Arvel and Beda.

As soon as he saw his father's face, Rees braced himself for the storm he knew would surely come. "You're late and you didn't do your work."

"Leave it now, Bran," Gwen Kenyon said.

"Leave it? I'll not be leaving it! It's an answer I'll have from you, boy!"

"That's right. Where's the timber you were supposed to bring in?" The speaker was Arvel, oldest of Rees's half brothers. He was a copy of his father, bulky with scrubby brown hair and eyes to match. "We couldn't get the work on the schooner done, because you didn't bring the wood in."

"It'll be at the yard in the morning," Rees said. He sat at his place and his mother brought a plate, but his father sat staring at him.

"You've been at that doctor's house again."

"Yes sir, I have."

"I've told you I'll not put up with such doings. You'll do your work."

"I did my work," Rees said quietly. He bowed his head and said a silent grace, but when he looked up, as he had expected, his father was glaring at him with dissatisfaction. "The wood wasn't cut as the man had promised. I had to wait."

"Why didn't you come back and help with the schooner?"

"I always go on Thursdays to study with the doctor, sir; you know that."

"And foolishness it is! You have no sense in you, boy. You're wasting your time. You'll never become a doctor."

"Yes, I will," Rees said quietly. He continued to eat, but the meal was spoiled for him as his father and his older brothers harangued him. It was something that went on every week when he went to visit Dr. Crawther for his study.

His mother came over and blocked the view of his father. She reached out and touched Rees's hair. There was a special love in Gwen Kenyon for this son of hers. He was like her, not in body but in spirit. Her husband and his three sons by his first wife were rough, uncultivated men, and she had never known exactly why she married him.

"How are Seren and the baby?" Rees asked to get away from his father's constant criticism. He had a deep love for his only sister and had missed her after she married Huw Tenney.

"They're fine."

"I'll go see them tomorrow."

"You'll be sneaking off to that sawbones," Bran Kenyon said.

Rees Kenyon was an easygoing young man, as he had been an easygoing child. Somehow the memory of many meals like this came to him, and without volition a stubbornness began to rise within him. He had felt it before on a few rare occasions. Once he had seen a man beating a dog, and although he had tried to keep himself out of it, he had finally been driven by a wordless, voiceless pressure to challenge the man. It had ended in a fight in which he had been badly beaten, for he had been but a lad at the time.

Now he felt something like that taking shape within him. It was a mixture of disappointment, anger, despair. The life he led had not been bad. He enjoyed building ships. He enjoyed even more going out to the forest to find the trees with the particular bends and crooks and forks that would be shaped into the knees and ribs of the vessels which would be the product of their strength. He also enjoyed watching the ships come together from nothing to become a fine vessel that would cleave through the water with speed, and he had pride in his work.

But from his early boyhood something had drawn him toward medicine. He had read what few books he could find, but it had been Dr. Crawther who had opened up a world that he knew he must share. Now as he sat there, a bitterness came to his lips, and finally his father said, "I forbid you to go to that doctor any longer."

"I do my work," Rees said. His words were quiet, but the years of listening to his father criticize him suddenly came together in a resolution.

Bran Kenyon stared at his son. "You'll not go back to that doctor's again, do you hear me?"

"I'm sorry, Father, but I will go."

Bran Kenyon blinked with surprise. He had unquestioned authority in this house always, and none of his other sons had ever challenged this. Now he slammed the table with his fist. "As long as you stay under my roof, you'll do as I say! I'll hear no more of it!"

Rees stared at his father for a long moment, and then he said quietly, "Then I will leave the house."

"Rees!" Gwen Kenyon came quickly to him, her hands fluttering. But she saw something in his eyes that stilled her.

Rees stood to his feet and waited for the sentence that he knew would come.

"If you leave this house, you'll not come back."

Rees did not answer. He was aware that his brothers were staring at him with shock. They were, in their own way, fond of Rees, and none of them could comprehend this rebellion. Rees said, "Mother, I'll be going to London to study with Dr. Freeman. He's the brother-in-law of Dr. Crawther. I will write often and I'll come back when I can."

Gwen Kenyon had long known this day would come, and now she drew herself up and came to him. She pulled his head down and kissed him, saying, "It's a thing I've seen in you all your life. You become a great physician, my son."

Rees knew that he would miss this woman who had done her best to make his life pleasant, but he was also conscious that a weight had been lifted off him. He turned to his father and said, "I hope you'll wish me well, Father."

Bran Kenyon somehow seemed to shrink. He had not thought such a thing could happen to him, and he scowled, "You'll come back. Mind my words. You'll come back."

"Never in this life," Rees said. He turned and left the room and his mother followed him. It took but moments to gather his few things together. He had saved a little money, not enough, but that did not seem to matter. Turning to his mother, he said, "It's you I hate to leave, Mum."

"You must go, Rees. It's what you were born for!"

"I thank you, Dr. Crawther, for all you've done for me."

Rees looked down at the smaller man, who seemed suddenly very frail, as though he had aged a great deal. The two were standing beside the coach while passengers boarded. "It's missing you I'll be, sir."

"Well, I'll be leaving here myself within six months, so we would have parted then anyway. Here." Fishing into his inner pocket, Crawther pulled out an envelope. "Give this to my brother-in-law."

Crawther then reached into another pocket and pulled out a small leather bag. It jingled as he held it out. "Here, you'll be needing this, boy."

"Why, I can't —"

"Do you question me? Quiet, you! Now take it."

Rees felt a lump in his throat as he took the pouch he knew was filled with gold coins. "There is proud I am to know you, sir. Like a father you are to me."

Crawther suddenly cleared his throat and removed his pipe. He looked off into the distance silently for a moment, and then he turned and blinked his eyes, saying fiercely, "Well, boy, get on the coach! Greet my sister and her husband for me. I'll come to see you when I can."

"Good-bye, sir."

Rees took his seat by the window and had time only to wave and call out good-bye again before the horses lunged against their harness and the coach lurched. He sat there watching the village, the only home he had ever known, wheel by. What came to him then was partly fear at leaving but also joy for all that was ahead. He watched until the village disappeared, then leaned back and began to think of what lay before him.

# Chapter Two

THE JOURNEY FROM LLANDUDNO TO LONDON WAS A PURE JOY FOR Rees Kenyon. He had traveled very little in his lifetime, and now every hour found him staring out the window in fascination at the changing scenes of the countryside. Even the small villages in which the coach stopped gave him pleasure. The farmland that he passed, long stretches on the way to London, flaunted itself as a beautiful woman might display her charms. The birds filled the air with their dulcet sounds. Their pure flute calls seemed to blend, then to sever and flow apart and mingle together during the morning hours. Over the land the fruit trees, tossed about in the wind, flung out pink and white flowers that spread wide in the sun. The hawthorns put on white flowers beyond their brittle thorns, and once when the coach stopped at an orchard, Rees walked among them, inhaling the sweet scent that blew with the gentle breeze.

When they stayed overnight at Banbury, Rees walked about the village listening to the babble of voices in the markets and finally went past the village limits, where a hot sun poured down on the earth and the air was thin and still. He passed into a section that had not been cultivated, where clumps of trees boasted their green leaves, and beside a creek where water reeds stood in brushy thickness along the banks.

He slept in a barn that night, and the next day they arrived at Oxford at dusk. Rees felt a reverence for the stones that made up the ancient buildings which rose out of the earth with a startling dignity. They seemed to say, "We are here forever. We will never change." He watched the young scholars with envy as they paraded in their black robes and mortar boards, going to classes, and he wondered if he would ever have half the assurance that the least of them seemed to have. *They know where they're going,* he thought. *But so do I!*

The travel was hard. The coach crossed rivers coated with dust by the heat of the summer, and late in the afternoons the roads were disturbed by its wheels throwing up plumes of dust. The spongy odors of summer and spring were always with Rees, and he found he missed most of all two things: his mother and the sea.

Finally the journey ended when the coach pulled up inside the environs of London. As soon as he stepped out, Rees knew this was another world. He retrieved his bag, made of carpet, from the top of the coach, and then for a time he simply walked the streets of London. He was in no hurry and was anxious to get acquainted with this place which would be his home for a long time. He threaded his way through the heavy traffic, dodging between vehicles and pedestrians. Carts and coaches made such a thundering, it seemed as if all the world went on wheels. At every corner he encountered men, women, and children — some in the sooty rags of the chimney sweeps, others arrayed in the gold and gaudy satin of the aristocracy gazing languidly out of their coaches. Some of them were borne in sedans by lackeys with thick legs. Rees took in the sight of porters sweating under their burdens, chapmen darting from shop to shop, and tradesmen scurrying around like ants, tugging at the coats of the men who fought their way through the human tide that flowed and ebbed through the streets.

"Watch yourself, boy!"

Rees felt his arm pulled, and he was dragged away from his place beside the building just in time to avoid a deluge of slops that someone had thrown from the upper window. "Nearly gotcha that time!" The speaker was a short, thin young man half a head beneath Rees's height. He wore a worn shirt, a disgrace of a pair of knee britches, and stockings with rents and holes. Still he had a cheerful aspect and laughed, saying, "Not a good way to start the day, gettin' baptized with slops. You're new in town, ain'tcha?"

"Yes. From Wales."

"Wales, is it? Well now, you want to be on your care, or you'll be ducked with somethin' not quite so sweet as wine."

"The people here just throw their slops out the window?"

"Where else would they throw 'em?"

"Well, at home we have better manners."

"You ain't 'ome now, sir, so I'd be careful if I was you. Look, you ain't seen nothin' like *that*."

Rees followed the man's gesture toward a ditch about a foot wide and six inches deep, in the center of the cobblestone street. "What's that for?"

"That? Well, that carries the slops and garbage away when it rains. Ain't it wonderful what a change modern improvements make? Why, most cities just let the garbage and slops pile up till they rots — but not London."

Rees listened as the man went on about the glories of London, and when he looked off, he suddenly felt his coat being brushed. He whirled quickly, his big hand shot out, and he captured the thin wrist as it was coming out of his pocket, holding his purse. He squeezed hard and felt the bone give.

"Ow, let go! You're breakin' me bloody hand!"

Rees relaxed his grip but did not release it. "You're a thief," he said.

"A man's got to make 'is way in this world. Let me go!"

Rees hesitated, then released the wrist, but not before retrieving his purse. Cursing, the man whirled and walked away.

Rees transferred the purse to an inner pocket, realizing that he was no longer in a small village relatively free of such things.

As he moved along the streets, he was appalled by the harlots that seemed to be everywhere. They came out of alleyways, some of them young, their faces painted, wearing dresses cut so low that he was shocked. One of them grabbed his arm and pressed herself against him, saying, "Come along, 'usband, I'll show yer a good time."

"I'm not your husband!"

Rees freed himself, and the woman, no older than seventeen, cursed him horribly, then turned to pluck at the sleeve of another man.

Dr. Crawther had taught Rees a little of the treatment of venereal disease. *Be a good business for a physician in this place, I'm thinking.* He had absolutely no idea how to find Dr. Freeman's house, but he asked several responsible-looking citizens, and finally, after spending the largest part of the day getting lost, he found himself in the proper neighborhood. He looked up and saw a sign over a large brownstone house set well back from the street. "Dr. Freeman," the sign indicated in plain block letters. The house rose three stories high and smoke was pouring out of one chimney. It was an ancient house, Rees could tell, and set off behind it was what appeared to be the carriage house and a house for servants.

Now that he was here, Rees was filled with apprehensions. He had heard only good things about Dr. Freeman, but still Rees had known nothing but the simple life of a Welsh village. Now it troubled him to be thrust into the large, curiously active city of London to meet the man in whose hand his fate rested.

Straightening his shoulders, he muttered, "We will go in, is it?" He climbed the steps, knocked firmly on the door, and a few moments later it swung open to reveal a young woman.

"Yes? Are you here to see the doctor?"

"Not as a patient. My name is Rees Kenyon."

"Oh yes! Well, come in, Mr. Kenyon." The speaker was an attractive young woman wearing a light linen dress in royal blue with a square neck and long sleeves. It had a snug bodice separated with a single green ribbon bow and revealed a pert, trim figure. "I'm Grace Freeman, Dr. Freeman's daughter," she said. "You can put your bag over there."

Rees set the bag down, feeling awkward. The room in which he stood, evidently a foyer, was filled with delicate furniture, and he felt he might break it simply by passing by. The ceiling was high, and a glass chandelier with a few candles burning in it gave off light. Clearing his throat, he said, "I don't want to bother the doctor if I've come at a bad time."

"No, he is with a patient now. Come into the parlor. Would you have tea while you wait?"

Rees entered the parlor, which was far more ornate than any room he had ever been in. It was a large room carpeted with floor-cloth painted in brilliant colors of crimson and green and gold. On one wall was a biblical tapestry such as he had never seen, but he recognized the Passover and the Death of the Innocents somehow woven into the material with metallic threads. Other pictures in rich wood frames covered the walls. Rees had rarely felt so out of place in his life.

The young woman smiled, saying, "I'll be right back with the tea."

"Thank you."

Rees waited tensely, not knowing whether to sit or not. The chairs all looked rather fragile, and he was accustomed to the chairs he or his brothers had built of heavy oak. These had gracefully curving members and scarcely looked strong enough to support his weight. Instead of sitting, he moved around the room looking at the pictures. He turned at the sound of footsteps and saw the young woman step inside with a tray bearing a teapot, two cups, sugar, and cream, in dainty blue and white pottery.

"Please be seated, Mr. Kenyon. Will you have sugar and cream?"

"Yes, please."

As the young woman prepared the tea, he took advantage of her diverted attention to study her. Her hair was a rich yellow and lay neatly pulled back over her head in a single part. The sunlight coming in through the windows touched its surface, and he noted a reddish gold glow. She was smiling, her lips curved in an attractive line. Her complexion was fair and smooth and her throat showed a delicate ivory shading. The sunlight that touched her was kind to her, showing the full, soft lines of her body, the womanliness in breast and shoulder. When she looked up, he saw a small dimple appear at the left of her mouth, and the light danced in her eyes. "Our family has been looking forward to your coming, Mr. Kenyon," she said, handing him his tea.

"I'm surprised to hear it."

"Oh yes. My uncle has been lavish in his praise of you." She took a seat opposite Rees.

A slight color touched Rees's cheek and he shook his head. "There is surprised I am."

"Why should you be surprised? You've been friends for a long time, haven't you?"

"Well, it's proud I am to call him a friend and indeed he has been that."

"In one of his letters he said that you built ships."

"Yes, miss. That's true enough."

"Did you like that sort of work?"

"Yes, I rather did."

"I love ships. Nothing is more beautiful than swift vessels skimming across the waves."

Rees warmed to the young woman. "Yes, that's true. Have you done a bit of sailing?"

"Some. Not as much as I'd like. But tell me about yourself. Uncle Howell says you're a fine medical student."

"He's too kind. I picked up a bit sitting at his feet, but I'm not at all sure I can ever learn enough to be a doctor."

Grace Freeman leaned forward. "That's not what my uncle says. I'm sure you're far too modest."

"Well, I have a great deal to be modest about. Nothing to buy a stamp for I am. You should have been in my village." Rees smiled, holding the cup carefully between thumb and forefinger. "Most everyone there says I'm not smart enough to be a doctor."

"Don't listen to them," Grace said firmly. "My uncle says you're very bright, and he should know."

At that point footsteps sounded outside the parlor, and a man entered. They came to their feet and Grace said at once, "Oh, Father, it's Rees Kenyon who's come to us."

"Well, I'm glad to see you, Mr. Kenyon."

Howard Freeman was a short man with a wealth of brown hair and warm brown eyes to match. He had a neat mustache and his expression was lively and full of welcome. His clothing was simple enough but of an expensive cut. He was wearing a dark green suit of fine wool with a small, turned-down collar and turned-back cuffs. It was worn open to reveal a dark green waistcoat buttoned from top to bottom. The embroidered ruffled edges of a white silk shirt showed at the neck and wrists. His breeches were loose-fitting and ended just below the knee, held in place with buckles, and he wore a pair of white silk stockings and shiny black boots. Dr. Freeman stuck his hand out and when Rees shook it, his hand swallowed the older man's. "My, what large hands, and strong too!" Dr. Freeman said. "That can come in handy in the operating room."

Rees was surprised. He pulled his hand back and stared at it ruefully. "I have always thought that small hands would be better."

"Well, a certain amount of dexterity is necessary, but strength too comes in handy." Dr. Freeman looked up and smiled at Rees. "What a tall fellow you are! You must bump your head continually in those low-ceilinged cottages there in your village."

"Yes indeed, sir. I have my share of knots from them." Rees shifted uneasily. He felt the eyes of the young woman on him and then suddenly blurted, "Sir, I've been worried ever since I left home about coming to you like this."

"Worried? What is there to worry about?"

"Well, I don't want to force myself upon you."

"Nonsense," Dr. Freeman said, waving his hand. "My brother-in-law and I have gone over all this through the mail."

"I appreciate that, Dr. Freeman, but let me say at once that if I can't do the job, I'll not be a burden on you. I'll find work in the shipyards or someplace."

"Never take counsel of your fears, my boy," Dr. Freeman said expansively. "From what I've heard of you and now seen, I feel we'll get along famously."

"There's kind of you to say so, sir."

"Well, well," Dr. Freeman said and turned to his daughter. "We'll fix the room in the attic for Mr. Kenyon."

"Of course," Grace replied. Then she said to Rees, "And you must be starved. I'll have Cook fix something extra special tonight."

"Go along with my daughter, Rees. I have a call to make but we'll have time to talk after dinner tonight." He put out his hand once again and said, "Welcome to London, Rees Kenyon."

The meal was better than anything Rees had tasted in a long time. It consisted of roast beef covered with delicious gravy, thinly sliced mutton, and well-cooked fish that had been seasoned in a way that Rees had never tasted. The dining room was small but elegant. Two floor-length windows on one wall were draped with yellow damask curtains. The walls were pea green with green-and-yellow-flowered wallpaper bordering the windows. The light from candles flickering in brass sconces on the wall was reflected in numerous mirrors, and the heavy oak dining table was covered with a snowy white linen tablecloth. Across the room from Rees a large mahogany sideboard was filled with an array of dishes, and an oak serving table was heaped with the evening's main courses.

Rees had been relatively silent during the meal but had listened as the family spoke. Elizabeth Freeman finally turned her attention to him. "My brother tells me you build beautiful ships, Rees."

"Well, ma'am, it's my father's business, and I might say that we have produced some nice vessels from the yard."

"I've passed the shipyard many times," Mrs. Freeman said. "It's always puzzled me how ships are built. I can understand a house, which is built straight with even timbers, but ships curve, don't they? The parts, I mean."

"Yes ma'am, they do."

"Well, however do you make the wood bend?"

Rees liked Mrs. Freeman a great deal. She was a slight woman with delicate features, blond hair, and intelligent gray eyes. She also had a sense of humor, he had discovered, and he suspected she had passed it along to her daughter.

"Well, Mrs. Freeman, you have to go into the woods and find a tree that's already bent. For example, if you want the knees of the ship — that's the part that holds the stern onto the rest of the frame — it has to be bent almost in the shape of an L. So we find a large oak tree with a branch growing out at a right angle. When we chop the tree down, we save that bend. Then we take it to the yard and whittle away at it with adzes or hatchets, axes, and chisels until we have what we want."

"And you've been doing that most of your life, my brother tells me."

Rees smiled ruefully and held his hands out, palms up. "Yes ma'am. You can see from my hands I've spent some time working with wood."

"Well, we're so glad to have you here," Mrs. Freeman said, smiling.

"There is happy I am to be here, ma'am, but I don't know if I am bright enough to become a physician like your husband or your brother."

"Well, we'll soon find out," Dr. Freeman said, nodding. He dabbed at his lips with a snowy white handkerchief. "You'll have a room in the attic, plenty to eat, and there's plenty of work around here for you to do."

"Indeed, sir, that would please me greatly. I am rather handy at fixing things."

"Well, thank heaven for that," Elizabeth Freeman said. "Things are always breaking down around here, and our handyman had to leave us recently."

"You show me tomorrow, Mrs. Freeman, and I'll get right at it."

He leaned back in his chair, filled with relief. *A fine family this is,* he thought. *A man who couldn't make it in a place like this should go to his death.*

Night had come, and as Elizabeth Freeman stared out the window, she found herself admiring the new moon, which was tipped on one of its horns. It made a bright arc in the heavens and wore a few stars as though they were a mantle surrounding it. She wore a loose-fitting nightgown and her nightcap covered her head, and as she turned and came to the bed, she said, "It's time to go to sleep. Put your book up, Howard."

Blowing out the light on her side of the bed, she got into the high poster bed and turned to face her husband. He obediently blew out his lamp, then settled back with a contented sigh.

"How is Rees doing?" she asked. Reaching over, she lay her arm across her husband's chest.

Drawing her close and putting his arm under her head, Howard Freeman said, "How long has he been here now? Two weeks? Three, I think. He's doing fine. He's made a big difference in the yard and the house, hasn't he?"

"I've never seen such a hard worker. He's amazingly good at helping John with the flowers, too, but how's he doing with his studies?"

"Very well indeed! He doesn't know much of course, but more than I expected. I'll tell you, Elizabeth, he has a mind that's like ... like *glue!* Howell gave him an anatomy book before he left home. I tested him on it. He can name every bone and muscle in the body."

"He's very bright."

"Yes. He's worried about his hands. They're so big, yet it's amazing what delicate work he can do. But his strength is handy, too."

"Really?"

"Oh yes. Three days ago we had a patient with a bad break in his leg. You know how strong the leg can be, much stronger than a man's arm. It's always hard to stretch the leg out until you can pop the bones back into place."

"But Rees was a help?"

"Yes indeed. We tied the patient's shoulders to the top of a bed, and I was dreading getting that leg set. I told Rees what to do, and he took hold of that leg and just as easy as you please, as easy as kiss my hand, he stretched the leg out, and I popped the bones back in. It was a treat to see that."

"You really think he can become a doctor?"

"No doubt in my mind about it."

The two lay there silently. Howard was almost off into a sound sleep when his wife dug her elbow into his side. He grunted and said, "What? What is it?"

"Have you noticed that Grace likes your student very much?"

"What are you talking about?"

"I'm talking about your own daughter here, and she's interested in that tall young man."

"But he has nothing, and he has a long way to go."

"I know that, but she always makes it a point to speak to him."

"He's a homely young man. Not handsome at all."

"Well, not all women can have handsome husbands, as I do."

Howard laughed. "Go to sleep, Elizabeth. It's late."

# Chapter Three

THE SUNLIGHT RAN FRESH AND FINE OVER THE LEAVES THAT LAY scattered across the expanse of yard. It was, however, a cold sunlight that seemed to give no warmth, for September had brought cold weather to London — colder than usual. As Rees raked the crisp leaves into piles, he tilted his head back and stared up at the sky, thinking of the old calendar that someone had left in his room. It was a year out of date, but the hired man who had lived there during that period had marked each day with a comment, and on this very day a year ago, September the tenth, he had written, "Warm sunshine. Hot for this time of year." He had also put a verse from the Bible beside each date, and Rees smiled as he thought of the verse he had read earlier in the day: "My brother Esau is a hairy man, but I am a smooth man" (Genesis 27:11).

As Rees thought of this, humor bubbled up in him. It amused him that the verses had nothing to do with spiritual life. It was as if the man had opened the Bible and let his finger fall on the verse and copied it down. He could not understand such a thing, for to him the Bible was a treasure to be searched for truth, not a game in which one simply picked a verse at random.

As he continued to rake the leaves for burning, he was aware of his surroundings. London was a crowded place, but the sky overhead was clear this day except for the pillars of smoke that rose out of the myriad chimneys. He studied a flight of swallows which appeared, dividing the air in evanescent shapes and making a pleasing pattern. At the broken stems of the garden, he saw a red admiral butterfly move in its peculiar flight, fluttering like a leaf, the colors of his wings glittering like flakes of sunlight. "It's too late for you, butterfly. Go from here now before you freeze yourself."

"Good morning."

When Rees turned, he saw Grace Freeman walking across the yard toward him. She was wearing a light wool dress and over it a coat of wool of a darker blue. Her cheeks were flushed and she had a smile on her face, as if she were pleased with herself and with the world around her.

"Good morning, Miss Grace. A fine day."

"It is, isn't it? I love the fall weather! I wish we could keep it all year round."

"That wouldn't be too good for the crops," Rees said, smiling. He towered over her, and always when they stood together, she gave him the impression of being even younger than she was. She was well shaped for a young woman, and now as she looked up at him, he felt somewhat embarrassed. She made him feel oversized and awkward, although she had never done or said anything to give him that idea.

"I guess you're right, and I don't want to complain. I hate complainers, don't you?"

"Why, I suppose I do."

"I stay away from them, as far as I can. Probably when Moses was leading the children of Israel out of Egypt and struck the rock and brought the water, I'd guess there were some who complained because he didn't use a fancier stick."

"I never thought of such a thing." Rees found himself pleased with her. She stood before him, making a pleasing picture in the cold sunlight. Finally she looked over to where the family dog was digging a hole industriously. "Hodspur, stop that!" Grace cried sharply. When the dog ignored her completely and continued to send a shower of clods into the air, she shook her head and said in a vexed tone, "That dog never minds."

"Why, I can make him mind, Miss Grace," Rees said with a grin.

"I don't believe you can."

"You just have to know his ways. Watch this now." He raised his voice and said, "Hodspur, keep on digging the hole." Turning to Grace, he said, "You see. He minds perfectly. He just has to have the right command."

"You're awful, Rees! You're always making fun of me."

"Making fun? Indeed no, miss! The day I'd make fun of a fine lady like you, why, look for me on the floor!"

Grace laughed. She had a pleasing laugh, as if it came from deep inside. She shook her head, saying, "You've been here four months and you've never done anything but work."

"Oh, Miss Grace, that's not exactly right."

"It *is* right. You're either studying with my father or going on rounds with him or else you're out working on the yard or the house."

"Well, I do go to church."

"Indeed you do. I don't think you've missed a single Sunday in all the weeks you've been here. But" — a pixieish light came into her eyes — "man shall not live by church alone."

Rees laughed aloud. "I've never heard that particular version of the Scripture. Is it in the Bible?"

"It will be when I write it in the margin."

"Do you do that often? Write your own text for the Holy Scripture?"

"Only when absolutely necessary. But you haven't seen any of the sights of London yet, have you?"

"No, Miss Grace, not yet."

"Then I declare that you should. As the Scripture says, 'Thou shalt visit the Tower of London.'" Her eyes danced and she said, "I'll write that on a piece of paper and put it in my Bible. Then it will be in the Bible, won't it?"

Rees loved the wit of the young woman. "The Tower of London. That's where they execute prisoners, isn't it?"

"Not so much anymore, but you'll see for yourself. When you finish raking the leaves, we'll get the carriage hooked up and I'll take you on a tour."

"What would your father say?"

"He won't be back until tomorrow."

Rees shrugged. "Someone has to rake these leaves, though."

"No, there's a wind coming up. It'll scatter them nicely. You get the horses ready and I'll go put on my riding habit."

The Tower of London was an education for Rees. Grace apparently knew every square foot of it, and she pointed out that it was Julius Caesar who, according to tradition, had founded it. She showed him the White Tower, the massive keep at its heart which was built under William I and William II. Rees was impressed by the yeoman warders, resplendent in their Tudor uniforms, and when he asked why they were called Beefeaters, she laughed and said, "Why, because they eat beef, of course! If they ate fish, they'd be called Fisheaters."

She took him to the magnificent collection of medieval armor, pointing out the very suit of armor that Henry VIII had worn. When he asked about the prisoners and the executions, she spoke of them at length. They included Sir Thomas More, Sir Walter Raleigh, Lady Jane Grey, and Anne Boleyn, and she informed him that even Queen Elizabeth had been a prisoner in the Tower before she became queen.

The excursion was a delight to Rees Kenyon. He had read somewhat of the sights of London, but to see them — and with such an attractive guide — was beyond his expectation. He found himself more at ease with this young woman than he had ever dreamed of being with a lady of quality.

At the restaurant where they went for high tea, he found himself the target of many questions. Grace was intently interested in his life in Wales. As they ate their shepherd pie and drank cup after cup of steaming tea, they found themselves speaking freely. She was especially interested in the coal mines, and when he described the horrors of them, she said, "I can't think of anything worse. They sound hellish."

"I think they are. Glad enough I was to build ships."

The mention of shipbuilding brought another series of questions, and finally Grace asked him, "What do you want, Rees?"

"What is it I want? What do you mean, Miss Grace?"

"I know you want to be a doctor, but beyond that what do you want?"

Rees's brow furrowed for a moment and he shook his head. "If I can think of it, it isn't what I want."

Grace's laughter made a musical sound amid the noise of the busy restaurant. "That sounds very philosophical."

"Oh, I'm no philosopher." He paused. "I suppose," he said finally, "I want what all other men want."

"And what is that?"

"Why, a wife, children, a home. Isn't that what all men want?"

"I'm not sure you can ever have that."

Rees was somewhat shaken by her reply. "Well, am I a rat with green teeth, then?"

"No, but you've got to know how to court a woman before you can marry her." She leaned forward, and her eyes were bright and her lips were parted in a half smile.

Rees watched the slight changes in her face, each small expression. Her hair was brushed back on the sides of her head, with a mass on top, and then caught into a fall behind. Her nearness suddenly sent off a shot within Rees. He had not known this to happen with any woman before, and as she spoke, he felt a warmth toward her. He knew she was teasing him, and he said, "Well, there is right you are. I wouldn't know how to court a London woman."

"Then I'll teach you. Can you dance?"

"Dance? Just a clog as our people do."

"Well, you can't go clogging when you have a London ball. When we get home, I'll give you a dancing lesson."

Rees laughed. "There is soft you are. You can't teach an awkward fellow like me to dance."

"I could teach anyone to dance," she said. "Come. Have you had enough to eat?"

Dr. Freeman arrived at his home, weary to the bone. He passed the larger of the two parlors in the house and watched his daughter and Rees doing some sort of dance. His daughter was singing and Dr. Freeman was amused at the sight. He watched for a time and then went into the library, where he found his wife sitting at the table, reading.

"What's going on with those two?"

Elizabeth looked up and smiled. "Grace is teaching Rees to dance."

"Can a man get to be as old as he without knowing how to dance?"

"I don't think the poor boy has had much opportunity. He's worked hard all his life."

"You're right about that. He deserves some time off. I've never seen anyone work harder or make better progress."

"Well, so you think he will be able to finish his training and set up a practice of his own?"

"I think he's going to be a fine doctor. Better than I am."

"No. No one's better than you."

Howard Freeman sat and put his hand on Elizabeth's shoulder. He caressed it for a moment and smiled and said, "I think you overestimate your husband's virtues."

Elizabeth put her hand on his and shook her head. "No, I don't. God blessed me by bringing you into my life."

The two listened to the sound of Grace's voice. Howard Freeman said, "Do you think she'll ever get him to a ball or anything that frivolous? He's a very serious young man."

"You know Grace. She can make you do anything she chooses."

"Wait a minute! That's not exactly so."

Elizabeth laughed. "Yes, it is. She could always get anything she wanted out of you — and I expect she'll do the same with Rees Kenyon."

Rees stood before the mirror, staring at his image. He had felt guilty spending so much money on a suit to wear to a ball, and now he muttered, "There is handsome you are! And there is insane you are, spending so much on a suit of clothes!"

The suit was dark green, made of the finest wool. The overcoat came down below his knees and had a small, turned-up collar and turned-back cuffs. The coat was worn open to reveal a fully buttoned dark green waistcoat with embroidered edges. The white silk shirt that showed at his neck and wrists was almost blinding. The breeches were gray and were tied just below his knees, and the white stockings set off the black leather shoes with the large brass buckles. He stared at himself, and then a smile turned the corners of his broad mouth upward. "For an ugly fellow, you look very good," he murmured. "But you can't make a silk sow out of a purse's ear. I mean . . ." He could not get the proverb right, and suddenly he heard his name called and turned to face the door. He left the room, and when he descended to the foot of the stairs, he found Grace waiting for him.

"Now, let me look at you."

"I feel like a fool," he said.

"Don't talk like that. Let me see." Grace moved around Rees, and when she came to stand before him again, she said, "You look absolutely delightful. If you drop dead, we won't have to do a thing to you."

Rees laughed. "What a thing to say, Miss Grace."

"Please, if you'd stop calling me Miss Grace, I'd appreciate it. Grace is good enough."

"But you're my employer's daughter."

"That doesn't matter. Come along. I want to show you off at the ball."

"Right. We will go, is it?"

Grace suddenly smiled at him. "I love your Welsh way of speaking, Rees. It has a lilt to it that pure English lacks. Here, give me your arm." Taking his arm, she looked up and said, "Now off to the ball!"

The ballroom almost stopped Rees in his tracks. It was at the home of a Dr. Monroe, a colleague of Dr. Freeman, and was given expressly for his two daughters. Rees had entered with Grace on his arm but was stunned by the room in which the ball was to be held. It was a tremendous ballroom, oval in shape, with white pillars encircling the entire room. He scanned the walls, which were painted a bright white. Each cornice, ceiling trim, and doorway had been covered in gold leaf. Staring up at the high ceiling, he saw that each section had a different scene etched in gold. He was practically blinded by the large crystal chandelier that glistened with flickering candles throwing their brilliance over the scene beneath.

At one end of the room was a huge fireplace of marble, the mantel covered with silver candlesticks, and on each side of the room were tables overlaid with white damask tablecloths. Silver trays of food, cut-glass crystals, and fine china covered the tablecloth completely.

"Close your mouth, Rees. You're going to swallow a fly!"

Rees realized that he was gawking and snapped his jaw shut. He looked down at Grace. She was wearing a beautiful gown, an azure blue of lightweight velvet material. It had a low-cut, square neckline and was edged with white lace. The bodice was white with small lace insets, and the petticoat was full, layered with pale yellow lace that was edged with delicate embroidery.

As Rees gazed at Grace, he understood that she was a young woman with a great deal of vitality and imagination. Her mouth was soft and well shaped, and the glance that she turned upward to him was self-possessed and yet still had some of the little girl in it. But Rees was conscious that this was no little girl but a woman, with a woman's softness and fullness that somehow troubled him and at the same time drew him toward her. She was watching him carefully with a strange expression, her lips softly together and points of light dancing in her eyes. "Come now. I must see if my dancing lessons have been successful."

"Nothing to write home about my dancing is," he murmured. But she had taught him well enough that at least he did not step on her feet. She was as light as a feather in his arms, and he knew that his own dancing left a great deal to be desired. Yet he saw the pleasure in her fine greenish eyes, and she encouraged him as they moved around the floor. When the dance ended, she said, "Now come. I want you to meet Dr. Monroe's daughters."

She led him to one end of the room, where he met the doctor and his wife. His two daughters whispered to Grace while Rees conversed with him. Nella, the oldest daughter, said, "He's so tall — but not very handsome."

"He's dignified. That's better than handsome," Grace said. "I want you to dance with him, Nella. He's very shy. Try to build his confidence up."

Rees felt a touch on his arm and was introduced to Nella. Feeling Grace's eyes on him, he blurted, "Would you give me the pleasure of this dance, Miss Nella?"

"Certainly."

Grace engineered Rees's evening from that point on, seeing that he danced with several of her girlfriends. Finally she herself danced with him, and Rees said, "Like an old mule I am, Grace. I can't talk about anything but shipbuilding and medicine."

"What did they want to talk about?"

"Oh, music and theaters and plays and balls. It's only a dance I want, but I feel as out of place as a bullfrog in this fine house."

"Surely you can find something to talk about."

"Well, I told that last young woman — what was her name?"

"Heather."

"I told Miss Heather about the amputation I helped your father with, but she didn't seem interested."

Grace suddenly laughed aloud. "Well, of course she wasn't interested! Don't talk about things like that, Rees."

"What will I talk about, then?"

"I'll teach you how to make meaningless talk. We'll have to go to at least one opera and one play, and you can make those do with young women."

Rees shook his head. "I don't think I'll ever be able to do that. I don't care about those things."

"But other people do," Grace said, "and you'll be dealing with people all your professional life. So we'll start your education tomorrow."

Dr. and Mrs. Freeman left the ball early but Grace begged to stay. "We can get a carriage home. It isn't far," Grace argued, and they agreed.

"Don't let her keep you out all night. We have a busy day tomorrow, Rees," Dr. Freeman said, smiling. As he walked out with his wife, he said, "I believe you're right. She's got him under her thumb — just as she has me."

Rees found himself enjoying the dance. He had to work hard to find an appropriate subject for discussion, and he had difficulty remembering the names of the young women. He gave up finally, and when he and Grace were on their way home, he said, "It was a fine ball. The best I ever went to."

"Why, I suppose it was! It was the only one you've ever attended."

"Still, it was the best. Thank you so much, Grace, for taking so much trouble with me."

Grace sat quietly in the cab. The horse's hooves beat a syncopated rhythm on the cobblestones. Suddenly she turned to him, saying, "What do you expect to find in a woman, Rees?"

Surprised by her question, Rees could not answer for a moment. Finally he said, "I don't know much about women."

"But what are you looking for?"

Rees rubbed his chin thoughtfully. He was very much aware of her presence. Her arm brushed against his and he could smell the lilac scent she wore. It was chilly outside and she had put on a heavier coat. "Do you know what a keystone is, Grace?"

"Yes. It's a wedge-shaped stone at the top of an arch."

"It's the keystone that holds the arch together. If a keystone trembles, the arch will carry the warning along its entire curve. And if the keystone is destroyed, the arch will fall. It will just leave a few lesser stones heaped close together with no design."

He turned to her and smiled. His face was homely enough, but when he smiled, there was a certain masculine attractiveness about this man, and Grace responded to it.

"And you think a woman is like a keystone in an arch?" she whispered.

"That I do."

"Do you think you'll ever find a woman who will be like that?"

Rees did not answer for a moment, and then he said, "You know, once I found a hidden note, written by a lover, I think."

"A hidden note? What do you mean?"

"It was in our village back in Wales. I had gone down to the river to a place where lovers often go. Oh, I was simply going to catch a fish, but I found this note stuck under a stone. I still have it somewhere, I think."

"What did it say?"

"It was a woman's handwriting, and it said, 'I just couldn't come — I hope you'll understand.'"

"That's all it said?"

"That was all. Somehow those few words moved me."

Grace suddenly put her hand over his. Her eyes were misty, and she said, "How did it move you, Rees?"

"There was something wrong between the two," he said simply, "and it grieved me that they couldn't find each other. I never knew either of them, but there was a little tragedy there and it hurt me to think of it."

"You're such a sweet, gentle man, Rees."

Rees had not known until that moment how lonely his life was. Her face was turned toward him, and he saw that his little parable had touched her. He felt the pity in her, and now without thought but with a great longing he took her in his arms, and suddenly, as she came to him, there was a sweetness and a richness that made him, for that moment, full and complete. When he kissed her, he felt the gentleness of her lips, and yet there was a power in her that lifted him up, out, beyond himself, and Rees Kenyon was suddenly conscious of that which he had only had a vague hint of before: he suddenly knew the glory a man and a woman might know.

The fragrance of her hair touched his senses, and she lay against him, and then when he lifted his lips, he whispered, "There is sweet you are," and waited for her to speak.

Finally she did speak, and her voice was soft, yet there was a tension in it. "I have never loved a man, Rees, but I think you are a man I could love."

Her words surprised him and he released her and shook his head. "Why, I'm not the man for a fine lady like you!"

"I'm only a woman, Rees."

And then Rees Kenyon knew a sudden peace. It was for all the world like coming into a harbor after a long voyage. And as he sat beside Grace Freeman, he knew that in her his loneliness had found a haven.

# Chapter Four

"YOU'RE RATHER PROUD OF YOUR PROTÉGÉ, AREN'T YOU, HOWARD?"

Dr. Howard Freeman glanced at the speaker, a tall, heavyset man of fifty with a pair of frosty blue eyes and luxurious muttonchops. "I have the right to be, Dr. Morton," he replied. "He's going to be one of the finest physicians in the kingdom."

Morton turned his head to one side and winked. "And I suppose you'll be losing him when he finishes his apprenticeship. How long does he have to go?"

"He's been with me two and a half years. Another six months and I think he'll be qualified."

"He's not much on looks, but you say he's a good man with a saw and a knife?"

"He has the surest hands of any young fellow I've ever seen, Stanley! He's very strong and can stitch up a wound as delicately as any surgeon in London. And he's tireless! This epidemic has been bad, but that young fellow can go for twenty hours without stopping."

"It's the worst cholera outbreak we've had in years. And there's really nothing any of us can do for the poor people! Let's pray that it runs its course soon."

The two men were speaking quietly in a room where a group of London physicians had gathered to observe various surgical procedures. Actually, Howard Freeman was somewhat nervous, for the finest of physicians from the city were here, and he wondered if perhaps he shouldn't perform the surgery himself. *It might not be fair to allow Rees to work under such difficult conditions,* he thought. Howard well knew how critical other doctors could be, and he toyed with the idea of filling in for his young assistant. But as he looked across the room at Rees, who was smiling as he spoke to Dr. Edmondson, he could see no trace of nerves. *He's as steady as a man can be. No, I'll let him go on with it.*

As the two doctors moved across the room toward Rees and Edmondson, Freeman heard Rees say, "Well, sir, I think perhaps we'd better put a fine edge on my instrument."

"That's an art in itself," Edmondson said. He was a small man, frail almost, and not over five three. He had to look up, craning his neck to stare into the face of Rees. "I've never been much of a hand at that. I always had my assistants do it."

Rees shook his head slightly, as if to say that he would not trust such a duty to another set of hands. He turned and removed four stones from the bag he had brought, two coarse and two very fine, all of them the best oilstones that could be purchased. He had found, strangely enough, that his days as a shipbuilder were useful in this respect. He had learned from his youth to put a razor edge on an adze or an ax or chisel, and he had found that the same principle reigned over scalpels and other blades used by surgeons.

For just one instant Rees glanced around at the doctors, all of whom were watching curiously. Inwardly he smiled, for he knew that there was a competition among doctors that would have surprised most laymen. They were all jealous of their trade secrets, even extending to the drugs they used. It grieved him to think that any man could be selfish enough to withhold something that might help another doctor's patient, but he knew that such a spirit existed. It was not in Dr. Howard Freeman of course, for he was as generous a man as Rees had ever known.

Rees spat upon one of the coarse stones and ran the scalpel over it with only five passes, succeeding to the next grade of stone with only two. He put several drops of oil on the fine stones and carefully moved the scalpel across the surfaces. Finally he held his arm up and with a sure hand moved the blade quickly. Holding his arm out, he said, "There, sir." To Dr. Freeman he said, "There is a lovely blade, Doctor."

A murmur of appreciation for the blade went around, and Dr. Morton said, "What surgery are you performing today, young man?"

"Not a complicated one. Sure, I'd be standing back for Dr. Freeman or one of you other gentlemen if it were. No sir, it's only a suprapubic cystotomy."

"You call that *simple!*" Dr. Morton exclaimed. "I've known quite a few physicians who had difficulty with that."

"Dr. Kenyon has done four of these already under my supervision," Dr. Freeman said quickly. "I daresay he's as expert in this particular operation as any man I've ever seen."

"I suppose we'd better get to it, then, if you gentlemen will accompany me." Rees led the three doctors out of the small room and into one much larger. A platform had been built on three sides, and a considerable number of medical students sat ready to observe the procedure. Rees had schooled himself to simply blot out the audience to his work. He had found that he had a singular ability to focus his attention, including his hearing, on the patient. It was as if his ears were muffled and all of his sight, except that which lay immediately in front of him, were blotted out in a dark haze.

The patient was a man of some forty years of age, large and well muscled. As was his policy, Rees had made it a point to meet with the patient, whose name was Peter Jenkins. Rees had discovered that the more confidence a patient had in him, the more success he was likely to have with his surgery. Now he focused his attention as he came to stand beside the man and said, "Well now, Jenkins, we're ready."

"Yes sir."

The eyes of the patient were wide so that the white showed much more than was normal. He was tied down by leather-padded chains and had been drugged with forty drops of laudanum. His belly had already been washed and shaved, but the drugs had not driven away the fear.

"This is going to be a little painful, Jenkins, but it will soon be over, and you'll be a well man again."

"Thankee, Doctor. Thankee."

"Now I'm going to pour some wine over your belly to take away the pain."

One of the medical students whispered loudly, "Better to let him drink it. All he can hold."

Rees heard this vaguely but ignored it. He took the bottle of alcohol and applied it to Jenkins' stomach and then handed the bottle to an assistant. "Now, you've been drugged to take away some of the pain, but you're going to feel some. Please, Jenkins, don't jerk any more than you can help, or I may not be able to do my job."

Jenkins forced himself to relax. He closed his eyes and his lips and said grimly, "Go ahead, sir. I'll try my best to hold still." His lips became a white line and his muscles were tense.

"Tighten the bonds a little if you please, Mr. Matson."

The assistant tightened the chains a full length, and then without hesitation Rees made the incision. He was pleased to see that despite the pain, Jenkins was going to be a good one. No man could remain perfectly still while his stomach was being opened, but Jenkins was far better than most. As Rees worked, he spoke calmly, explaining to the medical students what he was doing, and from time to time he would reach out and touch Jenkins, speaking a word of encouragement. He moved efficiently, with economy, and the operation was over in a surprisingly short time.

As he finished the last stitch, Rees said quietly, "You may remove the chains now. Jenkins, I'm very proud of you. Everything went well. Lie still and I'll be by to see you tomorrow."

"Thank you, Doctor." The words were gasped rather than spoken, and a film of perspiration covered Jenkins' body. He opened his eyes and managed a smile. "I did my best."

"You did fine. Very fine indeed."

The patient was carried out on a stretcher. Dr. Morton was the first to speak. "I've never seen anyone use wine like that, Kenyon. Where did you come up with that?"

"I'm not sure it has a great deal of value, but I always like to let the patient know that I'm going to avoid giving pain wherever possible. However, Dr. Duraton from France always used it when he opened an abdomen," Rees said, mentioning the name of a famous French surgeon.

As Rees left, Dr. Templeton, the head of the hospital, walked beside him. When they were inside the adjoining room and Rees was exchanging his bloodstained white apron, Templeton watched. He was not a prepossessing man, except for his eyes, which were always active. "I congratulate you on your surgery, Kenyon. Very fine work indeed."

Rees turned and nodded, his face flushed with the praise. "There is kind you are, sir."

"No kindness in it." Templeton shrugged. "I've seen many a young surgeon make his beginnings here — and seen quite a few who went on to great things." He hesitated, then smiled slightly. "I think you might be one of those."

"Very kind of you, sir."

"As a matter of fact, I've been speaking with some of the staff. You'll be through with your training in about six months, will you not?"

"So Dr. Freeman informs me — although, as you know, I have much to learn."

"This may be a good place to learn it."

Rees stared at Dr. Templeton, not catching his meaning. "I don't understand you, sir."

"There will be a place for you here in the hospital if you would like to join us."

Rees could not believe what he was hearing. He had spent enough time with other medical students during the two and a half years of his training, much of it at this hospital, to learn that such invitations were not given lightly. He felt a quick gust of pleasure at the invitation but did not hesitate. "I thank you very much, Dr. Templeton, for your gracious invitation. I will never forget it, sir, but I will be working for Dr. Freeman for some time."

"He's a fine doctor but your career might go better here with us."

"I have no doubt of it, sir, but perhaps you know I owe a great debt to Dr. Freeman."

Templeton stared at the young man. He had never in all his experience been refused, and now he was somewhat at a loss for words. Finally he said quietly, "Loyalty is a fine thing, sir."

"I'm afraid my answer is final, Dr. Templeton — but again let me say how much I appreciate your offer."

Templeton suddenly smiled more broadly, and he was not a man given to smiling. "Dr. Freeman is a fortunate man, Kenyon. Let me know if I can be of any help to you."

"Thank you very much, Doctor."

Rees watched Dr. Templeton leave. "Well, there is proud I am," he whispered. "But I owe it all to Dr. Freeman."

Later that day, during the carriage ride home, Freeman kept waiting for Rees to mention the offer extended to him. When Rees said nothing of it, he brought it up himself. "You haven't said anything, Rees, about Dr. Templeton's offer to join the staff at the hospital."

"Well, indeed I was flattered, sir."

"You ought to take it."

Rees stared at the older man. "No sir! No indeed!"

"It would be the best thing for you. You'll have no financial worries and you can rise very quickly."

"Does that mean you don't want me to work with you, Doctor?"

"No, certainly not! I didn't mean to imply that. It would be a good thing for me but not so good for you."

"I'll stay with you, sir, as long as you'll have me. I'm not forgetting who gave me my chance. You've been good to me beyond my desserts."

"So be it, then," Dr. Freeman said, smiling. "I know one who will be glad to hear it besides myself. Well, two really. Elizabeth and Grace."

"I'll be taking her to the theater tonight. She's trying to make a silk purse out of a sow's ear."

"Be sure you work into your conversation this opportunity you had. It'll make her value you a lot more."

"I don't think your daughter is that influenced by things like that," Rees said with a smile.

"No, you're right. Well, I'll tell her myself. She'll be proud of you."

Rees left the theater with Grace clinging to his arm. She spoke rapidly about the performance but Rees said little. He listened in the carriage as they made their way home. When they arrived, he would have stopped in front of the house, but she said, "Go ahead and put the horses up. I'll ride with you."

Rees nodded and drove through the gate. As he unhitched the horses and put them in their stalls, she stood watching. When he came to her, she said, "Look, the moon is so bright tonight and so beautiful."

"It is, now," he said quietly. "Would you like to sit out awhile or are you tired?"

"No, I'm not tired at all."

The two of them sat on the steps, and he waited until she finally said, "Father told me about the offer you received from the hospital. He was surprised you didn't take it."

"Well, that disappoints me. I would have thought he might have known I had no plans to leave him."

Grace took his arm and held on to him. She looked up at him, and the moon washed its silver light over her face. "I'm glad you're not leaving," she said simply.

"I want to do some good in the world."

"You will."

Rees wanted to express more of what he felt, wanted her to know how he felt, and he said, "There are so many things wrong in this world, Grace. Things are always being destroyed. People are breaking down and I want to help them." He looked at her and said, "I want to see God, too. Sometimes I think that when I try to find him, I see only the soles of his shoes, and I weep. But that's all a man can ever see of God in this world perhaps."

"No, you'll see more of him."

"Do you think so, then?"

"Yes. He that seeketh findeth."

"You're a woman of great faith."

"I am glad you think so. And I'm glad you're a man who has a heart to know God."

"That was my mother's doing, and I'm afraid I'm not the Christian I should be."

"Who of us is? Sometimes when I throw one of my fits, I'm so ashamed of myself that I can't even pray to God to forgive me. I have to let several days go by until I have the face to go to him."

"Why, Grace, do you think God changes in those times? Go to him when the sin's red-hot in your hands!"

"Is that what you do?"

"Ah, you have me there! I feel like you do." She seemed to understand his whole vision, and he turned toward her and said, "Grace, I must tell you how grateful I am to you."

"Grateful to me? For what, Rees?"

"Why, for the thousand kindnesses you've shown. Teaching me how to dance and how to speak. I was like a wild Welshman when I came here, and you've helped me more than I can say."

"I'm glad you feel that way."

The air was chilly but there was a warmth in Rees Kenyon. He did not know exactly when he had fallen in love with this young woman, but it had happened. There were a thousand little things that had brought him to this affection, and now he knew he must speak. Cautiously he said, "Grace, don't you think that friends should express their gratitude from time to time in a . . . in a physical way?"

Grace smiled and said at once, "I certainly do, Rees Kenyon."

Rees saw the surrender in her eyes. He put his arms around her and kissed her, and she came to him with an openness and an ardor that told him without words that she cared for him. When he lifted his head, her face was completely expressive — more so than he had ever seen it. He knew that what he saw in her eyes registered delight in the shadow of her feelings. He knew she was a young woman who had a fullness of heart which flowed for others, and now a stirring came to him and he cried out, "Oh, Grace, there is so proud I am to love you!"

"Do you love me, then, Rees?"

"You know that I do," he whispered. "I remember every moment we've had together. My heart counts those times like a bank teller counting money, but the memory of you is more than the rustling of paper or the ringing of gold coins. It's my flesh and blood saying I love you."

And then she put her arms around his neck and drew his head down. "I love you, too, Rees."

"Will we be married, then?"

"Yes!"

Rees's life turned a corner the night Grace Freeman agreed to marry him. It seemed to him that the air he breathed was fresher and more invigorating and that the skies contained more stars and that they glittered more brightly. He spent every available moment he could with Grace, and everything else seemed pushed away from the foreground. He could not believe that other things had once been so important, when now only this slight young woman seemed to fill his whole horizon.

Grace's parents were happy for her. Without reservation they welcomed Rees as their future son-in-law, and this was a humbling thing to Rees himself. He stumbled over words trying to tell them what he felt for them and promised repeatedly that he would do all that a man could do to make Grace happy.

But it was Dr. Freeman who brought him back down to earth by saying, "I know a man in love hates to think of other things, but we have real problems in the city with this cholera epidemic."

Rees immediately sobered and shook his head. "I've tried not to think about it. It is bad, isn't it?"

"We all hate to think about it but we have to. If we only knew how to treat it. But we must do what we can. If it continues to spread, Rees, I don't know what we'll do. Already every doctor in the city is working overtime."

Cholera swept through the city, invading palace and hovel alike. Rees worked long hours, and often when he came home very late, he would find Grace waiting for him. He came in on a Saturday night just before twelve o'clock and was shocked to find that she had prepared him a meal.

"You shouldn't have stayed up, Grace."

"I knew you wouldn't take care of yourself. Now sit down and eat."

"I am hungry." He sat, bowed his head as always, and then cut off a piece of mutton and chewed it. "You're a terrible cook, but no matter," he said solemnly.

"You beast! You know I'm a wonderful cook!"

"Well, if I starve, so be it," Rees said soberly, and then he had to laugh. "You *are* a wonderful cook. You are wonderful at everything. You're going to be a wonderful wife."

Grace sat down, urging more food upon him, and finally she joined him, pouring them both strong cups of tea.

Quietly she said, "I worry about you and about Father. You are exposed to this terrible illness constantly." She put her hand on his, picked it up, then held it between her hands. Her eyes grew misty and she said, "I don't know what I'd do if anything should happen to you, sweet."

Rees leaned over and kissed her on the cheek. A lock had fallen over her forehead and he pushed it back. "Nothing's going to happen to me."

"You can't know that."

"You just take care of yourself."

"Oh, me, I never get sick!" A thought crossed her mind and she said, "Let's make a pact, Rees. I've seen such sad things when wives have lost husbands or husbands wives."

He stared at her. "What kind of pact?"

"Let's agree that if anything happens to me, you won't overly grieve. You'll go on with life."

"Don't speak like that!"

"I think it's important."

"I won't hear of it," he said. He laughed suddenly and stood, and she stood with him. Leaning forward, he put his arms around her and picked her clear up off the floor. "I need another dancing lesson," he said.

"Put me down, you crazy thing!" Her feet dangled as he swept her around, and she continued to protest. Finally he put her down, kissed her, and said, "Now, we'll be all right. It's late."

Rees was leaving the hospital when he saw Howard coming in and knew by his face that something was wrong.

"What is it, Dr. Freeman? Is there more infection on the east side?"

Freeman's face appeared to be frozen and it seemed difficult for him to speak.

"It's not . . . that."

When Freeman could not say more, Rees suddenly had a premonition. "What is it? Tell me."

"It's Grace. She's ill."

Rees felt a cold hand close around his heart and begin to squeeze it. "Not cholera! Tell me it's not cholera."

"I'm afraid it is cholera. We'd better go home."

Rees had been struck once in the pit of the stomach in a boxing match when he was a young man. It had not been particularly painful but it had taken away his breath. He could not breathe, and this moment was like that. The air seemed thin and he felt a dizziness. He forced himself to shove the feelings aside and stumble after Howard Freeman, but inside he was crying, *It can't be! She can't die. God, she can't die!*

Fear ran through Rees as he bent over Grace, for all his experience told him that what he had dreaded most had come to pass. He forced a smile and said in a hearty voice, "Why, what's this? You have a touch of fever, my dear." But the sight of her pale face, sunken eyes, and dry lips spoke of cholera. Placing his hand on her brow, he sat on the bed and picked up her wrist. Her pulse was erratic and her skin, both on her arm and on her brow, was burning! "We'll get this fever down and you'll feel much better."

"I . . . I think I'm very ill, Rees . . ." Grace's mouth and lips were so dry that her words came in a threadlike whisper. Her eyes were yellowish and Rees read the fear in them.

"Nonsense! Here — let me get you some water to drink; then we'll get that fever down with cool water."

For the next hour Rees worked to bring Grace's fever down, but it was stubborn. She never complained, but despite his brisk chatter he was aware that both of them were desperately afraid — and both were determined to keep the dreaded word *cholera* unspoken.

After a time Rees said, "I'm going to get some more cool water, dear. I'll be right back." Leaning over, he kissed her forehead, and the heat from her skin seemed worse than when he'd first come.

He left the room and as he went to get water, Grace's father entered the house. He came to Rees at once, his eyes speaking the question he could not frame in words. Rees shook his head. "I . . . I'm afraid it's cholera, though I haven't told her."

"She knows, Rees." Dr. Freemen was a strong man but his lips trembled as he spoke. He stood before the younger man, his shoulders stooped, defeat and dejection written on his features. "I'd better get my wife," he said quietly. "She'll want to be with Grace."

"It might be better to keep her from the room," Rees said, but he knew well the answer he would get.

"She would never agree to that." Dr. Freeman turned and walked slowly out of the room.

When the door closed, Rees quickly filled the basin with cool water and returned to the room. Before he entered, he paused and stood holding the basin, his face twisted with pain. *Lord, please! Don't let her die!*

# Chapter Five

THE CHOLERA EPIDEMIC HIT LONDON WITH A TERRIFYING FORCE. The most frightening thing about it was the mysterious nature of the disease. Medical science simply did not know what caused it, nor was there agreement on the treatment of patients. Both Rees and Dr. Freeman did their best to join others in doing what was thought to help the situation. The clothes of the victims were disinfected and even burned. Carbolic acid and chlorine of lime were used extensively to disinfect the victims' homes, but nothing seemed to halt the waves of cholera. Treatments for the patients were crude, and Dr. Freeman finally said wearily to Rees, "We're not doing any good, my boy."

Rees was tired to the bone. Deep circles shadowed his eyes, and his hands were not steady. "There must be something we can do."

"It's one of those diseases we haven't learned enough about."

"One thing I'm sure of," Rees said grimly. "The people who die seem to have just dried up. Their hands and feet turn into claws. Their skin practically crackles when you touch them. And their lips, they crack. Why, they can't cry and don't even have spit."

"Yes, I have noticed in postmortem an exorbitant desiccation of tissue."

Rees nodded. "What I'd like to do is to try keeping them as hydrated as possible. Oh, we can keep on with our disinfectants, but it seems to me most of those dry the patients out anyhow. Look at your own hands."

The older man looked down at his hands and noticed that they were stained yellow and that the knuckles were swollen. "You're right," he said. "And at least it would give them some comfort. From now on we'll instruct all the families we're treating to make sure that the patients get as much water as possible. If they're unconscious and can't drink, then let one of the family members drop water into their lips just a drop at a time. We'll try it, but — " Howard Freeman did not finish what he had started to say. He was thinking of his daughter and rose up abruptly. "I'm going home to check on Grace," he said.

"I have one more call to make. I'll be there as soon as I visit the Stanleys."

"That's a bad case, isn't it? Four children, and three of them down with the cholera. What are those poor parents going to do if they lose them?"

"It's worse than that. Mrs. Stanley's down now, too."

Howard threw up his hands in a gesture of futility. "Well, God help them, and do the best you can. . . ."

James Stanley lived with his family in one of the worst slums in London. The stench of sickness lingered over the whole area, it seemed, and when Rees stepped toward the door, it opened and he found himself met by the pastor of his church, Reverend Josiah Coleman. "Why, Pastor, I didn't expect to find you here."

"I just came by to try to console the family." Reverend Coleman was a powerfully built man, a little under six feet, and looked more like a blacksmith than a pastor. His face was square, and his hands were hard, for he had been a farmer in his youth and still retained much of his early strength.

"How are the Stanleys?"

"The smallest child, Thomas, just died an hour ago."

"I was afraid of that. He was very weak the last time I was here."

"The other two aren't much better."

"How is Mrs. Stanley?"

"How are any of them, Doctor? She's in poor condition."

"I'd better have a look at them."

"I'll wait. Perhaps I can pray with James. He's almost out of his mind."

The visit was frustrating to Rees Kenyon. The mother was barely conscious and already showed signs of the cholera that probably would lead to her death. The two younger children were frightened and James Stanley was beside himself.

"Doctor, can't you do something?" he begged, his eyes pleading with Rees.

"I wish we could do more, James."

"My little Thomas taken away before he had a chance to live!"

"I know it's hard," Reverend Coleman said, "but we must remember that God is merciful. He's taken Thomas to himself." He had prayed with the father but James Stanley was dazed and angry.

"Why did God have to take him? The poor little chap never had a chance to live!"

Rees said nothing. He listened as the preacher quoted Scripture and did his best to comfort the distressed father. But finally, when Rees and Reverend Coleman had left the house, Rees turned to him and said, "I'm no better than that poor man, Pastor. I can't understand why God lets such terrible things happen. All over this city children are dying, and there's nothing I can do about it. Why would God allow such things?"

"You know your Bible better than that, Rees Kenyon. It's because of sin."

If Rees had not been so worn down by his duties and frantic because of his concern for Grace, he might not have spoken out. He had been a Christian for many years, but his faith had withered somehow in the onslaught of the tragedy that he faced almost hourly. "Why should helpless children die because Adam sinned?"

Josiah Coleman felt a gust of pity for this tall man whom he knew to be a good Christian. He spoke softly about the sufferings of good people, mentioning the patriarch Job. "Don't let this destroy your faith, Dr. Kenyon."

For a moment Rees stood there, and then his mind went to the young woman he loved so dearly. "I don't think my faith is strong enough. If I lose Grace, I lose everything."

"Don't talk like that, man. We all have to face up to this world we live in. None of us are going to get out of it alive. Some will go in this epidemic. Some will live to be old men and women. But in the end we all face God, and your Bible tells you he is merciful and long-suffering. I know it's hard to see that when we're faced with tragedy. But we've got to go on with life."

"With my head I know you're right, but there's a dark cloud hanging over me, Reverend Coleman."

"Suppose I go along with you. We'll see how Grace is. We'll trust that God will do a miracle in her."

"There is kind of you," Rees said.

The two men got into the carriage and made their way through the city. When they came to the Freeman home, Rees left the carriage in front, telling the preacher, "I'll take you home after you've had your visit."

The two men went inside and were met at once by Howard Freeman. Elizabeth came behind him and she was weeping.

"She's taken a turn for the worse, I'm afraid," Dr. Freeman said, his lips tight and his face strained. "You'd better go in to her, Rees."

Rees nodded and walked across the floor, moving stiffly. He entered the room and went at once to Grace's bedside. Shock ran through him, for he recognized instantly that she was in the last stages of the disease.

*She's dying and there's not one thing on God's earth that I can do about it!*

Standing over her bed, Rees Kenyon was intensely aware of the frailty of life. His physical strength, all the medical training in the world, the prayers that had been lifted up for this young woman — none of it availed. She was slipping away and he wanted to shout, to beat his fists against something. But what? How could one fight this sort of thing? Never in his life had Rees felt the futility of human effort and endeavor as he did at this moment.

He leaned over, kissed her cheek, and then put his arms around her. She felt fragile, and the disease had turned her body into a miniature furnace. Her lips were dry and the beauty had been leached out of her by the disease. Rees tried to hold back the tears but it was useless. They began to flow and his shoulders began to shake. Finally he sobbed, holding on to her, crying out, "Oh, Grace, I can't bear to lose you! Don't leave me!"

The daylight had gone and the night had come, but it meant nothing to Rees. Grace was dying and he stood stiffly, his fists clenched and his mind rebelling against it. He stood back in the corner while Grace, who had regained consciousness, was saying her farewell to her parents. He heard her voice but it was not like her voice at all. The voice he loved to hear had been so rich and so full. Now it was just a mere whisper, scratchy and fluttering, without strength.

His name was called and he stumbled to the bed. He leaned over, picked up her hand, and stroked her forehead. She was saying something and he put his ear to her lips. He made out the words, "I must . . . leave you." Then a silence. And finally, "Try not . . . to grieve too much."

"Oh, Grace, I can't bear it!"

The slight form seemed to grow tense, but he heard her say, "I have loved you . . . my dearest one . . ."

Those were the last words that Grace Freeman spoke upon this earth. She lapsed into unconsciousness, and two hours later she slipped quietly away.

All was confusion to Rees. He heard voices and was aware that Reverend Coleman had come and put his arm around his shoulder, whispering something. He himself went to Howard and Elizabeth, but he could never remember what he said. The darkness outside the house had become almost palpable in his soul. It was as if the sun had gone out in his spirit and left him in utter blackness.

Josiah Coleman was sitting in his study and now glanced outside the window. The sun was beaming down. August had come and brought with it the heat of full summer. He looked again at Dr. Howard Freeman, noting that the man was in poor condition. The cholera epidemic had for the most part passed away, but it left behind the wreckage of many homes, not the least of which was that of this fine physician who had come to sit in on church business. *He's lost*

*weight, and the joy has gone out of life for him,* Reverend Coleman thought. *He and his wife were so wrapped up in Grace, and it's all they can do to keep moving ahead.*

"It's been two months, Howard. A hard two months," he said slowly. "Almost every family in our church has lost someone. Indeed, we've lost entire families. The Stanleys — husband, wife, and all four children buried."

"It's been worse than a war," Howard said, nodding. "That takes the strongest men, but this terrible illness has struck down women, children, old people. I'll never get over it, I don't think."

"We must trust in the mercies of God." Reverend Coleman suddenly slapped his hands together. "I hate it when I do that!"

"Do what, Pastor?"

"Utter these blasted platitudes!" Reverend Coleman got up and walked to the window and stared outside. A group of sparrows were fighting over crumbs, rolling in the dust. The preacher stared at them, and a line of poetry — *If birds in their nest don't agree, why should we?* — came to him. He stared at the birds fighting as viciously as their human counterparts and finally turned around and said, "When a loss such as yours comes, there's really nothing to say."

"You must say something, Pastor. It may mean little, but the saying of it is important."

"I stand rebuked, Howard. The words of the Lord sometimes are like seeds. We put them in the ground and we don't see any results for a long time. In any case, this has been the hardest period of life for me." He sat down heavily and then looked up and asked, "What about Rees? It's been two months and he hasn't been to church since we lost Grace."

Howard Freeman shook his head. He passed his hand over his face and then dropped it back to his lap. "I've never seen a man grieve so. He's changed. He was so lighthearted and cheerful, and now it's as if his heart were frozen."

"He may lose his health if he doesn't learn to cope with his grief."

"I've told him that. He goes through the motions of living but that's all." Suddenly Freeman slapped his fist into his palm. "We may as well have buried him with Grace, Pastor. He's even been drinking to drown his grief."

"He's such a fine young man. So much promise. Come, Howard, let us pray for him — and for ourselves."

The two men got on their knees and prayed fervently and brokenly. The sunlight came down, anointing them with golden rays, but when they rose, both men's faces were wet with tears.

Rees stared down at the Thames as it purled along its banks, making small whirlpools. He had come often the last few days to stand on the bridge, and now silently he stood there, a tall, bent figure without expression on his craggy features. He glanced up and looked at the Tower of London. Thoughts of his visit there with Grace came trooping through his memory. He was blessed — or cursed — with a vivid recall, and he could see her face as she laughed and pointed out the suits of armor on display. She had been filled with life. Her lips had been red, her cheeks flushed, and her eyes dancing. He too had been full of life that day, but now the bitterness of his loss came to him.

The sound of voices came to him from time to time, and a beggar approached and said, "Spare a bit for the poor, master?" Rees reached into his pocket, gave the man the change he found there, but never heard the man's thanks. Standing with the hot sun bearing down upon him, Rees remembered vividly the dream he'd had last night. It had been a simple dream. He had dreamed that he had been happy with a group of small children. They had filled his ears with their happy cries, and his eyes with their healthy faces. They had begged him to be allowed to go out and pick flowers in the field, and he had let them go. But they had never come back. He had waited until darkness came, and he had been filled with a poignant sense of loss, an agonizing knowledge that they would never come back. And the flowers that they had gone to pick were bitter fruit indeed.

"A man's a fool to hope for anything in this world."

Rees Kenyon whispered the words to the waters far below. Without realizing it, he had come to murmur aloud. The whiskey did that to him. He hated strong drink, what it did to men, and knew he was a fool and that it displayed a weakness. Still, it provided oblivion for a time. Now his head ached and his mouth was furred and his stomach was soured because of the whiskey he had filled himself with. "All hopes are doomed. They're like sailors who come and visit for a time, stay a day or two, and finally sail off, and a man sees them no more."

Bitterly he turned away and walked to the bank. Blindly almost, he passed by the docked ships, unaware of the activity, of the men who loaded them and unloaded them. He thought suddenly of the letter he had received from his mother, congratulating him on becoming a doctor. She had not yet heard of Grace's death, and he knew he must write and tell her. But there was no heart in him for such things. Indeed, there was no heart for anything. He glanced at the river and the bridge that crossed it. The thought slipped into his mind as a thief slips into a house in the darkness and the owner does not even know he is there: *How easy it would be to jump off that bridge and end it all.*

Such a thought shocked Rees, for it went against everything he had ever believed. The subtlety with which it had crept into his mind alarmed him. He knew it was the liquor that had allowed him to reach this stage, and finally he said aloud, "Go from here now, Rees Kenyon." Alarmed by his thoughts and befuddled by the alcohol, he walked rapidly for two hours. Finally he paused before a pub. He entered and asked for a glass of water.

The innkeeper studied him and said, "Just water?"

"Perhaps a glass of ale. But water, and it's thirsty I am."

He drank two large tumblers full of water, then nursed the ale, studying it as it gave off its amber color under the flickering lanterns and lamps that lit the pub. He had seen too many lives destroyed by alcohol to have any illusions and knew that he had come to a point in his life when something must happen. There was no going on as he had been.

The room was filled with smoke and noisy. He watched the men seated at a worn table, their tankards before them. One man was dressed in the uniform of a sergeant in His Majesty's forces. He was of no more than medium height, but there was a sturdiness about him and a ruddiness in his cheeks and a light in his eye that spoke of a vivid life within. Rees listened and soon discovered that the sergeant was just back from Boston. Rees was aware of the troubles that were occurring in the colonies. It had seemed very remote from him, but since coming to London, he realized that the issue was a live one. So he listened carefully as the sergeant spoke of the rebellion brewing far across the seas.

Eventually the sergeant's companions left, and the soldier looked across the room at Rees and smiled. "Good day to you, sir."

"Good day, Sergeant. May I buy you a pint?"

"Well, I don't see why not. There's no 'arm in it."

Rees got up and moved over to the table. He ordered the drinks and paid for them, and then he said, "I'm afraid I don't know much about what's going on in the colonies."

"A rebellion is what's going on, flat and simple. My name's Carwell."

"I'm Rees Kenyon. Proud I am to know you, Sergeant."

"From Wales, is it?"

"Yes indeed!"

"So am I." He named the village where he was born and had grown up, and the two men spoke warmly of their homeland, as men will who love the place of their birth.

"Would there be a place for a man over in Virginia?"

Sergeant Carwell shrugged. "That's as may be. What might you do for a living, Mr. Kenyon?"

"I'm a physician."

"A sawbones, is it!" The sergeant's eyes glinted. "Well, you might sign up in our regiment. Always a place in the army for another pill roller."

"I don't think I'd be fitted for military life, but I need to get away from London."

"Not thinking of going back to Wales?"

"No, I think not."

"Well, you'd do well in the New World."

"In the middle of a rebellion?"

"That won't last long." Sergeant Carwell waved his hand. "England has the finest army — and the finest navy — in the world. Those colonists are a bunch of shopkeepers and farmers. They'd run like sheep the first time they heard a shot. No, Doctor, they're talkers but it won't amount to anything."

"So I might find a place for myself, you think?"

"Indeed, I think so. A London doctor is a prize in the colonies."

The sergeant drank two more pints while Rees nursed his. He was fascinated with the idea of a long trip at sea and a new place. Finally Sergeant Carwell said, "I have a cousin there in Boston. I'll give you a letter to him if you'd like. His name is Henry Knox." He took a drink of his ale and then shrugged. "A fine, fat fellow. Sells books, but he knows everybody in Boston. I think he could put you right, Doctor. Be a good place for you to start your new career. But if you go, be sure you don't get involved with any of those revolutionaries."

"I'll not be likely to do that, Sergeant."

"It truly is a new world over there, Dr. Kenyon. There's room enough for a man to swing his arms. When we get this rebellion snuffed out, I might be going back myself. I'll be needing a good doctor. I'm getting married this week. Expect to have at least ten young Carwells, so we'll keep in touch. Right?"

"Right, you. And thank you, sir."

Dr. Freeman stared at Rees and turned suddenly to exchange glances with Elizabeth. They both had been shocked when Rees had come in to tell them he was leaving London.

"But where will you go?" Howard asked. "I had such great plans for your future here. You'll do well, I'm sure of it."

"I'm very much aware of your kindness, Dr. Freeman, but I've got to go someplace where — well, where every sight I see doesn't remind me of Grace."

Elizabeth understood at once. "I know, dear," she said. "It's hard for all of us. Where will you go?"

"I'm leaving for America."

"With all the trouble over there?" Freeman asked at once.

"I don't think that will amount to anything. But I've been told that a London physician can depend on a good practice there."

The three spoke for a time and then Freeman said, "Do you need money, Rees?"

"No, no! You've been too kind." Actually, Rees did not have a great deal of money. His sister had been having difficulties and he had been helping her. But he shook off the good doctor's further efforts to help him and said, "I'll be leaving day after tomorrow."

"We'll miss you, Rees," Howard said. "You may not like it there. You can always come back here."

Rees spent most of his remaining time with the Freemans. He loved them both dearly, but even they brought memories of Grace, and he knew that despite missing them, there would be a relief in finding new faces.

He bid them farewell two days later, then headed for the docks. As the cabby took him toward the ship, he found himself grieved to leave the Freemans but at the same time filled with anticipation and hope that in America he would find release from the grief that bound him and a life that had meaning once again.

# Chapter Six

A BLACK NIGHT HAD CLOSED OVER LONDON, DARK CLOUDS BLOTTING out the stars overhead. The fog had rolled in with its miasmic thickness. It was not a London Particular, a fog mixed with the smoke of thousands of chimneys burning coal. This fog came in from off the sea, with none of the bite of the thick clouds that filled the streets of the great city.

Callie Summers made her way cautiously along the street. Looking out over the Thames, she could see the lights burning on some of the ships. The tide moved the vessels, and the yellow lanterns were reflected in wavy images on the water. The fog was too thick for her to see across the river, but if she could have seen the other side, Callie would have known every foot of it, as she knew the side she moved along now.

She turned onto a street lined on both sides with shops, which gave way farther down to the taverns and inns, all with their lights shining brightly though it was after ten o'clock. The street was not crowded, for most of the men and the women out at this time of night had found a place to drink themselves into insensibility. It was that sort of street but Callie gave danger not a thought. This was her world and she had learned to survive.

"Hey, sweetheart, come along and give a man some lovin'."

A sailor with a greasy pigtail down his back and a striped shirt had lurched across the street, more than half drunk. He grinned, exposing broken teeth, and lust burned in his eyes.

Callie fended off his outstretched arms, shoving him backward. His feet got tangled together and he sat down hard on the cobblestones. "Keep your blinkin' 'ands to yourself, sailor boy!" she said. Callie laughed at his curses and ran lightly away as he struggled to get up.

Keeping a careful watch, she made her way down the street by the yellow light of the lanterns illuminating the tavern signs. Most of those she saw were drunken men, but as always the harlots of London were out in force. Some of them were no older than Callie, who was sixteen. Others were ancient and covered their ragged faces with pasty makeup. Their voices were screechy and Callie ignored them. She ignored the calls of the men, too, although once when a big man grabbed her arm, she reached under her coat for the dirk she always kept there. It had a six-inch blade and was sharp enough to shave the hair from a man's arm — or do worse. She did not have to pull the blade, however, but was quick enough to jerk away. Moving rapidly, she stepped into the door beneath a sign with no words, only a picture of a red horse.

The room Callie entered was some twenty feet in width and perhaps twenty-five in depth. On one side was a bar built of hardwood, with glasses and bottles lined up on shelves on the wall. Mismatched wooden tables were scattered around, and chairs and stools. Under the dim lights Callie quickly eyed the customers. The smell of tobacco was rank, and the odor of spirits was almost thick enough to make one drunk simply by inhaling. The air was filled with laughter laced with the shrill cries of the prostitutes who hung on to men sitting at the tables.

Callie moved to the right, headed for the wall which lay in partial darkness. She had to step over the body of one man, dead drunk, who lay stretched out on his back, his eyes closed in a peaceful rest. Bending over, she felt his pockets, but before she could complete her task, her arm was seized and she was pulled up and around. The man who held her was bulky, had a huge stomach covered by a filthy white apron. His face had been battered, and the cauliflower ears and the broken nose and the scars that brought his eyes down at the edges marked his former profession, or hobby, as bare-knuckled brawling.

In a voice surprisingly high for such a huge man, Timothy Ryan said, "All right, Callie, I've thrown you out of here too many times."

"I wasn't 'urting nobody, Tim."

Timothy Ryan frowned. "You're too young for all this."

"I ain't either! I'm nearly seventeen and I ain't done nothin'!"

Ryan, the battered owner of the Red Horse Tavern, shook his head. "That detective Simon Gore, he's been catchin' lots of gals like you." He held her easily in his massive hand and added, "You get caught stealin', you'll end up in Old Bailey — or on the end of a rope."

Callie laughed at him, turning her face up. "Never was a tec wot could catch me, Tim my boy."

Ryan studied the young woman. Under her open coat she was wearing a gray dress too large for her, but even that failed to conceal the curves of her youthful body. She had blond hair that would have been blonder had it been washed. A floppy cap concealed part of it. Her smooth complexion was somewhat grimy, but her enormous eyes were her best feature — they were well shaped, like almonds, and were a peculiar shade of green, sometimes dark and sometimes light as the sea itself. Despite the way she made her living, there still was on the girl some trace of innocence that caused the saloon keeper to lecture her severely. He had two daughters of his own not much younger than this one, and he knew that her end would not be pleasant if she were taken by the law. "Why don't you get a job, Callie? It ain't too late for you to make a fresh start. Get out of London. This place ain't no good for you."

"I don't know 'ow to do nothin' else, Tim. Besides, I won't get caught."

"You won't get caught in this place. Leave here now."

Callie pulled her arm back as the big man released it, and she smiled up at him cynically. "There ain't nothin' else for a gal to do, Tim, and don't worry about me." She turned and started to leave, but her quick eyes picked out a well-dressed man sitting alone at a table to her right. He was already half drunk. She had learned to gauge drunkenness almost scientifically, and she knew that soon he would stagger out, unable to do much more than walk.

She turned and went back to Ryan, who was watching her. "Give me 'alf a pint of gin, Tim."

"I'm not selling you liquor."

"I've got the cash. And it ain't for me."

"Who's it for, then?"

"It's for my friend Maggie. She's got a cold, she 'as."

Shaking his head, Ryan went behind the bar, filled a half-pint bottle with the colorless liquid, capped it, and handed it to her. "Go on home. It's late."

"I'm on my way, Tim. Good night to you."

Callie stepped outside but she did not go far. Crossing the street, she slipped into the shadows and waited. As she did, she pulled a small bottle from an inner pocket, uncapped it and the bottle of gin, and carefully counted off five drops. She replaced both caps, shook the bottle of gin thoroughly, then set herself to wait.

The wait was longer than she thought, but forty-five minutes later she was rewarded. The well-dressed man appeared suddenly and came out onto the street. He was using the careful walk that drunks used, as if they were walking on the edge of a very thin board. Callie let him get out of the light and then at once left her hiding place. She came up boldly to the man, took his arm, and smiled up at him. "Yer wants a good time, sweetheart?"

"What's that?" The man tried to focus his eyes. He was a small-ish man, not much taller than Callie herself. She squeezed his arm and repeated her invitation, and for a moment she thought he would refuse. But finally a foolish grin crossed his face.

"Why, sure I want a good time — but where is your place?"

"Right down the street. Come along, 'andsome. Here, let's 'ave a drink." She took the bottle out, removed the cap, lifted it to her lips, but she covered the opening with her tongue. She swallowed, then handed him the bottle and wiped her mouth with her sleeve. "Good stuff!"

Her victim took the bottle, drank from it several times. As she went down the street, twice more she urged it on him. He had drunk half its contents by the time they had gone a block. Callie capped the bottle and saw that already he was going out. They were quickly coming to the alleyway she had picked out, and she said, "Come on. It's down 'ere."

The man made an unintelligible reply. He stepped into the alley, Callie keeping his arm. "It's dark in here," he mumbled.

"Just a few more steps."

But a few more steps were too many for the man. His knees began folding, and he cried out in a confused manner and then fell headlong.

In the darkness Callie expertly removed his watch, the ring from his finger, and his money from his inside coat pocket. She started to take his shoes but caution came to her and she rose. Staring down into the murky darkness, she laughed. "I 'ope you had a good time, sweetheart." Then she turned and left the alley.

Making her way through a labyrinthine set of streets and alleys, she arrived at a building on the waterfront and saw a small light in an upstairs window. Quickly she climbed the rickety steps and banged on the door. "Lemme in, Maggie. It's me!"

She heard footsteps sounding then and the door opened. The yellow light loomed behind the young woman who stood there. "You're out late tonight, Callie. Come on in."

Shutting the door behind her, Callie put the bolt in place and then removed her coat and tossed her hat onto the peg driven into the wall. "I 'ad a piece of good luck tonight. Look at this."

Maggie Price was wearing only a thin shift. She was in her early twenties and the rough life had begun to mark her. There were still traces of beauty, however, and now as she came forward, her eyes gleamed. "How'd you get these?"

"Same ol' way." Callie related her adventure and the two laughed. "He'll wake up in the mornin' with a splittin' 'ead, no watch, no money, and not even a memory of a good time. Here, you take 'alf the money, Maggie."

"No, it's yours."

"You split with me when I was broke. Now, you take it. I'll sell the watch and the ring tomorrow. I'm gonna buy somethin' real nice."

"Are you hungry?"

"No. I'm tired, though."

"Go to bed."

Maggie watched as the young woman stripped down to her underclothes, lay on the thin mattress on the floor, and went to sleep almost instantly. She went over, picked up a thin coverlet, and pulled it over the girl. With a wishful expression she studied the younger woman's face. "If I was as young and pretty as you, I'd get out of this place," she muttered. Then wearily she went back to her own bed, fell into it, and soon was snoring.

The fence had no name that anyone knew. He was called Rattler, which was almost certainly not his name. No one knew where he lived or anything else about him except that he could be found on the waterfront early in the mornings. He conducted all his transactions at that time rather than at night, in the old, deserted shack he called home. Rattler was a tall man with a skeletal frame, but he wore respectable clothes and could pass down the street without being noted by the police. He had white hair and pale blue eyes, which now he fastened on the watch and the ring that Callie had brought him. "Not a good make, Callie. I can't no ways give you over three pounds for both of them."

"Three pounds!" Callie's eyes flashed indignantly. "You'll get forty pounds when you sell them!"

Rattler smiled. He had a rather beatific smile and looked more like a deacon than a fence, one of the underworld's aristocracy. "Why don't you go sell them yourself, then?"

Callie could not answer, for both knew very well that if she tried to sell them, she would be spotted and the police would be on her immediately. "Come on, Rattler, 'ave a 'art."

"Well, seeing as it's you, I will have a heart. Ten pounds. My final offer."

Callie sighed and shook her head. "All right. Give me the cash." She took the coins Rattler extended, put them in her pocket, and looked at him curiously. "Don't it 'urt your conscience none to rob an orphan?"

Rattler laughed aloud. "Did it hurt your conscience to lift this off some bloke? Why, it's like you're robbing his wife and children."

Callie was a good-humored young woman despite her harsh circumstances. She saw the humor of Rattler's remark. "You're right," she said. "We're both of us bound straight for the pit."

"Now, now, don't talk like that. We'll repent someday when we're rich and don't need to steal any longer."

"You're a villain, you are! Good-bye, Rattler."

"Be careful," Rattler called out his warning. "The tecs are out. If they catch you with stolen goods like this, you'll do the dance for the hangman."

Callie paid no heed except to give him a cheerful smile and a wave. She then went directly to one of the better streets on the west side of London. It was like another world, for here the respectable people moved. They wore good clothes. They had rings and watches, and the ladies had parasols made with ivory, and they smelled better. Callie had an acute sense of smell and she herself tried to stay clean. It was almost impossible, considering the lack of bathing facilities.

She moved slowly along and finally she stopped in front of one of the shops. Peering in through the window, she could see counters and bolts of fine cloth, and taking a deep breath, she held her head up and went inside.

No sooner was she inside than a woman came over to her. She was in her middle thirties, Callie guessed rather accurately, and wore a gray dress with a pearl brooch at her bosom. "You can't come in here, girl."

"I've got money that'll spend as good as anybody else's."

The woman stared at her, and then when Callie held out a handful of coins, she shrugged her shoulders. "Very well. Buy what you want but you'll have to leave soon."

Callie was accustomed to such talk but she would not be hurried. She stayed for half an hour, and when she left, she clutched a bottle of expensive scent that the woman had assured her had come all the way from Spain. In a small package was a delicate lace shawl. She had no place in her life to wear it, but she knew she would take it out at home, run her hands over the beautiful material, and put it on over her rough clothing.

Callie hurried home, anxious to show Maggie her purchases. When she got there, however, the place was empty. Maggie was unpredictable, so this did not bother Callie. She opened her packages, breathed the scent, and put less than a drop on her neck and smelled it ecstatically. "Ooh, that's so good," she said. She unwrapped the lace and sat with it across her lap, running her hands over it, enchanted by it. She had a love for fine things, which was surprising, since she'd never had any. She remembered her parents only vaguely, for they had both died in a cholera epidemic when she was only ten. She had survived somehow, and the miracle was that she had not gone out on the streets at some point. If it had not been for Maggie, she probably would have, but the woman had taken a liking to her and protected her from the worst of street life.

Finally Callie hid the purchases under a board under her mattress and went out looking for prey. She had no luck all day long and came home hungry. When she opened the door, she called, "Maggie?" but there was no answer.

*Where can she be?* Callie knew Maggie could not write, so there was no way she could leave a note. Callie set about making herself a meal out of what was available in the small box nailed to the wall — cheese and hard bread. She washed it down with ale that was too warm and ate a few raisins she had saved for dessert.

The evening passed by and still no Maggie. This had happened before, and Callie knew that Maggie was probably with some man. She went to bed finally but knew that she would have to search for Maggie the next day. Maggie had once been beaten unconscious by a brute, and it had been Callie who had found her and brought her home. As she lay in the darkness, Callie thought once of praying, but then she laughed cynically. "I don't think God would hear a girl like me." She turned over and finally fell into a fitful sleep.

# *Chapter Seven*

THE RED HORSE TAVERN SEEMED WORN OUT FROM ITS EXCESSES of the night before. As Callie entered, she took no note of the odor of stale tobacco smoke and raw alcohol, but quickly her eyes went to Timothy Ryan, who slumped at a table in the rear, his head on his forearms. A greasy old woman making ineffectual swabs at the floor took a slow look at Callie, then ignored her. Moving across the room, Callie studied Timothy. A bottle before him had only a couple inches of liquor left, and an empty bottle lay on the floor beside him. The big man was snoring softly, but he started and lifted his head when Callie spoke to him. "Timothy?"

Snorting roughly and sitting up abruptly, Ryan lifted his hands in a defensive gesture, his eyes wild, but after an instant he slowly began to focus on the girl in front of him. His eyes were red, and the cold morning light streaming in through the window revealed the rough life he had led. The lines were ingrained deeply in his face, and his cheeks were sunken and his hair stringy and falling over his forehead. "What do you want?"

"I'm lookin' for Maggie, Tim. I've looked everywhere for her. 'Ave you seen her?"

Ryan stared at her steadily, then picked up his glass. He poured it half full, drained it, and then as the liquor hit his stomach, he coughed loudly and shut his eyes. When he opened them, he said, "Ain't you heard?"

"Heard wot?"

"Maggie. It was her you were askin' for."

"'Ave you seen her, Tim?"

"She's been taken."

Callie's face seemed to freeze and for a moment she could not speak. "When?" she whispered.

"Don't know, but she's been took. I tried to warn her, same as I did you. The tecs are out to get everybody they can. Especially the women. You best lay low for a while or get out of town."

Callie turned and walked away without another word. Ryan called out, "Ain't no need tryin' to help her. She's beyond that." When Callie did not even turn, Ryan picked up the bottle and, ignoring the glass, took several swallows. His Adam's apple went up and down, and when he lowered the bottle, gasping for breath, he gripped it hard, then stared at it as if it were a mortal enemy. Suddenly he threw it across the room, where it shattered against the wall. The old woman looked up but said nothing. Ryan stared at the splotch that the bottle had made on the wall and cursed, then slumped back down with his head on his arms.

Old Bailey rose against the sky, and it took all the courage Callie Summers could muster to force herself to approach the guard. All her life she had heard stories about this place, and she'd been frightened out of her wits by an execution in which two men and three women were hanged. She could not even remember who took her there, but Callie still, after all these years, had vivid dreams about the crowds laughing at the victims as they stood on the gallows. She still remembered that one of the women was no more than fifteen or sixteen, and her face was drained of all color. Another woman was fat, and even the threat of death could not take the color from her reddened cheeks. She had cursed until the very end, when her voice was cut short by the snap of her neck at the end of the rope.

The guard stared at Callie as she approached. "I'd like to see one of the prisoners," she said.

"Well, you ain't goin' ter."

Callie well understood that all things were possible inside Old Bailey — for cash. She had come prepared for this and took a coin out of her pocket. A few minutes later, after the price was negotiated, she was allowed inside. She was led down a mazelike corridor of the prison, sickened by the smell of death and frightened by the gloomy shadows.

Finally she was locked into a large room where at least thirty prisoners sat or walked aimlessly, all illuminated by two high, barred windows that admitted feeble, pale shafts of light. Her eyes went around the room and she saw Maggie lying on the floor, flat on her back. Quickly she went over and knelt beside her. "Maggie," she said urgently, "are you all right?"

Maggie Price opened her eyes at once and sat up. She ran her hands through her tangled hair and passed them over her face, then shook her head. "You shouldn't be here."

"I 'ad to come and see you."

Maggie took a deep breath. She seemed to have aged ten years in the short time since Callie had last seen her. She made a ghastly attempt at a smile, but then the fear that lay in her etched across her face. She stiffened her lips and said hoarsely, "You may as well go, Callie. There ain't nothin' you can do."

"I'll see a lawyer."

"What good will that do? I was caught red-handed."

"Who was it wot caught you?"

"It was Simon Gar, that's who." Maggie cursed and shook her head. "May he rot in the fires forever!"

Callie tried desperately to think of some encouraging thing she might say, but nothing came. The hand of death was on Maggie in one form or another. Finally Callie said, "I've got some money saved. I'll get a good lawyer."

"Don't do that. He couldn't do nothin' but take your money." Maggie closed her eyes and placed her head back against the wall. "There ain't no hope. I'll get at least ten years. I'll kill myself before I let them put me in that place!"

Callie suddenly leaned forward and embraced Maggie. The woman clung to her and began weeping. Callie held her until the weeping subsided, and then she said, "Don't give up. We'll get 'elp."

"Get out of this life, Callie. You'll end up like this."

Callie stayed for another fifteen minutes, trying to encourage the doomed woman, but both of them knew her words were worthless. Finally she kissed Maggie, then turned and left, saying, "I'll be back."

"Don't come back no more. It won't be no good."

The lawyers were thick as fleas on Fleet Street but Callie knew none of them. She passed several signs and finally went into one of the offices. It was a dim, musty place lit by two candles and a whale-oil lamp. The outer room was empty, but through a door Callie could see a man sitting at a table, reading a book. "Please, sir, can I see you?"

"What do you want?" The man looked up from the book, and when he saw her, he stood up and entered the room she was in. "What is it?"

"I've got a friend. She's in trouble." Callie explained the situation and said, "I don't have much money."

The man had a pale, thin face with eyes set close together. He moved forward and put his hand on Callie's shoulder. She could feel his fingers digging in and took one look at his eyes and knew well what his next words would be.

"You and me will work out somethin'," he said knowingly. He suddenly put his other hand on her shoulder and attempted to embrace her, but Callie's hand was quick. She brought out the gleaming knife, held it to his stomach, and her voice was cold.

"Take your 'ands off me!"

The lawyer stepped back immediately and cursed her, but she did not stay. She left the office at once.

For the next hour she went from office to office, and her concept that lawyers were grasping creatures became firmer. Most of them had ideas such as that of the first. Others questioned her almost at once about how much money she had.

Finally she encountered an older man who listened to her story. He was wearing a white wig and was decently dressed. He had invited her to sit across from him and made no suspicious movement. Callie found herself hopeful, but when he spoke, he dispelled those hopes at once.

"My dear young lady, you would be wasting your money to give it to me or to any other attorney. The very most we could do would be to persuade the judge to send your friend to the prisoner's colony at Botney Bay instead of sending her to the noose. I'm not sure," he said quietly, "that would be doing her a favor."

"But please, sir, will you try? I'll give you all I've got."

Cyrus Andrews stared at the girl with compassion in his eyes. "I won't take your money, young woman, but I will stand for your friend. It won't do much good but I'll try."

"'Ere, I want to pay," Callie said quickly and pulled out the sum she had decided she could spare. She rose and approached him and when she saw denial in Andrews' eyes, she said almost fiercely, "I don't want no charity. I wants to pay just like anybody else."

"Well . . . well, this will be enough." He took four of the coins and nodded. "I suppose you'll be in the courtroom."

"Yes sir. I will."

Maggie's trial was a travesty. If it had not been for Andrews, she would have been sentenced without a word to the noose, as were two other felons. But Andrews had spoken out, and the judge, somewhat surprised to see so reputable an attorney, had listened and finally been persuaded to change the sentence from death by hanging to ten years in Botney Bay.

Callie had watched Maggie's face and seen the hopelessness, but she had done her best. She went at once to the attorney and thanked him.

"As I said before, I'm not sure I've done her any favor. But I do have some influence there. Perhaps I can get her sentence shortened."

"I'll pay you."

"There's no need, child. Just one letter is the least I can do." Andrews hesitated and then said quietly, "I'm concerned about you, Callie. I'd hate to come here one day and find you up there in the dock."

The lawyer's concern touched Callie. She ducked her head and tried to frame an answer, and then she looked up and said simply, "This life is all I know, Mr. Andrews."

Two weeks had passed since Maggie was shipped out with other lawbreakers. Callie had gone to see her twice and told her what Mr. Andrews said about shortening her sentence. The news seemed to cheer Maggie up, and at the last meeting she echoed what she had said before. "It's all up with me, dearie, but not with you. You ain't never hit bottom like I have. Why don't you get yourself a job as a maid or somethin' like that."

"Maybe I will. I'll try." Callie had known that such a thing was hopeless, but she did not want to discourage Maggie.

Tonight Callie sat in their room, very conscious of missing her friend. Maggie had been rough at times but the best friend she had ever had, and now the lull seemed almost unbearable. Callie drank very little but Maggie had left a bottle of gin, and she drank enough of it to dim the memory of their last visit.

Finally she rose and went out into the night. She wandered the streets and eventually Giles Toper appeared before her. His eyes were bright, though his tongue was somewhat thick with the gin he had been drinking. "Come on, Callie, I got us a mark."

"Not tonight, Toper."

"There won't be nothin' to it. I'm tellin' ya, he's got money like a prince." Toper pulled at Callie's arm. He was a middle-aged man with few skills and had spent some time in prison. He sounded almost desperate. "Come on. You can take one look at him and tell he'll be an easy mark."

Callie stared into the man's face and knew he was weak, but she remembered that she had given most of her money to Mr. Andrews. She struggled for a moment, remembering the advice Andrews and Maggie had given her, but a sense of despondency had gripped her ever since she had become involved with Maggie's hopeless fight. Half of her said that they were right, but she could think of no way to extricate herself from the life she had lived since she was a child.

"All right, Giles," she said, "but it'll 'ave ter be safe."

"Oh, don't worry about that," Giles said eagerly. He shrugged his thin shoulders expressively. "It'll be nothin' to it. Come on now."

Callie followed Giles to a tavern that was far more respectable than those she was accustomed to, it being in a better part of London, and she said, "I ain't goin' in there."

"You don't have to," Giles said. "Stand here and when he comes out, you can do a job on him."

The wait was not long, no more than forty-five minutes. She was almost in a haze, thinking of Maggie being transported to Botney Bay. Callie was a sensitive young woman in spite of her rough surroundings. Even as a child she had been so, and now despite the wall she had adamantly built around herself for protection, still inside something cried out for affection as well as for the finer things of life. She did not know that those who wore silks and had money and fine homes were often as miserable as those who roamed the waterfront.

Callie's thoughts were interrupted when a man lurched through the doors of the saloon. She watched cautiously as he swayed from side to side, then turned and began to walk unsteadily down the sidewalk. Callie followed him, keeping ten feet back and glancing around often to see if there were any witnesses. The street was deserted except for two men on the far side. She followed the drunk, and when the two men turned into a doorway, she quickened her steps. The man was talking to himself as drunks sometimes do, and Callie made her decision. Moving forward, she took the man's arm and smiled up at him, saying, "Come along, 'andsome — let's us 'ave ourselves a good time."

The man stopped dead still, swayed dangerously, and stared at her. His eyes were glazed and he tried to focus on Callie's face. He attempted to speak but he could only mumble. "What ... what'cher say?"

"Come along now, I've got us a fine place." She pulled at his arm and the drunk laughed meaninglessly and stumbled after her. He was trying to talk to her but made no sense at all. Looking ahead, Callie saw a dark form move out of an alley. She kept her eyes on him and made out the face of Giles Toper. She pulled the man along, encouraging him, and when they reached the alley, Toper reached out and pulled the man inside. Callie moved into the murky alley and found that Toper had thrown the victim to the ground and was holding his hand over the man's mouth. "Get wot he's got, Callie — and be quick!"

Expertly Callie extracted the struggling man's watch, his wallet, and stripped his ring from his finger. "Got it," she said, panting. "Let's get — "

"Hold it — or I'll blow yer 'eads off!"

Callie tried to run, but she had taken only a few steps when a fist struck her in the back. She fell to the ground and was seized at once. A strong hand pulled her up and her captor yelled, "I've got the woman, Ed. You get the man?"

"Sure, I got him, Sergeant!"

Callie was dragged out onto the street, and her heart failed when she saw that her captor was Simon Gore. If she had entertained any hope of mercy, it fled at that moment. Gore pulled her face around, stared at her, then called out, "You take the bloke in, Ed. I'll take care of this one."

A hearty chuckle came from the other policeman, and then Gore took a firm grip on Callie's arm. "You come with me."

"Where . . . where are you taking me?" Callie cried out.

But the bulky officer growled, "Keep yer face shut or I'll shut it for you!" He moved along the street, hauling Callie with him.

Gore knocked on the door and turned to leer at Callie. "You ain't a bad-lookin' bird," he said. "But you won't be takin' in no more marks."

"Wot is this place?" Callie asked, fear rising in her. "Take me to jail!"

Gore grunted. "Ain't no profit for me in that." The door opened and he said, "Hello, Slasher — got a volunteer for you."

"Bring 'er inside."

Callie struggled with all her strength, but Gore slapped her face, and the power of the blow stunned her. She felt Gore's hand drop but her other arm was seized at once. She turned and faced a huge man, even larger than Gore, and she knew him at once — Slasher Murdock! Callie had seen him before and knew his reputation, as did everyone in the lower east side.

Slasher Murdock made his living from young women — and was not at all careful where he got them. Many a young girl had been drugged and had awakened to find herself in the power of Slasher Murdock. "Please, take me to jail!" Callie cried out, but she knew it was hopeless. She watched as Murdock pulled some bills from his pocket and thrust them toward Gore. "Find me some more like this 'un," he said, laughing.

Gore pocketed the cash, gave Callie a leer, then said, "I'll pay a fiver for her, Slasher."

"Not likely!" Slasher laughed roughly. He tightened his grip on Callie's arm and ran his free hand over her body. "I got plans for this 'un! Got a bloke who'll pay 'ansome for a fresh young gal like this!"

Gore shrugged, then turned and left the room. Slasher pulled the frightened Callie down the hall, opened a door, and thrust her into it, saying, "Try to get away and I'll make you wish you was dead." Then he laughed coarsely and shut the door. The darkness that covered Callie was not nearly so black as the fear that flooded her spirit. She slumped on the floor and began to weep — but she knew tears would bring her no pity from the beast that now held her.

# Chapter Eight

"I'M AFRAID THERE'LL BE A LITTLE DELAY, SIR."

Rees had arrived at the dock with his small trunk and two bags. He had entered the shipping office and announced that he'd come to take the *Orion* bound for America. Now he was anxious to get away but the clerk shrugged. "The loading won't be finished for another twenty-four hours, sir."

"All right. I'd like to leave my baggage here."

"Certainly, sir. I'll take care of it myself and see that it's loaded."

"Thank you."

Rees turned and left the office. He walked down to the water-front and looked at the *Orion,* a trim, three-masted ship, and noted that the deck was swarming with men carrying cargo up a wooden gangway. He pulled out his watch, studied it, and then turned away. Night had not yet begun to close in, and Rees walked along the shore studying the ships and taking in the faces of the people. Mostly they consisted of workers connected in some way to shipping — sailors, stevedores, laborers of all sorts rebuilding a dock.

Finally he began looking for a place to stay.

He found himself in front of a tavern with a badly drawn picture of a knight on a horse. Studying it, he supposed it was intended to be Saint George. The dragon was faded and looked rather pathetic, as if he knew he was about to be cut down by Saint George's famous sword.

Entering, Rees found himself in the room reserved for food and drinks, and he waited until the short, thickset man who appeared to be the tavern keeper was free.

"Do you have a room for the night?"

"Yes sir. One night only?"

"Yes. I'll be leaving tomorrow on the *Orion.*"

"Oh, bound for America!" The tavern owner had a thick Irish accent. He studied Rees for a moment. "Going to the colonies, are you, sir?"

"Yes."

"Bit of trouble over there."

"I know. Could I get something to eat?"

"Yes. I'll have my wife cook up something. Chops be all right?"

"That'll be fine."

"The room's upstairs. Third door on the right. Why don't you go get settled, and your supper will be ready before long."

Rees nodded and went up the stairs. He found the room, stepped inside, and looked around. It was rough enough but at least there was a bed. Walking over to the window, he pulled a chair up and sat. He watched night close down over the waterfront, and looking up, he saw the moon, which seemed to have two horns.

The silence of the room somehow depressed Rees. He was in a bad mood and could not get the memories of Grace out of his head. They ran through his mind like a drama upon a stage — things they had done together, her laughter, the way humor had danced in her eyes. Suddenly the silence became intolerable. He left it and went downstairs. He found the tavern keeper watching him and said, "Is the meal ready?"

"Yes sir, that it is. Sit down over there." Rees took a seat, vaguely aware that the room was crowded now. There was gambling at several of the tables, while others were filled with men drinking or eating.

A heavy woman wearing an apron came and put a plate down in front of him. "Will you be 'aving somethin' to drink, sir?"

"Yes. Ale."

"I'll bring it, sir."

Rees ate slowly. He dreaded the thought of going back up to the room and wondered if he wouldn't have been better off to have simply insisted on going aboard ship.

After he finished the meal, he asked for whiskey, and for over an hour he sat trying to pull his thoughts together. He tried to concentrate on the future rather than the past, and lost track of the drinks he had consumed. Finally, when he set the glass down hard on the table and noticed that the sound was muffled, he knew he'd had too much.

He pushed the bottle away and looked around the room. The smoke haze was highlighted by the lanterns, and he began to pay attention to four gamblers who sat at a table not far away. One of them was a man who was hard to miss. He was sprawled in his chair and he seemed to be as broad as a man could be. He was running to fat, Rees noticed, but the snuff brown suit he wore was stretched tightly, straining against the muscles in his arms. One look at his face revealed that he had at one time been a fighter or perhaps still was. One of his ears was a shapeless mass, and a tiny network of scars crisscrossed the corners of his eyes. His nose had been smashed, and his hands were so huge that the cards looked tiny in them.

The big man seemed to be losing and it made him ill-tempered. He turned and put his eyes on Rees, and after losing a hand, he cursed and turned back and said, "Get me some more whiskey, girl — and don't try to get away!"

Rees noticed the young woman who had been standing against the wall of the tavern. She was very young, he saw, and her face revealed none of the traces of debauchery that such creatures usually have. Her blond hair escaped from a cap she was wearing, and the worn and faded dress, though somewhat loose, revealed her figure. Her face seemed to be frozen, and at the big man's command she went at once to the bar, where the innkeeper gave her a bottle. She brought it back and put it down. As she did, the big man suddenly grabbed the front of her gown and, bunching it up in his hand, pulled it down until her face was even with his. "Well, give us a smile, can't you?" When he got no response, he shoved her away, muttering, "I'll teach you to smile!"

As the game progressed, the big man continued to lose. He grew violent and continued to drink. Rees would have left, but the silence in his room kept him downstairs, where at least there were lights and people. He watched as a large pot built up and saw that the big man was confident he had the winning hand. He leered at his opponent, a tall man with a pair of steady gray eyes, and said, "You ain't winnin' this one, Barker."

"It'll cost you to stay in, Slasher. I raise you twenty pounds."

Slasher was more than half drunk. He began to search through his pockets and finally said, "You'll have to take me marker for it."

"Cash only, you remember."

"You know I'm good for it!"

"Cash only. Either call or it's my pot."

The big man cursed and looked over at the innkeeper. "Let me have ten pounds, Nick."

"I can't do it, Murdock."

Murdock glared at him and suddenly his eyes fell on the girl. His mind seemed to be working slowly but then he lurched to his feet. The girl shrank from him, but he grabbed her by the upper arm and pulled her away from the wall. "Here you go, gents. A real bargain. She'll give any man of you a good time."

Rees was conscious that the big man's eyes were suddenly fastened on him, and then he heard the man's rough voice saying, "What about you? You wants to buy this girl? I'll sell her to you for twenty pounds."

Rees, though far from sober himself, was shocked. "No," he said. "I don't think so."

"Come on now. Be a sport." The big man turned to face the girl and saw that her face was drawn into fear. He cursed her and slapped her. "Smile, can't you!" The force of his blow rocked her.

Something came to Rees Kenyon at that moment. He had been too drunk to think very clearly, but now he suddenly realized that the girl bore a startling resemblance to Grace. Her face was similarly shaped. She was taller but there was something in her that reminded him so strongly of the woman who haunted him that he could not bear it.

"You don't have to beat the girl."

"She belongs to me. I'll do what I want with her — " And here Murdock's eyes narrowed. "Will you buy her, then?"

"Yes."

Rees Kenyon heard himself speak but it did not seem to be his own voice. He knew then that he was drunker than he thought, and he would have risen and left but Slasher Murdock was too quick. He dragged the girl over to stand in front of Rees and said, "There she is. It'll be forty pounds."

"You said twenty."

"I got to have a profit, ain't I? Give me the coin or else keep your face shut!"

Rees had read once of a man who was condemned to stand on a ledge for all eternity. For some reason that old story or fable came back to him just then. He felt somehow that he was standing at an interstice in his life and that what he did right here would be a turning point.

"Please, sir, 'elp me."

Rees's eyes fell on the girl, whose face was twisted with torment. She was poor and her face was grimy and her hair was unwashed, yet still there was that unmistakable resemblance to the only woman he had ever loved. She had the same green eyes and blond hair he had so loved in Grace.

The scene seemed to blur then before Rees's eyes, and he swayed, nausea rising in him. He knew he had drunk far too much, and he could not think properly. Then he knew he was going to be sick. He turned and staggered away, but as he did, he saw the big man snarl and strike the girl again. Desperately Rees reached into his pocket, pulled out some bank notes, and thrust them at Murdock. "There," he said. "Now leave her alone." He could say no more, for the whole room seemed to be spinning around, and he knew that if he did not get away, he would fall unconscious. He turned and left, and there seemed to be a roaring in his ears. By the time he got to his room, the nausea had overtaken him, and it was all he could do to reach the basin on the washstand. He threw up until he was weak and trembling and then staggered over and fell onto the bed. As he closed his eyes, it seemed that the bed was turning over and over and that the room itself was spinning.

A noise came to him, and a voice, and he turned to see that the door had opened and the girl had stepped inside. "Go away," he said.

"I can't," she whispered. "'E'd find me."

"You have to get out of here."

"I ain't got no place to go," she said. Her face seemed to become enlarged to fill the whole room, and Rees shut his eyes and plunged into a darkness as black as anything he had ever imagined.

Consciousness came oozing back like a creeping tide. Rees had no memory and for a few moments panic struck as he tried to determine where he was. Finally he began to remember and groaned deep within his chest. He lay there for a moment, gathering strength, and then painfully sat up. He was fully clothed and the first thing he thought of was his money. He reached frantically and found that his wallet was intact.

"It's still there."

The voice startled Rees and he came off the bed to see a young woman standing there. Then the memory came back fully. He stared at her for a moment, trying to think, and when he tried to speak, his voice was harsh. He was so thirsty that he suddenly couldn't bear it. He turned and went to the washbasin, picked up the pitcher, and drank from it. When he could hold no more, he was still thirsty. Putting the pitcher down, he turned to her and said, "What are you doing here?"

"Murdock will be waiting for me, and he'll take me to his bawdy 'ouse."

The problem seemed too great and Rees knew he was not thinking straight. A thought came to him and he rammed his hand into his pocket and pulled out his watch, thankful it was still there. "I've got to go."

"Please — take me with you."

"Take you with me? What are you talking about?"

"They'll get me and take me to jail if you don't."

"I can't take you with me. I'm going to America."

The girl came forward, and Rees saw that her face was tense with strain. He had not seen her properly the night before and now he studied her. He remembered that he had paid the big man his money because she looked like Grace, but he could not see much resemblance now. The dress she was wearing was worn and dirty and her face was smeared with grime. The broad daylight revealed that the hair he had thought to be so like Grace's was not the bright yellow he remembered but a darker color.

"What's your name?"

"Callie Summers."

"Who is that man I gave the money to?"

"His name is Murdock."

"Who is he? A relative?"

"No, he keeps a fancy 'ouse and he was taking me there."

The starkness of her answer sobered Rees. "You don't have to go if you don't want to."

"I can't stay around 'ere. One of the tecs caught me."

"Tec? What's a tec?"

"You know, a detective. The police. He caught me stealing and he was goin' to turn me in. I'd get 'anged or sent to the prison colony across the water. But he gave me to Murdock. If I stay 'ere, either Murdock will get me or the police. Please, you got to take me with you!"

"It's impossible," Rees said. The sun was strong at the window and he knew he had to get out of this place. He went to the washstand, found a clean basin, and washed his face. He needed a shave but there was no time for that. The girl, he was aware, was keeping her eyes on him, and he was trying to think of a way to get rid of her. Taking her was of course impossible. He dried his face and turned to her. "Callie, is that your name? I don't have much money, and I'm going to a land where I don't know a soul. I can't possibly take you with me."

The girl began to tremble. He could see her holding her shaking hands together to keep them from being so obvious, and there was a vulnerability about her that brought pity to him. He began to speak quickly, trying to explain how impossible it was, and then, seeing that she could only stand and stare at him, he murmured, "Look, I'll give you a little money. I don't have much, but — "

"I don't want your money. I just want to get away from 'ere!"

"Well, I'm sorry but I can't take you."

He grabbed his coat, put it on, clamped his hat over his head, and then, picking up his small bag, he paused long enough to hand her a bill. "Here, take this." When she did not, he dropped it on the floor and said, "I'm sorry," and left the room.

When he was out in the hall, he heard the sound of crying and stopped and stared fixedly at the wall. Reason told him to get away, and setting his teeth, he turned down the hall and went downstairs into the drinking area. He stopped at once when he saw two men talking. One was the tavern owner, and the other was the big man who had sold the girl last night. Instantly Rees understood what was happening. As if to confirm this, the big man turned and said, "You're leaving, eh? Well, I hopes you had a good night with the girl, but she's mine."

Those words "she's mine" seemed to resonate in Rees's mind. The idea of slavery was abhorrent to him in any case, and for this brute to claim ownership of a helpless young woman brought anger rising up in him. Without a word Rees turned. Retracing his steps, he reentered the room and found the girl sitting on the floor, her head on her arms. She looked up and he saw her tearstained face. "Come on," he said roughly. "We're getting out of here."

He watched as the girl scrambled to her feet, and then he said, "I'll get you out but you can't go to America with me. Watch it. Be careful now. Murdock's downstairs waiting for you."

"Please don't let him 'ave me!"

"I won't." His words gave some comfort to the girl, he saw, and he turned and walked purposely down the hall, aware that she kept slightly behind him. When they entered the barroom, he saw the big man with his feet planted, a fixed grin on his face. "You ain't goin' no place."

"Get out of my way, Murdock," Rees said and kept walking.

Evidently something that the big man saw in his eyes made him alert. Murdock reached into his pocket and brought out a wicked-looking knife. "I'll cut your gizzard out!"

But Rees advanced toward him. He saw Murdock wielding the knife in expert fashion, but he continued to hold the big man's gaze, and when Rees got close enough he suddenly lashed out, kicking with all his might. The tip of his boot caught the big man in the groin and Murdock dropped the knife, uttered a piercing scream, and fell to the floor, holding himself in a fetal position.

"Come on, girl," Rees said. He turned his eyes on the barkeep and said, "Are you in this?"

"No, not me. None of my business."

"Good enough. There is smart you are." He turned and walked away and heard the sound of the girl Callie behind him. When they were outside, she caught up to him.

"He'll 'ave the law on you. He will. He's a cruel man, he is."

Rees made up his mind at that instant. "Come along. The ship will be pulling out."

"I can come with you?"

Rees turned and studied the girl. "I'll have to pay your fare."

"I'll work. I'll pay you back. I'll do it, mister!"

"My name is Rees Kenyon."

"Mr. Kenyon, then." Callie's face was alight, Rees saw, but the tearstains were still there.

"Come along. Where are your things?"

"I'll show you. It ain't too far from 'ere."

"It'd better not be. We have to hurry."

Callie nodded. "I'll show you," she said.

The *Orion* lifted with the swell of the waves, and Rees steadied himself, hoping he would not be seasick. He had heard how bad such a thing was, and now that the sails had filled and the clipper ship had picked up speed, he waited but felt fine. He looked at the girl beside him. It was almost dusk now and he studied her face, thinking how strange it all was. Memory came of how they had gone to her room and she had thrown everything she could think of into two large sacks. They had hurried then to board the *Orion*, and now the coast of England was fading fast.

"How do you feel? Are you going to be sick?"

Callie was looking out over the water. She shook her head but did not speak.

Rees Kenyon had never felt like such a fool. He remembered how the captain had grinned knowingly and winked lewdly when Rees brought the girl on board. Rees had stared the man down, but now he knew that everyone on board thought that this girl was a plaything he had brought for his own enjoyment. The thought troubled him, and he stood there silently until finally it grew dark.

They had already eaten, so he said, "Come along. It's getting late."

He turned and they made their way down the hatchway into the corridor leading to the cabin. He opened the door and she stepped in, and when he closed the door, he saw that her eyes were narrow as she watched him. The cabin was small, with only two bunks, an upper and a lower. She had brought in her sacks, but he had put his luggage in storage except for one bag. He turned to her and waited for her to speak. He suddenly felt a compassion for her. She was obviously a waif of the streets, and he could only imagine the kind of life she had led in such a place. But she was all alone with a stranger, headed for a land she had never seen. He felt that he had acted the fool, but it was too late for that. He stepped forward and put his hand on her shoulder. "Callie," he said, "I want you — "

Callie made one quick movement and then she had a knife in her hand. Rees saw the determination in her eyes and said, "You don't have to be afraid of me."

Callie's laugh was harsh. "You're a man, ain't you?"

"I'm telling you that I won't bother you."

"I've 'eard that before!"

Rees Kenyon stared at the girl. "Like an old porcupine you are!" He turned and began to take off his coat. He pulled off his boots, his socks, and then lay on the bed. "There's sleepy I am. You do what you please."

Callie watched cautiously, keeping the knife ready. She waited until his breathing was regular and then, fully dressed, climbed into the upper bunk. She lay there tensely, and once she leaned over and peered at his face. His features were relaxed and she breathed a sigh of relief. Lying back, she wondered what sort of man he was. He was of a kind far above her, and she had known no one like him.

Later when she was almost asleep, she heard his voice and instantly stiffened.

"Grace!"

Callie warily leaned over and saw that Rees Kenyon's face was twisted with pain. He was reaching out and whispering the woman's name over and over.

Callie waited and finally heard him say, "Grace, where are you?" Then he fell silent.

As Callie Summers lay in the bunk, feeling the roll of the ship, she clutched her knife and eventually dropped off into a fitful sleep.

The *Orion* sailed over the waves, carrying its burden of human life toward America. The moon came out and dark clouds fretted it for a time, then covered it completely as the ship plunged over the fathomless sea, headed for America.

# Chapter Nine

REES CAME AWAKE WITH A START AND FOR A FEW MOMENTS FEAR took him. He was aware that he was not in his own bed but in a strange room. Then memory came flooding into his mind and with it came relief. He lay still, his eyes fixed on the ceiling, and thought with distaste of the scene in the tavern. The details were cloudy and the knowledge that he had been half drunk disgusted him. *I made a fool of myself!* But even as he lay there berating himself for what happened, a single, clear image — the girl's face — came to him in one of those unexpectedly clear recalls. He could see every detail: the dirty blond hair, the full, trembling lower lip, the smear of dirt on her left cheek. *She was so afraid and so alone; that's why I couldn't help what I did....*

A slight sound broke into his thoughts, startling him, and he came off the bed with one quick motion. Turning his head, he saw the girl standing in the shadows at the corner of the small cabin. She had her back to the bulkhead and for a moment Rees could not see her features clearly. He felt a surge of irritation to find her there and spoke gruffly. "What are you doing here, girl?"

For a moment she said nothing; then she lifted her head and met his eyes. "I didn't 'ave no other place to go."

Rees blinked his eyes, licked his dry lips, and suddenly realized he had a raging thirst. Moving over to the small chest, he picked up the pitcher and drank deeply. The water was tepid but it seemed to soak into his parched tissues. As he drank, he sought for something to say to the girl, but nothing seemed appropriate. To cover his uncertainty, he moved to the small washstand and poured the pewter basin full of water. He had not shaved the day before, and he was a man who hated two-day-old whiskers on himself or anyone else.

Turning to the small bag he had brought, he fished out his razor and shaving soap and worked up a lather. There was no mirror, and his hand was not as steady as it should have been, but he shaved slowly, the silence in the room being complete and somewhat oppressive.

Finally he finished the job, rinsed out the basin, and emptied the water into the chamber pot stashed under his bunk. *What in the world can I do with her?* Turning to face the girl, he said, "Wash your face, girl," then abruptly left the cabin.

When he reached the deck, he stopped and looked out over the sea. He had not realized what an immensity the ocean was. Always before, his world had been blocked by trees and mountains and fields. Now in every direction the gray ocean stretched out, with not even another ship in sight. Somehow this depressed him, and he leaned against the rail, staring out at the horizon. A noisy group of gulls circled the stern of the ship, and he saw a sailor throwing something overboard. The gulls descended, rending the air with shrill cries as they fought over the garbage. Rees turned his attention to the sails overhead and thought they were beautiful. He had seen ships but had only been on small fishing vessels, and now the white sails were swollen and somehow lent an air of distinction to the vessel. The ship rolled slowly as it moved through the waves, and he was grateful that he had not experienced seasickness.

*What am I going to do with that blasted girl? Why did I have to make such a fool of myself?* It was not the first time Rees's impulses had gotten him into trouble, and now as the ship moved along, seeming to keep pace with the clouds that drifted along slowly overhead, he racked his brain trying to think of some way to handle the situation. Nothing came. Finally he turned to notice that the girl had come out of the hatchway. Seeing him at the rail, she stopped abruptly. He knew he had to do something, so he moved toward her and said tersely, "Let's see if we can find something to eat." She did not speak and he did not urge her. He tried to remember her name but it escaped him. "What's your name, girl?"

"Callie Summers."

Her gaze was fixed on Rees in a way that troubled him. He stopped a sunburned sailor, asking, "Can you tell me where we might find something to eat?"

The sailor, a short, muscular man with yellow fangs for teeth and a pair of bright blue eyes, grinned and nodded. "Go down the hatchway and ask for the galley. Breakfast was over some time ago, sir, but the cook will give you something."

"Thank you."

Rees made his way down the steps, followed by Callie, and found the galley, which was manned by a lanky cook with a wooden peg leg. "Could we have a bit of breakfast?" Rees asked. The cook scowled but put them in the dining area, and soon he brought eggs, some cold beef, and two mugs of coffee.

Rees applied himself to the food. He was not hungry and his stomach was rolling, but he felt he should eat.

"Did you sleep?" he finally asked rather brusquely.

"Yes." Callie's eyes were clear, he saw, and she had washed her face, which lent a glow to her skin. He was sure she was filthy except for her hands and face, but considering her background, that was not unusual. The dress she wore was loose but still revealed the growing feminine curves, and he finally asked, "How old are you?"

"Sixteen."

"What about your family?"

"Ain't got none!" The words were clipped and there was a defensiveness about the girl that somehow irritated Rees. She was sitting rigidly, her spine straight and her shoulders thrown back. Her chin was lifted and she was giving him glance for glance.

Rees could think of nothing else to ask, and finally when the meal was finished, he abruptly got up and left. Not wanting to go back to the tiny cabin, he went topside and stood at the rail. He noticed that the girl had followed him, taking her place five feet away. He continued to watch the ocean and had almost put her out of his mind when she said, "Wot do you do?"

Rees turned to find her watching him. He was somewhat surprised. He had thought her eyes were blue, but now he saw that they were an unusual shade of green. Her blond hair was stiff with grime and tied back. He could see that there was a curl in it, and now as the sun touched her head, he was reminded more than ever of Grace.

"Are you deaf? I asked wot you do. Are you rich?"

Rees suddenly laughed. "There's dull you are, girl! Me — rich!"

"You talk funny."

"I'm from Wales."

"Well, wot is it you do, then, if you ain't rich?"

"I'm a doctor."

He saw the girl watching him with a fresh interest, and he was about to turn back when she suddenly asked, "Who is Grace? Is she your wife?"

"No. She's not." The wound seemed to open in Rees and he turned quickly and walked away from the girl.

Callie stood watching him leave and whispered, "I reckon she must of been his woman — and she must of did 'im dirt." She turned to the sea then, watching the waves as they rolled in endless swells. She was fascinated by the water that boiled whitely along the edge of the *Orion*. Somewhere she had picked up the habit of speaking to herself quietly, and she did so now. "Wot'll I do in America? I can't stay with 'im!" She slumped suddenly, afraid of what lay ahead, but then she held her head up high. "'E don't like me. But I'll make out — see if I don't!"

Callie had made friends on board the *Orion*, mostly among the sailors. They had flocked to her of course, as they will to a young woman. Some of them made coarse remarks, and she had answered them in kind, which made them laugh. She kept herself always on guard, but once she had been caught when walking the deck, and a brawny sailor had pulled her into the shadows of the mast at dusk and mauled her. She had turned her lips away from his kiss and pulled the knife out, touching the point of it to his chest. He had not been afraid but had laughed and stepped back. "You've got life in you, sweetie. I likes to see that in a gal." His grin was broad and he had winked rudely as she left.

Five days had passed and Callie knew the deck well. She even knew the names of the sails that towered over the ship, for William

Knox, the third mate, a tall young man from Hastings, had named them for her. Knox had been surprised that she could identify them all. "You're bright," he said, "and pretty too."

Callie grinned at him. He was a shy young man, and this was the first time he had revealed the attraction he felt toward her.

"'Ave you ever been to America, Mr. Knox?"

"You can call me Billy."

"And you can call me Miss Summers," Callie rapped back. "Wot about America? You ever been there?"

"Of course I've been there! I've been to New York and Baltimore and lots of other ports. It's — "

Suddenly there was a wild cry, and both Knox and Callie whirled around. Callie caught the sound of something striking the deck and realized that one of the sailors had fallen from the mainmast. Knox said, "That's Nelson, the foretopman! He's probably dead."

Callie followed Knox to where the crumpled body lay. By the time they reached the sailor, the captain had already arrived. He was bending over and Knox asked, "Is he dead, Captain?"

"Almost, I'm afraid. He was setting the royal and slipped. I saw him hit the main yardarm. That broke his fall before he hit the deck but he looks bad." Captain James Rogers was a comparatively young man, compactly built. His eyes studied the fallen man and he shook his head. "Not much we can do for him."

"The last trip we had a doctor on board," Knox said, "but not now."

"There's a doctor on board." Both men turned to look at Callie with surprise. "Mr. Kenyon, 'e's a proper doctor."

"A doctor!" Captain Rogers exclaimed. "Go get him, miss, if you will."

"Yes sir!"

Callie ran along the deck, plunged down the hatchway, and burst into the cabin. "Mr. Kenyon, there's a man been 'urt bad. I told the captain you was a doctor, and 'e says for you to come quick."

Rees had been lying in the bunk staring upward at nothing, but he jumped out of bed immediately.

"Where is he?"

"I'll show you."

Callie led Rees topside and then to where the fallen man lay.

"You're a doctor?" Captain Rogers demanded at once.

"Yes, I am, Captain." Rees was bending over the sailor. He pulled the injured man's eyelids upward and stared at his eyes, then checked his breathing while taking his pulse. "Where did he fall from?"

"The very top of that mast."

Rees felt the man, making a quick examination, and stood up. "He has to have surgery."

"You tell us what you need, Doctor."

"I'll need a table and lots of light."

"Mr. Knox, see that Dr. Kenyon has everything he requires. Let me know how it turns out." He turned to face Kenyon. "Nelson's a good man. He has a family in Dorsetshire, three children. I hope you can save him."

Knox had commandeered a table in the officers' small quarters, and Nelson had been placed upon it by his mates. His shirt had been stripped and now Knox and Callie watched as Kenyon prepared to operate. The injured man had been tied firmly to the table so he could not move. His face was colorless but he was still breathing.

"He must have hit something coming down," Rees murmured as he examined the wound in the man's side. "Whatever he hit drove a splinter of ribs hard against the nerve." He suddenly looked up at Knox and Callie. "If you can't stand the sight of blood, you'd better leave now."

"I ain't never been sick," Callie said at once, but Knox muttered something about having duties and left. Callie shrugged, then asked, "Can I 'elp you, sir?"

"I have to be able to see what I'm doing, Callie. You can soak up the blood as I operate. Use those cotton rags."

Callie moved in closer and didn't flinch as Kenyon began to cut into the sailor's flesh. The blood welled up and at once she removed it. "That's good!" Rees said quietly.

Callie concentrated on her assignment, fascinated with how Kenyon's fingers seemed sure as he worked. From time to time she looked up at his face and saw that he was thinking only of the task before him. The patient groaned and strained against the leather straps, but never did the hands of the doctor falter.

Nelson gasped as Rees finished pulling the ribs back into place. After closing the incision, Rees quickly moved to the sailor's head, which had a terrible gash. Callie wondered if a man could live with a wound like that.

"His head wound looks worse than it is," Rees said. Quickly he pulled the scalp into place, and Callie watched, spellbound, as he used a curved needle and catgut to stitch it back together.

Finally Kenyon said, "Well, he ought to be comfortable enough unless there should be some infection. I'll need to stay close to him for a time, Callie." He smiled then, adding, "You did fine. Thanks for your help."

Callie flushed and shrugged her shoulders. "It wasn't nothin'."

"Yes, it was. Will you go tell Knox we can move him now?"

Callie left and soon returned with Knox. "He is alive, Doctor?" the third mate asked.

"Oh yes. I'll need to stay with him awhile."

"I'll see to it, sir. We'll have him carried down and bring a chair where you can sit, or maybe a cot."

"A chair would be fine."

At that moment Captain Rogers entered, his face tense. "How is he?"

"He's doing fine, Captain," Rees said. "He has some rib damage. They were pressing against a nerve, I think."

"What about his head? It looked like it was split wide open."

"No, it wasn't that serious."

"So he's going to be all right?"

"Oh yes, of course. I'll keep close watch over him."

Relief washed across Captain Rogers' face. "Thank God you were here, Doctor."

"I'm glad I was able to help."

"I'd like to have you join me and my officers at dinner tonight."

Rogers had glanced at Callie but halted abruptly. He knew that this was not Kenyon's wife, but it was a delicate matter.

Instantly Rees realized the captain's problem. His brain raced frantically as he tried to put a good face on Callie's presence. "Miss Summers is my . . . my ward," he said.

Captain Rogers could not quite conceal the smile. "Of course, you and your . . . uh, your *ward* . . . will be welcome, sir."

"Put on the best dress you've got, Callie."

"Wot for?"

"You know what for. The captain wants us to join him for dinner."

"I ain't goin'."

Rees stared at her. "Stubborn as an old mule you are! You'll have to go."

Callie's eyes flashed. "You paid for me, so you can make me do anything?"

Rees threw his hands up and rolled his eyes. "Will I look to you for an argument? You're going and that's all there is to it — so put on the best you have!"

Rees left the room, irritated with the girl. She had a stubborn streak in her and he knew he was going to have trouble. He loitered around until finally she came out, and he saw she was wearing a light blue dress. Her hair was still grimy but there was little to be done about that. "You look very nice, Callie."

She did not answer and Rees led her to the captain's table. There were four other officers there, including Billy Knox, and after introductions were made, the meal was brought in. It consisted of boiled beef, cabbage, and ship's biscuits. As they were served, Captain Rogers spoke of their destination. "Can't say much for the Americans."

"You don't like them?"

"They're as independent as human beings can be," Rogers grumbled. He bit down on a piece of beef, chewed it thoroughly, and then shook his head. "There's going to be a war over there, you mark my words."

"Oh, come now, Captain," the first lieutenant said. "There can't be a war." The lieutenant's name was Benning, a handsome man with a bluff red face and a wealth of auburn hair. "What would they fight with? They don't have any army and they certainly have no navy."

"They have one thing, though, Benning."

"And what's that, sir?"

"They have thousands of miles."

"I don't understand you, sir."

"You have any idea what it costs to equip a soldier and send him all the way from England to the colonies?"

"I'm afraid I don't."

"It costs hundreds of pounds, and you multiply that by an army, say, twenty thousand men. Who's going to pay for that?"

"But sir, if we occupy the country — "

"Do you have any idea how enormous America is, Benning?" The captain had studied the situation at considerable length, and Rees listened as he spoke of how difficult it would be to put a standing army in America. "As a matter of fact, we already have a military force there under General Gage, but the place is huge. The colonists would merely have to run off into the woods. Our men can't march in formation through that thick undergrowth, and there are rivers everywhere that can't be crossed."

"But can they fight, sir?" Knox asked.

"Not properly. They fight like Indians, shooting from behind trees instead of coming out in ordinary ranks as soldiers should."

Callie listened and understood little of it. She felt out of place, and as soon as the meal was over, she slipped away. "Your ward is shy, isn't she, Doctor?" Rogers said, smiling.

Rees looked the captain straight in the eye. "She's had a difficult time, sir. I'd appreciate it if you would be understanding. Now, I'd better go see about her. Thank you so much for the invitation. It was a fine meal."

After he left, Lieutenant Benning grinned knowingly. "She's not his ward, sir. I know that much."

"Yes, but he did us a favor in saving Nelson, so let's have none of you trying to have anything to do with that girl."

"Of course not, sir."

Rees caught up with Callie on deck. She stood gripping the rail and he leaned on the rail beside her. "Are you all right?"

"No, I ain't."

"What's wrong?"

"I don't know 'ow to act with them people. I ain't goin' back to eat in that place anymore."

"You've got to learn how to get along with people, Callie."

"I gets along fine with my own sort."

Rees had had time to think about the problem of Callie, and now he turned to her and said, "Look, I don't know where I'll be staying but I'll find us a place."

"I ain't livin' with you." A defiant look marked her features as she turned to look up at him. "You may 'ave paid money for me, but you ain't gettin' at me, see?"

Rees stared at her. "I'm telling you right now, Callie. I'm not interested in any romance with you."

"I 'eard that before — from lots of men!"

"Be quiet, is it? Now listen. I told the captain you're my ward."

"And wot's that?"

"It's when a man takes care of a younger person. When we get to Boston, we'll find a place. I don't know what you'll do but you can learn how to get along. I'll be learning myself how to get along with these Americans."

"Well, you bought me," she said bitterly. "I'll 'ave to do wot you says."

"I don't own you, Callie," Rees said quietly. "I don't believe in owning people." She grew quieter and he saw then the trace of fear on her face.

"I'll do wotever you say." She turned to him and he saw that her lip was trembling. "I ain't forgot wot you done for me, sir. There ain't many men who would of done it. I never met one, anyways."

She had let down her guard for a moment, and Rees saw that underneath the hard surface there was a young, desperately frightened young woman. "We'll be all right," he said. "I'll find some work and we won't starve."

"When will we get there, sir?"

"I'm not sure. It depends on the wind, I suppose." He hesitated, then said, "Are you afraid, Callie?"

"Yes sir, a little."

Rees laughed. "Right, you! I'm a little bit afraid myself, but the good Lord will help us. We'll both find our way when we get to the colonies."

"Who is this doctor you're goin' to see, sir?" Callie asked.

"His name is Joseph Warren. He's an old friend of a doctor I studied under in London. I have a letter for him and I think he already knows who I am."

The two were walking along the streets of Boston. They had landed only an hour ago, and Rees had arranged to come back later and pick up their luggage. They had asked directions twice, and now Rees said, "According to what that man told us, that ought to be the house right there."

"I'll wait for you out 'ere."

"Nonsense! You can't be alone in a place where you know no one."

The house was built of red brick and sat back off the street. Behind it was a carriage house and there was a look of prosperity about it. "Well, he's not a poor doctor if he owns a place like this," Rees murmured. He knocked on the door, and it was opened at once by a black woman wearing a brown dress and a white apron. "I'd like to see Dr. Warren."

"Come in, sir — and ma'am."

The two entered and the black servant put them into a parlor. "I'll tell the doctor you're here. Is he expecting you?"

"No, but I have a letter for him."

"Yes sir."

Rees watched the woman go, then looked around the parlor. It was a comfortable room with a large fireplace in the center of one wall. Pictures and decorations covered the others. A large bay window admitted sunlight and the carpet was light blue with a pattern in it.

A man entered almost at once, saying, "Yes sir, I'm Dr. Warren."

Rees turned and bowed. "We've never met, Dr. Warren. My name is Rees Kenyon. I believe we have a mutual friend."

"Oh, of course!" Warren was a tall man in his forties, fine-looking and dressed at the height of fashion. He came forward immediately with a smile on his face. "You're Dr. Freeman's friend. He's written about you several times. I'm glad to know you, sir." He turned then and said, "This must be your wife."

Rees blinked and saw the shock on Callie's face.

"No sir. I suppose you haven't heard. My fiancée died very recently."

"Yes, Dr. Freeman told me of your loss." Warren dropped his head, saying quietly, "I lost my own dear wife not too long ago, so I understand your grief."

"Thank you, Doctor. This is my ward, Miss Callie Summers."

"I am very happy to meet you, Miss Summers." Dr. Warren bowed.

Callie whispered, "Thank you, sir."

"Well, come along. We'll have tea and you can tell me all about your journey."

They soon were drinking tea, and Rees was astonished to learn that Dr. Freeman had written often about him. He soon discovered that Warren was one of the most congenial men he had ever met.

"What are your plans, Dr. Kenyon?"

"Actually, I have none. I just had to get away from England. There were too many memories."

"I know the feeling, sir. I'd like to get away from here but I can't be spared at this time." Warren's warm eyes studied the younger man, and then he said abruptly, "I've been meaning for some time to take on an assistant. I wonder if you'd be interested in such a proposition?"

Rees stared at the tall doctor. "But sir, you don't know a thing about me or my qualifications."

"But I know Howard Freeman and he's spoken highly of you. I'd be glad if you'd care to come on a trial basis. We'll see if we get on. We could work up to a partnership and there's plenty of work here."

"I would be most honored, Dr. Warren."

"Well, we'll talk about terms. Housing is a bit hard to find but I think we can solve that. I own a house that's empty — rather small but it's close to this place. It needs some work but it could be made into something very comfortable."

Rees saw that Callie was struck dumb by this offer, and he said at once, "Wouldn't you like that, Callie?"

Callie blinked with surprise and cleared her throat. "Anything will do me, sir."

"Well, then it's settled." Warren rose and said, "Come along. I'll show you the house and you can get settled in."

He led them outside and they walked three blocks, with Warren doing most of the talking. He stopped in front of a small house built of red brick, with a steep roof and two gables facing the street. "This is the place. Come inside."

Warren showed them through the house, which was small but snug. He took them upstairs and said, "I think this might be suitable for you, Miss Summers."

"It's fair beautiful, sir!" Callie was stunned. It was a very large room with a sloping ceiling. The furniture was beautiful and a dark, figured carpet covered the floor.

"This is very handsome of you, Dr. Warren," Rees said.

"Not at all! Not at all!" Warren was smiling. "It will take some of the work off me. I have more work than doctoring to do, you know."

"How is that, sir?"

"I'm very active with the Sons of Liberty."

"The Sons of Liberty?"

"You may as well know this, Dr. Kenyon. I'm very much into politics. I believe England has treated us unfairly." His face grew stern. "If you can't live with that, perhaps you'd better not come to be with me."

"Why, I'm not a political man, sir. I just want to be the best doctor I can."

"Fine, fine." Warren turned to Callie and said, "Miss Summers, make yourself at home here. I'll take Dr. Kenyon on a few calls with me. We'll need to get used to each other, but we'll all have dinner together tonight and get to know one another better."

"Thank you very much, Doctor."

Callie watched as the two men left; then she walked around the room. Her heart was full, for the room was finer than anything she had ever lived in, to say the least. She went around touching the yellow wallpaper with the fine figures, the smooth grain of the chairs.

Finally she sat on the bed and stared at the wall. She felt very much alone, but the kindness of Joseph Warren had been good for her. She sat there thinking of many things, and somehow her eyes grew misty, and then she was shocked to feel tears roll down her cheeks. She stood up at once and admonished herself. "Don't be a fool! You'll be all right." She walked to the window and saw the two men leaving in a carriage. Rees was sitting on the side nearest her, and she saw that he was smiling. Somehow this made her happy. "He's been good to me, he 'as!" She watched until the carriage disappeared, and then she moved away from the window, wondering what this new world would bring into her life.

# Part
# -2-

## Chapter Ten

CARRYING A TWO-GALLON BUCKET IN EACH HAND, HANNAH THOMAS made her way laboriously up the circular staircase, headed toward the top of the lighthouse. The builders had conveniently left at stated intervals small, foot-square windows which illuminated the steps in the daytime but which also admitted the snow and driving rain in bad weather. But March had come now, and with it the worst of the weather had passed.

As Hannah reached the summit and stepped outside, she put her buckets down, stretched her arms, and then leaned on the railing that surrounded the reflectors. Gurnet Point Lighthouse had been built by masons who were less than expert, but they had added in strength and solidarity what they lacked in artfulness. The brick walls were rough, with the mortar left untrimmed, some of it hanging off in gobs exactly as it had been applied in 1768. The structure rose forty feet in the air and at some point had been painted white, but now the white had been worn away by driving seas and wind and rain until the color of the original brick showed through in splotches. Still, the strength of the structure had proved the builders' determination, for it had weathered crashing waves some twenty feet high, and the freezing winters and burning summers had not managed to obliterate it.

As always, Hannah looked out with pleasure over the scene spread before her. She took in first the gray ocean, her expert eyes noting that the rolling swells were not dangerous. She looked upward and the sky bespoke fair weather. Far off she saw the white sails of a clipper ship under full sail, headed for Boston Harbor. She delighted in the fast craft, for to her they were beautiful, whereas the lumbering transport ships and men-of-war seemed slow and clumsy by comparison. She watched for a moment as the ship heeled over to make its way toward the harbor; then she turned and looked out over the land.

Everything she saw was familiar. She knew every square inch of the land, for she had lived at Gurnet Point Lighthouse since she was six years old. The spires of the churches of Boston lifted themselves toward the sky, and she knew that soon she would hear the tolling of the bells, for twilight was beginning to shade the earth. The land was rolling and hilly, but farms had been tucked neatly into the small valleys, and cattle grazed on the hillsides.

Turning her eyes downward and without meaning to, Hannah checked the domain she felt was hers. The lighthouse property consisted of six acres, most of it used either for garden or pasture, plus the lighthouse itself of course. She could hear the chickens clucking, and a smile touched her lips as she saw the sow trotting within her pen, followed by twelve piglets. Their squeals came to her, and she thought of the ham she was smoking, which must be nearly done. She gave one last look at the cow with the nursing calf, and the goats stretching their heads through the fence to get at the grass on the outside. The mare was grazing on the stubby grass and the sun caught the rough texture of her coat.

Turning with a sigh, Hannah began her work. As she filled the eight oil lamps — which took four gallons of oil each night — she thought about how people never considered how much work it took to make a lighthouse function. Three times a day someone had to climb the steps with buckets full of oil. If the reservoirs were not filled at the proper times, they went out. During windy nights it became difficult to keep them lit at all. Many a night she had stayed up protecting them from the driving wind, but people didn't think of things like this.

She cleaned the glass, which grew smoky because of the whale oil used, then finally heaved a sigh and turned to make her way down the stairway. There was no railing and the steps had become rounded and worn with time, so a fall was always possible. Leaving the tower, she walked on the raised boardwalk which led to the house itself — a single-story structure with a steeply pitched roof to accommodate two attic bedrooms. The house was built of the same brick as that of the tower, but the masons had taken more care, and the Thomas family always used fresh whitewash so the house glowed under the pale skies. Flower beds, the delight of Hannah's heart, surrounded the house, and she paused to poke her finger in the soil where she had planted geranium seeds. She pulled up a seed and saw that it had indeed sprouted and a tiny root was beginning to explore its world. Quietly she murmured, "That's you, Hannah Thomas, never patient enough to wait for God to do his own work. Shame on you!"

Smiling at her own foolishness, Hannah put the seed carefully back in the ground and then went at once to the smokehouse. The smoke nearly choked her, but she plucked a ham off the hook and quickly stepped outside and wiped her weeping eyes with her apron. Entering the kitchen, she set it on a table, then nodded with satisfaction.

She sliced the ham and put a thin slice on a plate, added boiled potatoes and fresh onions. Taking a goblet, she poured it full of milk and then, tossing a napkin over her shoulder, she left the kitchen and went down the short hallway and entered the main room of the house. Her father was sitting in his rocking chair, looking out the window as usual, and for just one moment Hannah paused, her heart suddenly stricken by a memory. Her father's arms now were thin and weak and his whole body seemed to be shrunken. She remembered when she was a child of six. Amos Thomas had put her on his shoulders and run full speed up the steps to the top of the lighthouse. She thought of how she had squealed and clung to his head fiercely, and she remembered how he had done that in the full glow of his strength. Now as she saw the cadaverous cast of his features, sorrow came to her, but she pushed it away and said, "Now then, time for you to see if I know how to smoke a ham."

Amos Thomas turned to his daughter and despite his ailments summoned a quick smile. He always took delight in her appearance, the flaming red hair and bright green eyes and the smooth skin. Now he said, "You should know. I taught you myself."

"You always want to take credit for everything I do. Don't you suppose I ever learn anything for myself?"

"I don't like to see women thinking. It's dangerous."

Setting the plate on the table beside her father's chair, Hannah tugged a lock of his hair, pretending to be angry. "You have no respect for women. Not even for your own daughter." She loosened her grip, pushed his hair off his forehead, and said, "Now, let me see you eat all of that."

Amos took the plate and began to cut the meat into small pieces. His hands had been the strongest on the coast of Boston for years when he was a fisherman. Now it was all he could do to cut the meat. The sickness that had come upon him nearly a year ago had drained the life out of him, and his early strength was only a memory.

Sitting across from her father, Hannah did the talking for both of them. She knew that the pain was almost always with him, and she checked the bottle with her eye, reminding herself she would have to get more laudanum from Dr. Warren. She forced herself to be cheerful and spoke of the little things that filled her life — tending the lighthouse, taking care of the farm animals, cooking, churchgoing — and finally, when he had finished half his meal and pushed the plate away, she said, "Can't you eat a little more?"

"No. Thank you, Daughter."

The room was still then, and Hannah watched as her father lifted his eyes to the painting of her mother that hung over the mantelpiece. His eyes often went there now, and she knew that the loss of her had hurt him more than this sickness that drained his life away almost daily.

"I miss your mother, Hannah."

"Yes. So do I."

"I'll be with her soon enough."

Hannah opened her mouth to rebuke him, but then she had always been an honest young woman, and now she took his hand in hers, and when he turned to face her, she whispered, "Won't that be fine, now?"

"I'm glad you don't try to fool yourself. I won't be on this earth long."

"We're all in God's hands, Father."

"Indeed we are. I'll hate to leave my children but I'll be glad to see my Kate. In a way I think I put myself in the grave with her."

"You know, Father, I think about you and Mother when I read those silly romances. They're so frivolous and I thank God I was able to see a real love affair."

"We were married for forty-six years and they were all filled with joy."

"Did you never quarrel?"

"Oh, of course we quarreled, but there was the fun of making up afterward. Even when we were quarreling, we both knew that had to pass." A smile pulled at the thin lips of Amos Thomas, and he said, "Someone asked your mother once, 'Did you ever consider divorce?' She got all huffy and said, 'Divorce? No!' and then she said, 'Murder, yes! But divorce, never!'"

Hannah laughed. "That's so like her." She squeezed her father's hand and then started to gather the dishes.

"Will Thad and Matthew be here soon, do you think?"

"They're working very hard. It seems everyone's getting their muskets ready. Thad's talking about taking on another assistant."

Amos turned his eyes out toward the sea and then murmured, "I wish Matthew had not agreed to become Thad's apprentice."

"It's an honest trade, rifle making is."

"I know, but Thad's wild. He's twenty-two years old and should be settled — but he's got a wicked streak in him. I think it came from my own father. He was rather a wild young fellow himself."

"He'll find himself, Pa." Hannah thought for a moment of her older brother's life. Thad was an expert at making and repairing firearms, but his personal life was bad. He drank too much. He had a reputation for chasing women and his gambling grieved both Hannah and her father. "Matthew knows better than to take after Thad in those ways."

"He's only sixteen, Hannah, and he admires Thad."

"We'll just have to pray harder. They'll be coming for supper tomorrow night. We'll have all their favorite dishes. Don't worry about your boys. They'll be all right."

Hannah took the dishes back to the kitchen and began washing them, but she shared her father's anxiety. Matthew Thomas, at his young age, was a prime candidate for following in his brother's footsteps. He was a gentler boy than Thad had been. Still, the world had a pull. *Lord, bring Thad to your own heart — and don't let Matthew fall into his ways!* She left the kitchen, the prayer on her mind.

Fat white clouds drifted across the sky, covering the face of the sun. Hannah approached the pigpen, and as she lifted the bucket over the fence and began to pour the contents into the trough, she laughed at the mad scramble the pigs made to get at it. They came squealing and shouldering each other aside, snapping at their siblings furiously. "You stop that, Simon Peter, you hear me!" Lowering her bucket, she clipped a reddish brown pig on the head and laughed at his squeals. "You leave Thomas alone. You're always persecuting him — and you, Judas, your soul is as black as your hide! Now stop that!" She continued to fight for the rights of the smaller piglets. She had named them after the twelve apostles, and she insisted that they had taken on the characteristics of their biblical namesakes. Judas was the only black pig in the litter and he lived up to his name famously. He was treacherous, sneaky, and could be violent on occasions, and nothing could tame the pig devil in him.

Hannah loved them as she loved all the chickens, the rabbits, and the goats that were her charge. She made excuses for the ornery ones and doctored the sick animals as best she knew how. Leaving the pigpen, she went over to lay her hand on Sukey, the cow, stroking her silken hide. "How are you today, Miss Sukey?" she asked and laughed as the cow nipped at her sleeve. Bending over, she held her hand out, and the calf she had named Esther licked at her palm, seeking the salt. "There's a good little calf." She stood there for a moment, not allowing herself to think of what would happen to most of these animals, who would be consumed by their owners. She preferred not to think of such things. Matthew always laughed at her, saying, "You eat like you're starving, and then you cry over every pig we kill."

Hannah knew Matthew was right, that she was illogical, and once when he pushed her too far, she had slapped at him, saying, "Let me alone, you awful boy! I can feel sorry for them even if I'm not reasonable."

Matthew had grinned. "I never expect a woman to be reasonable. Thad says that's asking too much. Anyway, I envy these pigs."

A smile came to Hannah's lips as she recalled the conversation. Matthew had continued, "They don't have any responsibilities, Sister. Somebody feeds them. They get sick, we have to take care of them. And they have one bad afternoon in their whole life. I wish I were a pig!"

Hannah laughed at the thought, for her brother Matthew had a wicked sense of humor but a good heart to go with it.

The sound of a voice came to her, and she turned quickly to see the wagon coming down the road. She saw Matthew sitting on the seat but he was alone. Disappointment came to Hannah sharply and keenly. *Thad could have come. He knows how Father expects him.* Anger touched her for a moment, for Thad was a thoughtless young man, especially where her father was concerned. *I'll give him a piece of my mind — and of my tongue too, you can believe that!*

As she came forward, however, she saw that Matthew's face was pale, and instantly knew something was wrong. "What is it, Matthew?" she cried as the wagon pulled to a stop in front of the house.

"It's Thad. He's been shot." Matthew leaped out of the wagon, wrapped the reins to hold the horse steady, and ran around to the back of the wagon. "Help me get him in the house."

Hannah's heart went cold when she saw the blood-soaked blanket wrapped around her brother. His eyes were closed and his face seemed leached of all blood. Fear seized her and she seemed to gain strength as she lifted his legs. Matthew, a tall, strapping boy, carried the upper part of Thad's body. They made it awkwardly to the door, which stood open, and Hannah said, "We'll put him in the downstairs bedroom next to Pa."

They had just laid Thad on the bed when Amos came in. He held on to the door frame and his eyes flew open. "What's wrong with him?" He moved closer and said, "Good Lord! What happened, Matthew?"

"He was in a duel and he got shot."

"Why didn't you take him to the doctor?"

"The English thought he was dead. They'd probably arrest him. The duel was with an English officer."

Hannah said instantly, "We've got to have a doctor. I'll go for Dr. Warren."

"Take the wagon," Matthew called. "We'll get the bleeding stopped. And hurry, Sister!"

Halting the mare with a cruel wrench of the reins, Hannah jumped out and ran to the front porch. She banged on the door and called, "Dr. Warren! Dr. Warren!"

Almost at once the door opened, and Dr. Warren's little daughter Abigail said, "What is it, Hannah? What's wrong?"

"It's Thad. He's been badly hurt. Dr. Warren has to come right now."

Abigail shook her head. "But he's not here. He went to Concord to deliver Mrs. Simpkins' baby."

For a moment Hannah stood there, unable to think. Her brother was dying. He might be dead already. "I'll see if I can find Dr. Smithston."

"Wait a minute!" Abigail said. "Father has a new assistant. He could help."

"Get him quick, Abby!"

Abigail turned and ran down the hall. Hannah heard her speaking and then a tall, dark-haired young man quickly appeared. "Yes? I'm Dr. Kenyon. What's happened?"

"It's my brother. He's been shot."

"Shot where?"

"I don't know. In the chest, I think. Please hurry, Doctor."

"All right. Do you have a wagon?"

"Yes. Hurry, please!"

Hannah went back to the wagon and climbed into the seat. She picked up the reins and saw the young doctor come running out of the house, pulling on his coat. He had a bag in his hand and he leaped in with ease. "All right. I'm ready."

Hannah slapped the reins on the mare's back, and she responded by moving forward at a fast trot. But Hannah was not satisfied and the mare was soon at a full gallop.

"Don't kill us getting there, miss."

"I'm afraid for him."

"What's your name?"

"I'm Hannah Thomas. My brother is Thad."

"I'm Rees Kenyon."

"You've got to help him, Dr. Kenyon!"

"I'll do everything I can. Can you tell me anything else about the injury?"

"Not really. My brother is his apprentice. He brought him in. He did say he was in a duel."

"That's not a very wise thing to do."

Hannah took her eyes off the road long enough to glance at the doctor. She'd noticed he was lanky, and now she saw that he had homely features, except for his eyes, which were a very dark blue.

"I hope we get there in time," Rees said simply. Something about the young woman touched him. She did not resemble his mother physically so much, but something in the way she held her head and shoulders reminded him of her.

"God will take care of him."

Instantly Rees turned and studied her more carefully. She had the most perfect complexion he had ever seen, and he was certain that she used nothing to decorate it. Her nose was slightly upturned, giving her an air of impudence, and her jaw was clean-cut, hinting of stubbornness. "I'm glad you think that way," he said quietly.

Rees expelled his breath and held up the bloody slug with a pair of tweezers. "There it is," he said. He looked at the table where Thaddeus Thomas lay. Matthew and Hannah Thomas had both insisted on watching. Hannah had kept the blood stanched as well as she could, and now her face was pale as paste. "Is he going to be all right, Doctor?"

"I think he is — barring infection. There's always the danger of that."

"What can we do?" Matthew said. Admiration was in his eyes and he suddenly blurted, "I'd give anything if I could do what I've just seen you do."

"You probably could if you set your mind to it."

"Me become a doctor?"

"Why not? I did."

"But I'm just an apprentice gunsmith."

"And I was just a shipbuilder."

Thad moved suddenly, his legs twitching, and then his eyes opened. Rees leaned over and said quietly, "You're all right, Mr. Thomas."

All three watched as the wounded man's eyes moved around the room, and then they fell on Matthew. "I missed him. He cheated, Matthew. He didn't wait the full count!"

"Don't talk about that, Thad," Hannah said quickly. She put her hand on his forehead and said, "You must rest. You're very weak."

But Thaddeus Thomas was angry. It showed in the glint of his eyes, which were only half open. "Bloody British lobsterback, I'll pay him back for that! See if I don't."

Rees said, "I think I'd better stay the night, just to be sure nothing breaks loose."

"That would be so kind of you, Dr. Kenyon," Hannah said. "I'll fix something to eat."

Matthew lingered awhile after his sister left. "When did you know you wanted to be a doctor?" he asked, his eyes fixed on Rees.

"I think when I was about six years old," Rees said, smiling. "That was when I started following Dr. Crawther around. I made myself a pest until he showed me a few things."

"I'll bring you some tea while Sis's fixing a meal. Then maybe you'll tell me some more about doctoring."

"Go from here now and bring the tea, and then I'll tell you all you want to know." Rees Kenyon watched the young man as he turned away. He seemed to be seeing himself, and as he sat down, he looked at Thaddeus, who had gone to sleep. "There's a young one with a future, but I don't know about you. Getting yourself shot in a duel is stupid." He got no answer, as he knew he would not. He let himself relax, settling back in the chair, for operations always tired him. He sat there very still, thinking of his mother and sister and wondering how his family was doing back in Wales.

# Chapter Eleven

BREAKFAST WAS A DISASTER! THERE WAS NO OTHER NAME FOR IT, for although Callie had given it her best efforts, she still had not learned more than the fundamentals of cooking. She had attempted to make porridge, and now she stood staring down with disgust at the lumpy mass that filled the bowl before her. She snorted, then walked to the kitchen door and threw the bowl's contents out in the yard. When she came back, she found that Rees had entered. His face was glowing from a fresh shave, and he was wearing the brown suit that looked so good on him. She had not bathed and the dress she wore was none too clean. The difference between the two of them irritated her, and she snapped, "I tried to fix porridge but it didn't turn out right! I ain't no cook at all!"

"Well, we'll make do," Rees said. "Why don't we just have battered eggs. Nobody can go wrong there."

Callie, who was ready for an argument, stared at him, but there seemed to be no reasonable protest she could make. "All right," she said, nodding. "You can 'ave some toast and cheese while you're waiting."

"That'll be fine." Rees sat at the table. As usual, he had a book, and he opened it at once and began reading it. Callie pulled down another bowl and broke six eggs in it and began beating them furiously with a spoon. The fire had warmed up the kitchen, so she was perspiring, and from time to time she mopped her face with a limp neckerchief tied around her neck. She poured the eggs into a blackened skillet sitting on the fire and watched carefully. At least she knew how to do this. While the eggs were cooking, she stole a glance at Rees. She studied the straight black line of his brows and noted that his raven hair was shaggy. He was not a handsome man but this had never troubled her at all.

She carefully stirred the eggs until they were done, adding some salt and thinking about the strangeness of their life together. The little house had been at first a delight to her. She had her own room upstairs, and Rees was gone most of the time, so she had the house to herself. When he came home, there was a constraint, however, the two of them warily walking around one another as if a charge of dynamite could go off if they so much as touched.

For the first few nights and days Callie had kept her knife handy, but Rees had made no attempt to force himself on her. As a matter of fact, he had practically ignored her, and this for some reason had begun to irritate her. *He don't even know I'm alive,* she thought as she poured the eggs into two wooden trenchers. Coming to the table, she set the plates down with more force than necessary, then filled his cup with fresh tea and poured some for herself. "The toast is burned," she said.

"Well, I always liked burned toast. It makes it crunchy."

She saw deviltry making its thin point in his eyes and knew he was teasing her. He never did so in such a way that she could put her finger on it and challenge him, and now she began to eat using the big spoon she had stirred with.

"Why don't you try one of the silver spoons?"

"This is good enough for me."

"If you get that thing caught in your mouth, it's strangled you'll be."

Actually, Callie admired Rees's manners, but a perversity in her caused her to keep using the large spoon. "I'll eat my own way and you eat yours."

"There's a stubborn mule you are," he said and suddenly grinned. "Eat any way you please. It's all the same to me."

"I will."

Rees finished the meal, drank the rest of the tea, and then leaned back in his chair. "Did you ever see a lighthouse?"

"No."

"Would you like to?"

Callie studied him carefully. She was bored with the house and had walked around the neighborhood, so there was nothing new to be seen. "You mean go with you?"

"I have a patient out on the coast. If you've never seen a lighthouse, perhaps it'd be a good excursion for you. Get out and stir around a little."

"All right. I'll go."

Rees said cautiously, "Right, you. But you'll have to wash your face and put on a clean dress."

"Wot's wrong with this dress? And my face is good enough for me."

Rees shrugged. "All right. Keep a dirty face, then. Be like an old pig."

His words challenged Callie. "All right. I'll do it."

"Go you, then. We need to get a quick start."

Callie took in the city of Boston as they drove through the streets. Rees seemed lost in thought and said nothing but she was fascinated by the scenes. They passed distilleries, fisheries, rope yards, shipyards, and she was surprised at how many soldiers they saw in the streets. Their red coats made them stand out like brightly plumaged birds, and she finally asked, "Why are there so many soldiers 'ere in this place?"

"Because there's likely to be some fighting."

"Who will they be fightin'? The French or the Spanish?"

"Neither. It'll be a revolution. A civil war. Haven't you ever heard of this?"

"I 'eard a little of it sometimes in the tavern but I ain't never understood it."

"It's hard to understand, Callie. But basically it comes to this: England spent a great deal of money fighting the French and Indian War, and a great part of that war's aim was to keep America in British hands. Now the war is over, and the Parliament is asking the colonists here to pay their part of the cost. But Americans don't want to do that."

Callie sat listening while he explained. As they left the main part of town and the countryside began to open up, she was amazed at the cleanness of the air. Accustomed as she was to the thick atmosphere of London, she found the fresh country air exhilarating and intoxicating. Her eyes constantly shifted as she noted the neat farms that lay just outside Boston, and they passed through wooded areas that delighted her. She had never been in the woods in her life, and once she almost asked Rees to stop so she could get out and walk among the trees. But he was hurrying along, driving the mare at a fast pace.

"Wot's that bird?" she finally asked, pointing at a strange-looking bird with a red head and a striped body.

"Some kind of woodpecker, I think. I don't know its name. I don't believe it's an English bird. Now, if we were back in Wales, I think I could tell you the names of most birds."

"I don't know the names of any of 'em except sparrows."

"There was one bird that stayed close to the shipyards back home. I never knew what kind it was, but I called it the go-away bird." He looked at her and grinned. "His cry sounded like that. 'Go away! Go away!'" He suddenly turned his head to one side. "A bit like you he was."

Callie stared at him. "Wot does *that* mean?"

"That's what you are always telling me. Go away."

"I never said nothin' like that to yer!"

"Callie, everything about you says go away. You've built a wall around yourself and you don't want any man coming close."

Callie suddenly uttered an oath and glared at him. "If you 'ad to fight off as many greasy, nasty men as I 'ave, you'd say the same!"

The anger that flashed out of Callie surprised Rees. He had tried to be gentle with her, but there was indeed a wall about her that he could not break through. "Your life has been bad. I know that. I'm sorry for it."

Callie did not answer. She had few pleasant memories, and this man who was so far above her socially could no more understand her than he could the mind of a wild beast.

Finally he said, "Callie, if you want to write any friends back in England, I'll post a letter for you." She still did not answer and he turned to look at her. "Did you hear what I said?"

She turned to him, her face stretched tight over her cheekbones, her lips drawn together. "Don't yer make fun of me!"

Rees was surprised beyond measure. He stared at her open-eyed. "Make fun of you? All I asked is if you want me to mail a letter for you."

"I . . . I can't write . . . and I can't read neither."

Rees could not answer for a moment. It had never occurred to him that the girl couldn't write, although he knew there were many of her station who had never learned this art. He felt he had insulted her, innocent as he had been. He saw that she had turned away from him, and he tried to frame an answer that would take away the straightness of her back and put her at ease.

"You're a bright girl," he said. "I'll teach you to write and to read, if you'd like." She did not move and he thought perhaps he had said something wrong again. Finally she did turn, and there was something in her face he could not understand. Some of the guardedness had left and she seemed vulnerable somehow. The rich, yellow gleaming of her hair had caught the glint of the sun, but it was her face that he noticed. She had washed carefully, he noted, and he saw again that her face was beautifully fashioned. The hint of strong will was on it, and despite her background there was still pride left in her. He saw it in her eyes and in her lips and in the set of her shoulders.

"Would yer really do that for me, Mr. Kenyon?"

"Of course I would, if you'd like."

"I'd like it frightful well!"

Rees nodded. "We'll do it, then. We'll start tonight and you'll be reading before you know it."

"Well, there's the lighthouse," Rees announced.

"They live in that tall thing?"

"No. They live in the house right there beside it. See? That white one with the tile roof."

"Then wot do they do with the tower?"

"They light it up. They keep it lit so ships at sea can see it. The captains use it as a marker. It keeps them from going onto the rocks and losing their ships."

Callie said no more and they soon pulled in front of the house. Rees got out of the carriage but she did not wait. She saw a young man coming out of the door, and she leaped out and stood watching him as he approached.

"Good morning, Matthew. How's the patient?"

"Very well, Doctor." Matthew's eyes went to the young woman, who said nothing. "Come inside."

"Of course. This is my . . . ward, Miss Callie Summers." He hesitated over the words, although that was the story they had agreed on. He wished now that he had never thought of such a thing, but the damage was done.

"I'm mighty pleased to meet you, Miss Summers," Matthew said.

Callie nodded. "Likewise." She saw that he was watching her, and as always she was guarded around men, even one so young.

"Come inside, Dr. Kenyon. My sister's just put on some fresh coffee and she's making donkers."

"I don't know what they are but it sounds good."

Callie saw Rees step back and allow her to go first. She flushed and walked toward the house. Matthew ran ahead and opened the door. When she entered the house, she fell silent, for she did not know how to speak. They were met by a young woman, and Rees said, "This is Miss Hannah Thomas. Miss Thomas, this is Miss Callie Summers, my ward."

Callie murmured some reply but she was intimidated by meeting strangers.

"Matthew, why don't you show Miss Summers the lighthouse while the doctor attends to Thad," Hannah said.

"Of course. I'll be glad to if you'd like to see it, Miss Summers."

"Yes, I would."

As soon as the two left, Rees asked, "How's your brother?"

"He seems to be doing well. Come along — and thank you for coming."

Rees followed Hannah into the bedroom and found Thad Thomas sitting up in bed, his back braced with pillows. "Well, Doctor, I'm still alive."

"I'm glad to hear it, sir." Rees took Thad's wrist. He noted that the pulse was regular, and looked into his eyes and examined him briefly. "Now let's see what that wound is like."

"It itches. That's what it's like."

"Well, be sure you don't scratch it."

"He's like a child, Dr. Kenyon," Hannah said. She had come to stand on the other side of the bed, and she was smiling slightly. "I have to practically tie him in bed."

Rees removed the bandages and noted with satisfaction that the bleeding had completely stopped. "You're already starting to heal. The wound looks good. There was some cloth in with the ball. If I hadn't gotten that out, you would have been in trouble."

"I appreciate the help, Doctor." He was a fine-looking young man but now an angry expression crossed his face. "Did they tell you how it happened?"

"Not really."

"Well, it was that Englishman with an odd name. Banastre Tarleton. Isn't that a stupid name?"

"What was the quarrel over?" Rees was cleaning the wound and began applying a bandage around Thad's chest.

"It was over a lady."

"She was *not* a lady, the way you told it before, but some tavern wench," Hannah said.

"Well, perhaps she wasn't a fine lady but it doesn't matter. I'll see him later. He cheated."

"There. That ought to do it. You can put on your shirt now," Rees said.

Rees watched as the young woman helped her brother don his shirt and then said, "Are you having another duel with him?"

"He's got to answer for what he did. He was already turned when we counted off our steps. He turned at nine. I had no chance at all."

"Come you now. Be grateful that you're not dead. You could easily have been."

"Dr. Kenyon is right. God gave you your life, Thad."

Thad Thomas could not meet his sister's gaze. "I suppose it was a fool thing to do." He looked up and said, "You're fresh from England, I understand?"

"That's right."

"What do they say in England about the trouble over here?"

Rees began cleaning up but Hannah came over and said quietly, "I'll do that, Doctor." He turned to Thad and sat on the chair. The young man was interested in him. If he was a typical American, the English troops would have their hands full. Rees knew that young Thomas was an expert shot, for Dr. Warren had told him that. He not only made guns but had won many shooting contests. He was well built, not fat nor overly muscular but with a lean strength. "There's a great deal of difference over there. The king, I understand, is going to insist on you people paying your share of the war debt."

"That blasted stamp tax! We'll not pay it! We'll fight first!"

"Don't get excited. It's not good for you."

Rees sat there listening, trying to get to the sort of man Thad Thomas was. His sister had left the room and now returned with tea, and Rees stood. She put the tea down and then sat to join them. "Tell us about your practice, Doctor," she said. "Is it like what you had in London?"

Rees said, "I was only in practice there for a brief time." He changed the subject, speaking of ships and the sea, and discovered that these American colonists were rather nice after all.

Callie stared out over the sea, delighted with the view. "You can see so far," she whispered.

"You see those rocks over there? No, this way. They're just barely sticking up." Matthew moved closer to Callie, extended his arm, and said, "Right over there."

"I see 'em."

"Two years ago a ship ran onto those rocks. It was in the middle of a storm. The wind was so bad that it blew out the lights here. We rang the bell all night, all of us taking turns, but at dawn we saw that the ship had struck the rocks."

"Wot happened then?" She turned to him and he noticed how wide and beautifully shaped her eyes were.

"There was no way for them to get ashore. Their boats were all wrecked, so we rowed out and we got twelve of them."

"In the middle of the storm?"

Matthew nodded. "It was quite a chore, Miss Summers. We almost drowned ourselves."

"You can call me Callie."

"That's an unusual name."

The two stood there talking and finally he asked, "What about Dr. Kenyon's political feelings?"

"I don't think he 'as any politics."

"Well, he must be a patriot if he works with Dr. Warren. You know, Dr. Warren is a member of the Sons of Liberty."

Callie turned to face him. "Wot's that?"

Matthew was astonished. "You don't know about the Sons of Liberty? Why, they are a group come together to fight against English oppression."

Callie watched as the young man grew excited. "I'm a member of the Sons of Liberty myself."

"Would you fight against England if a war come?"

"Why, of course I would."

Callie was fascinated with the young man. He was clean-cut and seemed even younger than his sixteen years. They were in fact the same age but she felt a hundred years older. Finally he told her about his work as a gunsmith, but then he said, "I don't want to be a gunsmith all my life. I want to do something different."

"Different? Like wot?"

The wind was blowing Matthew's chestnut hair. He ran his hands through it and looked at her with puzzlement. "I don't know, but I know we only have one life, and I don't want to spend it doing the wrong thing. Somehow I want my life to count, Callie."

Callie did not understand this. It was beyond her. Eventually they heard a call, and looking down, Callie said, "The doctor's ready to go." She put out her hand, something she rarely did with men. "Much obliged for showing me the light'ouse."

"Why, I was glad to do it." Matthew shifted for a moment and something inside him struggled to find expression. Finally he said, "We're having a frolic next week."

"A frolic? Wot's that?"

"What you'd call a party. One of the young women from our church is getting married. Her parents are pretty well off, so they're giving a big party. Lots to eat, music. Dancing even. I think you should come."

"Me?"

"Yes. You could meet some young people."

"I wouldn't know 'ow. I don't know anybody."

Matthew suddenly grinned, his teeth very white against his dark skin. "You know me. Will you come?"

"You'll 'ave to ask the doctor."

"All right. I'll do that."

Hannah was thanking Rees again. She had followed him outside, and he said, "I'm glad to come. I'm happy your brother is doing so well."

"Are you meeting a lot of people?"

"Well, we've been pretty busy so far. Doctor Warren has a lot of patients." He thought a minute and said, "I've been invited to a dinner at General Gage's home. I don't know how I got that invitation."

"Dr. Warren didn't get one, I'm sure of that."

"No, he didn't." He saw that her demeanor had grown cooler, and wondered at the change.

At that moment Matthew and Callie came out of the lighthouse, and Matthew said, "Dr. Kenyon, there'll be a party next week, and I've asked Miss Callie if she would like to go. She says you'll have to give your permission."

Rees stared at Matthew and then turned his eyes on Callie. There was nothing in her face to tell her feelings, but he shrugged, saying, "If you'd like, Callie. I'm sure it would be a nice event for you."

Callie turned to Matthew and smiled. "I'll be glad to go."

Callie went to the carriage and prepared to climb in, but Matthew was there. He reached out his hand and at first she did not know what he wanted. Then she flushed, realizing that he intended to help her. She took his hand and got inside. He ran his hand through his thick hair and said, "I'll look forward to the frolic."

Rees spoke to the horse and as the carriage pulled away, he and Callie turned and waved.

"They're very nice people, ain't they?"

"Very nice indeed, Callie."

"Do you mind if I go?"

"Why, no. I may go myself."

He spoke to the horse again and as they picked up speed, he wondered about the change he had seen in Hannah Thomas. Then he realized her reaction was against the British General Gage. *Well, I'll have to go. I've agreed now,* he thought as he urged the horse on to a faster pace.

"I'm surprised that you're going to General Gage's house for the dinner, Dr. Warren."

Warren sat beside Rees in the carriage. He turned and smiled briefly. "I want to hear what he has to say, but I'm surprised he invited me. He knows I'm a member of the Sons of Liberty. I think he's going to try to convince me of British superiority."

The two men were approaching the house, which was rather ornate. It had belonged to a wine merchant, so Dr. Warren had told Rees, but the general had taken it over for his headquarters.

Callie sat in the back listening to them talk. Rees had insisted on her coming but she dreaded it. Uneducated as she was and with her background, she knew she would be out of her depth.

Finally when they stepped out of the carriage and walked up the steps, Rees said, "I hope you'll enjoy yourself, Callie."

"I wisht I was home. I didn't want to come 'ere."

"Don't be like that. Come you now. You'll enjoy it."

The door was guarded by two grenadiers in full-dress uniforms. When the three of them entered, they were led to an elaborate dining room by a lieutenant dressed in green. He introduced himself as Lieutenant Banastre Tarleton, and at the name Rees suddenly realized, *This is the man who shot Thad Thomas.* He studied the young man, who was short but well built and handsome in a heavy sort of way.

Lieutenant Tarleton took them to where the table was set in the center of the dining room. At one end of the room a group of officers and several women were gathered. Tarleton said, "Our guests are here, General Gage."

Gage came forward at once. He knew Dr. Warren and when Warren introduced Rees, Gage greeted him with a smile. He was a tall man, full-bodied, with a dignity and yet an openness that pleased

Rees. "Welcome to Boston, Dr. Kenyon. I understand you've come lately from London."

"Yes, General, that is so."

"Ah, London, how I miss it! But come and let me introduce you to the rest of our guests."

Rees heard several of the names and tried to remember them, but the only one he did was that of an attractive young woman. "This is Miss Elaine Gifford. Miss Gifford, Dr. Kenyon."

Elaine Gifford was wearing the latest in fashion and Rees was struck by her beauty. "How do you do, Doctor?"

"I'm happy to know you, ma'am, and may I present Miss Summers, my ward."

"I'm glad to know you, Miss Summers." Elaine Gifford had a pair of quick brown eyes and she at once attached herself to Callie. "You must tell me all about your trip. What part of London are you from? I spent three years there myself."

Callie was struck silent by the woman's attention. She knew the minute she opened her mouth she would be discovered, so she contented herself with simply agreeing with whatever the woman said.

Rees found himself seated by Elaine Gifford at the table. He caught the scent of her perfume and was somewhat dazzled. He had never been in such proximity to such a fine lady. He saw that Callie was miserable and thought, *I shouldn't have brought her here. She's not ready for something like this.*

The dining room where the party had gathered was large, with wall-to-wall green carpet. The walls were covered with bold green-and-gold wallpaper with diamond shapes. There were no windows in the room, but a set of French doors at the far end were covered with white lace curtains. Everything was lavish and expensive. The meal was finer than anything Rees had had and certainly intimidated Callie. Roasted venison in spiced wine sauce was the main dish. It was followed by a platter of roasted goose basted with butter. Bread was cut into tiny pieces and served in silver bowls. Everything was delicious, but Rees was very aware that Callie was scarcely touching her food. She was shrunk into herself, and Elaine Gifford ignored her, turning to talk to the rest of the group.

Politics of course became the topic of conversation. General Gage was a well-educated man, well spoken, and he handled the situation well. Banastre Tarleton spoke harshly of the colonists, but Gage had been in America for some time, and he had sympathy for the problems of the colonies. He tried to draw Dr. Warren out but Warren refused to commit himself. Once he said clearly, "General Gage, I fear that the men who rule England have no idea what a war would be like in this country."

Gage shook his head at once. "We must hope it doesn't come to that."

Warren had not responded and Gage had guided the conversation away. Later in the evening he took Dr. Warren off, and Rees suspected that the real purpose of the doctor's invitation would be made plain.

He found himself liking Elaine Gifford very much. She had a generous smile and was obviously at ease in any society. Her manner had an openness that he admired, and she gave her full attention to him in a most intense manner. "We have lost our family doctor," she said with a smile. "I will tell my father that we need to take advantage of London's finest."

"That's very kind of you, Miss Gifford. I'm sure Dr. Warren would be pleased."

"Don't be so modest. I meant *you*, of course." Elaine laughed, adding, "A modest physician! I didn't know any existed!"

Rees felt pleasure at her words. He was charmed by the woman, and he spent the rest of the evening speaking with her, forgetting all about Callie.

"I ain't never goin' nowhere with you again!"

The two were riding in the carriage, and Rees turned with shock running through him. His memories of Elaine Gifford were so much in his thoughts that he'd scarcely spoken a word to Callie, and she had not broken the silence once.

"What do you mean by that? I thought it was a fine party."

"I don't fit in there."

"Now, Callie, all you have to do is learn a few things."

"No, I'm stupid and I won't never fit in!" Suddenly Rees felt a strong twinge of conscience. He had ignored the young woman and he rebuked himself. Aloud he said, "It's just a matter of learning which fork to use."

"I wisht I was back on the streets! I knowed how to act there!"

"No, you don't." Rees put his right arm around the girl's shoulders, attempting to comfort her. "Now, Callie —"

Callie turned and her eyes were blazing. "You do your lovin' on that Gifford wench and keep your hands off me, you 'ear me!"

Rees moved his arm at once. Callie turned, bitterness welling up in her. She was so angry and mortified that she wanted to weep, but she clenched her teeth and refused to give in. One thing she knew. She would never go anyplace where that Gifford woman was present!

# Chapter Twelve

NOTHING IS MORE DIFFICULT TO KEEP THAN A MILITARY SECRET, AND for several days prior to April 18 many in the city of Boston were aware that the British were planning some sort of military expedition. General Gage had done all he could to keep the plan confidential, but a Boston lady who employed the wife of a British soldier as her maid learned many of the details. Once the essence of the plan was unveiled, spies from all over the city began to pick up various bits of information until finally there was little left secret.

In effect, a company of soldiers who would be commanded by Lieutenant Francis Smith and whose second in command was John Pitcarn were to lead the expedition. By the time the date of execution arrived, there was little the British could do to conceal their movements. The plan had been to march quietly out of Boston on the night of April 18 without telling the troops their destination. They were to march to boats waiting on a secluded part of the waterfront. Every effort was to be made to keep the march silent, but it is impossible to move large numbers of troops through the middle of a large city in secret — especially when practically every patriot is an unpaid spy anxious to uncover the movements of the king's troops.

Just before ten o'clock that night a knock came at the door of Paul Revere's house. The silversmith had been waiting for it, and after he opened the door and exchanged a whispered conference, he grabbed his cloak and hat and moments later was hurrying through the dark streets. He kept to the shadows and soon arrived at the door of Dr. Joseph Warren. Revere was glad to see that lights were still on in the physician's house, and he knocked urgently. The door opened at once and Warren invited him in. "Come in, Paul," he said. "You have news?"

Pulling off his hat, Revere nodded. "I do."

Revere started to speak but he noticed that another person was there. He had met Dr. Rees Kenyon before but now held his peace, casting a quick glance at Dr. Warren.

Warren at once said, "You'll excuse us, I'm sure, Rees. Mr. Revere and I have some business."

"Certainly." Rees bowed to Revere and left the room.

"Is he safe, Doctor?"

"I wouldn't want him to hear what you have to say, but if you mean is he a spy and would he go to the British, no. Regretfully, he's not been here long enough to find out how the situation is. What do you have, Paul?"

The two men faced each other and would have seemed most unlikely associates. Revere was a short, heavyset man with a flaring nose and quizzical brows over his dark eyes. He looked like a craftsman, which he was; he had even ventured into the role of surgeon dentist. He had made the two front teeth that showed between Dr. Warren's lips. He was the finest craftsman in the colonies in anything to do with silver or pewter, but what tied him to Dr. Joseph Warren was his fervent patriotism and his hatred of England. He was a member of the Sons of Liberty and was one of those who had blackened his face and become a Mohawk Indian for a night, helping to dump tea off the ships in Boston Harbor at the famous Boston Tea Party.

"The British are on the move and they're headed toward Concord. But they also mean to arrest Adams and Hancock."

"They'll have to be warned."

"Yes. That's why I'm here."

"Will you undertake the task?" Warren asked.

"Yes sir."

"All right. We'd better send two messengers. You'll be one and William Dawes will be the other. We'll have him ride by land and you will row across to Charlestown. Get to the members of the committee as quickly as you can — and above all warn Mr. Adams and Mr. Hancock. They mustn't be taken."

"Don't forget the powder that's hidden there in Concord. They'll be after that for sure."

"We're going to need that powder," Warren said, nodding grimly. "You know everything that's there; if you ride fast, most of it can be moved."

"I'll leave right now, Dr. Warren."

"God go with you, Paul!"

Hannah stared at Matthew in disbelief. "You're going to do what?"

Matthew had rushed into the house, his eyes blazing. He was so excited that his words tumbled over one another. He waved his hands around, saying, "I'll tell you, it's the truth, Sister. There's going to be a battle and I've got to be there."

"What are you talking about?" Hannah asked. "Calm down, Matthew."

"I'm going to Concord. The minutemen are gathering there. The British are on the march to steal our powder. We've got to stop them."

Hannah shook her head. "You can't do that. You don't know anything about it."

"Yes, I do. I've been going to the Sons of Liberty meetings, and besides, Will is going to be there and I want to fight the British with him."

Will Parker was the son of Jonas Parker. Jonas was the brother of Rebecca, who had married Amos. The two cousins had been close all their lives, and now Hannah saw the fire in her brother's eyes. He was usually a calm young man, but there was no calming him now.

"Be quiet. You'll wake up Father."

"I want to tell Thad."

"You'll do no such thing. He's still weak from that wound he's taken. He'd be the one to go, not you."

"I'm a man, Sister, and I'm going."

Something in Matthew's expression told Hannah that argument was useless. Quickly she thought and said, "You go to your uncle

Jonas and put yourself under his care. He's a sensible man. He'll take care of you and Will."

"All right. I'll do it. I just came home to get my musket." English law required able-bodied men to own muskets. Every man from sixteen to sixty was enrolled in the crown militia and could be called out by a draft in time of danger. Each man was to keep a good supply of powder, a bayonet, and be ready for the call of his king.

Matthew went to the wall and picked the musket that had belonged to his father. "I could have gotten one from the shop," he said, "but this one shoots truer."

Hannah watched helplessly as Matthew girded himself with the powder, the balls, and other supplies, then she said, "Here. I'll fix you a bag of something to eat."

"I don't have time to wait."

"Yes, you do. You'll get hungry, and you need to take a water bottle with you, also."

Matthew protested but finally gave in. When she had pulled together a bag full of meat and bread and fruit, he slung it over his shoulder, pulled her forward, and kissed her on the cheek noisily. His eyes were gleaming and he said, "I'll be all right. Don't worry about me."

"Of course I'll worry about you. Now you be sure to put yourself in Uncle Jonas's care."

She stood there watching as Matthew left, and then wondered whether she should tell her father. Instantly she knew that was wrong. Ordinarily she would have told Thad, but he was still weak from the loss of blood and could do nothing about it. As a matter of fact, knowing Thad, he might have gotten up and tried to go with Matthew.

"It'll come to nothing," she whispered as she stared out into the night and listened to the hooves of Matthew's horse as it disappeared into the darkness.

"You boys stay out of this," Jonas Parker said sternly. He looked at his son Will and then put his steady gaze on Matthew. "There'll be no fight here today."

"But Pa, the men have all got their arms."

"It's just a show of force. Why, we have no more than seventy men here." Jonas Parker swept his arm in a gesture that encompassed the men who had gathered on the green at Lexington. Most of them wore leather jerkins and broad-brimmed hats. All of them carried muskets, but Jonas Parker, their officer, had commanded them sternly that there would be no firing. "We'll make a demonstration of strength," he had told the men, "but we'll not begin a war this day."

A quick reply rose to Matthew's lips but he knew his uncle was a firm man. Matthew exchanged a despairing glance with Will and they moved to join the line. "I have my weapon loaded no matter what Pa says," Will said stubbornly. "So does everybody else."

"So have I," Matthew whispered.

The two took their place in line and then watched the road. The patriots had already been informed that the king's troops would be there almost at once, and soon they could hear the sounds of marching men.

"There they are," Will said with excitement in his voice. "There's a lot of them, too."

They kept their eyes on Jonas Parker, a great, tall man with a large head. "Pa doesn't think we can stop 'em, but I know we could if he'd just let us," Will said.

"I guess we'll have to do what he says. He's the officer."

What happened next seemed to occur more quickly than Matthew could have imagined. He was aware of the minutemen standing in line, and he heard his uncle call out, "Be still, men! No firing!"

No sooner had his voice fallen away than a multitude of red-clad soldiers came over the rise. They were cheering and advancing at a quick pace. Three mounted officers galloped ahead of the men and pulled up, and the foremost of them cried out in a loud voice, "Lay down your arms, you blasted rebels, or you're all dead men!" He brandished his sword over his head three times, and Matthew felt the sweat break out on his face as the British troops drew closer. The officer began to curse and continued shouting for the rebels, as he called them, to lay down their arms. After it was all over, there was great argument about who fired first, and Matthew did not know. He did hear a shot ring out, and he thought it came from Buckman's Tavern across the road, or perhaps from a stone wall beside it.

Instantly one of the officers ordered their men to fire, and the air was suddenly filled with the crash of exploding muskets.

Jonas Parker cried out and fell, struck by one of the balls. Will ran to him but he had no chance. Matthew had joined him and he said, "They're coming with bayonets. We've got to get away, Will!"

Tears running down his face, Will Parker joined the retreat, for all of the company began to run. The musket shots continued to sound, and Matthew looked back just in time to see a burly redcoat lift his rifle and plunge the bayonet into his uncle's body. He knew that Will had not seen it and was glad. The two ran for all they were worth, joined by their friends and fellow patriots.

When they finally stopped, Will was weeping freely. "They killed my pa," he whispered.

"And others too," Matthew said grimly. He suddenly stopped, for a group of men were approaching, obviously some of their own volunteers. A tall man with steady blue eyes said, "What's happened?"

"They fired on us. They killed my pa."

"They killed Jonas Parker?"

"Yes sir."

"I'm sorry, boy." The tall man put his hand on Will Parker's shoulder. "We'll have them for that. Join us. There are others coming."

Another man came up and said, "They'll have to go back down this same road to Boston."

"Yes, they will," the tall man said, "and we'll be waiting for them!"

Matthew could hear the shots plainly now. He was crouched behind a stone wall, his cousin Will beside him. Will's face was pale but tense. He had not said another word about the death of his father. The two of them had joined the tall man's group alongside the others who were gathering, all ready to take up the fight. The tall man, whose name was Sanders, had not been appointed commander specifically but seemed to be in charge. By now there were hundreds who had come from the countryside.

Sanders came by and said, "Boys, we're going to hunt them just like we would squirrels. Let them get into sight, and as soon as you get a dead shot, take them and then run further down the road. Find another good spot. We'll shoot them to pieces."

Matthew nodded and said, "Yes sir," and took his place.

He could hear the sound of the drum now and he said, "Here they come, Will."

Will did not say a word.

Matthew finally cleared his throat. "Do you think you can kill a man?"

"Yes."

The answer was spare and cold, and Matthew set his lips together in a firm line. "There they are," he whispered.

The column came into sight, marching down the road, led by an officer on a horse. The soldiers were obviously weary, and the officers had trouble keeping them going. They had marched all the way from Boston to Concord, but the word had come back that the supplies had already been moved.

Matthew waited and as the men came closer, he could make out individual faces. He leveled his rifle and looked down the length of it, aiming it at the chest of a tall soldier on the outer edge. He shifted it to another, a shorter, fatter man whose face was red with exertion. He was about to kill a man and something seemed to swell up in him. *Which one? I have the power to kill one of them — but which?* It all seemed so different! Everything had been theory until now, but his finger was on the trigger and a living human being was in his sights. He began to tremble and wiped the perspiration from his forehead.

Suddenly Will's musket exploded and a soldier grabbed his stomach and fell crying to the ground, kicking in agony.

"Shoot, Matthew!"

Matthew centered on one soldier, not looking at his face, and pulled the trigger. He saw the man go down and then Will grabbed his arm, saying, "Come on. We'll run down the road and get two more of them." As they ran, they heard musket shots and knew that the British were firing back.

Matthew felt sick and knew it would be a long time before he forgot the sight of the man he had shot in the breast falling limply back full length, obviously dead.

For the British soldiers and their officers it was a nightmare. They were fired at from all sides of the road, mostly from behind. People would hide themselves in houses until the troops had almost passed and then pick off the men in the rear. There were plenty of places for the rebels to hide, and they knew well how to take advantage of the stone walls that often lined the road. The incessant fire never seemed to die down, and Lieutenant Frederick McKenzie of the Royal Fusiliers was at his wits' end. He knew there was a relief column on the way, and if it didn't come soon, they would all be shot down. There was no way to do battle with ghosts!

He saw one of the enemy rise and aim his musket. Quickly McKenzie lifted his pistol and fired. He saw the shot catch the man in the throat. The man fell back and his throat instantly was covered with scarlet blood.

At the same time another shot rang out, and Corporal Higgins suddenly coughed. McKenzie turned. "Are you hit, Corporal?"

"Got me in the side . . ."

"Don't give up. The relief column will be here soon."

The corporal was holding his side, trying to keep his life from pouring out. His face was pale and he shook his head. "They'll kill us all, Lieutenant."

But five minutes later the relief column, under the command of Lord Percy, appeared. The fight was not over, and the British battled their way to the very outskirts of Boston. They had left dead men all the way from Concord and knew that all of them would have died if it had not been for the reinforcements.

The British soldier's face was ashen. He said, "Sir, General Gage asked if you would come and help with the wounded."

Rees Kenyon had opened the door to his house and found the single soldier there. "The wounded? There's been a fight?"

"Oh, yes sir. So many of our men are dead and many are dying. Please come, sir!"

"I'll get my bag." Rees quickly turned inside and found Callie standing there. "There's been a battle," he said. "I've got to go help."

"Let me go with you."

"No, there's no place for you, Callie. You stay here. I'll get back as soon as possible."

"Will you . . . be in a battle, Rees?"

It was the first time she had ever used his first name. Always before it was Mr. Kenyon or Dr. Kenyon or sir. He saw that she was troubled and said, "No, the battle's over, I think. I'll just be helping the wounded. Don't worry."

"Come back," she said as he left in a hurry. "As soon as you can."

As Rees rushed along beside the soldier, he asked, "Is it bad, Private?"

"Sir, you wouldn't believe it! There was a battle at Concord and all the way back. The colonists gathered beside the roads. Our men had no chance at all. The dirty cowards! They wouldn't come out and fight like men!"

Rees did not say so but he thought, *That's exactly what good soldiers would have done.*

The soldier led him to a large building which had been turned into a hospital, and for a moment as Rees stepped inside, he was stunned. The floor seemed covered with wounded men, many of them crying out and screaming.

Dr. Benjamin Church, whom he knew slightly, came to him. His hands were red with blood and he said, "Thank God you're here, Kenyon! Will you help?"

"Of course, Doctor. I'll do everything I can."

"Come along, then. We have an operating room of sorts, and you'll be of great service."

Rees threw himself into the work and for the next six hours he did not stop, except once to drink some tepid water. He amputated, probed for musket balls, but several men died before he and Dr. Church could get to them. Other physicians also had been pressed into service. As Rees was binding up the leg of a middle-aged man, he asked about the fight.

"We had no chance at all, and some of our men went out of control."

"What do you mean, Sergeant?"

"I guess we all went kind of crazy. They were shooting us and we couldn't see them. Some of the men went into houses and shot everybody in there."

Rees straightened. "You mean innocent civilians?"

The soldier put his hand over his eyes. "They went into one house, so my companion told me, and there was a woman who had recently given birth. Had the baby in her arms. They were going to kill her but she begged them not to."

"What did they do?"

"They let her get out and then they set fire to the house."

Rees shook his head but said nothing. "You'll be all right, I think."

"It's good of you, Dr. Kenyon."

He turned away and found himself facing General Gage. The general's face was tense but he said quickly, "I appreciate your service, Doctor."

"I'm glad to do what I can, General."

Gage stared at him and said, "I'm glad to see you here. Dr. Warren is no doubt tending to the rebel wounded."

"I can't say, General."

"Well, I'm glad to see you're loyal to the crown, anyway. Would you consider becoming a physician in the king's service?"

"I could not agree to do that at this time, sir."

"Think about it. Every man's going to have to make a choice, and I hope yours is the right one."

Rees understood what was being said. The general was grateful now, but it was obvious that a war had begun and that no man or woman could be neutral. Rees bent over a young soldier no more than seventeen or eighteen. He started to work on him and then he saw that the boy was dead. He rose, laid his hand on the boy's forehead for one moment, and knew that life in America was not going to be as he had imagined it.

# Chapter Thirteen

IF ONE THROWS A PEBBLE INTO THE CENTER OF A STILL POND, THE results are instantaneous. A circular ripple will begin in the epicenter and will spread out. Farther and farther the ripples will go, traveling outward until finally they will reach the shoreline. What was once a smooth, glassy surface is now marked by the dropping of one stone into the center.

So it was with Lexington and Concord in the beginning. Events were set in motion, and life was never again the same as it was before American blood was shed on the green fields of Lexington and by the bridge at Concord.

The day after the battle at Lexington, a British ship arrived in Boston Harbor with a peace proposal from Lord North. Basically, Lord North admitted that the crown had been too harsh with Americans, and generously offered not to tax those colonies that voluntarily paid their share of the cost of the French and Indian War. What would have happened if this proposal had come a week earlier will never be known, for Lexington had spurred the spirits of the colonists. Heralds went out from Massachusetts to all thirteen of the colonies, and a tall, powerfully built man named George Washington was so affected by the news that he packed the old red and blue uniform he had worn under Braddock and went at once to Philadelphia. The Second Continental Congress convened on May 10, 1775, and on that same day Fort Ticonderoga was attacked by American forces led by Ethan Allen and Benedict Arnold.

This circle was one of those resulting from Lexington, and it placed within the hands of the patriots priceless artillery and opened the gateway to Canada. As for the Second Continental Congress, more ripples became obvious. Men suddenly began to gain stature. Men such as Thomas Jefferson of Virginia, a tall, red-haired, wealthy aristocrat, began to be heard. John Adams, Ben Franklin, and others like them took control and began to speak loudly.

And the largest ripple of all, which was to affect the Republic more than any other, was the choice of a commander in chief of the fledgling American forces. George Washington was forty-three years old and had more military experience on the frontier than any other man in America. He had commanded the militia of Virginia, and when John Adams nominated him for commander in chief, he was unanimously elected by the Second Continental Congress.

When offered the command, Washington spoke in a low voice filled with hesitation. "Mr. President . . . I . . . declare with the utmost sincerity, I do not think myself equal to the command I am honored with. As to pay, sir, I beg leave to assure the congress that as no pecuniary consideration could have tempted me to have accepted this arduous employment at the expense of my domestic ease and happiness, I do not wish to make any profit from it."

More pebbles fell into the waters of politics. A steady stream of New Englanders flowed into Cambridge, surrounding Boston with a besieging force. No one kept a careful count, but by estimates they numbered close to fifteen thousand men. Their commander, Major General Artemas Ward, was ill with an infection of the kidneys. He was not a man of action, but one thing he did was to hold together the nucleus of what would become the Continental Army of the United States.

Yet another ripple that would affect the fury of revolution in America occurred on May 25. The *Cerebus* sailed into Boston Harbor carrying three generals sent to America to deal with the American crisis. The powers in London had decided that General Thomas Gage was incapable of dealing with the growing rebellion. Lord North, the prime minister, had finally chosen these three men to scrub the uprising that was creating agitation throughout the British Empire.

Ranked along the rail as the *Cerebus* pulled in, the three generals stood looking out over the harbor. The senior of the three was forty-five-year-old William Howe — tall, dark, and an excellent soldier. He was a strict disciplinarian respected as a tactician and well liked by officers and men. He did enjoy the company of women, perhaps too much, although he was said to be fond of his attractive wife, whom he left in England. He had been a major general for three years, but his capacity to lead an army had not yet been tested in battle.

Next to Howe in seniority was Major General Henry Clinton. Clinton was an officer of severely limited talents who had risen to his rank through the influence of powerful friends. The general was shy, with a sense of insecurity that made him appear quite touchy and suspicious. He was in effect a lonely, aloof, introspective man quick to take offense at the slightest provocation.

The third British general to arrive in Boston, John Burgoyne, had aristocratic connections. Fifty-three years old, he was believed to be the illegitimate son of a high-ranking nobleman. He had risen in the army by proving himself to be a successful and distinguished cavalry officer. He was even better known as a man about town and as a writer for the theater. He was believed by many to be a vain and vicious man — which was true to some degree.

As the three men stood speaking of the problem they faced, Clinton turned to his two fellow generals and said gloomily, "The whole affair seems to have been poorly handled so far. Here we are, the British army, pinned down in Boston by an undisciplined and leaderless rival force. I think it's a disgrace!"

Gentlemanly John Burgoyne, as he had been called behind his back, smiled expansively. "Well," he said, "now that we are here, we shall be able to make a little elbow room."

Unfortunately, his remark was heard by a corporal, who repeated it to his fellow soldiers, and soon Burgoyne was to hear the cry "Make way for General Elbow Room!" whenever he made an inspection.

The three generals looked at the dark, brooding hills beyond Boston. If they had been able to read the future, they would have perhaps stayed on the *Cerebus* and sailed back to England. Before this business was over, the "small crisis" in the colonies was to prove to be a graveyard for the reputation of British generals.

While the city of Boston seethed and General Gage tried desperately to find a way to put out the smoldering ashes resulting from Lexington and Concord, Dr. Rees Kenyon found himself busier than he could have dreamed. Dr. Warren threw himself into matters political with all his might, leaving Rees to take care of his burgeoning medical practice. It was a difficult thing for the young physician, for he was relatively unknown in the city. Furthermore, his politics were not clear, so he was regarded with suspicion among the patriots.

Rees rose early and came in late, often wrung out with the demands of the day. He knew himself to be unfit to handle many of the cases that came to him, and he managed to persuade Dr. Warren to see those who were most critical. But the bulk of the work fell on him.

Somehow during the busy activity of fulfilling these obligations Rees became unhappy with one aspect of his responsibility toward Callie. He well knew that people were suspicious of their relationship. No one said it to his face, but he understood grimly that most people who examined the situation were convinced that Callie was his mistress. There was no way to fight such an accusation, so Rees kept his lips sealed, but he determined that there would be no grain of truth in such accusations.

He saw little enough of Callie, usually briefly in the morning. She would rise and cook breakfast for him. They would eat together, making conversation, and then he would bid her good-bye and leave. Inevitably, when he came home at night, she would have food cooked. Although she was not a good cook, she was learning. Many nights he would sit at the table so tired that he could barely eat, and it was on one of these nights, a Friday late in May, that he had come in totally exhausted. Callie had a meal cooked and she told him to wash up, which he did, and then he sat at the table. He tasted the soup and looked up at her. "This is very good, Callie."

"Oh, anyone can make soup. See 'ow you like the fish."

The fish was so fresh and white and flaky, it fell apart under the fork. There were also slices of mutton, and the meat was tender, and the bread was surprisingly good.

"Did you make this bread yourself?"

Callie flushed. "No, I bought it at the bakery, but I'm going to learn 'ow to bake."

"You're doing a fine job. You're a good housekeeper and a fine cook."

"I bought the cider from a vendor. See if you like it."

Rees sipped the cider, which was cool and sparkling and fresh. "It's very good," he said.

"I got some fruit too but it's gettin' scarce. The army takes most of it, I think."

Rees ate the berries and other fruit that she put before him and then sat back. "That was good," he said.

"Did you 'ave many hard cases today?"

"About the same as usual. I'm afraid there's going to be a great deal of sickness. I hope the plague doesn't break out, but with so many soldiers jammed into Boston, it makes for danger."

As Rees spoke, he watched Callie. She was wearing a simple, light blue dress with a white apron over it, and her blond hair was fixed up on her head in a way he had not seen before. She started to rise and gather the dishes, but he said, "I've been thinking about something, Callie."

"Wot is it?" she asked with surprise.

"I think we've neglected a very important part of life. I think we ought to start attending church."

Callie stared at him. "I ain't never been to no church."

Rees was shocked. "Oh, surely you've been to church at least once or twice."

"No, I ain't never been, and I don't wanna go."

Rees stared at the young woman. It was inconceivable to him that a British subject would never have attended church. He made up his mind suddenly, for he knew that though he was not close to God himself, there was at least a longing in him. "We're going to church Sunday."

"I ain't got nothin' to wear," she said.

Rees rose and reached into his pocket. He pulled out some coins and laid them on the table. "There," he said. "Go buy you some clothes. This is Friday. You have all day tomorrow to pick out something. I don't want to be hard but this is something I think we need to do. No discussion, is it?"

"If you say so."

"Good night, then," Rees said and turned and went wearily to bed.

Callie leaned over and picked up the coins and held them in her hand, touching the polished surfaces. She was troubled, for this was something new for her. She had passed enough churches in London and seen the people, but mostly they were what she called "swells." At the same time something stirred within her. Staring down at the coins, she was aware of a longing to be different. Never before, back in England, was this so strong as it had been lately. Now she sat there, and the lamp cast its amber corona over the coins and twisted shadows into shapes, shedding yellow on the walls and the floor. She was unhappy and could not imagine why. Finally she closed her hand on the coins, got up, and began to clear away the dishes.

The streets of Boston were crowded and British soldiers were evident. Callie arrived at the shops. She had ignored the raw comments some of the soldiers made to her, keeping her eyes straight ahead. The day was warm and the sun was bright, and she was conscious of her coins, which she had stuffed into a small purse. She moved along the streets until finally she saw a dressmaker's shop and turned to go inside.

"Well, can I help you?" The speaker was a short, rounded woman of some forty years, with sharp black eyes and hair bound up under a mop cap.

"I wants ter buy a dress."

"A work dress?"

"No. A fine dress." Callie had no idea how to buy a dress, for she had never bought one. She stared defiantly at the woman, saying, "And I've got money, don't ya see?"

The proprietor hid her smile behind a hand and then nodded. "Well, I think we can find something that will suit you."

"And I want somethin' to put on me face."

"You mean rice powder and something to make your cheeks rosy?"

"That's wot I wants. And perfume. Somethin' wot smells sweet."

"It's rather dear, you know. It has to be shipped from France."

"Didn't I tell ya I got money?" Callie produced the purse and let the coins clink out into her palm. "There. My money ought to be good enough for ya."

"I'm sure it is. Well now. Let's see. Why don't you try on this one?"

"No, that ain't got enough color in it."

"Oh, you want color? Well, I think we have just what you want...."

Later Callie left the shop with a large package containing her purchases. She was excited and actually looked forward to going to church. *He'll be proud of me, Rees will. 'E ain't never seen me dressed up like this — and I'll smell good, too!*

Rees turned at the door, saying, "I'll have to go visit Mrs. Lewis before the service. You know where the church is?"

"I'll be there."

"Good. I shouldn't be late. I'll see you there."

Rees left the house and hurried across town. Sunday morning was calm and cool, and he felt good about his decision to start attending church. As he rushed along the streets, he noticed that worshipers were more numerous this morning. *Perhaps trouble draws people to God more. I don't remember this many people going to services before the bloodshed at Lexington.* The thought passed through his mind and then he shoved it aside.

He arrived at the Lewis house, and as he had suspected, Mrs. Lewis wanted attention more than she wanted medicine. She was a good woman but it took all of Rees's tact to assure her that she was not going to die immediately. He prescribed a harmless dose of the most evil-tasting medicine he could concoct, then smiled and said, "You'll be fine, Mrs. Lewis," and left the house.

The bells had already rung throughout Boston, signaling that he was late for the service, but as he hurried along, he saw that he was not the only one. His eyes brightened and he hurried to catch up with Hannah Thomas, who was obviously on her way to church. She was wearing a light blue dress with a square neck and long sleeves. A snug bodice decorated with a single green ribbon bow added color, and as she turned to face him, he was aware of how attractive she was.

"Good morning, Miss Thomas. On your way to the service?"

"Yes, I am."

"So am I." She did not answer and somehow Rees felt uncomfortable. "I've been meaning to come by and check your brother's wounds."

"He's doing very well."

Her words were cool and so were her eyes. Rees found himself searching for words.

"And your father. How is he? I've been meaning to come by and see him too."

Hannah's lips drew tight with displeasure. "You were too busy with the men who killed my uncle, sir."

Rees could not answer for a moment, he was so surprised. He knew he had not incurred the favor of the rabid patriots in town for patching up the British wounded, but her attitude caught him off guard. "It was something I had to do," he said. He saw that she did not intend to answer, and he wished he had not joined her. He nodded, saying, "I hope you enjoy the service," and let her pass. He loitered long enough to let her get to the church and enter, and then quickened his pace. When he turned the corner, at once a bright flash of color came to him, and as he approached, suddenly his heart sank. "Oh no," he muttered, slowing his steps, "surely she knows better than that!"

Callie was wearing one of the most brilliant red dresses he had ever seen. It was made of smooth material and caught the sunlight. It was so bright that it almost hurt his eyes. *I shouldn't have let her go by herself. She has no idea how terrible that dress is for a church service in Boston.*

He stopped beside her and instantly saw that the dress had not been her only purchase. Her face was covered with powder and her lips and cheeks were tinged with rouge. *She looks like a harlot,* he thought with utter dismay, and then he took a deep breath and was almost stifled by the strong, musky odor of the perfume she wore. Desperately he tried to think of something to say. Callie was watching him, a smile on her lips. "Do you like my new dress?"

"It's . . . very unusual," Rees stammered.

"It is, ain't it? It was the brightest one they 'ad, and I got me some perfume and somethin' for me face, too."

"Yes, I can see that." Rees was trying to think of some excuse for not entering. They couldn't possibly go into the house of God with Callie dressed like this!

"Well, good morning, sir."

Rees whirled to find Elaine Gifford with a man standing beside her. He was short, round, and wore a wig, and his eyes were fixed on Callie, his mouth parted with surprise.

"This is my father, Mr. Robert Gifford. Father, may I introduce Dr. Rees Kenyon? I told you about him."

"Yes, you did. A pleasure, sir."

"Happy to meet you, Mr. Gifford." Rees was aware that Elaine Gifford was concealing her humor, but her eyes were dancing, and she could not quite control the smile. "And this is Dr. Kenyon's ward, Miss Callie Summers."

Callie stuck out her hand like a man, and when the surprised Mr. Gifford took it, she squeezed it hard. "Glad to meet yer," she said.

"We're all late," Elaine said. "Come, you must sit with us."

"Oh, we wouldn't — "

"I'll have no argument, sir," Elaine said. "Come along, Miss Summers. You and I will lead the way. Let these men follow."

Rees felt like a reluctant actor caught up in some terrible drama. They entered the church, and as he woodenly followed the two women, he saw every head turn to catch a glimpse of the young woman wearing the brilliant scarlet dress. He groaned inwardly but there was no help for it. He hoped for a seat near the back but Elaine led them down to the third row. When they were seated, Rees found himself between the two young women. The odor of Callie's perfume was miasmal, and everyone within ten feet obviously was affected by it.

Rees slumped in the pew, his face fixed and reddened by the shame of it all.

"So glad you could come. I hope you'll be a regular visitor," Elaine said to Rees. He turned to meet her eyes, which still sparkled with amusement. "Do you know the minister?"

"No ma'am, I do not."

"He's a fine preacher. That's him looking at your ward. I think he's attracted to her." Elaine covered her mouth with a fan and said, "His name is Reverend Lucas Bennington." She proceeded to whisper, but her voice seemed to carry, drawing more attention. "He lost his wife a year or so ago. He's raising their two children. Every mother in the congregation wants to marry their daughter off to him."

"Are you in the race, ma'am?"

"No, he's too holy for me. Those are his children over there — Miriam and Caleb." He looked at the two children, who were in the front row, between two rather large women. They both had fair hair and blue eyes, like their father. "Their mother, Leah, died of yellow fever."

From time to time as Elaine whispered, Rees looked around and noticed that few people were paying attention to anyone except Callie. His eyes went to her face and he saw that she was pale beneath the paint and powder. *She knows she's done the wrong thing*, he thought. *She looks awful! Why did I ever trust her to do this herself? It's all my fault!*

Reverend Lucas Bennington, with a great deal of tact, rose and kept his eyes away from the young woman whose red dress was like a magnet for the eyes of the worshipers. He was a young man of thirty-three, of medium height, with blond hair and fine blue eyes. He opened after the song service by introducing his text. "'What must I do to be saved?'" He read the story of Paul and Silas, who, while confined in the jail at Philippi, had prayed and sung until midnight even though their backs were bleeding. He was a forceful speaker with a magnificent baritone voice seemingly too large for so spare a man. Indeed, he was too thin, and it was said that he was still grieving over his dead wife.

He plunged into his sermon, which was as simple as he could make it. He began by reading Romans 3:23: "'All have sinned, and come short of the glory of God.'" Bennington looked out at the congregation and asked, "How many of you would like to have everything you've ever done revealed to this congregation? None of you would, I'm sure, for we all have our deep, dark secrets, our shames, the sins that are still on our minds and in our memories. Surely I do not have to convince any of you of the truth of this Scripture. We have not all sinned alike — but we have all alike sinned."

He continued to speak, and once Rees turned his head enough to catch a glimpse of Callie. He saw that she was humiliated and thought with surprise, *Why, she's taking all this personally! She thinks somehow that the minister is preaching only at her.* He could not imagine what it was like to come into a church for the first time in one's life and suddenly be exposed to the accusation of sins. He thought, *Maybe I ought to just stand up and take her out of here,* but he knew that would not work.

The minister spoke clearly and forcefully. "And what is the result of our sin? We find the answer to that in Romans 6:23: 'The wages of sin is death.'" He then spoke quite graphically of the anger and wrath of God upon sinners. He read the story of the beggar and the rich man, emphasizing that the rich man in hell was conscious and in terrible pain.

Finally Bennington lifted his head and said, "But the good news is also found in the twenty-third verse of Romans 6. For it says, 'The gift of God is eternal life through Jesus Christ our Lord.' That is the good news. That is the gospel. No matter what else might be our problems or our difficulties, we can all cling to this verse. Jesus Christ brings peace and forgiveness of sins."

*I'll be glad when this is over,* Rees groaned inwardly. Never had he endured a worse time in a Christian church in all his life.

Callie had known from the very moment Rees had walked up that something was wrong. She had seen it in his eyes, and her happiness over having such a fine dress and preparing herself as well as she knew how suddenly turned to ashes. And when the woman and her father had come, she had seen the looks on their faces. They were laughing at her, that she knew full well, and she realized that the only reason would be that she had violated some code.

She had walked into the church — or been pulled in by Elaine Gifford — and all through the service she had felt inward tears. She was too proud to let it show, so she had kept her head high, fixing her eyes on the minister. She had never heard of such things as he said. She had heard the name of Jesus only in curses and profanity, and by the time he had come to the last of the sermon, in which he spoke more gently, she was so filled with humiliation and shame that she could no longer hear.

Finally everyone was standing, and she rose quickly. She stepped out of the pew, and her legs felt wooden, and she wanted to run screaming from the church.

It was difficult getting out, for the church was crowded and the lines moved slowly. People were staring at Callie with open curiosity, and when one man who had moved beside her let his eyes dwell on her a moment with such avid wonder, Callie said loudly, "Keep your bloody eyes off me!"

She knew that the silence which followed her statement was terrible for Rees, but she found herself hating him too. She clamped her lips together, and when they finally reached the door, she found the minister standing there greeting people. He shook hands with Rees, who muttered something, and then he started to speak to her.

Callie had reached the end of her endurance. She said loudly in a harsh voice, "I'd rather go to 'ell than be with the likes of all you hypocrites!" She turned then and ran outside, leaving Rees to repair the damage as best he could.

When she reached the street, she shoved her way through the crowd, paying no heed to anyone. The need to get away was so great that she could not bear it. Finally she arrived at the house, went up to her room, and ripped off the dress. She threw it on the floor and kicked it, and tears came to her eyes. She was mortified in a way she had never been back in England, even in the worst of the taverns. For a time she walked the floor, and then she heard a knock at the door. "Wot do you want?" she cried.

"Can I come in?"

"I don't care wot you do," Callie said. She saw Rees open the door, and when his eyes fell on her, he stopped short. She glanced down and saw that she was wearing only her shift, but she did not care. "Wot do you want?"

"Well, Callie, a little talk — but later."

She saw his eyes drop and he averted his face. He turned to leave and she stepped forward. "I'll never go to that place again, you 'ear me?" She slammed the door and for a moment stood there; then she whirled, ran across the room, and threw herself on her bed, stuffing her fist against her lips to contain the sobs that rose from deep inside her heart.

# *Chapter Fourteen*

FROM ALL OVER THE COLONIES CAME THE CRIES OF RAGE AGAINST Great Britain. No longer was she spoken of as the mother of the colonies. She was now the enemy! Typical of most of the cries that went up against England, yet perhaps more eloquent, were the words that fell from the mouth of Patrick Henry in his speech to the Virginia Convention. "There is no retreat but in submission and slavery! Our chains are forged. Their clanking may be heard from the plains of Boston! The war is inevitable — and let it come! I repeat it, sir, let it come! Gentlemen may cry peace, peace — but there is no peace. The war is actually begun! The next gale that sweeps from the north will bring to our ears the clash of resounding arms! Our brethren are already in the field! Why stand we here idle? What is it that gentlemen wish? What would they have? Is life so dear, or peace so sweet, as to be purchased at the price of chains and slavery? Forbid it, Almighty God! I know not what course others may take; but as for me, give me liberty or give me death!"

Dr. Warren was a loving father. He had lost his wife, and now with four children under his sole charge, he took what time he possibly could find to be with them. It was on a morning in June that Warren had invited Rees to go to town with him. He had taken the day off from his political activities, and Rees arrived at the house and was greeted at once by the children. There were two boys and two girls, all under the age of eight. Rees had become very fond of them, and now as they walked along the streets of Boston, he carried the youngest, a girl named Abigail. She was a beautiful child with the fair hair and blue eyes of her father, and she talked to Rees constantly.

Dr. Warren looked over and smiled. "Abigail, you chatter like a bird."

"Yes, she does," Rees said. He suddenly tossed her in the air. She squealed with joy, and he laughed and said, "She's going to be a heartbreaker, Dr. Warren."

"She's beautiful like her mother," Warren said, and for a moment a shadow crossed his face. He was holding hands with another daughter and the youngest boy, and his eyes rested on each of them. He said nothing about his wife, but Rees had heard him speak of her so often that he knew the physician was thinking of her. He was a cheerful man, this Dr. Joseph Warren, and a good man. Rees had never found another whom he liked better, except of course for his old friend Dr. Howell Crawther, and perhaps Dr. Howard Freeman. It was strange that these three physicians had played such a strong role in making him what he was.

"Let's go in and see how young Thomas is doing," Dr. Warren said. He led the way into the gun shop and said to the young man who came to greet them, "Good morning, Thad. It's good to see you back at work again."

"Good morning, Dr. Warren, and to you, Dr. Kenyon."

"Good to see you," Rees said. "How's the wound?"

"Nothing. Nothing at all. You did a good job, Doctor."

Rees was warmed by his words and also by the smile the young man gave him. He had not forgotten the cold treatment he'd received from Hannah Thomas, and he wondered if she still felt animosity toward him.

Rees carried Abigail around, letting Dr. Warren and young Thomas speak. The two boys were busy looking at the firearms on display, and once Rees saw his employer and Thad Thomas put their eyes on him. *He's wondering what I'm going to do about this war. Well, I wonder myself.*

He was right, for Thad had asked the doctor in a lowered tone, "What's Dr. Kenyon going to do, do you think?"

"About the war? He'll have to take sides. Everyone will. Kenyon is a good man. He's just new to all this."

"My sister thinks ill of him."

"Why is that?"

"Because he doctored the British wounded."

"Well, she's foolish, then, Thad. Hannah should know better. We doctors have to tend the sick, regardless of their nationality or what uniform they wear."

"Maybe you'd better tell her that, sir."

"I will the next time I see her." Dr. Warren turned then and said, "Are you ready to go, children?" He received a chorus of ascents and they left the shop.

"That's a fine young man," Warren said.

"Yes, and his brother also. I hate to think about them being caught up in this rebellion."

Warren did not speak for a time. "This is going to be a hard time for all of us, Rees. In a war people don't think logically. When they see someone they think is an enemy, they strike out."

Rees turned to face the doctor. "Are you trying to say I should leave?"

"It may come to that."

"I'll stay with you as long as you'll have me, Dr. Warren."

"It won't be me who would make you leave, but there will be others who won't understand."

"Why, Dr. Kenyon, how nice to see you!"

Rees had been making a call in the residential area of Boston and was pleased to see Elaine Gifford standing in front of a brownstone house, smiling at him. "Miss Gifford, a pleasure it is to see you." Taking his hat off, Rees moved to stand before her and gave a slight bow. "You're looking well."

"Is that a professional judgment, Dr. Kenyon?" Elaine's eyes danced and she laughed at his confusion. "I'm sorry, I couldn't resist. When a physician makes a remark about how I look, I always think he's making a diagnosis."

"Not at all!" Rees protested. "You certainly do appear to be healthy, but I was thinking about how you can cheer a man's day just by smiling at him."

"Why, Doctor, I begin to think you're a courtier! Or is this your bedside manner?"

Rees laughed. "No indeed! When I'm speaking with a patient, I try to look very wise and put on a most solemn air. But when I meet an attractive woman, I stand straighter and try to weave a little poetry into the conversation. For instance, I might say, 'You walk in beauty, Miss Gifford, like the night of cloudless climes and starry skies.'"

"Indeed, you might do well on the stage," Elaine said, smiling. "Are you going to town?"

"As a matter of fact, I am."

"Then you must share my carriage. I want to hear more of your poetry."

Rees laughed again and shook his head. "I'm afraid I just exhausted my stock — but I'll make some up."

"You Welshmen are a danger to young women! Come along, you can tell me all about your patients."

Rees helped Elaine into the carriage, and when he joined her, she spoke to the driver. "Edward, drive very slowly."

"Yes, Miss Elaine. Slowly it is."

Rees had supposed that Elaine Gifford would be proud, but he soon discovered that she was just the opposite. She had a quick wit and was able to poke fun at her own follies as well as those of other people. Rees found himself completely at ease, and when they reached the center of the shopping district, he volunteered to carry her purchases. For the next couple of hours the two of them moved from shop to shop. They eventually entered a tea shop and had lunch. Rees discovered that Elaine was a very close listener, and found himself talking much more than usual. Finally he threw up his hands, exclaiming, "I'm becoming an old bore! Why don't you tell me to hush?"

Elaine smiled and said, "I like to listen to you, Doctor. Your Welsh accent is so musical — and you have an interesting point of view about life. Now, you may call me Elaine, for I propose to call you Rees. Come now, we have more shops to explore."

Rees had always wondered why people spent so much time shopping, for he himself wasted no time on such business. But shopping with Elaine Gifford was pleasurable, and when she finally announced that she had to go home, he said, "This is a dreary world, Elaine, but there are bright spots in it — and this time with you has been one of those."

"What a lovely thing to say!" Elaine gave Rees her hand, and when he squeezed it, she said, "Come to dinner tomorrow. Just you and Father and I — and we'll find some way to get rid of him!"

Rees had pondered Dr. Warren's words of warning ever since they were spoken. Actually, it was two days later, when he was coming out of the house, ready to start his rounds, that he thought of them again. Warren had left for a meeting with Sam Adams. Rees looked up to see a horse and rider coming down the street at a rapid gait. The steel-shod hooves of the animal rang on the cobblestones, and Rees recognized young Matthew Thomas. At once he grew alert. *I'm afraid it's his father, from the look on his face.* He was right, for as Matthew came off the horse, the words tumbled out. "You've got to come, Dr. Kenyon."

"What is it? Your father?"

"Yes. He's bad. Is Dr. Warren here?"

"No, he's not available, Matthew, but I'll come at once. Let me get my horse."

"Hurry, Doctor. He's going fast, I'm afraid."

As soon as Rees looked down at the face of Amos Thomas, he knew in his soul there was little hope. The disease that had drained him of all his strength was now mounting its final assault. Rees went through the formality of taking his pulse and checking his temperature. The sick man's eyes fluttered, and his lips barely parted as he whispered, "There's nothing you can do, Doctor."

"I'd not be too quick to say that, Mr. Thomas."

But Amos Thomas had no time to waste on words. He shook his head, thanked Rees, and then said, "Children, come — "

Rees moved to the wall and put his back against it. There was nothing he could do, and he saw from the faces of the three who gathered around the bed that they harbored no false illusions. He had seen men die before, and now he remained silent, but he missed nothing of what took place.

Amos lifted his hand and it was seized at once by Hannah. Matthew and Thad went around to the other side of the bed. Thad took his father's hand and whispered, "What is it, Father?"

"You've all been good children. I thank God for you."

Matthew Thomas put his hand on his father's shoulder. "I love you, Pa," he said, his voice husky, and the tears ran down his face.

"Matthew, you've been a good son. Your mother loved you so much."

The dying man's eyes went to Thad.

"I've been a disappointment to you, Pa."

"You haven't found your way, Son, but God has told me that you will." He spoke a few more words to Thad and then turned his head painfully. He looked up at Hannah and saw the tears in her eyes. "Don't cry, girl. It's to glory I'm going."

"Pa—" Hannah could not speak then, but she bent over and kissed his hand and then laid it against her cheek.

Rees felt his own eyes grow misty. He did not know Amos Thomas well, but he knew he was a good man, and he wished fervently there was something he could do. But there was nothing. Amos Thomas was beyond human help and was now in the hand of God.

The silence was broken by the labored sound of the dying man's breath. From time to time he would say something to one of his children. He mentioned his wife often, and finally he said, "Would you be singing the song that I love so well."

Hannah stifled a sob but lifted her voice. She tried to sing but her voice broke, and the two sons of Amos did little better.

Suddenly a clear tenor voice came, and all three of Amos Thomas's children turned to look at Rees. He sang the words of the old song with such sweetness. His voice was soft and yet there was the hint of power there, and it was obvious that had he chosen, he could have filled the whole house with the strength of his voice.

Alas! and did my Savior bleed
And did my Sovereign die?
Would He devote that sacred Head
For sinners such as I?
Was it for sins that I have done
He suffered on the tree?
Amazing pity! grace unknown!
And love beyond degree!
Well might the sun in darkness hide
And shut His glories in,
When Christ, the great Redeemer died
For man the creature's sin.
But drops of grief can ne'er repay
The debt of love I owe;
Here, Lord, I give myself away
'Tis all that I can do.

For a moment as Rees's voice died away, he was afraid he had interrupted, but then Amos Thomas whispered, "Lovely, my son! You glorify the Lord Jesus."

Tears came to Rees's eyes and he dropped his head.

"He had tears in his eyes. Did you see it?" Hannah whispered.

"I saw it. Pa saw it, too," Thad said.

The end had come twenty minutes after Rees had sung the hymn. He had left the room immediately afterward and waited in the parlor, feeling that the time was sacred to the family. When they came out, Hannah had come to him and taken his hand. "Thank you," she had whispered. She had seen that his eyes still were damp.

He had whispered, "Anything I can do," and departed.

Now Hannah and Thad stood in the center of the parlor. "He has a heart, Thad."

"Yes, he has — but not a head. He doesn't know what's going on. He thinks the English will show mercy to us, but they won't."

"But he sang for our father and blessed him. I'll never forget that."

"I won't, either," Matthew said. "He has a voice like an angel's. That's what Pa said, isn't it?"

"Yes, he did," Thad said. "None of us will forget Rees Kenyon."

Rees was on his knees and he smiled as the blindfold was placed over his eyes. The oldest boy, whose name was Joshua, said, "Don't forget. You're Buff." Then he said, "How many horses has your father got?"

"Three," Rees answered, knowing the game well.

"What color are they?"

"Black, white, and gray."

Joshua shouted, "Turn about and turn about and catch whom you can!"

Rees came to his feet and turned around rapidly three times. He moved slowly, and he could hear the children giggling and scrambling around the room. Finally he felt a touch, whirled and reached out. He knew it was Abigail, for she was the slightest. "I've got you!" he cried. "Now you have to be Buff."

They continued to play blind man's bluff, using different counting games to decide who would be Buff.

> Eenie, meenie, miney, mo.
> Catch a tiger by the toe.
> If he hollers, let him go.
> Eenie, meenie, miney, mo.

Another game that Mary, the oldest girl, liked was:

> Apples and oranges, two for a penny,
> Takes a good scholar to count as many,
> O–U–T, out goes she.

Joshua's was a little more complicated:

> Ena, mena, mona, mi
> Panalona bona stry,
> Ewe,
> Fouls neck
> Hallibone, crackabone, ten and eleven,
> O–U–T spells out and out goes Y–O–U.

This was the sort of thing that endeared the young Welsh physician to the Warren children. He wrestled with them, allowing them to crawl all over him as they wallowed on the floor, and laughed with them as they pulled at his hair and his clothes.

Dr. Warren's voice cut into the fun, and immediately the children turned Rees loose, and he got to his feet.

"Children, I'm going to have to send you to your uncle's house."

"You mean in New Hampshire? We're going to New Hampshire?" Joshua cried. "Are you going with us, Father?"

"No. You'll be going with Sam Gibbons. He'll take care of you."

"You come with us," Abigail said, going to take her father's hand.

"I'll be there in a few days, but you know you always have a good time at your uncle's house."

Rees stood back, seeing the strain on Warren's face. He knew something was wrong but did not speak. Warren looked at him and said, "Wait until we get the children ready and then we'll talk."

"Yes sir. Can I help?"

"Just stand ready, Rees."

The children had left in a carriage, waving and crying out their good-byes to their father. Now, standing in front of his house, Warren turned and his expression was grave. "There's going to be trouble and I don't want the children caught up in it."

"Maybe it will come to nothing, sir."

Dr. Warren looked older than his years. "There's no avoiding it this time." He hesitated, then said, "There's going to be a battle, Rees. The British are moving troops now, and our militia has gathered over at Bunker Hill."

Rees was stunned. "I had hoped all this would pass away."

"There's no hope now for that, and I may as well tell you. I'm not going as a physician."

"Sir?"

"No, I'll be going as a common soldier."

"But I heard you had a commission given by the Continental Congress, Dr. Warren."

"It isn't valid yet, so I'll just be one of the men in the line with a musket."

Rees suddenly knew what he must do. "I'll go with you, sir. Not as a soldier but as a physician."

A warm smile came to Warren's face. "We'll need you, Rees. You realize of course that it may put you in a bad light with the British."

"Only going to be a doctor I am. I insist on it, sir."

Warren suddenly put out his hand and his smile was warm and winsome. "I'm glad you'll be there. There are going to be men shot. Some will be killed but others will need a doctor."

"Well, I helped the English wounded after Lexington. I can do no less for the militia, Dr. Warren."

"We'll carry all the medical supplies we can, and we must hurry. They won't wait for us to get there."

# Chapter Fifteen

THE FOUR GENERALS SEEMED TO FILL THE SMALL ROOM AS GENERAL Gage stared at the map laid out on the table. Generals Clinton, Howe, and Burgoyne waited impatiently, for each believed he was more capable of conducting the battle against the colonists than Gage himself. "You see the terrain here, gentlemen," Gage said rather nervously and put his finger on the map.

"It looks like two tadpoles, doesn't it?" Burgoyne said.

Indeed, Boston Harbor did contain two peninsulas that resembled tadpoles. Boston itself, with its population of some sixteen thousand, was confined to a peninsula connected to the mainland by a narrow strip called Boston Neck. North of it lay another peninsula, also with a narrow strip of land connecting it to the mainland. This tadpole contained the village of Charlestown and was dominated by two hills. One was called Bunker Hill, which lay close to Charlestown Neck, and the other, closer to the shoreline, was Breed's Hill. "Gentlemen," Gage said, speaking very rapidly, "the Americans have decided to defend this ground here just north of Charlestown. They have thrown up some defensive fortifications, a redoubt on Breed's Hill — right there."

"Why, I know that spot well," Clinton said, stepping forward. "We have them, then! All we have to do is put troops ashore at Charlestown Neck and we'll have them bottled up. It will be a simple operation."

But Gage had already made another plan. "We must remember, gentlemen, the enemy has troops stationed at the neck. How many we do not know. To put five hundred men between two enemy forces, each of which may outnumber them, seems a very dangerous tactic to me."

"I agree, sir," General Howe spoke up. "We can move in with our war vessels, disembark the men, and take the rebels' position easily. Morton's Point here" — he touched the map with the tip of his finger — "is an ideal place to land troops. I looked over this ground only the day before yesterday. It's a half mile from the water's edge to this American position on Breed's Hill. They will have no way to oppose our landing. I suggest we send a flying column of light infantry here to the north. They can move around behind the enemy on Breed's

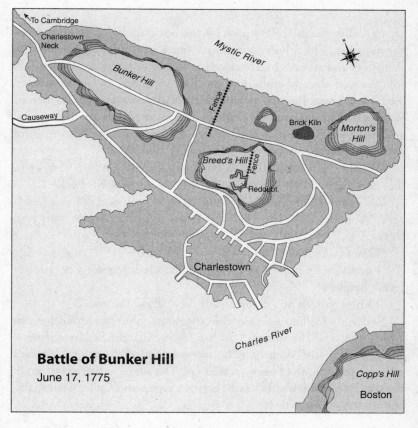

**Battle of Bunker Hill**
June 17, 1775

Hill. Nothing shakes up raw troops so much as an attack from the rear."

"But what if the Americans choose to make a stand inside that redoubt on Breed's Hill?" Gage asked.

"I doubt that very seriously," Howe said. "They finished that work in only one night, and even regular troops are not capable of building defenses with a single night's work. The hill is open. It's easy enough to ascend. We can carry it, sir."

Gage's face showed relief. "Very well, then. That is the plan. You, General Howe, will be in charge of the attack."

Three of the generals looked satisfied but Clinton had a sour look on his face. He did not protest, for that would seem cowardly, but doubt was plain in his features.

As Callie watched Rees pack his medical supplies, she felt a queer nervousness. The whole town knew there was going to be a battle. Whispers and rumors had changed to shouts of warning. The British soldiers had already embarked on their warships and were headed for Charlestown Peninsula. She knew also that many of the men of Boston had grabbed their muskets and gone to join the defenders, and there was word that others were coming from New Hampshire and the closer colonies.

"Would you get those extra bandages for me, Callie? They're in that chest over there." Rees waved toward the supply chest.

Callie moved at once and brought out an armload of fresh bandages. "You won't never be able to carry all this. Let me go with you, Rees."

"Don't be foolish! Women don't go to battle."

"I could 'elp you with some of the wounded. I'm not a doctor but I ain't helpless!"

"I know you're not, Callie, but I'd be afraid for you."

Suddenly Callie understood her feelings. She was afraid for this lanky man, and the intensity of her feeling caught her by surprise. She watched him silently as he moved around the room, his face reflecting the depth of his own feelings. The sunlight filtered through the window, throwing its beams on the carpet, and Callie tried to put her emotions into words.

"I . . . I don't like to be left 'ere all alone."

"Why, you don't have to be afraid, Callie. This battle will be over and I'll be coming back."

"How do you know that? Men get killed in battle, don't they?"

"I won't be fighting," Rees said with a shrug as he continued to stuff bottles of laudanum into the large bag, which was already bulging. "I'll be taking care of the wounded."

Callie spoke up suddenly. "Please be careful."

Surprised, Rees turned to face her. "I'll be in no danger."

Callie took in the lines of Rees's face. She had grown accustomed to him, and now she realized that she was more dependent on him than she had ever thought. "I'm sorry I've acted like I 'ave since that day at church."

"Why, don't think about that. It was nothing."

"I know you was ashamed of me."

"No, no, don't say that."

"You was, and I was ashamed of myself. I don't know 'ow to act. I'm just a stupid girl!"

Rees was taken aback. Callie had kept her distance from him ever since the episode at church, but now he noticed that her back was straight and her fists were clenched. He went to her and put his hand under her chin, for she was staring down. When she lifted her eyes, he saw embarrassment and shame. "Well, there is soft you are," he said quietly. He was taken by the smoothness of her cheeks. She had begun bathing more, and her hair was soft and glowed in the sunlight, as yellow as any he had ever seen. For that brief moment she reminded him of Grace but he shoved that memory aside. She was looking at him in a strange way and he was somehow embarrassed, not knowing exactly how to talk to this girl or young woman, whichever she was. He put his hand on her shoulder, feeling the firmness of the muscle and flesh, and said, "Don't be worrying about me, Callie."

"I ain't got nobody else."

"Well, I don't either, I suppose."

"You bought me and I'm your girl."

At once Rees shook his head. "That's ridiculous. I've told you to forget about that."

"No, I ain't gonna forget it. Not ever." Callie suddenly put her hand over his where it lay on her shoulder.

The action surprised Rees, for she had never voluntarily touched him. "You're really worried, aren't you?" he said quietly.

"Yes. I don't want nothin' to happen to you."

"Well, there's little likelihood of that."

Callie was aware of the strength of his large hand, and she wished he would reach out and touch her with his other hand, and suddenly to her amazement a thought came to her. *I wish he would kiss me.* The thought was shocking, because for so long she had fought off the attentions of men. But now she felt vulnerable and helpless. It was a new experience for Callie Summers, for all her life she had been building up an inner strength. Yet that seemed to have fled now, and as she stared into Rees's dark blue eyes, she wanted him to touch her with some gesture of affection.

"I wish you wouldn't worry, Callie. I'll be fine. You cook me up a nice supper and I'll be home to eat it tonight." He squeezed her shoulder and turned back to his packing. Callie said no more but an emptiness came to her. She helped him complete his task, and then he put the bag on his shoulder and picked his hat off a peg and stuck it on his head. "Well, I'll be off now."

"Take care."

"I will." Rees waved his hand and then turned and walked away. Callie moved to the door and watched him as he mounted the horse waiting for him. He turned the animal, gave her another wave, and the horse moved away at a fast trot.

Callie watched him until he disappeared, and the strange emptiness and fear that had been growing in her suddenly became worse. She went into the kitchen. She stood staring out the window, not really seeing anything, and then she shook her head and muttered, "He'll be all right — 'e's *got* to be all right!"

All seemed confusion to Rees. He somehow had expected the army of the rebels to be in uniform, but he saw no evidence of this. The men all looked like farmers and tradesmen, except for one man he saw talking with Dr. Warren. Rees dismounted and waited until

Warren glanced in his direction and called out, "Kenyon, come over here!"

When Rees approached, Warren said, "This is General Israel Putnam. General, this is my colleague Dr. Rees Kenyon. He'll not be fighting but he's come to help tend the wounded."

"We'll be needing him, then. Glad to know you, young man."

Israel Putnam had the body of a bear and the voice of a bull. He had a great, round, owlish head and at fifty-seven was still a commanding figure. He had led an adventurous life, having been taken prisoner by the French at Montreal and shipwrecked while leading an expedition against Havana.

"I brought what supplies I could, General."

"They'll be the only supplies here," Putnam grunted. He swept his hand around at the redoubt, which was merely raw dirt piled into makeshift walls. Men were moving back and forth around it, talking and laughing as if they were out on a holiday.

"They won't be laughing soon," Putnam said.

"Is this all the men, sir?" Rees asked.

"No, reinforcements are back there on Bunker Hill. They need to be here, blast it, for it's obvious the British are going to attack. We need every man and every musket we can get, but I couldn't talk General Ward into the notion. I'm hoping he'll move forward to this place when the attack starts."

The three men stood there, Rees merely listening as Dr. Warren and General Putnam discussed the battle to come. They were soon joined by another man, whom the general greeted as Colonel Prescott. "Well, Prescott, how many men did you bring?"

"Nearly twelve hundred, General."

"We can use them. See that they're put into place."

Prescott looked suddenly at Warren and said, "You're a senior to me, sir. I beg you to take charge of my men."

Warren shook his head. "No, Colonel, I'm not here as an officer today. My commission hasn't been approved. I will fight in the line as a soldier."

Prescott suddenly laughed. "Modesty in an officer! I thought I'd never live to see it, but I commend you, Dr. Warren. Now I think we'd better get ready for what's going to happen. It will be warm work, gentlemen."

"You'd better go back to Bunker Hill with the reinforcements, Rees," Dr. Warren said.

"Why, no sir, this is where the battle will take place, and it's where men will be wounded. I'll be needed here."

"Good man," Warren said, smiling. He slapped Rees on the shoulder. "We'll teach the English a thing or two this day. They've been laughing and making fun of our fighting ability. We'll see how they feel about it at sundown."

One of the king's ships, the *Lively,* began firing on the Americans. Rees, with the rest of Prescott's men, quickly took shelter within the six-foot walls of the redoubt. The roar of the cannon seemed very loud even though the ships were half a mile away, and cannonballs began to fall, some of them inside the fortification. The younger soldiers were amused, for when the cannonballs hit, they rolled, and it became a game to recover them. Rees was watching this, wondering how men who might be facing death within an hour could be so light-hearted. He heard his name called and turned to find Matthew and Thad Thomas coming toward him.

"Well, Doctor," Thad said, putting out his hand, "you've got your-self on the right side."

"It's good to see you, Doctor," Matthew said, his face beaming. "Do you have a musket?"

"No, I'm here to do what I can for the wounded."

"There won't be many," Thad said. "We can stay behind this wall and pick them off like squirrels."

Rees saw that both young men were cheerful, and he could not understand it. Very soon the finest troops of England were going to be marching, and they had rarely been beaten in battle. Here were a group of farmers and shopkeepers, most of whom had never heard a shot fired in anger, and as far as he could see, there was no fear whatsoever.

"I hope I'll be able to help," he said.

Matthew suddenly said, "Hey, Asa, you'd better get down! You'd be disgraced if you got blown up by an English cannon."

The young man laughed. "They couldn't hit anything. After this is over, Matthew, let's you and me go celebrate."

"Right you are," Matthew turned and said. "That's Asa Pollard. He's one of my best friends."

"I wish he'd get down. Those cannonballs are bad," Rees said.

Just how bad they were was evident five minutes later. Asa Pollard was walking back and forth atop the pile of dirt, laughing and shouting derisively at the English. Rees was watching him and suddenly, following the boom of a cannon, young Pollard's head was torn off by a solid shot. In horror Rees and Matthew stared as blood pumped from the gaping hole.

Almost before the body fell, pouring out its crimson flood on the earth, Colonel Prescott was there. "Quick, Sergeant, bury this man! All the rest of you men get to work. There's a whole breastwork waiting to be finished down there on the other side of the hill."

Matthew moved over and stared at the body. His face was now white, as if his own blood had been drained away. "But sir, not without prayers?"

"Pray all you want to! Just bury him and then get back to your post."

"He was your friend. Do what you can for him," Rees said. He watched as Matthew and Thad, joined by others, carried the body away, trailing blood on the ground. He noticed that nobody was laughing now. The balls from the ship continued to fall, and then someone cried out, "Here they come. The lobsterbacks, they're coming up the hill!"

Rees lifted his head above the pile of raw, red dirt, and there below he saw the line of English troops. They were coming in perfect order, as if on parade. Flags were flying and he could hear clearly the fifes and the rattle of the drums.

The soldiers were brilliant in the sunlight, which danced on the tips of their bayonets. The landing had been completely unopposed and the line was marching forward. General Putnam rode back and forth on a bay stallion, crying out, "Don't fire until you see the whites of their eyes — then fire low!"

Rees dreaded what was to happen. He saw the English march up the slope of Breed's Hill, and all was silent behind the breastworks and the rail fence. He was aware of the searing sun and saw that the tall bearskins of the grenadiers had brims to keep the sun out of their eyes. The British stumbled sometimes in the thick grass, and as they came closer, Rees saw individual faces, some young, no more it seemed than sixteen or seventeen, others lined with long years of service. All the faces were red with the heat and perspiration was flowing down them. The soldiers began to gasp from the heavy packs they wore.

Suddenly everything was noise and fire. The line of men behind the redoubt became a line of flashes as the muskets exploded with a concentrated roar. Rees stared aghast as the faces of the British troops in the front lines were turned into masses of pulp and the soldiers were knocked over backward by the musket balls. Others grabbed their stomachs and began to writhe on the ground like severed worms.

Over a hundred men lay sprawled on the bloodstained earth, yet still Howe pressed his charge forward. Flame and smoke belched forth, and men began to fall behind the redoubt as the English returned their fire. But every man in Howe's personal staff was either killed or wounded, and no one was ever able to explain how General Howe himself, who watched at the head of his troops, survived.

Finally Howe called for retreat, and as the British soldiers fled down the hill, the Americans were exultant.

"We've beat them! We've beat them!" Matthew cried. "See what they think of us now."

Colonel Prescott walked about, his face beaming, congratulating the men. But he said to Dr. Warren, "They'll come back."

"We'll fight them off again."

"We're down to a hundred and fifty men."

"We've lost that many?"

"Most have run away — and we're low on ammunition."

"Won't the general send more from Bunker Hill?"

"He's not a man to take initiative." Colonel Prescott chewed his lip. "I doubt if we'll get any help from him."

While the two men talked, Rees was working furiously. Some men lay dead. Others had taken balls that would mean amputation. He moved from man to man with no one to help him for a time, and then Matthew and Thad came to assist him as best they could.

Thad's face was stretched tight. "They're going to come back. I don't see how but they will."

Rees said, "Hold your finger right here, Matthew." He watched as Matthew put his finger on the artery that was spewing blood. "Hold it there until I can get the artery tied off."

At that moment Prescott's voice rang out. "They're coming again! Every man back to his post!"

"I've got to go, Doctor," Matthew said.

"Just one moment and then you can go." Rees stitched quickly. "Be careful, Matthew. Your sister would be hard hit." He smiled then and said, "There is proud I am to have you for a friend. You're a brave boy."

"Not so brave," Matthew said, his face pale. "I was so scared, I didn't think I could stand up."

"But you did stand up. You'd better go to your post."

It was on the third assault that the tragedy came. Matthew turned and said, "Thad, I'm out of powder."

"So am I," Thad said grimly. He looked over and said, "Colonel Prescott, we're out of powder."

"Then use your musket as a club."

"We can't fight off those bayonets!" Thad exclaimed.

Prescott did not answer. He was furious, for although there were plenty of men and a good supply of ammunition back on Bunker Hill, nothing he could do would persuade General Artemus Ward to release either. Ward was a fearful, timid man and should not have been in command. Prescott had raged but now he knew there was no hope. "All right, get ready to get out of here! We can't hold this place."

Rees was bandaging men as fast as he could. He had long since run out of bandages and had begun stripping the dead of their clothes to make do.

He heard the shouts of the British as they approached and was aware that many of the Americans were in full retreat. When he turned, he saw a sight that froze his blood. The British were piling over the redoubt, their bayonets flashing. He saw Americans with no ammunition swinging their muskets, but they were no match for the expert thrust of the British. The redcoats were howling like madmen and Rees knew he had to get away.

He rose to his feet and then he saw Dr. Warren and stood stock still.

Warren was being attacked by a tall soldier and others were coming up behind him. The doctor was surrounded, and without thought Rees stooped and picked up a musket. He knew it was not loaded but he grasped it by the barrel. He saw a soldier come over the edge of the redoubt, level his rifle, and pull the trigger. Dr. Warren was driven backward, and with a cry of rage Rees advanced. He was not quick enough to prevent one of the soldiers from plunging a bayonet into Dr. Warren's stomach. Rees swung the musket and the butt of it caught the soldier in the head, making a solid sound. Weeping and raging and filled with battle madness, Rees Kenyon fought until finally something struck him on the head. The world had been all explosions and fire, but now all faded into a silence more profound than any he had ever known.

# Chapter Sixteen

CALLIE STOOD WITH HER BACK AGAINST THE HOUSE, STARING OFF into the distance. The hills to her right were covered by a sullen haze and seemed to be brooding some brutal thoughts. A light rain had fallen earlier in the day, glazing the earth and bringing a freshness to the air. And now as she watched, a jay lit and proclaimed his brilliant blue that seemed to mock the sky. Overhead the sun was a white hole in the sky that poured forth heat even at this late hour.

Suddenly a movement caught her eye, and Callie turned quickly as a man came around the corner. She thought at first it was Rees, but almost instantly she saw that she was mistaken. A bitterness came to her then, and she suddenly flung out her hands expressively and half ran, leaving the house and moving down the street. She had no clear idea where she was going, but the cannons that had been audible earlier were silent now and had been for hours.

She reached the downtown section, and children and adults and dogs were eddying along the streets. The air was filled with the babble of voices, and a tall, heavyset man paused to look down toward the area of the docks.

"Wot's happenin', mister?" Callie asked quickly.

"The battle's over. The rebels got what they deserved." His voice was triumphant and he nodded, his eyes flashing with delight. "They're bringing the wounded soldiers back, but they beat the bloody rebels, they did."

Callie's heart sank and she turned away half sickened. What could have happened? She had never taken an interest in politics but now it had become real. She had a vivid imagination, and suddenly a picture of Rees lying still on the green grass, covered with blood, came to her. Blinking her eyes, she shook her head, whispering, "No, 'e can't be dead."

The crowd seemed to be headed toward the docks and she joined them. Many soldiers had also joined the throng, and when she reached the docks, she saw that a ship had pulled up and small boats were coming ashore. She shoved her way through the people and waited and found that several of the boats had landed and men were being picked up. Some of them were sitting, holding themselves carefully as if they might break, their faces pale and streaked with blood. Others lay still, and when the sailors unloaded them, it was as if they were unloading cordwood. All were English soldiers, however, and Callie had little hope.

Still, she stood there lonely and confused, watching as the wounded men were placed into carts and wagons. Their groans filled the air and from time to time a pitiful scream came to her. Fear now quickened her breath and drew her lips taut. Suddenly her name sounded, and she turned to see Hannah Thomas pressing her way through the crowd. Callie moved to meet her, and as soon as they were close enough, she asked, "Are your men safe, Miss Hannah?"

"Thad's all right," Hannah said, her face tight with strain. "But Matthew didn't come back."

"Wot did Thad say?"

Hannah seemed unable to speak for a moment. She swallowed and said, "He got away but he said one of the men told him that both Matthew and Dr. Kenyon were trapped by the last charge. They say Dr. Warren was killed."

"Oh no!" Callie said, gasping.

"Maybe it's not so. Thad didn't see it with his own eyes."

Hannah studied the face of the younger woman and said, "You don't need to go home alone. We'll try to find out if they were taken prisoners."

"How will we do that?"

"We'll have to go to the commanding officer's house. Come along."

Grateful to be with someone she knew, Callie hurried along beside Hannah. Hope was within her, but the fear she had been struggling with was there, too. The possibility that Rees was dead laid a frost on her nerves, and she saw the strain on Hannah's face and knew that she was enduring the same torment.

Rees came out of an immense darkness into the light. It was faint at first, an opalescent brightness like that of a cat's eye. He was aware that his head was one solid mass of pain and also that he was lying flat on his back on a hard surface. Sound came to him then, a hollow sound with the buzz and hum of voices, none of which he could make out.

Carefully he opened his eyes fully and saw forms moving in the sooty darkness. He tried to sit up, and the pain came then, like a dagger driven through his temples. He groaned, reached up, and found that his hair was stiff with blood and his scalp was torn. Automatically he said, "The bleeding isn't stopped yet," and then he was aware of someone beside him. Gritting his teeth, he tried to sit up, and then he felt an arm beneath him. "Take it easy, Doctor."

"What is this place?"

"We're in a jail. A warehouse, really."

Rees cautiously sat up. His movement seemed to have started the blood flowing, and he felt it running down his face. The man beside him moved slightly and the faint light from a window high overhead fell on him. "Matthew," he said. "You're here?"

"Yes, they got me too," Matthew said gloomily. "Thad got away, though."

"That's good."

"How do you feel? Your head looks awful. I thought you were dead when they loaded you in the boat."

"I'm all right, except I need to get my head sewed up."

Matthew shook his head and his tone was bitter. "You're not likely to get it here. Half of these men are wounded. And look. That one over there died about half an hour ago. Bled to death, I think."

"There's no doctor to take care of these wounded men?"

"I reckon not."

Rees's vision was returning quickly now and he was growing accustomed to the darkness. Most of the men were lying down.

Many were sitting braced against the wall. The place was one continuous groan and somewhere a man was crying like a child.

"I've got to get this bleeding stopped," Rees said. He rose to his feet and swayed and for a moment thought he would pass out. Finally the nausea and the dizziness passed. He moved across the room carefully to avoid stepping on the wounded. When he reached the door, he could see light coming in from the outside. He banged on the door and said, "Guard. guard!"

"What do you want, rebel?".

"I'm a doctor. I need to see to these men."

The voice was rough. "Go to blazes! Let 'em die!"

"You can't let these men die!"

"You wanna bet?"

The door suddenly opened and Rees was blinded. He squinted and said, "Just let me get some medical supplies and I'll take care of the wounded here."

"There wasn't nothin' said about that."

"What's this, Corporal?"

An officer had come, a tall man in a red uniform.

"This rebel says he's a doctor. He wants to take care of the wounded."

"Is that right? You're a doctor?"

"Yes. My name is Kenyon."

"What were you doing fighting with the rebels, then?"

"I went there to treat the wounded."

The officer had a thin, pale face and he stared at Rees Kenyon with distaste. "We don't have any medical supplies."

"Surely you have something — just something to sew up some wounds, and some laudanum."

"Get him a needle and thread, Corporal," the officer said, laughing harshly. "He can sew 'em up with that."

A laugh went up from three other soldiers who were serving as guards. One of them said, "I got it in me pack over here." He moved to a pack lying against the wall and ruffled through it. He came up with a grin and said, "There you are. Needle and thread, Doctor. Sew yourself up."

Rees took them and said, "If I could get word to someone, I could have medical supplies sent here."

"We got our own men. You know how many of our soldiers were killed in that battle? Over two hundred, some of them gut shot. Don't tell me about your wounded!"

Rees felt a hand on his chest and was propelled backward. He fell over wounded men, who cried out in agony, and then the door slammed shut.

Getting to his feet, he was aware that Matthew had come to stand beside him. "Not very friendly, are they?"

"No, but I've got to sew up this wound."

"You mean, do it yourself?"

"Unless you want to do it."

"I don't think I could."

"I think you'll have to, Matthew. I can't get at it. Come over here." Moving to the light, Rees took some of the coarse thread. It was not catgut but it would have to do. His hands were steady as he threaded the needle and then knotted it. "Here," he said. He turned to hold his head to the light. "Just sew it up as if it were a boot."

Matthew took the needle and stared at him. "I've never done anything like this."

"Just start where the wound starts, shove the needle through the flap of skin, push it through the other flap, and then draw it together. You can do it."

Rees felt the boy's irresolution and said quickly, "It'll hurt a bit but it'll be worse if it's not pulled together. Come on, boy, do it. You wanted to be a doctor. Here's your chance."

Rees braced his hands against the wall and took a deep breath. He felt Matthew's unsteady hands on his head and said roughly, "Do it as if I didn't have any feeling. Shove that needle in!" And then the pain came. He had not known what a sensitive part of the body the scalp was. He felt the needle go through again and again, and when Matthew pulled the skin together, it was agony, but Rees, his eyes shut, braced himself against the waves of pain. He thought of those on whom he had operated with only mild anesthetics and forced himself to remain rigid.

Finally it was over, and Matthew said in a voice not quite steady, "There it is, Doctor."

Rees straightened, reached up and touched the wound. He ran his fingers along the stitches and then turned to Matthew. "That was a good job. Maybe you'll make a doctor one of these days." Weakness came to him then and he murmured, "I'd better sit down, I think." He felt Matthew's hands guiding him to the wall and he slumped down. He leaned back against the rough wood and wondered what would come next.

"I think the casualty list is complete now, General Gage."

William Howe was standing in front of a window and the light blotted out his face. His voice was steady as he continued. "There were one thousand and fifty-four men shot and two hundred and twenty-six of those are dead. Others probably will die. Certainly those with belly wounds. I can't believe it, General. How did those shopkeepers stand up to our best troops?"

"They are better men than we thought," Gage said bitterly. "What about their casualties?"

"They lost about a hundred and forty men. We don't know how many were wounded."

"Well, at least we took the hill."

"A dear victory," General Howe murmured. "Another such will ruin us."

"Perhaps this will discourage them."

"I don't think so. I believe it's just the beginning."

The two men stood speaking more of the battle, and although Howe could not know it at this time, the Battle of Bunker Hill would mark him more strongly than anything else in his military life. In the future he would be less likely to go charging in against an enemy whose strength was unknown.

There came a slight knock on the door, and a lieutenant said, "General Gage, a young woman is here to see you."

"A young woman. I can't see her," Gage said abruptly.

"She says you know her, sir."

"What's her name?"

"Miss Callie Summers."

Gage shook his head and tried to think. "Well, let her in. There'll be others, I'm sure. Probably come to see about one of her sweethearts."

The lieutenant stepped inside and allowed the young woman to come in. Gage did not recognize her. "What is it, miss? We have little time."

"My name is Callie Summers, General. I was at your 'ome once."

"My home?"

"Yes sir. I was with Dr. Warren."

Memory came then and Gage felt a touch of anger. "Yes. If you've come about Dr. Warren, I'm sorry to tell you that he's dead. He should have stuck to his doctoring." His voice was harsh despite his best attempts.

"I know, sir, but it's about Dr. Kenyon that I've come. Dr. Rees Kenyon. 'E was with us at the dinner that night."

"I don't know anything about him and I don't have time, young woman."

"I know something about him." General Howe turned to face the young woman. "He's a prisoner."

"Yes sir, I know, but 'e's a doctor, not a soldier."

"You're mistaken! I was with the men. I saw him when he was taken. He was fighting alongside Warren. There was no doctoring to it."

Callie saw the coldness of General Howe's eyes and knew there was no mercy. "Please, sir, can I see 'im?"

"We don't have time for you now, woman," Howe said. "Now get out of here!"

The two men saw the young woman flinch. She started to speak again but Gage went over, turned her around, and guided her out the door. "Come back later. Perhaps something can be done." He closed the door and said, "What's this about a doctor?"

"He's the young doctor from London Warren took in to be his assistant. I told her the truth. I was with the men on the last charge. When we came over the hill, Kenyon was fighting like a madman. He should be grateful he wasn't bayoneted like his friend Warren."

"I'm sorry to hear that. I'm sorry about Warren too. He was a good man. Just embraced the wrong cause."

"We'll have to be careful. We're going to be besieged by people wanting us to release their relatives. This man Kenyon. Forget he's a doctor. He's an enemy soldier. I want him kept a prisoner."

"Of course, General. Of course."

Hannah endured the rough remarks of the soldier who led her to the jail. She knew that a miracle had taken place, as she had finally arranged to get a pass to see Matthew. Every English officer she had seen was rough with her, but she had been so persistent that one of them finally cursed and said, "Well, go see your blasted brother, then! You won't see him for long."

"What do you mean?"

"They ain't prisoners of war. They're traitors. We English shoot traitors."

Hannah had not answered him but had dropped her head and bitten off the reply that had risen. Now she approached the building that had once been a warehouse but had been converted into a prison for the captured patriots. She waited until the private who had brought her here said to the guard, "This woman's got a pass to see one of the prisoners."

"You want me to let her in or bring him out?"

"Let her in and if anybody tries to get out, shoot 'em in the head."

The guard, a short, round man with a red face and a pair of cold eyes, said, "Nothin' I'd like better." He opened the door. "Let me see that pass." Taking the slip of paper, he said, "Matthew Thomas. All right. You got fifteen minutes."

He opened the door and Hannah saw that the prisoners were all confined to one very large, dimly lit room. She noticed there were no beds. Men were lying on fetid straw; some were walking around. She stepped inside and the guard bawled, "Matthew Thomas!"

"Here!"

Hannah turned to see Matthew coming toward her. It had been only a week but he had been marked. His cheeks were sunken and he had lost weight. "Sister," he said, his voice glad and his eyes alight.

"Matthew!" She took hold of him and smelled his rankness. Obviously, there were no bathing facilities, but she hugged him and then kissed him on the cheek. "Are you all right?"

"Yes. I wasn't wounded or anything."

"What about Dr. Kenyon?"

"There he is, over by the window. He got his head split but I sewed it together with some thread a soldier gave us." Matthew managed a grin. "Maybe I'll be a doctor yet."

"Call him over here."

"Rees!"

Rees moved toward them and bowed. "Miss Thomas." His face was drawn, and she saw the rough surgery Matthew had performed on the side of his head. "How did you manage to get in to see us?" he asked. "There haven't been any other visitors."

"We had to do some bribing. Callie went to see the generals, but they wouldn't give her any hope or permission to visit. She's very worried about you, Dr. Kenyon."

"And I'm worried about her. She doesn't have anybody."

"This is terrible. Isn't there anything being done for these wounded men?"

"They feed us when they think of it, and bring us water. No medicines. No medical attention at all."

"Except what Rees has done," Matthew said. "He's been a big help."

"What can I do for them without medicine or bandages? The guards won't listen to me. Yesterday two men died who would probably have lived with just a little care."

"I'll try to get General Gage to allow us to bring in medical supplies."

"It would make a big difference."

Hannah spoke quickly, for her time was short. Finally she said, "Can I give Callie a message for you?"

"If you would show her some kindness, I'd take it as a great favor, Miss Hannah."

"Of course. I'll see to her, Dr. Kenyon."

The visit was soon cut short. Hannah hugged Matthew again and then shook hands with Rees. "I'll try to see that some medical supplies are permitted. I'll do everything I can."

"God bless you, Miss Thomas."

"Wot's going to 'appen to them, Hannah?" Callie asked. "Will they 'ave to stay in jail until the war's over?"

"That's what they say, Callie. But of course there's such a thing as an exchange."

"Wot's that?"

"We capture some of their men and we trade those men for some of ours."

"Well, can that 'appen?"

"I don't think we captured any of them in the battle but it could happen. But of course maybe there'll be no more fighting."

"That's not wot people say," Callie said dully. She had been hoping for better news and now she turned away from Hannah. "I worry about 'im so!"

Hannah had already made up her mind. "You can't stay here by yourself. I want you to come home with me."

"Come with you?"

"Yes. I'm all alone now. Thad's out with the other soldiers, keeping the British penned up here in Boston. Father's gone and Matthew's a prisoner. We need each other."

Callie turned and tears were in her eyes. "I couldn't do that," she said. "I ... I'd just be in the way."

"Nonsense! Let's pack your clothes. I brought the carriage."

Callie smiled tremulously. "It would be good for me, I think."

"And good for me too. Come now. Let's get packed."

# Part
-3-

# *Chapter Seventeen*

FOR CALLIE WRITING WAS A MYSTERIOUS ART, AND AS SHE DIPPED the goose quill into the ink and watched it soak up, she felt again the shock of surprise that she could perform such a wonderful ritual. The light streamed down over the paper in front of her, and as she put the tip of the quill to it, she felt something akin to joy as the letters seemed to make themselves, stretching out from one edge of the paper to another. The straight lines, the curls, the sweeping script had become a pleasure to her ever since Rees introduced her to writing. A sensuous pleasure lurked somehow in the very act of transferring the ink from the bottle to the paper, and even the scratchy sound which broke the silence of her room gave her a profound sense of satisfaction.

A movement caught her eye, and she turned her head to catch sight of the lithe form of Midnight, the ebony cat, whose only color was in his golden eyes. He leaped up on the table with that contemptuous ease that felines have, and Callie wondered, as she always did, how Midnight knew exactly how high to leap. Never too high, never too low. Always exactly right. Shifting the quill to her left hand, she ran the palm of her right hand down the silken back, which arched under her touch. "Wow!" Midnight said in a surprisingly deep growl for so slight an animal.

"'Wow' yourself." Callie smiled and continued to stroke the cat for a moment, then put her hand under the belly and, lifting quickly, put the cat on the floor. "I'm writing, Midnight. Go catch a rat and make yourself useful." She turned again and as she continued to write, the tip of her tongue extended from her lips, as it usually did when she concentrated on her work.

She'd recently written her first letter, to Rees's mother. Callie had obtained the family's name and address from the front of one of his books. She'd been frightened by her own boldness in contacting his family, but the time had passed and she had received a reply from Gwen Morgan, thanking her for her letter and for her attempts to help Rees.

Callie finished her second letter with a flourish, adding extra curls to the letters of her name. Carefully she wiped the quill free of ink and put it down, capped the bottle, and then, taking a bottle of fine white sand, sprinkled it over the surface. Lifting the sheet, she moved it rapidly from side to side, then poured the sand into a box she kept for just such a purpose. Holding the letter up to the light, she read it aloud somewhat proudly.

*My dear Mrs. Morgan:*

*I take my pin in hand too inform you that yur son Rees iz as well as cud be expected under such conditions. It iz hard to gett in to see a prisoner far the British are madd at everyone in the collony. I tried three times to tak him food, but each time I was run off. Finally I found that if I shared the food with the gards, I cud get in to sea the officer whose name is Lutenant Raymond Boggs. I am shamed to say so, but he has formed a attachment for me. I cant say the same for myself for he iz a fat, ugly young man who takes libertees. I take him pies or pastries an sumetimes rum, and he lets me in to see Rees. It aint what I like, but it iz the only way I can get inn to see him. I have to pretend to like Lutenant Boggs, which I do nott.*

Callie paused then and scratched out one of the words which did not seem to be spelled correctly. Her spelling, she knew, was bad, but she was learning rapidly, for Hannah, who had become her tutor in Rees's absence, was a good teacher. Reading through the rest of the letter, she folded it and sealed it as well as she could. She got up from the small table she used for a desk and went downstairs, where she began putting together a pie.

Cooking was another mystery to Callie. She could never understand how Hannah could cook five different things so they all came out hot and done just right at the same time. Whenever Callie tried it, some things turned out raw while others were burned to a crisp. However, she had persevered and had at least become an expert in pies and cakes and sweets of all sorts. As she worked, she took extra care with this pie, for it was another bribe for Lieutenant Boggs. She was well aware of what he wanted, but as long as she did not see him outside the prison, she felt safe enough.

The sun came in through a window to her right, lighting up the kitchen, and she walked over and glanced out. She felt a sense of security that had gradually become a part of her existence. The lighthouse was home, and even now as she watched the two young goats frolicking, butting each other and leaping high into the air, she wondered what she would have done had not Hannah Thomas brought her here after Rees was imprisoned. She had been tense at first, not really knowing the woman, but only a few days had passed before she had come to realize that there was a goodness in Hannah she had never encountered before.

She finished the pie and put it into the large black pan and set it in the ashes at the fireplace, going over in her mind the work that needed to be done. She had begun helping with all the livestock, feeding the chickens and learning how to milk the nanny goat. She had become proficient in taking care of the light and hauling the oil up to the tower. She had learned to keep the glass lenses polished so the light shone clear, and she had also begun to learn the rudiments of keeping house, which to her surprise she found was the most pleasant work she had ever done. Cooking, of course, and even cleaning was not a chore that disturbed her. As she turned from the fireplace, the thought came to her. *I can hardly remember what it was like living on the streets.* This was not strictly true of course, for she had bad memories that would force themselves upon her, but they were not so frequent now.

A faint whistling came to her, and she went back to the window to see Thad returning from the tower. She went at once to open the door, and when he came in, he grinned at her. "Good morning, Callie. You're looking mighty fetching, I must say."

Callie never knew exactly how to take Thad's teasing. She knew he was a man familiar with women, for even Hannah had revealed this to her. She had not needed Hannah's words, however, for she was wise enough in the ways of men to know that his practiced ease with her came from habit long formed. He was a fine-looking man and far above her station in life, but he was kind and she had seen how much he cared for his sister and his brother. They were a tight-knit family.

"I'll cook breakfast for you," she said.

"Good. Then sit down and eat it with me." He suddenly placed his hand on her head, then let it run down her back. "You have beautiful hair. As a matter of fact" — he nodded and winked merrily — "you are a beautiful young woman."

Callie laughed and pushed his hand away. "I know wot you are, Thad Thomas."

"What am I?"

"You're a man wot knows too much about women."

"No one can know too much about women." Thad laughed easily, sat at the table, and watched her as she made the breakfast. She put together the food quickly — battered eggs, toast, and thick slices of hickory-smoked bacon — while Thad spoke of the matters of the army. He had been with General Washington's forces that surrounded Boston but had been sent to town by his officer to check on the movements of the British. None of the Americans had any uniforms, so the British had no way of telling a soldier from a civilian.

"Did you see Matthew when you went to the prison Thursday?" he asked.

"Why, sure I did!"

"How was he?"

"They ain't none of them any good. It ain't right for them to treat human beings like that, Thad! They don't feed them and they don't do nothin' for the wounded men. One young man died just before I got there. Only seventeen 'e was."

Thad frowned and pounded the table with his fists. "I'd like to break into that place and kill all the guards and set all of our fellows free."

"Why don't you do it, then?"

"Because I'm not the general and the town's full of English soldiers. Do the prisoners have lots of visitors?"

"No. Hardly none."

"How do you get in?"

"Because I give food to the guards and they let me in to see the officer." She flushed and said, "He's ... he's sweet on me, so I give 'im food and rum and 'e lets me in to see them."

Thad Thomas stared at the young woman and saw the troubled look on her face. "Does it bother you to have to do that, Callie?"

"I've done worse."

"Worse! What do you mean?"

Callie had not revealed a great deal of her life to the Thomases. She was ashamed of her past and wished the conversation had not taken this turn.

"I don't like to talk about it," she said.

At that moment Hannah came in and sniffed. "You're cooking one of your pies, aren't you?"

"Yes, I am. I'm goin' to the prison today."

"Good. I'll help you get some things together. Good morning, Thad." Hannah went over and ruffled her brother's hair. "Why aren't you out soldiering?"

"I came in to see what the lobsterbacks are up to. Lieutenant Gibbons tells me the officers want to know everything that goes on, so I'm a spy."

"Well, don't get caught. They hang spies."

"I wasn't born to hang." Thad grinned and reached up and hugged his sister. "I was born to be rich and good-looking."

"Don't have anything to do with this one, Callie," Hannah warned, but she was smiling. "He has too many sweethearts as it is."

The three ate breakfast; then Thad left to see what he could discover in the city. Callie and Hannah put together the food for the prisoners, as well as enough for a bribe. "I 'ate to think about those pigs gettin' this good food," Callie said, her mouth tight, "but it's the only way to get in and get any of it to Matthew and Rees."

"You're doing the right thing. Just be careful with that lieutenant. Has he ever tried to put his hands on you?"

Callie suddenly laughed. "Of course he 'as. Wot did you think?"

"What do you say to him?"

"Oh, I just stay away from 'im as much as I can. He keeps wanting to meet me out in town but I put 'im off."

"That's good. You don't have anything to do with him." She came over suddenly and put her arm around Callie. "It's good to have you here, Callie. I couldn't do what you're doing now, I don't think."

Callie was suddenly suffused with a warm glow. The weight of Hannah's arm felt good to her and she smiled shyly. "I'm glad you brought me 'ere, Hannah. I don't know wot I would've done without you."

"You're family now, Callie," Hannah said with a smile. "Now let's hide some goodies so the guards won't get them."

As Callie approached the building that housed the prisoners, she was oppressed by it for some reason. The locals called it the Stone Gaol, and it had at one time been used as a local jail, but it was now old, moldering, and more recently had been used mostly to store grain. The rats that had come to feed on the grain still abounded there, and Callie had been frightened out of her wits when one of them ran over her feet on her previous visit.

Two British soldiers stood guard outside the front door, and Callie had discovered that the only way she could get inside was to give them food. She had learned from their conversation about how poorly British soldiers were fed. The two always demanded part of what was in her basket. This time she had brought them each a shepherd's pie, and she smiled brilliantly as she came up. "Good mornin'. Good day, Frank, and to you, Private James. I brought you somethin' very nice."

Private James took the pie, and his counterpart, a tall, hulking soldier with a face pocked with smallpox scars, grabbed his.

"Let's have a bit more, sweetheart," James said.

"No, your lieutenant wouldn't like that. But next time I'll bring you some tarts."

James argued but Callie held her ground, and finally Private James opened the door. As Callie went in, he reached out and ran his hand over her body. There was no way of avoiding this and she had come to expect it. "Don't be naughty," she said, forcing a smile. Stepping inside, she had to give away two more shepherd pies before she found herself at the door of Lieutenant Raymond Boggs. She knocked and when a voice said, "Come in," she entered.

"Good morning, Lieutenant. I've come to visit my brother." Callie had come up with the idea of claiming Rees as her brother and had undergone considerable interrogation. She had no papers to prove it, but she had smiled and weaseled Lieutenant Boggs until finally he had accepted her story.

"Well now, here's my pretty." Boggs was of no more than average height and homely, with a thatch of rusty red hair and a pair of watery blue eyes. He had a mouth like a catfish, and a potbelly that swelled against his uniform. He came over and reached for Callie but she put the basket between them. "I've got somethin' extra nice for you today, Lieutenant Boggs."

"You can just call me Raymond."

"Oh, that wouldn't be proper, you being an officer and all."

Callie managed to keep the lieutenant's attention with the kidney pie and the tarts she had brought. Indeed, the smell seemed to fill the office, and Boggs took them in one hand while grabbing her arm with the other. "Give us a kiss now."

"Why, that wouldn't be fittin', sir. Wot would my mother think?"

"Well, your mother ain't here. Come on, Callie. You're a sweet thing."

Callie turned her head in time to take the rather moist kiss on her cheek, then pushed him away. "There now, that's all. I've got to hurry."

Boggs grumbled but he put the pie down and took her to the door that led to the large room where the prisoners were kept. There was another door like it on the second floor, and as the guard opened it, Boggs managed to caress Callie before she could pull away. "I'll see you. There's a play tonight. Why don't you meet me after I get off duty?"

"I'll 'ave to do that sometime but tonight my mother is ailin'. I ain't able to, sir."

Callie argued with the lieutenant, knowing that somehow she had to stay away from him. She did not particularly mind deceiving him, for her life had been filled with deceit, but sooner or later she knew that Raymond Boggs would manage to get her alone. She still kept her knife handy for just such an occasion.

"I thought I'd never long for the food I got on a British ship of the line in His Majesty's navy, but I wouldn't mind a bit of burgoo." The speaker was a slight man of thirty-five with dark hair and dark eyes. His complexion was swarthy and he spoke with a pronounced accent. Stefan Chudzik was Polish by birth but had traveled greatly. He had served for a time in the British navy, but not as a volunteer; he had been impressed into service. He had managed to jump ship and had lived in Boston for five years. He had been enthusiastic about his adopted country and had been a willing volunteer with the recruits who had joined to fight the British at Breed's Hill.

Matthew grunted. "We ain't likely to get anything better until Callie brings it to us." He had lost weight and the flesh was shrunken on his face. The confinement had been hard on him, as it had been on everyone. Now he looked at Rees and said, "You think she'll come today?"

"I'm sure she will if she can. She's a bright girl to get in here."

"That's right," Stefan said, nodding. "She's about the only visitor who gets in, and she has to bribe her way at that. Has to give these swine part of the food she brings to us."

Stefan had become a good friend to Matthew and Rees. He had made the lonely confinement bearable, after a fashion, for he was a voluminous talker. He sometimes embellished his stories, but he was witty and remained cheerful despite the dismal circumstances. The three men had formed a little trio, as men will do in prison. Rees did what he could to treat the wounded and the sick, but with almost no medical supplies, that was not much. Stefan was highly impressed with education and was continually after Rees to share his knowledge.

"My youngest boy is healthy but my oldest has a cough a lot. What do you think that is, Doctor?" Stefan asked.

Rees laughed. "Stefan, you've asked me that before. There's no way I can tell without seeing the boy, but children get coughs and sneezes. They just go through it, as with mumps or measles."

"Look, the door's opening," Matthew said. All three men had been sitting on the floor, and now they stood as they saw Callie come into the room.

"I hope she has something sweet in that basket," Matthew said. "I do love sweets."

Rees watched with something like awe as Callie made her way across the room. Men were lying on the floor, some too sick to get up, and she spoke to many of them. He was amazed that she had learned the names of so many of the prisoners. When she came to stand before them, he smiled, saying, "You came again."

"Why, told you I would. Now, 'ere's all the food I could get in with."

"Let's see what you have there, sister." Matthew eagerly began to explore the contents of the basket.

Rees picked up an apple. "If you don't mind, I'd like to give this to young Finley."

Matthew nodded. "Sure."

"Why don't you give it to him, Callie. He looks forward to your coming, and" — Rees lowered his voice — "I don't think he's going to make it. Be kind to him."

Callie gave him a sudden look and he saw the grief in her eyes. She did not speak but took the apple. Rees watched as she went across the room and sat on the floor beside a young man who had been shot three times — twice in the leg and once in the side. He was dying and Rees could do nothing for him. Rees watched as Callie produced a knife, cut the apple up, and began slicing it into very small pieces, feeding the young man as she would a bird. Rees could hear the murmur of her voice but could not make out what she said. He saw her put her hand on the dying man's forehead and leave it there for a moment.

"She's got a heart, that girl," Stefan muttered. He was chewing slowly on a bit of mutton. "This is good," he said. "It's keeping us alive, I think."

Indeed, Stefan's words were true. The food Callie brought was keeping the three alive. They would have liked to have shared it with everyone, and they did share some, but Rees was aware that the one basket she was allowed to come in with could not feed everyone. He had said to Stefan and Matthew, "I know it seems selfish, but if we are to have any chance at all of surviving this, we've got to do it. We can't feed everyone."

When Callie came back, her face was troubled. "Poor chap! 'E's so young!"

"There's nothing I can do for him. Even if I had all the medicine in the world, it wouldn't help."

Callie looked at Rees and saw that the confinement had worn him down. She did not speak her thoughts but was as cheerful as she could be.

"Did that beast Lieutenant Boggs give you any trouble, Callie?" Matthew asked.

"Oh, I 'ad to give him some of the food like I always do."

"I'll bet he's tried to put his hands on you," Matthew said with a grunt. He had bitten into a tart, and the juice was running down the corners of his mouth. He wiped it away with the back of his hand, then licked the hand. "He's a swine. Stay away from him."

"Oh, he ain't no beauty, is he? But I can 'andle him."

"Did you get a chance to go see my family, Miss Callie?"

"That I did, Stefan. Your wife and children are doing fine. I brought this 'ere letter in for you."

Stefan snatched at the paper she held forth and at once began to read it. The others continued to speak, but Rees noticed that when Stefan looked up, his eyes were misty with tears. "Bless you, Miss Callie. This is good of you."

"Don't you worry none about your wife and boys. Hannah and I will see to them — and Thad's 'ome a great deal, too, Matthew."

"I wish I was there," Matthew said in a disconsolate voice.

"You will be one day. Don't worry," Callie said cheerfully. She stayed until the guard suddenly opened the door and called out, "All right, time to go! Visitin' is over!"

Quickly Callie squeezed Stefan's arm. "I'll tell your wife and your children that I've seen you, and when I come back, I'll 'ave another letter."

"Bless you, miss!"

Callie suddenly kissed Matthew on the cheek. She saw his look of surprise and giggled. "That's from Hannah." She turned then and for one moment Rees thought she was going to kiss him too, but instead she put her hand out. He took it and she said, "Be careful."

"Thank you, Callie. You're a light in this dark place."

Callie picked up the empty basket and made her way out. She turned at the door and waved to them, and then the door closed behind her. "Next to Hannah, that's the best woman in the whole world," Matthew said.

Stefan agreed at once. "Yes, she is a good woman. She's like my wife."

The three men sat down again and Stefan began to speak of his love for America. "It was bad in Poland," he said. "When I came here, it was good. Anna and I, we had our boys, and I wanted them to grow up in a free country, where a man's children would have a chance." Gloom took him then and he shook his head. "It don't seem as though it will be that way."

Rees could not answer. He knew all the prisoners now and all of them had the same dream of freedom, and he could not settle in his mind the ideas he'd had about England. He had always thought it the greatest country in the world, but now he had lost that confidence.

As soon as the meal was over, Bran Kenyon started to rise with his sons, but his wife said, "Sit you there. There's something I have to say."

Bran looked up with surprise but settled back in his chair. "What is it, Gwen?"

"I have another letter from the young woman who knows Rees, who's been visiting him in the prison."

Bran grunted. "She can't be a good woman if she's so free."

"Close your mouth, Bran!" The words were sharp and Bran stared at his wife with astonishment.

"You tell me to shut my mouth?"

"Yes, and listen to this letter. And you boys listen, too." She read the letter slowly and when she was through, she said, "This woman has done all she can to help our son. She has to bribe the guards to get in to see him, and I'm sure they abuse her. If he doesn't get food, he's going to die, and she's our only hope. Winter's coming on, Bran, and you know how he always hated winter."

"That's true," Arvel said. "He likes the hot weather best."

Bran listened as his wife spoke. He was master of his own house and did not like to be crossed. He still had not reconciled himself to Rees's decision to leave his roof, and now he said, "Fine. The young woman may be all right. I'm glad he's got a friend."

Gwen Kenyon pulled herself up straight. "We're sending money to this woman. Money to help our son."

"That we are not!" Bran said.

Gwen Kenyon's eyes glowed. She had a temper in her that she did not often show, and now Bran was suddenly reminded of it. "I am not asking you. I shouldn't have to. You're his father and you should love him enough to see that he doesn't suffer."

"We're sending no money — and there's an end to it!"

"I'm sending that which is left of my dowry, and I'm going into the chapel to stand up and tell them what sort of father you are that you begrudge your son a filthy lucre. That you love it better than you do your own flesh and blood! I'll tell the neighbors what sort of father you are. I'll steal from you, Bran. I'll leave you and the boys to cook and take care of your own meals."

Gwen Kenyon had never spoken like this, and the four men sat there staring at her with astonishment — Bran most of all, but the boys also were stunned. Finally she said, "I am not asking for favors. I'm telling you this is how it will be. Now, what do you say, Bran Kenyon?"

For once in his life Bran was unable to speak. He cast a quick glance at his sons, and Dafydd, whose eyes were wide with shock, said, "Well, Mother, I've got some money. Glad enough I'd be for Rees to have it."

Instantly the other two boys agreed. It troubled them to see their mother like this, for they knew she was a loving woman, but there was a steel in her now that they had never seen before.

Bran Kenyon shrugged his shoulders and looked down at his hands. A long silence fell over the table, and then finally when he lifted his head, there was a queer look in his eyes and a set of his mouth that none of his sons had ever seen. He cleared his throat and said quietly, "All right, Gwen, it will be as you say."

At once Gwen Kenyon went around the table, bent over and kissed her husband on the cheek. She kept her hand on his shoulder and then pulled his face around until she stared into his eyes. "He's your son, Bran, and I'm proud that you see it as you do." She straightened and said, "We'll send the money tomorrow."

# Chapter Eighteen

THE WINTER OF 1775 CLOSED DOWN ON NEW ENGLAND LIKE AN iron fist. The citizens of Boston shivered inside the houses, for firewood had grown so scarce that there was only enough to cook with. The British soldiers had a rough time of it. Food was scarce and they resorted to tearing down houses to make fires to warm themselves as they stayed on guard.

One warm spot in Boston was the headquarters of General Howe. He stood in front of the fire warming himself while staring at General Clinton, who sat at a table drinking spiced rum. Clinton felt that he was more able than Howe to end the war in America, and he had not always taken care to hide it. Now he was in the midst of a rather fervent exhortation concerning tactics. His round face glowed with the rum he had put away, and he nodded firmly, striking the table with his knuckles for emphasis.

"Now is the time, General," he said to Howe forcefully, "to end this thing."

"End it! And how would you propose to do that?"

"Why, General Howe, by all reports Washington's army has mostly drained away."

"That's all a rumor. We have no certain word about it."

"I think the word of our scouts may be trusted. One of them said that a whole regiment walked away just two days ago. Just simply walked out, and there was nothing Washington or anyone else could do about it."

Howe had become a much more cautious man. He had been severely influenced by Bunker Hill and was determined to take no chances of another such tragedy and loss of men. "We're in the middle of winter, General Clinton. Washington's men are freezing and they're bound to be hungry. They're not committed, as our soldiers are. When they get hungry enough and cold enough, they'll walk away. Why, by spring there won't be a thousand men left. We'll go out then and round them up. Nothing could be simpler."

Clinton continued to argue ardently but without much hope. Howe was a stubborn man and not likely to pay attention to a subordinate. Finally Clinton shook his head and said no more.

Seeing that Clinton had given up the argument, Howe said, "Come now, General. It's the middle of December. Christmas will be here in a week or so. We'll have a celebration. Tonight there is a play and I'm sure it will be enjoyable. Come. Let's enjoy as best we can the circumstances. By spring it will all be over and we can go home again."

Clinton did not answer but disillusionment was written on his face. He knew Howe would not move, and he knew Washington did not have strength enough to attack Boston itself. He foresaw nothing but a hard, boring time of it, and as he got up, he was thinking, *A play. We're soldiers and all he can think of is a play.*

As soon as Clinton left, the door opened and Howe's aide, a fuzzy-cheeked lieutenant, said, "General Howe, that young woman is here again."

"You mean the one who keeps begging for us to let that Dr. Kenyon go?"

"Yes sir. Won't you please see her? She's come every day."

"No, I won't, and you can tell her for me to stop coming."

"I've already told her so."

"Well, tell her again."

"Are you sure you can manage all this, Callie?"

Hannah was holding a petticoat in her hands and looking at Callie, who was standing before the fire in her shift. Hannah shook her head, saying, "It's going to be too heavy for you."

"No, it won't. Come 'elp me put it on."

Hannah raised the petticoat and slipped it over Callie's uplifted arms. When it settled down, she tied the drawstring, looking doubtful. "It's liable to simply fall off and then you'll be found out."

"Look, take some tape. We'll make some suspenders to go over my shoulders. They won't show under my coat."

Hannah shook her head again. "This frightens me."

But Callie laughed loudly and turned around. The petticoat did not swing out but hung straight down, for it was weighed down with items that had been sewn into pockets. "It's going to work beautifully. We 'ave it all padded so it won't make any noise. It's going to be fine."

It had been Callie's idea to make pockets in a petticoat and fill them with medical supplies. The bottles and the basic surgical instruments had been well wrapped with cloth and sewn into the fabric. She had convinced Hannah against her will, but now as she stood there, Callie's face was alight. "It will be easy. No one will ever suspect a thing."

"Well, we'll have to make sure it doesn't fall off." Hannah worked until she had tied linen tapes over Callie's shoulders, and then slipped the outer dress on. "It looks all right," she said. "But what if someone touches you?"

"The only one who'll be trying to touch me is that pig Boggs, and I'll stay away from him. Anyway, it's always up here he's trying to touch me." She touched her upper body and laughed. "He's such a fool! It ain't 'ard to trick him."

Hannah examined the young woman with a fond gaze. "It's a wonderful thing you're doing for Matthew and Rees, and for the rest of the men too."

"I'm glad I can do it. You've done so much for me, Hannah. Now, is the basket packed?"

"Yes. Too bad we have to give those English soldiers so much."

"Well, it gets me inside the prison. I'll come back as soon as I can."

"Do you have the letter for Stefan?"

"Yes, I 'ave it. You know, I think I'm cut out for this kind of work. I believe I'd make a good spy."

"But if they catch you, I don't know what will happen. Be very careful, Callie."

Callie took Hannah's hug, then pulled on her coat and slipped the bonnet over her head. Taking the basket from Hannah, she smiled, her eyes dancing. "It's all right. They'll never catch me."

Callie arrived at the prison, bribed the two guards with fresh bread and slices of ham, and then fought off Boggs, giving him a whole baked chicken. He swarmed all over her and insisted he wouldn't let her in until she agreed to meet him.

"Sometime — but not right now. My mother is sick. Maybe next week."

Boggs let her go and Callie passed through the door and went at once to the prison room. She spoke to many of the prisoners who had learned her name and was as cheerful as she could be.

She saw that Matthew was lying with his eyes closed, and she whispered, "Is he worse?"

"He's not good, Callie," Rees said quietly. He told her Matthew had developed a fever of some sort, as many of the men had. It was simply called "jail fever" and there was little anyone could do for it. "He needs warm blankets. All the men do."

"I don't rightly know 'ow I could smuggle blankets in."

"Bless you, girl. You're doing a wonderful job," Stefan said.

Callie said, "I 'ave more than the basket this time." Her eyes sparkled and Rees stared at her. "I've brought you some medical supplies."

"Medical supplies!" Rees whispered. "Where are they?"

"Wait, now — the guard might be lookin' in through the bars." Callie moved over against the wall. "Now you two stand in front of me and look the other way."

"Why should we do that?" Rees said.

"Because I'm going to take off my petticoat."

Rees blinked with surprise and exchanged glances with Stefan. The two men shielded Callie, and reaching under her blouse, she untied the knots that held the petticoat up. Then, lifting her skirt, she untied the drawstring. Carefully she held the skirt so it would not fall. Slipping out of the petticoat, she said, "You can look now."

Rees turned back and saw she was holding up a petticoat that seemed lumpy. He felt it. "Well, what's this?"

"It's all kinds of medicine. It's all sewed up in the pockets, and there's a scalpel too, and some other doctor's things that I got from your office."

Rees stared at her and then smiled and shook his head. "Child, you are a wonder!"

"I am not a child!" Callie said firmly.

"No, you're not. Well, you're a miracle, that's what you are," Stefan said.

"Here, Stefan. I brought you a letter from your wife."

"Bless you, miss." Stefan at once began to read, and Rees stood listening as Callie gave him the news from the outside.

When time grew short, Callie said, "Hannah told me something yesterday."

"What was it?"

"She said she'd been praying and that God 'ad talked to her." Callie turned her head to one side and looked puzzled. "God never spoke to me. Did he ever talk to you?"

"I don't think she meant in a voice."

"How, then?"

"Well, Jesus said, 'My sheep hear my voice.' But he simply meant that he would let them know things. What did Hannah say God told her?"

"That you were going to get out of this prison."

"Well, she's a godly woman. I'd like to believe it."

"I don't understand it. But anyway, I got a letter from your mother."

Eagerly Rees took it but said, "I'll read it after you leave. I want all the time I have with you."

"She's a fine woman, your mother! And she sent money too. Thad had to go get it changed into American money. It was some kind of a draft on a bank, but we 'ave the cash now. And your mother said to buy things for you and use it to get you out of here if that's possible."

"Bless her heart! I don't know how she got my father to agree with it."

"I wish I could meet her. She seems so sweet."

"Yes, she is."

Callie stayed until the guard called her out. As soon as she left, Rees sat beside Matthew and felt his face. "He still has a high temperature but maybe this medicine will help. We can rip up the petticoat for bandages, too."

Stefan, still holding his letter, said, "That's a smart girl, she is. You shouldn't let that one get away, my boy."

"What are you talking about?" Rees murmured.

"A man would be lucky to have a wife like that."

Rees stared at Stefan. "I'm not thinking about anything like that," he said stiffly.

"You're not the brightest man in the world," Stefan said, shaking his head. "Now let me read you about my boys and what they're doing."

Thad came bursting in and both Hannah and Callie turned to face him.

"What's wrong?" Hannah asked quickly.

"Nothing's wrong. I have good news."

Callie, as always, was glad to see Thad. She saw that his eyes were alight and he was practically dancing with excitement. "Wot in the world 'appened?"

"First, I'm going to be a hero, so I want a hero's welcome." He put his arms around Hannah, swung her around, and laughed at her protest. He kissed her on the cheek and then put her down. He grabbed Callie, who tried to stop him, but he was a strong man. He picked her up the same as Hannah, and she cried, "Let me down, you big ox!"

Thad laughed, kissed her soundly on the cheek, and said, "I'm going to be a hero. You really ought to be kissing me."

"You keep your 'ands to yourself," Callie said sharply.

"Why, you can trust me. I'm harmless."

"No, you're not!" Hannah said. "And you stop kissing Callie like that. Don't bring your barroom manners into this house. Now, what's your news?"

"What have you got for supper?"

"Tell us the news first."

"No, supper first, then the news."

Thad enjoyed teasing the women, and finally they sat down to a meal of corn on the cob, radishes, and baked chicken. He ate heartily, then shoved his plate back and said, "Well, that was a good meal. I guess you deserve to know what's happening." He leaned forward and his eyes were gleaming. "We're going to get the British out of Boston. That's the news."

Both women frowned and Callie said, "How will you do that?"

"We haven't enough men to take Boston by a frontal attack, but if we get cannons, we can put them up on the hills and blast them out."

"But where will you get the cannons?"

"That's the good news. But don't say a word about this; we wouldn't want it to get back to the British."

"Don't be foolish!" Hannah said sharply. "Where will you get the cannons?"

"General Washington is sending General Knox with a force to Fort Ticonderoga. There are plenty of cannons there. Ethan Allen and Benedict Arnold captured the place, so all we have to do is go get the cannons."

"But that's a long way, isn't it?" Hannah said. "How will he get them back?"

"I don't know but General Knox says we can do it."

"You're goin' with him!" Callie exclaimed, her eyes big.

"Yes. I volunteered, and when we get back with those cannons, the British won't have a chance." Thad rose to his feet and walked around, waving his arms and speaking excitedly of the mission. Finally he said, "Now, give me a piece of that cake, and I'll let you both give me a hug before I go to bed."

"You can 'ave the cake," Callie said, "but no more hugs."

She served the cake and Thad grinned at her. "One of these days you're going to fall in love with me, Callie. I'm an irresistible fellow."

"Not likely," she said with a sniff, sitting down across from him. "Tell me some more about the cannons."

Hannah went to bed early but Callie stayed up to cook for her next visit to the prison. Thad went to care for the lighthouse, and when he came back, he found her still up.

"Well, not in bed yet."

"No, I'm too excited to sleep. Oh, Thad, do you think it will work? I mean, getting the cannons and running the British out?"

"It has to work. Come here and I'll show you."

Thad pulled her over to the table and got a sheet of paper. He began to draw a diagram, and he said, "Look. Boston is here, and here is Dorchester Heights. General Knox will put the cannons up here, and we just have to begin shelling the city. What can the lobsterbacks do? They'll have to leave."

"But there are so many of them. Why can't they just come and fight you where the cannons are?"

"We have enough men to take them on. It'll work." Thad spoke with excitement. Finally he asked, "How are you coming along with your reading and writing?"

"Not as fast as I'd like to."

"Do you want me to help you?"

"Would you?"

"Sure I would. Here. Let's have a spelling lesson."

For an hour they sat before the fire, and Callie eagerly soaked up the spelling lesson. Eventually she shook her head and a sadness came into her face. "I'll never learn to be a lady, Thad."

"What are you talking about? You're already a lady. A beautiful young lady at that."

"No. Your sister knows so much and I don't know nothin'! I couldn't even go to a ball 'cause I don't know how to dance."

"Well, I'm probably the best dance instructor in all of Massachusetts. Come on."

Thad seized Callie's hand, pulled her to her feet, and said, "Now, you just move along with me. I'll go slow." He began to hum a tune and to guide Callie around the room. She had never seen dancing like this, but she found quickly that she could keep step with him. "Is that all there is to it, Thad?"

"Oh, there's a little more. When I come back from Ticonderoga, I'll take you to a dance. But you'll need some more lessons."

Callie looked up at him suspiciously. "You're holding me too tight."

"Oh no," Thad assured her with an innocence in his face. "This is the way it's done."

Callie did not protest, for she was enjoying the dance.

Suddenly Thad pulled her forward and kissed her lips. She was taken by surprise, and for one moment she realized she was enjoying his embrace. She found herself kissing him back, and then suddenly anger raced through her. She pushed herself away, saying, "You take your 'ands off me, Thad Thomas! You're just like all the rest!"

"No, I'm not. Besides, you've got to learn how to deal with men."

"How to deal with men! I ain't no baby where men are concerned. I've been fighting 'em off since I was twelve years old. Now, you keep your 'ands to yourself and no more kissing!"

Thad Thomas shook his head sadly. "You got a hardness in you, Callie."

"It got there because I fought off men like you!" Callie felt foolish, for she saw that Thad was disappointed in her. But she did not know how to handle herself, and rebuffing men's advances was too deeply ingrained. "Good night," she said.

"Good night, Callie. I'll see you when I get back from Ticonderoga." He laughed and said, "We'll have another dancing lesson."

She turned, feeling bad about what she had done. "I'm sorry if I was wrong."

"You keep yourself straight, Callie. That's a rare thing in a woman these days. Good night."

Callie went to bed that night thinking about the kiss. It was the first kiss she had ever given voluntarily, and she went to sleep wondering if she had done a wrong thing.

The next morning, after Thad had left to join his unit, Hannah noticed that Callie had nothing to say. She was usually a cheerful young woman, and finally Hannah said, "Something wrong, Callie?"

"Yes." Callie turned to face Hannah. "I don't know wot to do."

"What's the matter?"

"It's . . . it's Thad. He kissed me last night and, well, I kissed him back. You think that's wrong, Hannah?"

"You have to be careful. You must remember that Thad has been somewhat wild."

"I didn't mean to do it, but he was teachin' me to dance. Suddenly he kissed me and I found myself kissing him back. I feel ashamed."

Hannah was disturbed. She loved her brother, but she knew that his morals concerning women were not the greatest. "I think it would be best if you kept your distance from Thad."

"Ain't there any good men?" Callie asked, and there was a plaintive quality in her eyes.

"Yes, of course there are. Thad's a good man. He's just got some wrong ideas about women. He'll be a good husband once he settles down. And of course there's Rees. You think he's a good man, don't you?"

"Yes, 'e is. I'd be in a —" She hesitated and then looked at Hannah. "I'd be in a fancy house right now if he 'adn't saved me."

Hannah's heart went out to the girl, whose eyes were now filled with grief. "Well, you see, you do know one good man."

"But he'll never marry anybody."

"What do you mean by that?"

"He was in love with a woman called Grace. He still is."

"Was he married to her?"

"No, I don't think so. He told me once she died."

"I see. Has he ever tried to take advantage of you, Callie?"

"No, 'e ain't never."

Callie stood silently for a moment, her eyes downcast. Finally she looked up and said sadly, "He'll never love another woman. I know that much." She turned and walked away before Hannah could answer.

Hannah stood looking after her and finally shook her head. She felt a great love for the young woman, and she wondered who Grace was. *Someday I'll find out. I'll just ask him,* she thought. Then immediately she shook her head and said aloud, "It's no business of mine."

# *Chapter Nineteen*

BOSTON, ENCIRCLED BY WASHINGTON'S HUNGRY, FREEZING MILITIA, suffered greatly throughout the winter of 1775. British discipline was harsh. One soldier, Private Thomas MacMahan, was sentenced to receive a thousand lashes on his bare back with a cat-o'-nine-tails for receiving stolen goods, and his wife, Isabella, was to receive a hundred lashes on her bare back at the cat's tail.

The officers in the beleaguered town did not suffer so greatly as the enlisted men. They put on plays, assemblies, and balls and otherwise entertained themselves. The town itself suffered also. The British established a riding school in Old South Church. The pulpit, pews, and seats were cut to pieces and carried away, and horses were stabled inside the sanctuary.

But a great change came when General Henry Knox performed a minor miracle in moving cannon and artillery pieces from Fort Ticonderoga. With these guns George Washington immediately seized and fortified Dorchester Heights, exactly as he had planned. The guns were put in place, defenses were raised, and the British were taken completely off guard. When the Americans' artillery began a heavy bombardment of the town, General Howe ordered a counterattack. But the British attack failed, for a storm swept across Boston and Dorchester Heights, and when Howe stood staring up at the Heights, he knew he was beaten. He turned to his aide and said, "We will have to leave Boston. Have the preparations begin at once."

Thad had brought the good news to Callie and Hannah, shouting that the British would be forced to leave almost immediately. Quickly Callie went to the prison and found the soldiers sullen and angry, for the news had reached them. It took her some time to persuade Lieutenant Boggs to let her in, but finally she got inside. She told the prisoners the good news and gave Rees a letter his mother had received from London and sent to Callie. While he read it, Matthew was practically jumping up and down. He hugged Callie and whispered, "Rees has been angry at the British. I think he will be a patriot when we get out of this."

Stefan, however, looked gloomy and shook his head.

"What are you so sad about? We won!" Matthew said, punching Stefan on the arm.

"No, they will move us from this place. I have heard the guards talking."

Callie sobered instantly. "Won't they let you go?"

"No. They'll put us on a boat and take us to Halifax. That's where they're going, the rumor is. They have prisoners already there in hulks."

"Wot's a hulk?" Callie asked.

"An old ship," Stefan said grimly. "They put prisoners down inside and they starve them. Much worse than this place. Most of the men don't get out alive."

It had never occurred to Callie that this was not a complete victory. She turned to Rees, who was folding up his letter. She saw that he was paying little attention to her conversation with Stefan, and when he didn't speak, she said, "That was from the woman's father? The one who died?"

"Yes."

"Won't you ever be able to forget her?"

"No, and I don't want to."

Callie stared at him, then turned and began trying to encourage Matthew, but she found that Stefan had plunged the young man into despair.

"We've got to get out of here, Callie. We can't go into those hulks. We'll all die."

"You won't. We'll do something."

Hannah and Callie were in the kitchen when Thad entered the house. His eyes were wide as he blurted, "Stefan says that the rumor among the soldiers is that all the prisoners are going to be taken to Halifax, wherever that is, and they're going to be put in the bottom of an old ship, where they'll freeze and starve."

Callie stared at Thad, saying, "We can't let that happen. Can't you do something?"

"We've got to find out more about it. If they're going to move them onto a ship, I don't know what we can do. We don't have a navy."

Hannah was quiet as the two discussed the situation. Finally she said, "Callie, I want you to go back and talk to Lieutenant Boggs. Get out of him exactly what the plan is."

"I don't think the generals share their plans with lieutenants," Thad said.

"No, but they have to make plans. They'll be getting boats ready and you know what gossips soldiers are. Boggs will know."

"Wot good will it do for us to know their plan?" Callie asked.

"I have an idea but we need to know more. Will you do it?"

"Yes, I'll do it. I'll 'ave to take more food."

"Take an extra portion of rum and get him drunk," Thad urged. "Men always talk too much when they're drunk."

"All right. I'll do that."

Hannah said nothing to anyone but kept mostly to her room. She was praying constantly. She had always been a woman who could discern God's will more often than most, and while Thad went back to report to his unit and Callie was out getting Lieutenant Boggs drunk in hopes of gleaning more information, she fasted and prayed.

The next three days were lonely but Hannah did not eat a bite. Then early one morning she helped Callie prepare food to take to the prisoners — and their captors. As soon as the young woman left, Hannah went to the top of the lighthouse and trimmed the wicks of the lamps and replenished the supply of oil. After she polished the lenses, she stood looking up into the sky. The cold was bitter but she didn't notice it. Her whole heart and soul were caught up with finding a way to deliver her brother and the other prisoners from the awful fate that awaited them. She said aloud, "Lord, I've prayed every prayer I know. I will just wait on you. You can do all things. Free our men, Lord. In the name of Jesus."

The wind made a sibilant whisper around the top of the lighthouse, and clouds were building up in the west, but Hannah paid no attention. She stood there and suddenly stiffened, for something had come into her mind. She was not sure whether it was her own idea or from God, so she waited and continued to pray. Finally she left the tower, went downstairs, and within an hour she knew that God had spoken to her. She made a small bowl of porridge, ate it, and drank several cups of tea.

Eventually Callie came home and shortly afterward Thad came in. He hung up his coat and slapped his hands together. "It's freezing out there," he complained. He turned at once to Callie. "What did Boggs say?"

"Well, I got him drunk enough this time," Callie said, her mouth growing tight. "He's a beast! I thought I'd 'ave to use my knife on him."

"I'm sorry you had to go through that, Callie," Hannah said. "Did he say anything?"

"Yes. It's all settled. The British are going to take every boat they can find, and the prisoners will be put on an old transport that will barely float, to hear Boggs tell it. It's called the *Persus*."

"We can find out which one that is — but what good will it do us?" Thad commented.

Callie said, "Boggs is mad and so are the guards. They say the boat is old and will probably sink on the way. He told me he hopes it does. They'd get off in the lifeboat and let the prisoners drown."

"But he said she was slow," Hannah said. "Is that right?"

"Yes. That's wot 'e said."

"All right," Hannah said. "I've been waiting on God and I know what we have to do." She smiled as Thad and Callie both stared at her with shock in their eyes. "We'll hire a boat and we'll put armed men on it. When the fleet leaves, the boat with the prisoners will follow behind. That's when the armed boat will move in. There'll have to be enough men to take over the *Persus*. How many guards will there be, Callie?"

"Probably no more'n five or six."

"That's not many."

Thad was staring at his sister. "This will never work. There will be other ships around."

"I think this is what God wants us to do. I've been fasting and praying and it came to me."

"But what will we use for a ship?" Thad asked.

"We'll go to Silas Moon."

Thad suddenly slapped his fist into his palm. "I forgot about him."

"Who is Silas Moon?" Callie asked.

"He was a good friend of Pa's," Thad said. "He has a fine sloop, one of the fastest ships out of Boston, and he hates the English. His son was killed at Bunker Hill."

"But he'll be risking 'is ship, won't he?" Callie asked.

"We'll go talk to Silas," Hannah said. "All of us. Come get your coats on."

Silas Moon was a tall, rawboned man of fifty-two. He had a set of thick muttonchop whiskers and a pair of direct gray eyes. He had welcomed the three into his house, where he lived as a widower, and had sat listening without saying a word as Thad spoke of the plan. When Thad finished, he chewed on his lower lip for a time and shook his head. "Don't sound probable, Thad."

"I believe it will work, Captain Moon," Hannah said. "There will be only half a dozen guards on the ship, and some of them are bound to be down below. It wouldn't be hard for the *Clara Belle* to catch her. She's a very slow ship."

"Oh, I know the *Persus*. The *Clara Belle* could catch her, no doubt about that, but there'll be over a hundred and fifty ships leaving. The British won't want to leave any behind. That's why I hid the *Clara Belle* down the coast six months ago. If we catch the *Persus*, one of the warships is bound to be close."

"There must be some way to do it," Hannah whispered. Her eyes were fixed on Captain Moon and she said, "Can't you think of anything?"

Moon had always felt a deep affection for the Thomas family. He and Amos had been shipmates and had been in the fishing business together for a time. He got up, went over to the window, and stared out. He was silent for so long that Thad gave a despairing look at Hannah, but she shook her head.

Finally Silas turned and said, "There's two things that will help us. First of all, she's slow anyway. Second, I know a trick that worked once back when I was on the frigate *Defiant*. Never heard of it since, but the captain was a smart 'un." He began to grow excited and paced back and forth and said, "Have you ever heard of a drogue?"

"A drogue? No. What's that?" Thad asked with a puzzled tone.

"It's a cone-shaped piece of canvas sewed up tight at the narrow end. The open end catches the water. If we could fasten a drogue underneath the *Persus*, it would slow her down still. The ships would all leave her behind." Seeing their puzzled look, he began to explain. "We'd have to do it after dark with a good swimmer, maybe two. We'd fashion a drogue maybe ten feet long out of stout canvas. We'd put ropes on it and fold it up, and swimmers could go under water. I'd doubt there'd be a guard out in this freezing weather. We'd fasten it underneath the ship, maybe to the rudder itself. Then we'd take a piece of very light line and tie the narrow end of the drogue to the rudder. It'll stay that way until the *Persus* picks up speed; then the little line will break. The drogue will level out and start catching water. It's an anchor, in effect, that'll slow the ship down."

"It sounds complicated to me," Thad said, "but I'll be willing to be one of the men to put it on."

"No, a couple of my boys can do a better job."

"Oh, Captain Moon, will you try it?" Hannah asked.

"I reckon as how I will. We can't let our Matthew and the rest of them boys stay in them hulks. Tell you what. It would help a lot if we could get an English uniform. When we pull alongside, they'd be more apt to wait if they thought it was an English officer calling to them."

"I can do that," Hannah said. "What kind of uniform?"

"One like you see them officers paradin' around in. Maybe a major's uniform."

At once Hannah said, "When will you need it?"

"We'll need it before we attack that ship, for sure." Moon suddenly laughed, a big, booming sound. "We'll have to get some men who have guns and know how to use 'em."

"I think I know where we can get those. Let me take care of that," Thad said, grinning.

"What are you thinking of, Thad?" Hannah asked.

"I think it's time we hit General Washington up for a squad of pirates. There are enough men in my unit who'd do it if he would agree."

"Go to General Washington!" Moon said with amazement. "Why, he wouldn't never listen to a private."

"I think he will, Silas. Anyway, I'm going to give it a try!"

# Chapter Twenty

"I THINK THIS SHOULD INFLUENCE OUR ENEMIES TO LEAVE BOSTON, Your Excellency."

General Henry Knox was dressed, as usual, in a flamboyant uniform made of shiny green fabric with white facings. His round face glowed with pleasure, and his complexion was heightened by the March wind. He kept a handkerchief always wrapped around his right hand, for he had lost fingers as the result of a hunting accident as a young man, but the other he waved freely. "They have not a chance, sir! Not a chance!"

General George Washington smiled, for Knox was a favorite of his. It had been a source of amusement to him that a bookseller who had rarely seen a cannon had become the head of his artillery, for Knox, by study of books and with enthusiasm, had learned practically all there was to know about guns. Now Washington said, "You have done your country a great service, Henry, and I am personally more grateful to you than I can express."

Knox blushed, for he idolized Washington, as did most of the other officers on the general's staff.

Just as Knox started to speak of the attack that was soon to begin, Lieutenant Scammel approached and interrupted him. "Pardon me, General, but there's a young man and woman here to whom I think you should give heed."

Washington turned to see a tall young soldier standing at a distance, a young woman by his side. "What is it, Scammel?" he asked.

"Sir, if you'd give them just a few minutes, I think you would find it interesting — at least I did."

Washington placed great trust in his close aides and had found Scammel to be a rather penetrating man of thought. "Very well. If you say so, Lieutenant."

As Scammel went to bring the young couple, Knox stared after him. "What in the world could they have to say? He's just a private."

"Sometimes good ideas come from the lower ranks. We officers become so lifted up, we miss the obvious. I always like to listen to them."

"General Washington," Scammel said, "this is Private Thaddeus Thomas and Miss Callie Summers."

"What can I do for you, sir, and you, Miss Summers?"

Thad was rather breathless at being in the presence of the august leader of the Continental army, but he had practiced his speech well.

"Sir, I know you are always concerned about all of us, the men in the army, I mean, and Miss Summers and I have a plan that would free all the prisoners who were taken during the Battle of Bunker Hill."

"Indeed! I'd be glad to hear it." Washington stood there, a tall figure, strong and with a noble bearing. His eyes were quick and sharp and he listened intently as Thad spoke. When Thad finished, he said thoughtfully, "So your plan is to take over the transport once the fleet gets under way?"

"Yes sir. I know it can be done."

"But we have no ships to spare for such an endeavor."

"Oh sir," Callie said, "we've already hired a sloop which has a fine captain. But we do need some soldiers to fight the battle."

Washington studied the two, wondering about their relationship. He was somewhat amused by the scheme. He had heard a number of wild, harebrained plans since assuming command, but this seemed to have something to recommend it.

Callie said, "Please, sir, they are good men. They'll die, most of them, if they are put in that old hulk in Halifax."

Washington turned to Knox. "General Knox, what would you say? Could you supply enough men for this expedition?"

"If you command it, sir, it shall be done."

The general faced Thad and Callie. "Very well, Private. I will be interested to hear the results of this. I know our fellows in that jail are in poor shape. Please inform me as to the success of this endeavor."

"Thank you, General," Thad said, beaming from ear to ear. "I know we can do it."

"Thank you, sir," Callie whispered, and when Washington nodded, she turned away with Thad.

Washington smiled, then turned to Knox. "All right, Henry, when do we persuade General Howe to leave Boston?"

"As soon as we get the shipment of powder from Philadelphia, we'll be ready to blast the lobsterbacks out of the city."

"Take care of that young couple. I'd like to see such a ploy work. It would be good for morale."

"Yes sir, it shall be done."

On March 17, 1776 — Saint Patrick's Day — Howe's soldiers and about one thousand Tories, colonists loyal to England, crowded onto the ships until they were packed to the gunnels. The loyalists knew what they might expect, for they had treated the patriots shamefully and knew they could expect the same in kind.

When all the ships were loaded, the order came to move the prisoners out of the Stone Gaol, and Lieutenant Boggs instructed the seven guards to keep a close watch. "Some of them may try to escape. If they do, just shoot them down. There'll be no loss." He stood outside the main cell as the prisoners were led out. Finally he asked, "Is that all of them?"

"Yes sir," a leather-faced corporal said, nodding. "That's it."

"Well, let's get them on the ship, then."

Stefan's eyes were darting right and left as they stepped outside. He whispered, "I'm going to make a break for it, Rees."

"Don't do it, Stefan. You won't have a chance."

"That's right," Matthew said quickly. "Once we get to Halifax, we can jump off that old ship and make our escape."

Stefan did not answer. He had become desperate. He had grown more and more unhappy during his incarceration, and as the prisoners were marched together down the street, he saw his chance. The guards were scattered rather widely and suddenly he broke and ran. A cry went up at once from Boggs. "Shoot that man!"

Two of the guards threw up their muskets and fired. One of the balls went harmlessly into the side of a tavern, but the other struck Stefan in the thigh and drove him to the ground. He got up at once, holding his leg, from which blood was streaming, but the guards, under Bogg's roaring command, went to get him.

"I wish you'd hit him in the head," Boggs snarled. "Get him on down to the ship. Make some of the others carry him."

"What's this?" A lanky colonel had suddenly appeared. His face was pale and there was a bitterness in him that seemed to burn in his eyes. "What's happening here, Lieutenant?"

"Prisoner tried to escape, Colonel Riggs," Boggs said.

Colonel Riggs drew himself up. "Hang him!" he said sharply.

Lieutenant Boggs was not a man of compassion but the order caught him off guard. "Sir? Hang him?"

"You heard the command, Lieutenant. Hang him!"

Boggs swallowed hard. All the prisoners had stopped, and now every eye went to Stefan, who was bleeding freely. "Please, sir," he begged the colonel, "don't hang me. I've got a family."

"You should have thought of that before you tried to escape. Any man trying to escape from His Majesty is a traitor. Hang him!"

"But . . . where, sir?" Boggs asked.

"Send your man up in that building and throw a rope out. Tie his hands behind him and then haul him up."

Boggs turned pale but ordered two of his men. "You heard the colonel. Go up over that tavern and throw a rope out."

Rees had been staring at the colonel in horror. Now he could not keep still. He stepped forward and said, "Colonel, you can't mean to hang him."

"Shut your mouth, rebel! Death is the penalty for trying to escape."

"But sir, you can't do it."

Colonel Riggs stepped forward until he was face-to-face with Rees. "If you don't shut your mouth, you'll hang beside him!"

"I don't have a family. That wouldn't matter so much, but he does. What will his wife and children do?" Rees pleaded, his face twisted with agonizing fear.

The colonel stood shaking his head, and finally Boggs said in a strange voice, "Colonel Riggs, the men are ready."

Riggs half turned, shouting, "Pull him up!"

Rees saw a group of three soldiers, two of them holding Stefan and one of them putting a rope around his neck. Stefan was crying and begging for mercy, and the sound drove Rees beyond the bounds of propriety. He grabbed Colonel Riggs by the arm and whirled him around. "You can't do this! It's inhuman."

Riggs's eyes flew open wide. He cursed and pulled the pistol from his side and shoved it against Rees's chest. "Take your filthy hands off me or I'll blow your heart out!"

"Go ahead! Shoot!" Rees said. He did not release his hold, and his voice lifted so that everyone heard it. "You're nothing but a murderer! You're not a soldier. You're a cold-blooded, godless criminal!"

Riggs's face turned a brilliant red, and for one moment it appeared he would indeed pull the trigger. Instead he raised the heavy pistol and brought it down on Rees's head. It drove Rees to the ground, and he felt the blood begin to pour over his forehead. The world seemed to be spinning, and he saw nothing for a moment but brilliant, flashing light.

"Get him up and get him out of here!" Riggs shouted. "If he says another word, shoot him!"

Rees felt hands lifting him, and he heard Matthew whisper desperately, "Don't say anything, Rees. He'll kill you!" Rees wiped the blood from his face with his sleeve and felt himself pushed along. He stumbled forward, but when a cry went up he turned around and then wished he had not.

What he saw he never forgot. Poor Stefan, his hands tied, had been hauled up until his feet were free of the ground. He kicked frantically, his feet making a tattoo, his face scarlet red.

Unable to bear the sight, Rees looked away and put his hands over his ears.

"Are you all right?" Matthew whispered.

Rees turned and saw that Matthew's face was completely drained of blood, as pale as paste. Horror was in his eyes, and as they shuffled along, a rage began to build in Rees Kenyon. He shook his head and did not answer Matthew. When they reached the dock near where the *Persus* lay anchored, he watched the prisoners being packed into the small boats to ferry them out. He saw Riggs watching him, and finally Lieutenant Boggs came over.

"That was unfortunate. I know he was your friend."

"Yes, he was." Rees's voice was cold.

"He shouldn't have tried to escape."

"He didn't know he was dealing with beasts. He thought the British had some compassion. He was wrong! None of you are anything but wild animals!"

"Oh, I say!" Boggs protested.

"Someday, if I ever get free, I'll kill as many of you as I can," Rees said. "You don't deserve to live."

Boggs could not meet Rees Kenyon's eyes. He turned at once and walked away.

Matthew came closer to stand beside Rees, tears flowing down his face. "They shouldn't have hanged him."

"They'll be sorry," Rees said, his teeth clenched together. "I'll make them sorry."

The soldiers loaded them into the boats, and Matthew stared at Rees, aware that something had happened to the gentle man he had known.

"You'll have to show me a little respect," Captain Moon said. He was walking back and forth on the deck of the *Clara Belle*, running his hand down his sleeve. Moon was wearing the uniform of a British colonel and was inordinately proud of his appearance. "We British officers deserve a lot of respect." He looked at Callie and Thad and his first officer, Nathaniel Dirk, who were all dressed in common sailor garb. Others on the ship, all armed and wearing the same type of clothes, were laughing.

Nathaniel Dirk shook his head, his face filled with admiration. "You make a fine British colonel, Captain."

"Until I open my mouth. Then they'll know better."

"We'll be aboard. All they have to do is see you, Captain Moon,"

Thad said. He carried a knife at his side and a pistol stuck into his belt. "This thing might work, but I'm beginning to doubt it."

"It'll work, all right," Dirk said, grinning. He was a muscular man over six feet tall, hardened by a lifetime at sea. It was Dirk who had slipped into the water and attached the drogue to the *Persus* the night before it sailed. Now he looked ahead at the transport, which was moving slowly down the river. "That drogue's doing the job. As soon as we get out of sight of land, we can take 'em."

"Have your men ready, Nathaniel," Moon said. "This'll have to be done quick."

"You want to take any prisoners?" Dirk asked.

"That's up to them. If they throw down their arms, don't kill 'em. We'll put them in a prison and see how they like it."

"Most of them are just sailors," Nathaniel said. "I don't think they'll put up a fight. If we get the guards, it'll be easy."

The *Clara Belle* was a swift ship, and Captain Moon sailed only under the mainsail, the rest being furled. He noted that the *Persus* had all sails set but wallowed in the water.

"She probably has six feet of water in her well now," Moon said with satisfaction. "And with that drogue she's not making more than two knots an hour."

Thad was standing next to Callie. She had insisted on coming, and since she had provided the money for leasing the *Clara Belle*, she'd held the high card.

"I wish you weren't here, Callie," Thad said, turning to her. "A woman doesn't have any business in a situation like this."

Callie's lips grew stubborn. "We've been over that. I don't want to hear it anymore."

"You are a headstrong young woman!" Thad's eyes roamed over her and he shook his head. "You'd better stay out of sight. One look at you and they'll know you're not a sailor."

Callie looked down and saw that her figure was indeed revealed by the sailor's shirt she was wearing. She flushed and said, "They won't be 'avin' no time to look for women."

"Why are you doing this, Callie? Is it because of Rees?"

Callie did not answer. She looked away from Thad, her hair captured under a soft cap. Finally she said, "I reckon I am. He's been good to me. I couldn't do nothin' else."

"Well, if this works, it'll be thanks to you."

Callie turned and smiled briefly. "I wanted to get Matthew out, too. I thinks a lot of 'im."

Thad put his hand on Callie's shoulder. "You're a good woman."

Callie was uncomfortably aware of the pressure of his hand. It made her nervous and she moved away.

"You are a real touch-me-not, Callie."

"It ain't no time for foolin' around, Thad. Somebody could get kilt in the next few minutes."

"You're right about that." Thad's face grew serious and he fingered the butt of the pistol. He looked back and said, "We're out of sight of land now and there are no ships around the *Persus.*"

At that moment Captain Moon's voice boomed out. "Get the topsails on her and the top gallants too. It's time to have at those lobsterbacks!"

Callie knew nothing at all about sailing a ship. She was amazed at how the sailors knew exactly what to do. They made their way among the maze of ropes in an impossibly short time, and the *Clara Belle* was soon skimming over the water. Callie watched as the *Persus* grew larger, and she heard Nathaniel cry out, "They've seen us, Cap'n!"

"Right! I'm going to stand here. Nathaniel, pull up even with them. I'll shout somethin' but they don't have to hear it. All they need is to see this uniform."

"I hope this thing works," Thad said, his eyes narrow. "It's going to be active for a few minutes. You stay on board this ship, Callie, until we've overpowered the guards."

Callie was excited that the plan seemed to be working, but she had heard one of the soldiers say to another, "They may kill all the prisoners if they see they're going to get caught."

The distance between the two ships closed, and Callie could see Boggs but not clearly. He was standing at the side of the ship, hanging on to the rail and watching the *Clara Belle* as she drew near. Callie kept behind some of the men. It seemed unlikely that he would recognize her but she took no chances.

"What ship is that?" Boggs bellowed.

"*Clara Belle.* Message from the general," Captain Moon answered. He deliberately garbled his words and did not shout in his usual stentorian fashion.

"What's the message?" Boggs shouted.

"Concealed orders. Have to come aboard."

For a moment everybody on the *Clara Belle* was watching, almost holding their breath. The British guards were all on deck with their muskets ready. The American soldiers were crouched behind the rail and ready to spring into action, but it would be a bloody action at this range.

"Secret orders," Captain Moon repeated.

"All right. Come on board."

"Bring her alongside," Moon said to Dirk, "and then have the hands tie on quickly. As soon as we touch that ship, men, go aboard. Take those guards out but don't kill the lieutenant if you can help it."

The *Clara Belle* was well handled and slid smoothly beside the old transport. As soon as the two hulls touched, the sailors leaped aboard the *Persus* and began to fasten their vessel, and at that same time Thad called out, "Away, boarders!" He went up the side of the transport, holding the pistol in his hand, and the soldiers, with a wild yell, followed him.

Callie did not attempt to go with them, but she saw two of the guards level their rifles and heard Boggs scream, "They're the enemy! Shoot them!"

Shots rang out and one of the *Clara Belle*'s soldiers went down, holding his side. But the British guards were driven to the deck by a fusillade as the soldiers from Washington's army, yelling and screaming like madmen, emptied their pistols. For a few minutes the action was furious, but then all was quiet and Captain Moon said, "Well, they've done it, missy. Let's go on board. Weren't nothin' to it."

The action had not been as bad as Callie had feared. Drawing a sigh of relief, she scrambled up on deck and walked at once to Boggs. His eyes were wide with fright as he stared at the bodies of his men.

"Hello, Lieutenant," Callie said. She stepped in front of Boggs and pulled her cap off. Her blond hair fell down her back and she laughed at his expression. "I didn't bring you no bribe this time."

Boggs stared at her and his mouth dropped open. He tried to speak and finally he gasped, "What are you doing here?"

"I came to see that you're thrown into a prison, and I 'ope it's as bad as the one you kept our men in."

Boggs' face suddenly contorted as he shouted, "You'll hang for this!"

At that moment Thad appeared, grinning like a crazy man. He grabbed Boggs by the collar and stuck his pistol under the man's chin. "I ought to blow your head off!"

"No, don't kill me. Please don't kill me!" Boggs begged. He fell on his knees.

Thad stared at him in disgust. "Get up, you whelp! You're going to sit in prison through the whole war, and I hope you don't make it!" Thad turned to Callie and said, "Come on. I want to be there when Matthew and Rees find out they're not prisoners anymore."

Callie threw her head back, saying, "Yes, let's go find them."

Rees and Matthew and the other prisoners had heard the gunfire, but there was no way to look out of the lower deck where they had been penned in. All was darkness except for one feeble lantern.

"What could that be?" Matthew whispered.

"I don't know," Rees said. "Sounds like a fight of some kind but there were no cannons." They stood there hearing footsteps on the deck above, but Rees's mind was only half on the activity overhead. He was thinking about Stefan. He could not get the sight of the execution out of his mind.

Suddenly the door opened and people were piling in. Rees could not see who they were, despite the lanterns they carried, but then he heard a voice crying out, "Rees!" For a moment he thought he was losing his mind; then suddenly he felt the form of a woman pressed against him and arms around his neck. "Rees, you're free!"

"Callie! What — "

"You're free!" Callie whispered. She hugged him tightly and put her head on his chest. "I was so afraid for you!"

Rees's mind was whirling. He was aware that Thad was there, beating him on the back, and Matthew was shouting words he could not make out.

Finally Thad said, "Let's get out of this hole."

"Where are we going?" one of the former prisoners asked.

"Back to Boston," Thad said. "No British there now. You men can see your families again."

A cheer went up, and they climbed to the deck and stumbled out into the daylight. Rees looked up at the sun and the sky and the sea. Callie was standing beside him, and he asked, "How did this all happen, Callie?"

"I'll have plenty of time to tell you later."

Rees took her hand and lifted it to his lips. He kissed it and saw her face redden. "I'll never doubt God again," he said, "or you."

Callie did not say a word. She held his hand tightly and then looked back toward the land. "Now," she said, "I don't have to be afraid anymore."

"Were you afraid for me?"

"Why, course I was! Didn't you know it?"

"I'd almost given up, but in the darkest hours I remembered you. And I remembered Hannah saying we were going to be delivered."

"She never gave up, Rees. Not ever."

Rees Kenyon looked down at the young woman and for a time did not speak. Then he said, "Life's going to be a little different."

"Ain't you gonna be a doctor?"

"I'll use my medical skills but I'm going to do more than that. Did you hear about Stefan?"

"No. Wot happened?" Callie listened as Rees spoke in spare tones, and then tears came to her eyes. "Poor Stefan," she whispered. "And his family."

"We'll have to take care of them, Callie, you and me."

"We will," Callie said. "We'll do that. But wot will you do?"

"Probably become a soldier. If I'm going to live in this land, I'll have to fight for it."

Fear showed itself in Callie's face, but she did not speak, for she recognized the determination in Rees. She said no more, and the two stood at the rail watching as the two ships slowly turned and set sail for Boston.

# Part
## -4-

# *Chapter Twenty-One*

FALL HAD COME TO BOSTON AT LAST, RELIEVING THE TORRID DAYS of summer. Now, in the middle of September, the azure sky above pleased Rees Kenyon as he guided his gelding down a busy street. The countryside had already assumed a mid-September carnival color — riotous reds, splashes of yellow, and the crimson leaves of the maples decorated the woods that surrounded the city. The smell of burning leaves came to Rees as he studied the street before him. All was so different now that the British had been gone for six months. No longer did the bright red coats of the English soldiers appear, and in their stead the buff uniforms of the officers in the Continental army were seen.

"Dr. Kenyon! Oh, Dr. Kenyon!"

Pulling up the gelding to an abrupt halt, Rees turned to see a woman separate herself from a group gathered in front of a green-grocery. He had to search his mind quickly to identify her. Since taking over most of Dr. Warren's patients, he had stuffed his mind with faces and tried to match them with ailments. Now it came to him and he smiled, saying, "Good morning, Mrs. Tyler."

"Good morning, Doctor."

Amelia Tyler was a tall, rawboned woman whose husband Andrew was even taller, with bones more prominent. The details of the man's medical problems fell into place in Rees's mind, and he asked at once, "How is Andrew doing today?"

"Not as well as I'd like. I wonder if you would come by and visit him?"

"Yes, of course. I'd be glad to. I'll drop by late this afternoon."

"Oh, thank you, Doctor." Relief washed over Mrs. Tyler's face, and she watched as the tall physician nodded, then continued on his way down the street. Going back to her friends, she said, "You know, Abbie, I never thought I'd find a doctor I trusted like Dr. Warren, but this young man has a way with him."

"You'd better watch out. He's a single man and you know how they are." The speaker was an apple-cheeked woman, round and solid, with a pair of dancing blue eyes. "You wouldn't be looking for a little romance, would you?"

"Don't be foolish!"

"I ain't so foolish. Half the women in Boston with eligible daughters are teachin' them how to attract Dr. Kenyon's attention." She bit the end of her finger, then shook her head and laughed. "I hate to see a single man wasted. He could give a woman good comfort, he could!"

As Rees proceeded down the street, he was greeted by several other people, some of whom he did not know. For a time he'd been frustrated by the attention that a new doctor in town received, especially one attempting to stand in the place of Dr. Joseph Warren, an impossible task for any man! Rees knew that part of the welcome he'd received in Boston was due to Dr. Warren's staunch support of the patriot cause. Most people, he knew, assumed that he himself was a patriot — and although he had come to America with little concept of the politics of the revolution, he knew that at some point he had come to sympathize with the cause of liberty. He knew that sooner or later he would have to make his choice public, and he knew he would stand with the Americans.

Drawing up at the home of Robert Gifford, Rees stepped out of the saddle. He studied the house as he tied the horse's reins to the cast-iron hitching post. It was the home of a rich man, a Georgian-style house set back off the street more than most. The clapboards were painted salmon with green trim, and the two stories had a hip roof, with balustrades across the top deck. Massive red chimneys rose on each end of the house, and pilasters flanked the entryway with pedimented dormers. There was an air about it that almost smelled of money, which for some reason irritated Rees. Most of the houses in Boston had suffered during the occupation of the British. Many fine homes had been completely destroyed; others had been damaged so that it would take years to restore them to their original condition.

As Rees stepped to the doorway and knocked, he thought, *Robert Gifford has certainly come out well. He traded with the British while they were here, and now he's making money hand over fist serving the patriots.* He had learned this from Thad, who despised such men. The most rabid Tories had left on the ships, fleeing to Halifax, but there were several, such as Robert Gifford, who were like chameleons. They could meld into any background. For this reason, if for no other, Rees felt a vague distaste for Robert Gifford.

The door opened and Robert Gifford himself stood there smiling. "Well, Doctor, you're very prompt."

"I was in the neighborhood, Mr. Gifford."

"Come in. Come in, sir." Gifford was dressed in the latest fashion, a double-breasted coat of a striped black-and-gray material worn buttoned to the top and cut away in the front, a white silk shirt with ruffles at the neck and wrists. His tight-fitting white breeches ended just below the knee, where silk stockings with black embroidery at the ankles were revealed, tucked into black leather shoes with silver buckles. As with the house, his dress bespoke money.

"I haven't seen you lately, Doctor."

"No. I've been busy."

"Yes, by George, that was a stroke of luck, wasn't it, stepping into Warren's practice?" Gifford's eyes glowed and he shook his head. "I never had an opportunity like that. I had to make my own way."

Rees was well aware that this was not true, for Robert Gifford had inherited a large fortune from his father. He had never had to make his own way, but it pleased him to say so.

"And how is your . . . uh, your ward, Miss Summers?"

By this time Rees had become accustomed to the sly looks he received when Callie was mentioned. He had been relieved when Hannah invited Callie to stay with her. This had worked out well for everyone concerned.

"You say Miss Elaine is ailing, Mr. Gifford?"

"Why yes, she seems to be. Come along. I'll take you to her."

Rees followed Gifford up an ornate, winding staircase and then along a corridor, where Gifford knocked on a door and said, "Daughter, are you awake?"

"Yes. Come in, Father."

Rees stepped inside as Gifford opened the door and said, "I'll leave you with your patient, Doctor, but I'll see you before you go."

"Thank you, Mr. Gifford."

Moving over to the bed where Elaine sat propped up against a mountain of pillows, Rees could not help but note the lavish nature of the bedroom. He did not know much about the value of furnishings, but the thought came to him, *Probably more spent on this bedroom than the annual income of most people.* Aloud he said, "Well, Elaine, you're not feeling well, I hear."

"Oh, I don't know what's the matter with me, Rees. Or should I call you Doctor — since you're here on a professional visit?" Elaine was wearing a sheer nightgown made of some shiny blue material which clung to her in a most seductive fashion. She did not look like a sick woman, Rees noticed, but he took the hand she extended to him and bowed slightly. Her hair seemed perfect and her eyes were bright. "You don't look ill to me," Rees said, smiling. "What are your symptoms?"

Elaine put her hand over her breast and said, "It's my heart. It seems to be beating too fast."

Rees took her wrist and timed her pulse. "You have a regular pulse. About sixty beats a minute. That's very good."

"I suppose so, but something seems to be wrong in here." Once again she put her hand over her breast. "It frightens me a little."

Rees hesitated, then said reluctantly, "Maybe I'd better listen to it." He leaned forward and rested his head against her chest. Her heartbeat was strong and regular and he could detect nothing at all amiss. He was intensely aware of the softness that lay beneath his head, and she was wearing perfume that was faint yet insistent. He felt himself stirred by his actions, as a man will be in such a situation, and quickly stood up. Shaking his head, he said, "Your heart sounds fine to me."

"Well, it's good to know that I have such a fine heart. A woman needs a good heart, doesn't she?"

"And a man too," Rees agreed, smiling. "Any other symptoms?"

"Pull up a chair and sit down." Elaine waited until he had done so and then said, "I suppose I'm all right." A smile lifted the corners of her lips. "I haven't seen you since last week. I have to get sick to have you call."

"Well, as you can guess, I've been very busy. Dr. Warren's practice was large and I've inherited most of his patients."

"I know, and I'm so happy for you, Rees. Everyone's talking about what a fine doctor you are. Your patients are some of the most influential men and women in Boston."

"And some of the poorest too," Rees said. "Dr. Warren did a lot of charity work."

"I hear you went to see Sarah Thomasville."

"Yes, I did, as a matter of fact. How did you hear about that?"

"Why, she told me of course." Elaine laughed aloud and took Rees's hand. "Tell me. Was she very enticing?"

Rees suddenly felt quite uncomfortable. Her eyes were laughing at him and he shook his head quickly. "I couldn't reveal anything about a patient, Elaine. You know that."

"You don't have to reveal it. She's always after handsome young men, and doctors are especially tempting for some reason."

"Well, my mirror tells me that I don't fit in the category of handsome."

"But I'll bet some of your female patients have tempted you, haven't they?"

"Oh, constantly." Rees smiled faintly.

"I think it's nice that you won't talk about anyone. But listen, Rees, you know my father's giving a ball for the governor and for some of the other dignitaries."

"I hadn't heard about it."

"Well, it's in two weeks and I want you to be sure and come. It'll be good for your practice. You might pick up some more rich patients."

"Why, to be truthful, I have more than I can see now."

"Oh, you must come anyway! It'll be fun."

Rees was aware that this young woman usually got her way, and he found himself drawn to her. His own life had been filled with difficulties and hardship, and something about Elaine Gifford appealed to him. She was a beautiful woman of course, but there was a lightness about her that he liked. "All right, I'll come."

"Good. Now give me some medicine."

"You don't need any medicine. There's nothing wrong with you, Elaine."

"That's right. I just wanted to see you, so don't make me go through this again." Elaine put out her hand and when he took it, she squeezed it. There was an enticing light in her eyes.

Rees shook his head. "I'll come to the ball."

"Good. Now don't forget." Elaine waited until Rees stepped outside the door of her room and she heard his steps on the stairway. Jumping out of bed, she went to the window and stood watching him until he mounted his horse and rode away. Then she cried out loudly, "Nellie, come in here!"

Almost at once the door opened, and a short, heavyset young woman with a pair of direct blue eyes came in with a smile on her face. "The doctor look you over?" she asked.

Elaine turned to stare at her. "Don't be sassy, Nellie."

"There wasn't anything wrong with you."

Suddenly Elaine laughed. "You know me too well."

"Well, he ain't very handsome, is he?"

"No, he's not as handsome as some, but he's tall and I like that. And besides, he's the most popular doctor in Boston. Everybody says so."

Nellie knew her mistress well. She went over and began picking out a dress, saying, "Better a rich husband than a handsome one."

Elaine Gifford stretched, arching her back like a cat, and then she laughed aloud out of sheer exuberance. "He'd make a good husband. He doesn't know it yet, though."

"Oh, Callie, come in. I'm so glad to see you."

Marta Chudzik's face beamed as she pulled Callie into the house. She was a tall woman but well shaped, and her hair was the blackest thing Callie had ever seen. "You must eat with us today."

"How is Peter, Marta?" Callie asked as she removed her bonnet and coat. "Is he any better?"

"Oh, I think so. The medicine Dr. Kenyon gave him seemed to be just what he needed."

"I brought the boys a present."

"You shouldn't have done that."

"Oh, I wanted to. They're such good boys. Is Peter awake?"

"Yes. You go on back to their rooms and I'll fix us some tea."

The small house of the Chudzik's was not fancy but was practical. Callie had spent much time here since the death of Stefan and had become very fond of Marta, Stefan's wife, and their two sons, Jan, who was ten, and Peter, who was eight. She made her way into one of the two bedrooms and at once was greeted by both boys. Peter, who was in bed, shouted, "I'm almost well, Callie!"

"You're not either," Jan said. Both boys had the dark hair and dark eyes of their parents. Jan came over and looked at Callie's basket. "Do you have a present for us?"

Peter said, "It's not polite to ask for presents."

"Well, I always ask for presents myself," Callie said, smiling. She sat on the bed and said, "I brought you a book."

"What is it?" Peter asked at once. He was rather pale after his illness, but Callie had discovered that although he was physically not as strong as his brother, he had an active and inquiring mind. "I love books."

"Well, this is one that Miss Hannah sent you. It's called *Pilgrim's Progress*. It's Miss Hannah's favorite."

"Read it to us now!" Peter cried.

Callie laughed. "All right. We'll start it, but it'll take a long time because it's a long book." She opened the book, turned to the beginning of the story, and began to read. "'As I walked through the wilderness of this world, I lighted on a certain place where there was a den, and laid me down in that place to sleep; and as I slept, I dreamed a dream.'"

"Who is talking in this book?" Peter demanded. He was sitting up now, and his hands were folded over his knees as he clasped them close to his chest. "What did he dream about?"

"Be still, Peter!" Jan said. "You'll find out soon enough."

"Yes, you will. It's a story about a man called Christian, who had to make his way out of some real difficulties."

As Callie continued to read, she was conscious of how different her speech was from what it had been six months ago. Living in constant proximity to Hannah had worked wonders for her, as had the lessons in writing and reading and speech. Callie had been eager to learn, and she had managed to weed out most of her grammatical errors and now hardly ever dropped her *h*'s.

"'I dreamed and behold I saw a man clothed with rags, standing in a certain place with his face from his own house, a book in his hand, and a gray burden on his back. I looked and saw him open the book and read it and as he read, he wept and trembled.'"

"Why was he crying?" Peter said. "What was in the burden on his back?"

Jan suddenly took a pillow and stuffed it over Peter's head. "You be quiet! You always interrupt."

Callie wrestled the pillow away from Jan and managed to settle the two boys down. Peter could not help interrupting and Jan constantly berated him for it.

Finally, thirty minutes later, Marta came in with a tray. "Cakes and tea for boys who have been good. Have both of you been good?"

"I have," Jan said, "but Peter hasn't. He's always interrupting Callie."

"Oh, he hasn't been all that bad," Callie said. "I think both of you deserve some cakes."

"Here. You two boys have your own party. I need to talk to Miss Callie."

"But she's reading the book she brought us," Peter protested.

"She can come back. We need to talk a bit."

Callie followed Marta out of the room, and when they got to the kitchen, Marta said, "There. Sit down. We'll have our own tea party."

The two women sat and almost as soon as they started drinking their tea, Marta shook her head. "I don't know what the boys and I would have done after Stefan died if it hadn't been for you, Callie."

"Oh, it's been mostly Dr. Kenyon and Hannah."

"All of you have helped." She put her hand over Callie's. "You have a kind spirit, Callie. I depend on you so much."

Callie felt her face grow warm and she could not answer. Finally Marta asked about Thad, and Callie said, "Well, he's still with General Washington's forces in New York."

"What's going to happen there?"

"Thad says in his letters that the British are going to attack New York soon."

The two women talked, both of them aware of the voices of the boys in the bedroom. Eventually Marta looked down into her teacup and murmured, "I miss Stefan so much."

Pity came to Callie and she put her hand on the older woman's arm. "It must be terrible to lose someone like that."

Marta stared down into her cup as if it somehow had an answer there for her. Then she lifted her head and tears gleamed in her eyes. "I never had a cross word from him. He was such a good man and I loved him so much."

"And I'm sure he loved you, too."

"It's like . . . it's like part of myself has died, Callie. I wake up every morning and he's in my thoughts. And at night he's the last thing I think of. I don't believe I could ever love another man."

Callie could not answer for a time. Finally she heard a horse approaching and glanced out the window. "Look, there's Rees."

The two women got up and when Rees dismounted, they were there to meet him at the door. "I'm so glad to see you, Doctor," Marta said.

"How's that boy?"

"Oh, I think he's fine."

"I brought them something that may make them happy."

"You spoil them," Marta said and smiled. "Thank you so much for all you've done, Dr. Kenyon."

"Why, nothing at all it is. There's proud I am to be your friend. Now, let me see those young fellows."

Callie followed as Rees went into the bedroom, and at once both boys clamored for his attention. He had brought a boat with a sail which he had carved himself, and he said, "When you get well, Peter, the three of us will go out and I'll teach you to be sailors."

"Did you make that yourself, Doctor?" Marta said.

"Yes, I did."

"It's a beautiful boat."

"How did you learn to do such things?"

"Why, I've built ships all my life, but real ones. It's all my family knows." Rees took out a small leather bag and handed it to Peter. "Marbles for you, and a jackknife for you, Jan."

The boys shouted over the gifts, and then Jan said, "Look, Miss Callie's reading us a book. It's called *Pilgrim's Progress*."

"That's a fine book. One of my favorites. I wish I had time to stay and let Miss Callie read it to all three of us."

The boys immediately sent up a series of cries, but Rees said, "I'm sorry but I have to go."

Callie stepped outside while Rees said good-bye to the boys, and when he came out, he said, "I didn't expect to find you here, Callie. How did you come?"

"Oh, I walked."

"Walked! Why, that's a long way. Are you ready to go?"

"I suppose so."

"Come along, then. Thunder will bear both of us."

"I can't ride in a skirt."

"I'll handle that." Turning to Marta, who was standing at the door, Rees gave instructions about Peter's treatment, assuring her that he was fine. Then he said, "Come along, Callie."

"I'll be back to see you as soon as I can, Marta."

Callie followed Rees, saying, "I can't ride that horse. It ain't — I mean, it's not fitting." She corrected herself automatically and saw the light of approval in Rees's eyes.

"We will go, is it?" Rees grinned. He suddenly picked Callie up and sat her on the horse, with her legs dangling down one side. Then in one swift movement he leaped on behind her.

"We look silly," Callie said.

"What difference does it make how we look? We'll get home this way."

Callie said no more but she was very conscious of pressing against Rees's chest. He had his arms around her, more or less, to hold the reins, and after a time he began to speak. "I wish I was with Thad, doing the real fighting."

Callie turned quickly and her face was only inches from his. "You don't need to do that. You have so many sick people to take care of here."

"Any doctor could do that, but ever since Stefan was killed, I've known I'm going to have to do more than be a doctor. I've got to get into this revolution, Callie."

The two rode silently. Eventually he began to speak of his patients and finally mentioned calling on Elaine.

"What was wrong with her?"

"Nothing, really. I think she just wants attention."

Resentment rose in Callie. "She gets enough of that, doesn't she?"

"I suppose so. Oh, she did invite me to the ball her father is giving for the governor. I'll want you to go, too."

"I'm not going."

"Well, devil fly off, if you're not a touchy one! I thought you'd love to go to a ball."

Actually, Callie wanted to go, but perversely she said, "I'm not going and that's all there is to it."

Rees only laughed at her. "I never saw a girl who could refuse a ball. Maybe you can wear that red dress you bought to wear to church."

"I gave it away."

"You gave it away! Why?"

Callie could not answer. She had such terrible memories of how she had behaved the day she had worn the scarlet dress. "I just did," she said. "I didn't like it."

Rees did most of the talking as they rode along, and when they reached the lighthouse, they saw Matthew come running out. "I wonder what's wrong?" Rees said. "He looks excited. Of course, it doesn't take much to excite Matthew." Rees helped Callie slide to the ground and then dismounted as Matthew came to a halt in front of them. "What is it, Matthew?"

"It's the British — they've beaten Washington at New York!"

"There is sad I am," Rees said. "It's a bad setback for the cause."

"Washington's retreating. I wish I was there with them," Matthew said.

"So do I," Rees said, "although I don't know much about soldiering. Come on inside and tell us the rest of it."

They entered the kitchen and sat down while Matthew gave what news he had been able to obtain. He finally looked up and Hannah, who was standing next to the table, said, "The minister was here. He had heard about it, too."

Rees turned and eyed Hannah. Despite the bad news he suddenly smiled. "The minister comes here a lot these days. He must feel we're great sinners."

"No, he comes to see Hannah," Matthew said.

Rees laughed aloud. "Well, Hannah, I'm glad to hear it."

"Hear what?" Hannah snapped.

"Why, that you have a suitor." Rees turned and winked at Callie and Matthew. "Think how much time and trouble it will save you."

"What are you talking about?" Hannah demanded.

"Well, you'll be getting a couple of youngsters without going to all the trouble of having babies and all that."

Hannah stared at him and her face turned red. "You are an awful man, Rees Kenyon!" She turned and walked out of the room, her back stiff.

"You shouldn't tease her like that, Rees," Callie protested.

"Why, having a little fun I was. He's a fine man."

"Do you think she'll marry him?" Matthew asked.

"There's no telling about things like that," Rees said. "It wouldn't be a bad match for her."

"But does she love him?" Callie asked quietly.

Rees shook his head. "Well, you'd know more about that than I would. Women are the experts in romantic things. Come on, Matthew. We have to repair the fence those blasted goats keep getting through."

After they left, Callie went at once to find Hannah. "Rees didn't mean anything, Hannah. He was only teasing you."

"I know it. I shouldn't have gotten so upset."

"Do you love the minister?"

Hannah turned and smiled slightly, "I think I could, but it would be quite a chore taking two spoiled children."

"You could do it," Callie said. "I wonder what it would be like to be married."

"You'll find out one day. Come now. We have to fix supper."

# Chapter Twenty-Two

"CALLIE, WILL YOU SEE WHO'S AT THE DOOR?"

"All right, Hannah." Callie had been sitting at the table peeling potatoes. Rising, she wiped her hands on her apron and left the kitchen. When she reached the front door, she opened it, and her eyes flew open, for standing before her was one of the most impressive men she had ever seen.

"Oh, excuse me, miss, but I'm looking for Miss Hannah." The speaker was the husky young man Callie had seen several times but had never met. He was well over six feet, and the thin white shirt he wore was overflowing with bulging muscles. His deep chest strained against the fabric, and when he moved his arm, the sleeves swelled with enormous biceps. He had penetrating blue eyes, a square face, and a broad mouth, and when he pulled his hat off, his blond hair fell over his forehead.

"Why yes, she's here. Won't you come in?"

"Thank you, miss."

Callie stepped back and the doorway seemed to be filled with the visitor's bulk. He kept his hat in his hands and was studying her closely. "I don't think we've met. My name is Billy Gaston."

"I'm Callie Summers, Mr. Gaston."

"Pleased to know you."

"Oh, you're here, Billy." Hannah approached them and smiled at the young man. "I suppose you've come for the flip."

"Yes ma'am, I have."

"This is Callie Summers, a good friend of mine."

"Yes ma'am, we've already met."

"Billy's the village blacksmith and a very good one, too," Hannah said.

Gaston shrugged slightly. "You don't have to be very smart to be a blacksmith. Just a little bit smarter than the horses."

"I've never seen a blacksmith at work," Callie said. "You put shoes on horses?"

"Why yes, and I do other things too. You've never been in a blacksmith's shop? That's strange."

"Well, Callie grew up in the city of London."

"Why, there must be a lot of blacksmith's shops there. I have a mare to shoe. If you'd like to watch, it would be fine."

Hannah said, "I have the flip ready."

"What's a flip?" Callie asked.

"You don't know what flip is?" Gaston seemed astonished. "Why, it's the best drink there is."

"I don't know about that," Hannah said, frowning. "It's very strong. Come along and I'll show you, Callie." She led the two into the kitchen, pulled a cloth cover off a massive pot. "There it is."

Callie leaned over and looked inside. "What's in it?"

"Four pounds of sugar, four eggs, and a pint of cream. You beat the cream well and then you leave it to stand two days. Billy asked me to fix him up some."

"I'd like to sample it, if you have any beer," Billy said.

As was true with most people, Hannah kept beer, ale, and rum on the premises. The water was so bad at times that beer was much healthier.

"We'll give you your first taste of flip," Hannah said, pulling down three quart-sized mugs. "You pour these about two-thirds full of beer, Callie."

Callie went to get the beer, and when she came back, she watched as Hannah put great spoonfuls of her mixture into the mugs. When the mugs were almost full, she added rum. "All right."

Billy Gaston picked up one and nodded. "Your first taste of flip, Miss Summers. It's mighty good." He lifted his tankard and drained it without stopping, then shook his head with admiration. "That's the best flip I ever had."

Callie tasted the concoction and found it very strong. She drank almost no alcoholic beverages and the strength of it made her eyes water. "I can't drink all this," she protested, putting the mug down.

"Would you like for me to finish it for you?" Billy winked at her.

"Yes, if you'd like."

Billy guzzled her share of the flip, then put down the mug and wiped his mouth with his sleeve. He was a masculine young man and seemed a bit slower mentally than most other men. "I'm just down the street if you'd like to see me shoe that mare."

"Go on with him, Callie. Matthew and Rees are asleep."

"All right, I will." Callie was always interested in new things. Taking off her apron, she slipped on a coat and bonnet, and soon the two were on their way down the street. Billy Gaston was an entertaining young man with a ready smile, and when they reached the blacksmith shop, he showed her around with great pride.

"My pa was a blacksmith but he died two years ago, so I just took over. This is the mare I have to shoe right here."

Callie said little but she was intensely interested. Young Gaston spoke cheerfully, had a quick wit, and handled the heavy tools as if they weighed nothing. Callie was fascinated by how he drove the horseshoe nails right into the hooves of the horse.

"Doesn't that hurt them?"

"Not if you keep away from the frog."

"The frog? What's that?"

"The tender part of the hoof. You have to drive the nails slant-wise into this hard, horny part. You see? Why, it doesn't hurt a bit." He put the hoof down and rose, then stroked the mare's neck, speaking fondly to her.

"I don't think I'd ever be a blacksmith," Callie said, smiling.

"Why no, I reckon not," Gaston said, turning to face her. "You didn't say where you lived."

"Oh, I live in the lighthouse with the Thomases."

"You mean Thad Thomas?"

"That's him."

"We grew up together."

They stood there talking until finally Callie realized how long she had been there. "I must get back. I've stayed longer than I intended to."

Billy Gaston walked with her to the front of the shop, and when she thanked him for the demonstration, he said at once, "I'd like to come calling on you, Miss Callie, if you wouldn't mind."

Callie laughed. "You don't waste any time, do you, Mr. Gaston?"

"Just call me Billy. No, I don't waste time. Life's too short for that. I mean no offense of course."

She believed him. He had an open face and honest eyes. She could read his admiration for her, but it was different from what she sensed from some men.

He added suddenly, "I've always wanted to go up in the top of that lighthouse."

"Well then, come by some evening and I'll give you a tour as you've given me one."

"Thank you, Miss Callie. You can bet on that."

Callie returned to find Hannah mending socks. Hannah asked her how she liked the blacksmith's shop. She said, "It was very interesting."

Hannah smiled. "Did Billy flirt with you?"

"Not a bit. He was very much a gentleman. He asked if he could come calling on me, and I said he could."

"He's a fine young fellow. Strong as a horse. He'll make a good husband. He's very obedient to his mother."

Callie laughed. "Is that how you judge husbands — by how obedient they are?"

"Well," Hannah said, smiling slyly, "there are other things too."

Rees had been talking with Hannah for some time, and he finally noticed that Matthew was saying nothing at all, which was unusual. The young man stood staring out the window, and Rees asked curiously, "What is it you're looking at out there?"

"It's Billy Gaston."

"Billy Gaston? Who's that?"

"He's a blacksmith, a friend of Thad's." Matthew turned and his face was set in angry lines. "He came calling on Callie."

Rees was surprised and then said, "Why, he can't do that without my permission."

Hannah at once said, "Now, Rees, he's a nice young man. Just leave her alone." She was sewing and looked up from her work long enough to say, "After all, he's the first man she's shown any interest in since she's been here. She's had plenty of opportunities."

"What do you mean, opportunities?" Rees demanded.

"Well, I will be switched!" Hannah said with some spirit. "She's an attractive young woman. Why wouldn't men notice her?"

"But I'm responsible for her. If she wants to have any callers, they can see me first."

"Look at that," Matthew suddenly said loudly. "He has his arm around Callie. He's kissing her!" He suddenly whirled, left the window, and rushed outside.

"Matthew, come back here!" Hannah shouted. But it was too late. "Go out there at once, Rees. Matthew's too impetuous."

Rees got up immediately and left the room. As soon as he stepped outside, he saw Callie standing with a tall, broad-shouldered, solid-looking young man with blond hair. Rees hurried over but Matthew was there first. "You get out of here, Billy Gaston!"

Gaston was taken by surprise, and when he did not answer, Matthew suddenly and without warning struck him in the face. Gaston was too big a man to be moved by such a blow, and he returned it with interest. The blow caught Matthew high in the head, and Rees saw him go down in that peculiar, boneless fashion that unconscious men have. At once anger flew over Rees. He was aware that Callie was remonstrating with the young Gaston, but he did not wait. He bent down to check Matthew and found his pulse even, but a bruise was already beginning to show itself. Rees rose and grabbed Gaston by the arm to turn him around. It was like grasping an oak tree, but Rees was having one of his rare fits of anger. "You bully! What do you mean, coming on this place and beating up people? Get out of here!"

"I'll go when Miss Callie asks me to go."

"Billy, you'd better leave," Callie said with alarm. She would have said more but Rees was in no mood to wait. He yanked Billy Gaston's arm, but it was like pulling at a rock.

"Take your hands off me, sir," Gaston said, his face beginning to turn red.

Unable to move the big man out of his tracks, Rees gave him a tremendous shove. He was a strong man; his muscles weren't bulky like Gaston's, but years of hard labor had strengthened him. The shove caught Gaston off balance. He backpedaled, tripped over a root, and fell headlong. He came up at once, roaring, and threw himself at Rees.

Rees dodged one blow but took another in the chest. It hit him with a chilling effect, driving him backward. When he caught his balance, he waited until Gaston moved in, and struck him in the face. The blow had no effect whatsoever and suddenly Rees was caught in the mouth by a wallop that was a disaster. Even as he was falling, he felt the blood running from his cut lips. He scrambled to his feet, enraged. He was aware that Callie was shouting at the two of them to stop, but it was too late for that. The two men pummeled each other. Rees landed more blows, but every time he took one of the blacksmith's tremendous punches, he felt as if he were being destroyed.

Callie was yelling at them to stop and pulling at them. She saw at a glance that Rees was being beaten to a pulp, and she was crying, "Billy, leave him alone! Stop it!" But the big man was lost in battle fury.

Callie saw him drive a tremendous blow that caught Rees on the forehead and split his flesh just over the eyelid. Without hesitation she looked around for a weapon. The stove wood was stacked neatly in a pile, and picking up a healthy chunk of it, she swung it and caught Gaston on the back of the head. It made a solid clunk, and he grunted strangely and fell forward. He was not unconscious but remained on his hands and knees, waiting for his head to clear.

Callie was furious. "What do you think you're doing, Rees!"

"Me? He's the one!" Rees's face was bleeding severely, and his lips were already starting to swell. He knew he would look like a gargoyle the next day, but Callie was not interested.

Turning her attention to Gaston, who was getting to his feet slowly and feeling the lump on his head, Callie said, "You go on home, Billy."

Billy Gaston was confused. "I'm sorry. I didn't start this."

"I know, Billy. You go on home. We'll talk about it later."

Gaston nodded and then winced at the pain this brought to his head. He looked at Matthew lying stretched on the ground and at Rees's bloody face and shook his head. "This wasn't my doing." He turned and walked away. Callie did not even watch him mount his horse, but she turned to Matthew and knelt beside him. "Matthew, are you all right?" She lifted his head and pulled him to a sitting position. His eyes were opening and he began to twitch.

"Help me get him into the house, Rees. Don't just stand there like an idiot!"

The world was still not quite steady, but Rees managed to pick up Matthew and carry him into the house. Hannah had come out to meet them, and she said, "Put him on the settee." She looked at Rees's face and shook her head. "Now you're the one who's going to need a doctor!"

"Will you be still?"

"Well, that hurts!" Rees protested. Callie was cleaning out the wounds over his eyebrow as he sat at the table. His lips were so thick, he could hardly speak.

"It's got to be cleaned out, and it probably needs stitches."

"Bring me a mirror," Rees said. Hannah brought a mirror and he looked into it. "It'll be all right without stitches. We'll just put some sticking plaster on it. It'll heal up."

Matthew looked much better than Rees. He had a huge, bluish bruise on the left side of his face, but aside from that had taken no damage. "I should have shot the fellow!" he said.

Callie turned and her eyes were cold. "Get out of here, Matthew, and don't let me hear such foolishness!"

"Well, you shouldn't have let him kiss you."

"Didn't I see you kissing Betsy Fetterman just the day before yesterday?"

"That's different."

"Matthew, come along. Leave them alone," Hannah said briskly. She led him away, speaking to him as directly as Rees had ever heard her speak to anyone. He turned to Callie, who was putting away the cloths she had used to wipe the blood from his face. "Callie, you've got to come to me before you ask any men to call here."

Callie looked at him. Anger had etched lines into her face. "Do you ask me before chasing around after Elaine Gifford?"

"That's . . . that's different."

"That's right," Callie said, her tone deadly sarcastic. "You bought me for so many pounds, didn't you? So now I'm your slave." She whirled and left the room.

Rees was hurting. He had taken many blows, all hard ones. His ribs ached and he knew they would for a long time. Getting up slowly, he saw that Matthew had reentered the room. His face was white and Rees knew he had taken a tongue-lashing from Hannah.

"You should take a stick to Callie, Rees!"

"Don't be stupid. You shouldn't have hit that man."

"Well, you shouldn't have, either!"

"I did it because he hit you," Rees said. "It was none of your business."

"It was my fight; you should have stayed out of it!"

"Next time I'll let that elephant pound you to a pulp!"

The two stood there arguing, throwing recriminations, and finally Rees came to himself. "Matthew, really, we made fools of ourselves."

"But —"

"There's no buts about it, boy." Rees by now was cool. He felt terrible, both physically and from knowing he had been wrong. "You're going to have to apologize to both of them."

"Well, what about you?"

"I'll have to do the same thing."

Rees had taken the day off to wait for the swelling in his face to go down. By nightfall he looked considerably better, but his ribs still felt as if he had been trampled by a wild bull. He had stayed out in the woods all day, and when he finally came in, it was well after dark. He entered the house and found Callie alone. "Hello," he said meekly.

"Hello." Callie turned to him and studied his face. "Well, you're going to live."

"Just barely."

Rees saw Callie's tight lips and her half-lidded eyes. He had been composing his speech all day and now he gave it. "I was wrong to hit the young man. He can come to call on you anytime you like."

Callie had been ready for another fight, and now Rees's sudden and unexpected confession and his obvious humility silenced her. Her lips softened and she came over at once to stand before him. "Your poor face," she said softly. "I know it hurts a lot."

"A man who meddles with other people's business deserves what he gets."

Callie put her fingers on his bruised lips. They were still swollen and her touch was cool. "Did you put a cold compress on that?"

"Most of the day," he said. "Didn't help much. Callie, I meant what I said. You have that young man over whenever you like."

"Oh, Rees, I don't care whether he comes or not. He's a nice young fellow, and . . . I just need somebody to talk to."

"You get lonesome, Callie?"

"Of course I do. You're so busy all the time, but I don't have all that much to do, and I don't know that many people."

Rees felt a twinge of conscience. "I didn't know that."

"Well, I never see you, Rees. You're so busy with your patients."

Rees ran his hand over his black hair. He sought words and finally said, "Only a drink I want."

"How about some cider?"

"That would go down mighty well." He took a seat at the table and Callie went to where the cider was kept, poured two flagons, and brought them back. She sat down, putting one in front of him and holding the other.

"I'll have to be more careful," Rees said. "After all, we're family, aren't we?"

Callie had been drinking the cider and now she lowered it. "What do you mean, Rees?"

"Well, kind of like father and daughter we are."

"Don't be silly. We're almost the same age."

"Well, brother and sister, then."

"No, we're not like that either."

Rees did not understand the adamant tone in her voice. "Well, anyhow, I don't care what you say. We are like family." He tried to smile and flinched. "Ow, it hurts to smile."

Callie grinned and covered his hand with hers. "Matthew was jealous, that's why he hit Billy. Why did you jump on him?"

"Well," Rees said slowly, "I guess I was jealous, too. Of course, I was mad when he hit Matthew. I hope I didn't hurt him."

Callie laughed. She had a good laugh. It came from deep inside. "No, I don't think you hurt him much. *I* hurt him when I hit him with the stove wood."

Rees relaxed then, for he saw that her anger was gone. They sat there drinking cider, emptying their glasses. Halfway through another, he said, "There's something I want to do, Callie, and I want you to know about it, because I want you to be involved in everything I do."

Callie smiled widely and something came into her eyes. "Do you, Rees? Then I will be. What is it?"

"It's not enough just to doctor people. When Stefan was killed, a great anger came to me. Oh, there is anger that bites a man and drives him, and I've had that for the British ever since. This is not their land and they will not have it!"

"Are you going to join the army?" Callie asked with a frightened tone.

"No. Don't know if I'd be a good soldier or not."

"You would be. You'd be good at anything you tried, Rees."

"Do you tell me that?" Rees said with surprise. "Well, I'm glad you think so. No, I've told you what I did all my life before I went into medicine."

"Building ships."

"That's right. Now, that's one thing I can do."

"What kind of ships, Rees?"

"There's a new kind of war that I've been hearing about. Silas Moon told me about it and got me interested in it. It's what I want to do." He leaned forward and said, "These new ships — Silas Moon calls them spider catchers. I want to build one and I want to use it."

"What kind of ships are they? I don't know anything about ships."

Rees had been thinking about this for weeks now and had it all in his mind. He spoke earnestly and his eyes sparkled and danced. He looked more alive than Callie had seen him look for a long time.

"There are a lot of British merchant ships that travel along the coast, especially up around New York, taking supplies to the British. They don't have any guns, Callie, so the kind of ship I'll build will be small. It'll have a cannon in the front and one sail, but it'll have oars for maybe twelve to fifteen men."

"But what will you do with such a ship?"

"We'll wait along the coast. When we get word of a merchant ship unescorted by a warship, we'll go out and we'll challenge her to stop. If she doesn't, we'll put some holes in her waterline. They'll have to surrender, Callie, or be sunk."

Rees spoke for nearly an hour, moving his hands around as he gestured eloquently. Callie found herself caught up in it. She was thrilled that Rees had come to her and that he wanted her to be part of his plans. She leaned forward and said, "We can do it, Rees. Let me help you."

"Right, you!" His big hands closed around hers and he squeezed them. "You understand, they'll hang us if they catch us."

"They won't catch us. What will you name the ship?"

Rees's bruised mouth twisted into a smile. "The *Callie*."

Tears appeared in Callie's eyes, and she whispered, "You do have a way with you sometimes, Rees Kenyon — even though it's a dumb old thing you are at times!"

# Chapter Twenty-Three

THE WINTER THAT BROUGHT COLD, SOMETIMES FREEZING WEATHER, and snow that covered the ground like a carpet, did not bother Callie at all. November and December were the happiest times of her life, for she threw herself into building the spider catcher with a fervent enthusiasm. She knew nothing of shipbuilding of course but she learned quickly. As the days passed, she spent every free moment with Rees that he could spare away from his practice, and in truth he stole some of the time, for he too was consumed with an eagerness to strike a blow for the American forces.

Callie watched eagerly as Rees made drawings of the craft, and then accompanied him to various shipyards to buy the timbers, the planking, and the other necessary materials. One of the finest days came when they went to pick out the single mast from a forest that lay near Boston. They spent the day looking at trees and finally selected one, and when Rees felled it, she took her ax and helped trim it. They hauled it back by means of an ox they had borrowed from a neighbor, and when she saw the mast stepped and rising into the sky, she knew a joy she could not describe.

The shipbuilding enterprise was interrupted by Christmas, and it was a Christmas she would never forget. She had started keeping a journal, which she kept hidden from everyone, and her entry concerning that day revealed her excitement.

*December 25, 1776*

*I can hardly write these words because I'm so happy! It has been my first Christmas with a family, and what a fine day it has been! Hannah and I started cooking yesterday, and we got a huge turkey and a lot of other things. Matthew and Rees and I went out to the woods two days ago, cut a tree, and we decorated it with strings made out of pop-corn balls, and we put candles on it. And on Christmas Eve we lit them, and it was so beautiful.*

Callie looked at the page and felt a glow of satisfaction at the improvement she had made in writing. The time she had spent under the teaching of Rees and Hannah had paid off, and she suddenly felt immensely grateful to them.

*We had a fine meal. Thad wasn't here but Matthew was, and we ate until we couldn't eat any more.*

*Something happened this afternoon, and I will write it down. Not that I would forget, for I never will. Matthew had found some mistle-toe, and he put it on the ceiling of the house. I didn't know he had done it, but after we finished the meal, Rees and I were washing the dishes. When we finished, we started to leave the house to go check the oil in the lamps, and suddenly Matthew called out, "Look. You're under the mistletoe." I didn't know what that meant, so I asked, and Rees, who was standing right in front of me, said, "When a man and a woman find themselves standing under mistletoe, they're supposed to kiss." I told him he was making it up, but Hannah was standing there laugh-ing. "No, that's the way it is in this country," she said. "I don't know how it is in England."*

*Well, I had never seen mistletoe or heard of it, and they were all smiling at me. I looked up at Rees, and when I did, I thought of how kind he had been, and I smiled at him and said, "All right. If that's the way things are here." He leaned down, put his arms around me, and kissed me right on the lips. It was only a light kiss, and he didn't try to squeeze me or anything like that. But something happened. It was the first time, I think, that having a man kiss me didn't frighten me a little bit. He's so tall and I know him so well! I felt safe, and that's a feeling I've never known much. He lifted his head and he said, "You're a sweet girl, Callie Summers, and I'm lucky to have you in my life."*

*Well, I couldn't help the tears that came to my eyes, and I didn't know what to say, so I only said, "I'm the one who's lucky to have you, Rees."*

*We went out then and tended to the lighthouse tower, and Rees didn't seem any different, but I was different. I knew that I loved him. I think I've known it for a long time, but I've been so afraid of men, I was scared to even think it. But he's a good man. He would never hurt me. I don't know how he feels about me. He's always talking about how he's like a brother to me, and I think he doesn't really see me as a woman. He thinks of that dirty young girl with the bruises on her face whom he saw the first time in the tavern. But he will see me as a woman. I know he will someday.*

Matthew put down his plane, blew the shavings away, and stepped back to admire his work. "I think that ought to do it."

Callie looked at the gun mount Matthew had been working on. It was two days after Christmas, and she and Matthew had come out early and spent all morning working on the ship. The planking was all done now, and Callie knew every rib in the ship that was named after her. She knew every plank almost and had learned how to bore holes with the long, wooden-handled augers. It was hard work, but she had delighted in it, and then in driving in the hardwood pegs that held the framework to the ribs. Her hands were blistered from working with the caulking. Rees had taught her how to drive bits of oakum, a sort of rough rope, between the planks with a tool called an iron. It too was hard work but finally the last of the oakum had been inserted, and then they had gone over the hull, scraping it and planing it until it was as smooth as possible.

Callie stood in the bow and looked at the gun mount. It amounted to a track that looked like a ladder running from the extreme end of the bow to a brace about six feet back. She did not yet fully understand it, but she knew that the gun would be placed in the very front of the ship, mounted on a little truck with wheels. When the cannon was fired, it would drive the truck back until it was stopped by ropes to keep it from breaking through the brace.

"When will we get the cannon?"

"We already have it. It's a six-pounder. Not too big, but it'll knock the bottom out of any merchant ship that doesn't pay attention to us." Matthew's face was glowing, and he was fully as enthusiastic about the *Callie* as she was.

The two continued to work, ignoring the freezing weather. Callie was wearing some of Thad's old, rough clothes, including his trousers and his heavy boots. She had laughed as she displayed herself to Rees, saying, "I look like a man now."

He'd grinned at her and said, "What a shame to waste a good-looking woman in an outfit like that."

Now as Callie swept up the shavings and talked excitedly to Matthew, she found herself looking forward to the launching of the ship.

"I'm going to make Rees let me go out with the *Callie* when it attacks a British ship."

Matthew laughed and shook his head. "He'll never let you do that."

"He will too!"

"No, he won't."

"I can make him do it."

"He's bigger than you are," Matthew said, laughing. "He'd never let a woman go out into battle like that."

But Callie had made up her mind, and she knew there were certain things she could do to get her way with Rees. She had not had time in her rough life to learn many feminine wiles, but she had picked up a few tricks from Hannah, who could get anything she wanted from either Thad or Matthew. "You've got to be very sweet to get your way," Hannah had said with a laugh. "Cook them some nice things, some good food that they like. Fuss over them. Tell them how smart they are. Pretty soon you can get just about anything."

Callie had distrusted that advice, but after trying it out, she had discovered that Hannah was exactly right. Now as she continued to work on the spider catcher, she thought about how to persuade Rees to allow her to go with him on a mission.

"Hey, look, here comes Rees, and he has Elaine with him."

Turning quickly, Callie saw the expensive carriage that Elaine Gifford used. Rees was driving it and the two were laughing.

Disappointment filled Callie, and when the carriage stopped, she watched as Rees jumped out and then assisted Elaine out of the carriage. As they started forward, her feet slipped in the snow and she grabbed at him wildly. He put his arm around her to steady her, and Callie heard him say, "Do you want me to carry you?"

"Yes! You do that."

Rees picked her up easily and came forward, and when he got to the *Callie*, he grinned, saying, "I have a lazy woman here. Too lazy to walk."

"Put me down, you brute!" Elaine said and struck him in the chest. He set her down and she said, "Well, so this is the great gunship *Callie*." She looked at Callie and smiled. "Are you flattered, having a ship named after you?"

"Yes, I am," Callie said rather stiffly. She knew Rees had been seeing Elaine Gifford a great deal, but she had never trusted the woman. She realized some of her dislike came from the memory of how Elaine had made a spectacle of her when she had walked into the church wearing her flaming red dress. She knew for certain that if Elaine had been the right kind of woman, she would never have allowed her to go in dressed like that.

"So this is it," Elaine said. She studied the *Callie* for a moment and said, "It doesn't look very big."

"But it's fast," Rees said. "We'll put a lateen sail on it. It doesn't take much seamanship to use one of those. We'll have twelve rowers, the strongest men we can get, and all of them dead shots. Matthew and I will be the gunners and we'll have a steersman back on the rudder."

"I can do that," Callie said quickly.

Rees gave her a surprised look. "Why, I wouldn't let you go out on a raid."

"But I want to," Callie said.

"It's out of the question, Callie. Women just don't go into battle. I'd be afraid for you."

Elaine came over then and patted Callie on the shoulder in a condescending fashion. "You'll have to learn when you grow up, my dear, that men will have their stubborn ways."

"I am grown up! I'm seventeen years old."

"Are you really? You seem so much younger. Well, in any case you're a sweet child to help your guardian."

Callie glared at Elaine and her lips stuck out in a mulish expression. Rees saw it and said at once, "I'll tell you what, Callie. We'll be ready to launch probably later this week. You can go out while we break her in. How will that be?"

"Thank you, Rees." Callie said this rather submissively, but a stubbornness had come to rest with her, and she recognized it for what it was. *I'll go on one of the raids or know the reason why!* She stood back while Rees took Elaine around the ship, and finally he and Matthew got into an involved discussion about the problem of how to place the cannon.

Elaine came over and said, "It's a nice little hobby for Rees. He needs something to take his mind off his practice. He works so hard!"

"Yes, I suppose he does."

"You know," Elaine said, "it's fortunate you don't worry about your complexion. You can stay out in this weather. Most of us have to worry, but I don't suppose you care about things like that."

"Not much, Miss Gifford."

"Oh, just call me Elaine." Suddenly Elaine looked down and said, "Oh, your poor hands! They're all blistered. That's another thing." She held up her own hand, pulled off a glove, and examined it. "Most of us work at keeping our hands soft, but you don't worry about that either, do you?"

Callie knew that Elaine Gifford was putting her in her place. She suddenly spoke out, and in her anger she became the young woman she had been back in her London days. "I wonder as how you're tryin' to marry Rees," she said, her voice rough. "Ain't that the way it is?"

Elaine blinked with surprise, for there was such animosity in Callie's face that for a moment she could not speak, but she somehow found it amusing. "Well, it's possible. But if we were to marry, I'd make you a good stepmother. I could teach you how to dress and how to talk."

Callie had a bitter reply ready, but at that moment Rees came back, saying cheerfully, "Well, I suppose we'd better be going back."

"Yes, I think so. It's bitter cold out here," Elaine said. Then she turned to Callie and smiled. "You must come and see me sometime, Callie. Maybe I can help you with your clothes."

"That's a good idea, Callie," Rees said. "You need to get out more." He came over and put his hand on Callie's shoulder, and when she looked up, he said, "I know you want to go on a raid, but I can't have anything happen to you."

Callie glared at him, and the words came out hard and adamant. "I can take care of myself!" She whirled and stalked away blindly.

Matthew grinned. "I don't think you charmed her — like you did Miss Gifford."

"I just don't understand that girl," Rees said. "One minute she's sweet as sugar, and the next she's bitter as quinine."

"Well, come along, and I'll explain the ways of women to you, Doctor," Elaine said.

Matthew watched as the two got into the carriage and headed back. He turned then and went over to Callie, who was standing at the shore, staring out at the gray sea. "Are you ready to go?" he asked. "Can't do anything else on this gun mount."

"All right."

As the two trudged toward the horses they had ridden out to the building site, Matthew said, "You don't like Elaine, do you?"

"No, I don't."

"She sure is pretty and rich. I wouldn't be surprised but what Rees marries her. Then she would be your stepmother, wouldn't she?"

"I'd leave! That's what I'd do!"

"Ah, you don't have to do that, Callie. Wait a couple of years until I make a fortune and then I'll marry you. Think what beautiful children we'd have, both of us being so handsome."

Callie suddenly laughed and struck Matthew on the shoulder. "You don't have any modesty."

"Sure I do. I just keep it under control. Come on. I'm hungry. You can make me something good to eat when we get home."

Only eight days after the *Callie* was launched, Rees got word from Captain Silas Moon that a small British ship, no doubt filled with goods, was making its way along the coast. Moon had winked at him, saying, "Just about right for that dinky little spider catcher of yours. She ain't got no guns and she's slow as molasses."

Rees was electrified. "Right you are, Captain."

"You got enough good men?"

"We have twelve of the strongest, toughest men you ever saw. All of them are excellent shots and can row full-speed for hours."

"Well, good hunting, Doctor. Try not to sink the thing. Imagine if it has any supplies, we can use 'em here in Boston."

"I'm hoping it'll have something that'll help General Washington."

"Well, he needs all the help he can get. He's having to dodge around and hide from the British. And I hear food and uniforms and everything else are scarce."

"I know. That's why I'm doing this," Rees said, and his jaw tightened. "What's the name of that ship?"

"The *Hector.*"

"There she is," Rees said, his voice tight. The *Callie* was anchored in a small inlet and he had a clear view of the sea. He had a brass spyglass and he studied the ship that had appeared. "That's her," he said. "I know it is."

Matthew's eyes danced with excitement. "Let's go get her — and I get to fire the cannon."

Rees laughed. He suddenly felt exuberant. "Right you are, boy!" He turned to the crew, twelve hardened men, all dressed in warm clothing. Each had a musket beside him, having proved his marksmanship to Rees's satisfaction. "All right, men. We have a stiff breeze, so we may not need your oars. But keep your muskets handy. They may put out some sharpshooters when they see us coming."

Billy Gaston, who was the largest of the rowers, picked up his gun and said, "I hope they try it, Doctor." He had become a good friend of Rees and Matthew after they made up their differences, and had helped to recruit the rest of the crew. "Let's go get 'em."

The lateen sail was enough to propel the boat in the strong breeze. Rees had built the *Callie* to ride high in the water so it would glide over the waves. He stood in the bow with Matthew, his eyes fixed on the ship growing larger every minute.

"Do we give them a shot first?" Matthew asked.

"I think so. Load the cannon."

Instantly Matthew picked up a bag of powder and rammed it down the mouth of the cannon. He rammed the wadding down, then the six-pound ball. On top of that he put another wadding to ensure that the ball did not roll free.

Rees took the pick, a long piece of metal with a hook on one end and a sharp point on the other, and punched a hole in the powder bag inside the cannon. He then poured some light powder into the touch hole, letting it fill the base ring.

"Let me handle the linstock, Rees," Matthew begged.

"All right, Matthew. You're the gunner." Rees looked back and said, "Put us just coming straight into the side, Harry."

"Right you are, Captain."

The *Callie* was moving smoothly over the water, so quickly that by that time the *Hector* was only a few hundred yards away.

"Just put the shot in front of her, Matthew."

Using the quoins, Matthew and Rees put a proper angle on the gun, and then Rees said, "Fire!"

Matthew plunged the slow-burning match into the powder, and instantly the cannon roared. It was driven backward until it was caught by the tackle that held it. Matthew and Rees watched and saw a splash just on the far side of the ship.

"That ought to stop 'em!" Matthew cried and immediately drove a sponge down the barrel of the cannon and loaded it again.

But the *Hector* put up no fight whatsoever. Following Rees's orders, all the men had their muskets ready and trained. But a white flag was waved by a man in the bow, and Rees cried out, "We're coming aboard!"

"We did it! We did it, Rees!" Matthew whispered. "I hope she's full of stuff General Washington can use."

They pulled the *Callie* alongside the transport, and the crew held the boat in place and secured it. The *Hector*'s captain, a small man with a pale face, identified himself as Captain Horner.

"We're taking your ship, Captain Horner," Rees announced.

"You're pirates!" Horner cried.

"No, we're the Continental navy, and your ship is seized by order of General George Washington." Rees turned and said, "We'll take this ship back to Boston." He faced Horner again. "You and your crew will be released, Captain, since the *Hector* is not a warship."

Captain Horner was bitter. He longed for just one sloop flying the British colors to appear, but he knew that was unlikely. He surrendered with bad grace, and Rees accompanied him to his cabin, where Rees read the manifest. His eyes brightened. "You're carrying powder. Two hundred barrels of it. General Washington can use that. And muskets too, I see."

"It won't do you any good. You can't beat England."

"Why not?" Rees said. "We beat you, didn't we?"

When the *Hector* pulled into Boston Harbor, a crowd quickly gathered. Rees had sent some of his crew ahead on the *Callie* to alert the harbor master, and Callie was standing there with a host of others. Cheers rose as the *Hector* was eased into the dock, and when Rees and Matthew stepped off, the cheers grew louder. "Hooray for the doctor!" the cries went out. "That's the way to do it, Doc!"

Callie pressed forward, making her way through the crowd. When she reached Rees and Matthew, she threw her arms around Rees and said, "You did it! You did it, Rees! I'm so proud of you. I'm fierce proud."

Matthew said, "I fired the cannon, so I think I'm the hero around here," and Callie hugged him too.

"Come on," Rees said. "We'll have to talk to the officer in charge of the port. These supplies must go to General Washington."

This proved to be somewhat difficult. The port official wanted to claim the ship's supplies and take over the ship itself, but Rees faced him down. "General Washington will get the supplies as quickly as we can get them to him, and there'll be no more argument about it, Major."

Finally, after the arrangements were made, Callie said, "Let's go home. I'm going to cook you a meal you won't forget."

But they were not able to do that, for Elaine and her father appeared and insisted on taking them all to their fine house. Callie tagged along, feeling all the pleasure leave her.

The meal they were served at the Gifford house was fine, but Elaine dominated Rees's time, and Callie was forced to remain silent.

Perhaps the night would not have been completely spoiled if Callie had not seen what took place between Rees and Elaine. She had watched them jealously, and when Elaine left the room, pulling at Rees's sleeve, Callie had grown quiet. Finally curiosity and anger got the best of her. She moved toward the door the two had gone through, and when she opened it, she saw Elaine reaching up to pull Rees's head down. Callie stared at them as they embraced, then she turned and left the house.

Matthew followed her. "Where are you going?"

"I'm going home."

"Well, I'm ready to go, too. Come on, I'll drive you. Get in the carriage."

Matthew tried to carry on a conversation, but he found that Callie was absolutely silent. Finally he asked cautiously, "What's wrong, Callie?"

"I'm fine."

Matthew knew better than this but he had learned something of Callie's moods. He said no more until they got home, and when he pulled up the horse, Callie jumped out of the carriage and ran upstairs without a word.

Matthew stared after her, then shook his head. "She sure is one mixed-up young woman," he said to the horse. "Come on, Bessie. I'll get you unhitched."

# Chapter Twenty-Four

FROM THE DEPTHS OF ABSOLUTE DESPAIR OVER THE MANY DEFEATS by the British, the people of the colonies were brought to the heights of exaltation. The cause was the victory of George Washington and his ill-equipped, ill-trained army at the Battle of Trenton. Against all advice and with no encouragement from his staff, George Washington resolved to strike no matter what the cost. He decided to attack Howe's chain of posts and settled on Trenton. He knew he had to do something. He had to rally the fading cause that men were now leaving by the hundreds. He had to restore the spirits of Congress and of the American people. There was no other choice. The revolution was practically dead and it would take a miracle to revive it.

On December 23, Washington formed his army into ranks. Many of them had no shoes or wore mere strips of carpet tied around their feet. Some left bloody marks in the snow as they stood there while Tom Payne's words were read to them before the attack.

"'These are the times that try men's souls. The summer soldier and the sunshine patriot will, in this crisis, shrink from the service of their country; but he that stands it now, deserves the love and thanks of man and woman.'"

As a rule, words alone will not inspire beaten, worn, hungry men, but somehow these words did, and the soldiers moved to cross the Delaware River, which floated large chunks of ice. Twenty-four hundred men led by Nathaniel Greene and accompanied by Washington would compose the main force. The plan was to strike on Christmas night above Trenton and then press in to attack the city. As they advanced toward Trenton, all of the army, which was formed into two divisions, was enjoined to silence. The soldiers marched noiselessly and steadily, with cruel ice cutting through their flimsy footgear, and at eight o'clock in the morning they attacked the Hessian pickets and drove them in.

The action was short and violent, but Washington and his men were grimly determined. They overran the position and captured nine hundred and twenty Hessians, who were German mercenaries recruited by the British. Twenty-five Hessians were killed and ninety wounded. Two Americans had frozen to death on the march but not one was killed in the battle. Only two officers and two privates were wounded.

After the battle Major Wilkinson rode up to General Washington and announced that the last of the enemy had surrendered. Washington's face shone and he said with a fervent cry, "Major Wilkinson, this is a glorious day for our country!"

And indeed it was a glorious day. The word of the victories at Trenton and later at Princeton swept across the colonies, raising men's hope, and once again the revolution had been saved. Some would call it a miracle, while others would attribute it to the determination of General George Washington.

Rees was jubilant over the victory at Trenton, but when he expressed this to Elaine, he found she was not at all encouraged. They were sitting in the drawing room, and Rees had just risen to take his leave when he mentioned the battle.

"Oh, that doesn't mean anything," Elaine said at once. "It was just a small action. When spring comes, Washington and his pitiful little army will be defeated."

"I'm not so sure of that," Rees said. "I hear that the army is getting larger and becoming more well trained."

Elaine smiled, "You are an optimist and I like that most of the time. But you need to face facts." She saw the expression on his face and at once came to him. "Don't leave yet," she whispered. "It's early." She pressed against him and lifted her face. Rees kissed her and she put her hand on his chest. "You are much too attractive, Dr. Kenyon! I am jealous of all the deceptive women who tempt you — but I do it myself."

"Elaine!"

"No, you'd better go now before I . . . well, I don't quite trust myself with you."

Rees said, "You're a lovely woman, Elaine."

"Well then, come with me tomorrow to the ball that the Williams family is giving — and you can tell me more."

"All right, I'll be here early."

Elaine smiled and after he left, she walked to the window and watched him mount his horse and ride away. "He's so naive, like a small boy in some ways," she murmured. Then she laughed and turned away from the window, thinking of the ball. *Rees Kenyon is a strong man but he doesn't know much about women!*

Hannah brought the water in the heavy saucepan to a boil, then slowly poured in some yellow cornmeal. She stirred until the mix became so thick that the spoon stood up in it, and then she salted it thoroughly. Finally she ladled it into a small bowl, dropped some butter on it, sprinkled on ground nutmeg, and covered it with molasses. She sat down to eat it, but she was soon interrupted when the door blew open. The wind whistled and she rose at once to meet Rees, who came in, slamming the door behind him.

"It's cold out there, Hannah."

"I know it. Sit down. I just made some hasty pudding."

Rees pulled off his overcoat, hung it and his hat close to the fire. Slumping into a chair, he shivered, and Hannah said, "You have a cold, haven't you?"

"It's nothing."

"It could be something. You've got to take better care of yourself, Rees."

Rees started to answer but suddenly he sneezed explosively. Looking up, he grinned faintly. "Well, nothing for it. Doctors don't know how to cure a cold."

"Here. I just made this pudding, and you need to drink as much liquid as you can. Start with this coffee."

Hannah moved about the room, putting items before Rees. She was worried about him indeed, for he worked harder than any man she had ever seen. Finally she poured herself a cup of coffee, sat down, and asked, "How's the epidemic going?"

"I think it's fading, Hannah." He shook his head and said, "Very terrible it is, not to be able to cure people instantly." The smallpox epidemic that had brushed across most of the eastern seacoast had hit Boston hard. Washington had insisted on having many of his troops inoculated, but those not so treated had fallen prey to it. There was still a prejudice against inoculation in the colonies, and it took a stern order from the commander in chief to carry it out.

Callie entered and at once came and stood over Rees. "You look so tired."

"Well, I am tired for a fact."

"You need to take a day off and rest."

"There's no rest for the wicked—or for doctors either."

The two women exchanged glances, both of them worried about the tall man who was slumped before them, weariness in every line of his body. Finally he looked up and said, "It's a little late, Callie, but I'm going to treat you for smallpox."

"Why? I don't have it."

"No, and you're not going to. I've just come from Reverend Bennington's house."

"Why did you go there?" Hannah asked quickly. "Does he have smallpox?"

"No, he had it when he was a child. But his son does."

Hannah immediately grew agitated. "That poor man. He's tried so hard to raise those children without a wife to help him, and now this."

"Yes, and that fool woman who looks after them has left him flat." Rees snorted with disgust.

"You mean that?" Hannah said angrily. "And she's such a fine Christian, so she says!"

"I don't know what he's going to do. The best he can, I suppose."

"Well, I'm going over to see what I can do to help," Hannah announced firmly.

"You can't do that. You might catch the smallpox yourself."

"I've already had it. See this little mark right here?" She pulled her hair back from her forehead, revealing two small pockmarks. "I had it when I was only three years old. I'm going right now."

Hannah put on her coat and bonnet and left with a brief good-bye.

Rees shook his head in wonder. "Well, I will go to my death! When that woman makes up her mind, nothing stops her."

"She's a wonderful person, Rees."

"Yes, she is." Rees stirred himself, pushed the plate back, and said, "All right. Time for my next patient."

Callie protested but Rees would have no argument. "Roll up your sleeve," he said. He fumbled in his bag until he brought out a small glass vial.

Callie obeyed but watched him as he pulled out a sharp-looking instrument. "What are you going to do?"

"I'm going to make a small cut in your arm, and I'm going to put this in it."

"What is that? Some kind of medicine?"

"In a way it is. It's a scab I took off a patient."

"I don't want to do it! I'm afraid."

"It won't hurt you — not much, that is. You'll get the disease just a bit, and it'll leave a mark perhaps on your arm. But if it takes, you won't come down with a bad case of smallpox. You have to do it, Callie." When she hesitated and he saw the fear on her face, he said gently, "We will do it, is it?"

Callie was deathly afraid. It sounded terrible to her but she nodded. "All right, Rees, if you say so." She turned her head away while he made the small incision, and then finally he said, "All right. You'll be a little sick now. If Hannah is away seeing to the minister's son, we'll have to hire someone to take care of the light."

Callie turned to look at him and mischief danced in her eyes. "I'll get Billy Gaston to do it."

"Why, you can't — " Rees halted suddenly and then laughed when he saw she was teasing him. "Away with you before you have a couple," he said, lifting his hand in a mock threat.

Callie caught his hand and said, "You wouldn't hit me."

"That's more than you know."

"No, you wouldn't. I know it." She held his hand for a moment, then he pulled it away. "Now then," Callie said. "You need to lie down and rest for a while. You look like a ghost."

"Why, Miss Hannah!" Lucas Bennington said, surprise moving across his face. He stepped back from the door and said, "Come in at once. It's freezing out there."

Hannah stepped inside and turned to face him. "Dr. Kenyon tells me that Caleb has the smallpox."

"I'm afraid that's true."

"He also told me about Mrs. Jaspers. She left you to take care of him by yourself."

"Well, you can't blame the lady. She hasn't had smallpox and she's afraid of it, as everyone is."

"Well, I've come to do what I can."

"Why, Miss Hannah, you can't do that. You might catch it, too."

"No, I had it when I was a child. Now then. If he's awake, I'd like to see him."

"He was a moment ago. I was trying to feed him something but my cooking is pretty bad."

"Well, I'll take care of that. Now, where is his room?"

"I'll show you."

The two mounted the stairs and Lucas waved for her to the open door. As she went in, he followed her, saying, "Look, Caleb, you have company. Miss Thomas has come to see you."

Caleb Bennington was sitting up in bed. His face was flushed but he smiled faintly. "Hello," he said in a weak voice.

"I've come to see you and see if I can do anything to help until you get well, Caleb."

"Can you cook?"

Hannah laughed. "Yes, I can cook."

"Papa doesn't cook very well." He held up a bowl and said, "Look at this."

Hannah took the wooden bowl, which contained the remains of what appeared to be an egg. It was hard and when she touched it, it did not give. "Why, you can't eat this," she said.

Lucas looked sheepish. "I'm afraid, as I said, I'm not much of a cook."

"Well, I am. I'll wager you're hungry, too. Show me the kitchen." Before she turned, she said, "What would you like to eat, Caleb?"

"Some pudding with sugar on it."

"You shall have it. A quaking pudding coming up."

Lucas and Hannah left the room, and Hannah could not help noticing that the house was a complete mess. She held her tongue but thought, *Mrs. Jaspers must be the world's worst housekeeper. I'll see to that.*

She began to find her way around the kitchen as Bennington stood by helplessly. "Things are a mess, I'm afraid," he apologized. "I've been called out a lot, but it's been hard to get anyone to stay with Caleb."

"Where's Miriam?" Miriam was Bennington's six-year-old daughter.

"The Taylors are keeping her. I didn't want her to get this thing."

"That's very wise."

She pulled down the elements of a quick meal. As she began to prepare the food, Lucas took a seat and watched her. "You do that so easily," he said. "I get out everything there is and then either burn it or spill it."

"You shouldn't have to be doing this. I'll do the cooking and you can go out and do your work, Reverend."

"Oh, I couldn't ask you to do that. It's too much."

Hannah turned and looked directly at Lucas Bennington. "I believe the Lord would have me be a servant, so don't try to talk me out of it. I've heard you stress enough in your sermons how we need to have a servant's heart."

"Well, that's true, but —"

"No more talk about it. You go get yourself shaved. I'll fix a meal and I'll take care of Caleb."

Lucas smiled at her. "I thank you with all my heart, Miss Thomas."

"It'll be just Hannah. You don't use titles with servants." She laughed at his expression. "I'm afraid I'm a rather bossy person, Reverend."

"Please don't call me that. There's nothing reverend about me. I always hated the title."

"What shall I call you, then?"

"Well, when no one's around, my name is Lucas," he said, smiling shyly. "When others are present, I suppose you'll have to use the title, although I hate formalities." He hesitated, then turned to leave. But he stopped at the door and wheeled around to watch her. He started to speak but could not find the words. Finally he left.

Hannah continued to fix the meal. She knew it was right for her to be here, but her anger arose as she thought of Mrs. Jaspers. "Wretched woman! She ought to be whipped." Then she giggled, something rare enough for Hannah Thomas. "Who am I to judge her? Come now. You have a sick boy to take care of and a helpless man to feed!"

The mild case of smallpox Callie contracted from the vaccination came as a surprise to her. She had expected to become deathly ill and thought her face would break out, which she'd dreaded. None of this happened, however. The place on her arm had indeed formed one of the sores, but except for a slight fever there was no other evidence of smallpox. She'd had worse sicknesses many times, and as she healed, she was grateful that she now had some protection against the dreaded disease.

It was after noon and she was sitting at the table peeling potatoes when the door opened and Billy Gaston entered. He shut the door behind him and came near to tower over her. "Got the lamps all filled with oil. Nearly froze my nose off."

"Stand over by the fire and get warm, Billy."

"Don't mind if I do."

"I got some fresh johnnycakes and some of that apple butter you like. I'll fry you up some ham to go with it. Have a seat when you've warmed up."

Billy Gaston watched Callie as she fried the ham. Finally he seated himself at the table. He looked down at the plate loaded with food and grinned. "You must think I'm a hog, eating as much as I do."

"You're a big man, Billy. You take lots of food. Now eat."

As Gaston complied, he spoke around mouthfuls of food, mostly talking about the victory Washington had achieved at Trenton. He asked her once, "Have you heard from Thad?"

"No, not a word, but there's no way for mail to get through."

"I guess that's right." Gaston finished his meal, drained the large mug of coffee, and set it down. When she refilled it, he sat turning it around on the table. The cup looked small in his massive hand. "I don't know how to say this, Callie. I'm not much with fancy words."

Suddenly Callie was alert. She had known that Billy admired her, and now she dreaded what was coming, but she only said, "What is it?"

"Well, I think you're the finest young lady I ever met. I'm wondering if you could ever come to care for me."

"I do care for you, Billy. You're a fine man."

Gaston looked at her steadily. "But not the right man for your husband. Is that it?"

"I'm not even thinking about things like that, Billy."

Gaston looked at her, then shrugged. "I thought that'd be the way of it." He drained his coffee, got up, and moved toward the door. After he put on his coat, he pulled his hat down over his head.

Callie said, "I thank you for asking me, but I'm just not ready to get married."

"Well, you let me know if you change your mind."

He stuck out his hand, and when Callie put her own out, she felt the massive strength of the man. "Good-bye, Billy. Thanks so much for helping with the lighthouse."

"I'll come by tomorrow and fill the lamps again. Don't you be tryin' it," he warned, then he turned and left.

Callie felt an agitation. She moved around the kitchen, cleaning up, but could not get it out of her mind that Billy had asked her to marry him. He was a good man, she knew, a hard worker, and he would be a good match for her. Still, she felt nothing for him except admiration for his physical strength and gratitude for the help he had provided during her sickness.

She sat before the fire awhile, eventually picking up the Bible and reading it. She had become fascinated with the book of Revelation and had asked Hannah about it, saying, "I hardly understand a word of it, Hannah."

"Well, most people have difficulty," Hannah had replied. "But one thing about it — when you get to the end, you find out that those men and women who follow Jesus are the winners. They may not do well in this world but they will in the next."

Callie was reading doggedly, wondering what the beast out of the sea could possibly be, when suddenly the door opened wide and she felt the cold air rush in. She leaped to her feet, crying, "Thad!" She went to him at once and saw that he was thin and completely exhausted. "Come in. You must be frozen."

"I just about am."

"Are you hungry?"

"I'm starved."

"Sit down. There's plenty left."

Thad shrugged off his ragged coat and hung it on a peg and pulled his shapeless hat off and impaled it on another peg. "I'm just about pegged out, Callie," he said.

"Sit here close to the fire while I fix your food."

Thad sat down slowly and then relaxed with a sigh. "Oh, this feels good! I've been cold so long, I don't know what it is to be warm."

Callie scurried about, warming up the food, and when he came to the table to eat it, she sat across from him. "We've been so worried about you."

"Well, my enlistment was up, so I came home. A lot of fellows went home before their enlistment was up."

"Were you at the Battle of Trenton?"

Thad took a small bite of ham and chewed it and shook his head. "That's so good, Callie. We were a bunch of skeletons. Some fellows almost starved to death. Trenton? Yes, I was there — and Princeton too."

"Tell me about it."

Thad ate until he was filled. He related the story of the battle, making little of his own part. Callie listened intently. Finally she asked, "Will you go back and enlist again, Thad?"

"I don't know. I'm too tired to think."

"What am I thinking of, making you talk like this?" Callie said, rising from her chair. "Your bed is all made up."

"I'm too dirty to go to bed."

"That doesn't matter. Those bedclothes will wash." She came over and put her hand on Thad's head. "I'm glad you're back."

Thad looked up, surprised. Her touch had stirred him. He got to his feet and stared at her. "You know, you've grown up, Callie."

"Why, it hasn't been that long."

"Well, growing up is not always a matter of time. When I left here, my memory is that you were kind of a scrawny thing. Now you're a fine young woman."

"I know your soldier's ways," Callie said, laughing. She put her hand on his chest and whispered, "I'm so glad you're back safe. I've got to get word to Hannah."

"Where is she?"

"She's been taking care of Caleb Bennington. He has the small-pox and Mrs. Jaspers left the Reverend flat."

"Sounds like her," he said. Then he yawned. "I may sleep for a week." He put his hand on her shoulder. "That was a good meal," he said. "The best I had in months."

"Wasn't much."

Thad took his eyes off her and looked around the room. "I can't tell you how many times I thought about this place. Just to be here is a miracle." Suddenly he gave a short laugh. "Well, I'm going to sleep on my feet. Good night, Callie."

"Sleep as late as you want. When you get up, I'll fix you anything you want to eat."

Callie watched as Thad walked slowly out of the room. *He looks terrible,* she thought. *I hope he's not going back.*

# Chapter Twenty-Five

As Reverend Lucas Bennington sat behind his desk, surveying the three men who had come unexpectedly into his study at the church, the thought struck him that they somehow made the room seem smaller. All three of them were large men, with Cyrus Bing being the largest of all. He was also the most wealthy of Bennington's congregation and a man accustomed to having his way. He was flanked by Tobias Snelling on his right and Thomas Schultz on his left. Snelling owned much farming property and looked like the farmer that he was. Dirt was under his fingernails, and his hands were as large as hams. Thomas Schultz was as tall as his two fellows but not so meaty. He had made considerable money in the import business, and although the revolution had cut back on his profits, he was still comfortably well off.

The faces of the three men seated before him caused an alarm to go off in Bennington's mind. *They're not here for anything pleasant. As a matter of fact, I've never seen them look so uncomfortable.* Aloud he said, "Well, brethren, I'm glad to see you. Can I fix you some tea?"

"No, Reverend," Bing said at once. "This isn't a social call."

"Oh? Then it's a matter of church business."

"Yes, that's exactly what it is, and it's rather . . . unpleasant."

Tobias Snelling put his dark brown eyes on the pastor and said, "I'm just a plain man, Reverend Bennington, and I think you would appreciate plain speech."

"Why, certainly, Brother Snelling. I think that's always best."

"But we want to do this with a good spirit," Schultz said. He was by far the most cultured of the three, and it was obvious to Bennington that he was trying to find a way to put some unpleasant matter in the best light possible.

"Brethren, I believe we all know each other. I've been your pastor for four years now. You know me and I think I know and respect you. So why don't you just come right out with whatever the problem is."

The three men exchanged glances and by unspoken agreement, Thomas Schultz seemed to have been elected as their speaker. He was a fair-haired man with light blue eyes and had a pleasant enough countenance, but now he was troubled. "Well, Pastor, I'm afraid we're going to have to call your behavior into question."

Instantly Bennington knew what the visit was about. He had, as a matter of fact, been expecting it for some time, but he had no intention of giving the three elders any indication of this. "I'm sorry to hear it. May I have the particulars?"

"It's about the . . ." Schultz fumbled for words here and could not seem to find the right ones, and finally he cleared his throat and looked down at the floor for a moment. "Well, it's about your arrangement with Miss Thomas."

A silence hung over the room, and of the three only Cyrus Bing was able to meet the pastor's eyes. He was a good man but somewhat domineering. "I assume you know what we're talking about, Pastor."

"Miss Thomas has been a lifesaver to me and my children," Bennington said. "After Mrs. Jaspers left me, I had no help at all. As a matter of fact, not a single person from the church came forward to offer assistance."

This statement seemed to trouble Snelling and Schultz, but Bing shook his head, saying stubbornly, "I don't think that's pertinent, Pastor."

"Well, exactly what *is* pertinent?" Bennington asked pleasantly.

"To get to the point, it's not fitting for you, a single man, to live in a house with a single woman," Bing stated flatly. He held himself stiffly, as if awaiting the barrage of protest he expected from Lucas.

"Are you accusing me of some sort of misconduct with Miss Thomas?"

"Oh no, not at all!" Schultz said quickly. "There's no question in any of our minds but that you are totally innocent in the matter."

"Then what is the problem?"

"The problem," Bing said loudly, "is that there is a great deal of talk."

"What are people saying?"

"Why, you know what people would say in a situation like this," Snelling said. He shook his head and added sadly, "People will talk, you know."

Lucas realized he was at an impasse, but still he wanted the three men in front of him to make a direct accusation. He knew of course that they would not. He said quietly, "Was there ever talk when Mrs. Jaspers was my housekeeper?"

"Why no, of course not," Snelling said. "Not a word."

"And why do you suppose that was? I mean, after all, the situation is exactly the same. An unmarried minister living with a single woman."

"That was entirely different!" Bing protested.

"Different in what respect?"

"Why, as to that I can't say," Bing admitted, "but it's true enough."

"I think I can tell you why there was no talk," Lucas said. "It was because Mrs. Jaspers was plain, to put it bluntly, while Miss Thomas is an attractive young woman."

"Yes, that's exactly it," Schultz said quickly. "You understand, Pastor, how these things are."

"Yes, I do understand. You think I'm safe enough with a woman who isn't attractive, but I'm not to be trusted with a woman who is."

"Well, that's not exactly the right way to put it!" Bing said.

"I think it is, Brother Bing." For one moment Lucas was tempted to say what was on his mind, which was that this was exactly the sort of thing that had taken place in Salem years ago when accusations had brought the deaths of innocent people. He knew, however, that it was a useless battle, and being a man of considerable wisdom, he was compelled to say, "I know you are all good men and have my best interest at heart."

"Yes. I'm glad you see it like that, Pastor," Tobias Snelling said, relief washing across his face. "We just feel it would be better if you had another housekeeper. As a matter of fact, Mrs. Jaspers has agreed to come back."

It took all the grace Lucas Bennington had to keep what he felt from showing on his face. Mrs. Jaspers was a quarrelsome woman, always complaining. With her moody ways, she was bad for the children, and her cooking was an abomination — if not to the Lord, then to Lucas and his offspring. Still, he saw there was no alternative. "I must thank you for coming. I'm sorry if I've caused you any embarrassment."

Bing rose at once and his two fellows stood with him. "I'm glad we could settle this matter so easily. We must keep up appearances, don't you agree, Pastor?"

"Oh yes, we must do that." Bennington shook hands with the three men, and when they left, he stood for a moment staring at the books that lined the walls of his office. A bitterness came to him, but he quickly shook it off and said aloud, "Well, Lord, if these messengers are from you, they are certainly effective. Help me to always take this sort of thing with a meek and humble spirit." He sighed then and walked back to his desk and sat down. He tried to concentrate on the sermon he had been constructing when the three arrived, but his thoughts went to Hannah. *How in the world am I ever going to explain this to her?*

For the next three hours Lucas wrestled with his sermon, but he finally gave up. *What right do they have to criticize Hannah?* The thought angered him, and for a long time he simply sat slumped over the manuscript.

Then a startling thought suddenly leaped into his mind: *She's made our house a home!* Getting to his feet, he began to pace the floor, unable to shake off a line of thinking that drove all thoughts of sermon making out of his mind. Ever since Hannah had come, he had been not only grateful for her help but also acutely conscious of her as a woman — a very attractive woman. He was a minister and had learned to keep his guard up where women were concerned — but this had been different somehow.

This difference had troubled him, for old hungers had come to him, hungers he had quickly stifled. But now he could not help but think how she had a warm spirit which made a man feel . . . well, *easy* . . . in a way that was very pleasing. Only once had he touched Hannah and that had been an accident. She had climbed onto a chair to get a bottle of vinegar from a high shelf and had swayed, then cried out as she fell toward the floor. Lucas had been standing beside her and caught her as she fell.

For a few seconds Lucas relived that moment — as he had several times since the incident. As Hannah fell into his arms, for a moment the fullness of her body was pressed against him. She held on to him to steady herself, and in that instant looked up, her face only inches from his. The faint smell of lavender came to him, and for one instant Lucas had known a desire to kiss her.

But he had not.

Lucas could remember clearly how he somehow felt she *expected* him to kiss her. She said nothing, but as she lay in his arms, somehow he knew she felt the same needs he did.

He recalled that it took a distinct effort to step away from Hannah, and now he said aloud rather bitterly, "I must not be much of a man! Too holy to even kiss a fine and attractive woman like Hannah?" The sound of his voice and the words seemed to shock Bennington, but as he stood there thinking, he suddenly straightened and said defiantly, "Some way I'm going to get Hannah Thomas on that chair, and it's going to break. She's going to fall and I'm going to catch her, and then — " He laughed aloud and shook his head. "I sound like a . . . a boy in love!" The words caught him and he said almost angrily, "Well, what's wrong with that?"

Suddenly Lucas found that it was a foolish thing to stand in the middle of his study and think about Hannah. Taking a deep breath, he grabbed his hat and left the study, his face intent. "I have to go home, Lowell," he said loudly to the janitor, who was waxing the pews. "I may not be back for some time!"

Hannah was reading *Pilgrim's Progress* to the children when she heard the door close. "There's your father," she said.

"Miss Hannah, read some more. You're just getting to a good part," Caleb protested.

"At bedtime I'll read some more but now I've got to tend to supper." She tousled the boy's head. A great fondness for the two children had come to her in the short time she had been taking care of Caleb, and she had found that Miriam clung to her in a way that was very appealing. They both missed their mother, although Caleb could barely remember her.

"Well, what's going on here?" Lucas entered the room and came to stand over the children, who were sitting in small chairs he had made for them himself. "*Pilgrim's Progress*, is it?"

"Father, it's so exciting," Caleb said. "It's the best story I ever heard."

"I'm glad you think so."

Suddenly Lucas leaned down, picked up the chair with the boy sitting in it, and spun around. Caleb squealed with delight and when the game stopped, he said, "Do it again, Father."

"No, you're getting too heavy. One of these days you'll pick me up like that. And how is my darling daughter today?" He picked up Miriam and hugged her so tightly that she squealed.

"You're crushing me, Father!"

"I believe I'll do just that," Bennington said, squeezing her a little harder and winking at Hannah. "Give me a kiss." He took the kiss on his cheek, then set the girl down. "Well, I suppose they've been very naughty children today."

"We have not!" Caleb exclaimed. "We've been the goodest children in the world, haven't we, Hannah?"

"For the most part, yes. Now maybe you can talk your father into reading to you while I set the supper out. It's almost done."

Hannah moved to the door and looked back to see that the preacher had sat on the floor and picked up *Pilgrim's Progress*. He began to read it with great expression, waving his free arm around to illustrate the words. *He loves those children and just becomes a child with them. He's not like any man I've ever known.* Turning, she went into the kitchen and began to pull the meal together. When it was ready, she leaned into the hall and called, "Everyone come on. It's time to eat." She heard the scuffle of feet and the children came in, followed by Lucas. They all sat down and bowed their heads, and Lucas prayed a brief prayer of thanksgiving. Then he said, "This smells delicious and I bet it tastes better."

The meal began with soup and was followed by fish that was white and flaky. After this there was a joint of mutton and vegetables and fresh baked bread. They all drank cool, sparkling cider which had been brought up from the cellar. Finally for dessert there was freshly made custard.

"I'm going to weigh three hundred pounds," Lucas said, groaning. "You are too good a cook, if there is such a thing, Hannah."

"You'll never get fat. You're one of those men who'll stay trim even in their old age."

"How do you know that, Hannah?" Miriam asked. She was a very curious child and spent much of her time asking questions.

"Oh, I'm very wise, Miriam. I know all about what people will be like."

"What will I be like when I get big?" Caleb demanded.

"You'll be handsome and very, very smart."

Caleb looked at her and said, "Well, I already am."

Lucas burst into laughter. "You're not overcome with humility, Son."

"But he's right," Hannah said quickly. "You can't deny that."

"What about me?" Miriam asked, her eyes on Hannah. "What will I be like?"

"You will be very, very beautiful and everyone will love you."

"Not everyone," Miriam said. "Some people don't like me already."

"Who doesn't like you?" Lucas asked. "Tell me his name."

"John Ferguson doesn't like me. He says he doesn't like anyone with blond hair."

"I think I'll have a talk with that young gentleman. He needs an education in manners."

Hannah sat there and enjoyed the talk that went around the table. Obviously, the two children were precocious. They had been raised without a mother for the most part, but they had such an adoration for their father that it was plain to see. Finally the meal was over, and Lucas took the children to sit before the fire. He read some more of *Pilgrim's Progress*, explaining it to the children, while Hannah cleaned up the kitchen. Finally she joined them, and the four of them sat there enjoying the reading.

"It's nice to have a preacher read the story to me," Hannah said. "I'm getting a lot out of it that I missed."

"It's always been a favorite of mine. It's good of you to bring it to the children."

"They love being read to so much. They are going to be great readers themselves. They're already reading well for their age."

"You've done a lot to help them. I'm afraid I haven't had time for it."

"And Mrs. Jaspers doesn't care for reading," Miriam said.

"She can't cook, either," Caleb added, making a face. "Her potatoes always taste like dirt."

"Don't say things like that, Son," Lucas said.

"Well, they do. I heard you say so."

Hannah giggled. The sound amazed Lucas; he had never heard this kind of laughter from Hannah. He grinned sheepishly and muttered, "Well, they do taste like dirt. Now let's get on with the story."

"I always think it's a major victory to get those two in bed without a battle," Lucas said. He was sitting across the table from Hannah. The two of them were drinking tea, and Hannah felt pleasantly relaxed, but she noticed that Lucas seemed rather tense. She had learned to read his moods and knew he would take his time before sharing his problem.

"They're lively, aren't they?" she said. "I'm glad Caleb recovered without getting badly scarred."

"So am I, and now that we've had Dr. Kenyon vaccinate Miriam, she ought to be safe, at least from smallpox."

The two sat there talking, and to her surprise he began speaking of his wife. He had seldom mentioned her, but when she had remarked that the children missed having a mother, it seemed to trigger something in Lucas's thoughts. "She was such a good woman," he said simply. "I was fortunate to have her as long as I did."

"How did you meet her, Lucas?"

Hannah listened as he spoke of courting the young woman he was to marry and then of how happy they had been together. He fell silent and looked down into his cup. Finally he lifted his eyes and said, "She was a handmaiden of the Lord and it was hard to give her up."

"What was she like?"

"Why, she was very . . . solid, you might say. She arranged things so well." He thought for a moment and said, "She was such a fine woman but she had little imagination. Not like — "

Hannah smiled. "Not like me?"

"No, she wasn't like you in that respect."

"I suppose I have too much imagination."

"Not at all," Lucas protested. "You have a childlike spirit and that's refreshing in this world." He hesitated, then said, "I can't tell you how much I appreciate and am grateful for your help, Hannah. I don't know what we would have done without you."

Hannah felt a warmth then, but she put her eyes on him and said, "I'll be leaving, Lucas."

"Leaving?"

"Yes. I think it's necessary. I heard about the elders' plans to meet with you."

Anger touched Lucas Bennington. "Who told you?"

"You know it's impossible to keep anything secret in a small town. Thomas Schultz told his wife, and she told her sister-in-law, and her sister-in-law told me. I think she enjoyed it."

"Hypocrites!" Lucas blurted. "Why can't they mind their own business?"

"I don't think they're entirely wrong," Hannah said quietly. "I've felt for some time now that I should have left earlier."

"I suppose you're right. I've known it, too, Hannah, but I hated to see you go." He suddenly put his hand over hers. "You've been so good with the children. They love you as if you were their mother."

Conscious of his strong hand on hers, Hannah did not move. Something had been growing within her since she came to this house, and now she knew it was inextricably tied up with this man. She was alive to the shadows of his face, to the way his mouth turned and the way his blond hair fell over his forehead. She suddenly met his eyes and saw the understanding that had given him a great gift. She knew he had the gift of binding people to him, and in that still moment, with his hand resting on hers, she knew there was something in this man she had not felt for any other.

Standing up quickly, she said, "I'll be going tomorrow, Lucas."

But Lucas did not move, for he was watching her in a way she did not understand. And then suddenly he asked, "Hannah, have you ever thought of me as a man you might marry?"

A quick intake of breath marked the shock that Lucas's words sent through Hannah. His words suddenly made her recognize her loneliness. She had Thad and Matthew, but a woman needs more than this, and she had become more conscious of it. Living in this house, taking the meals with Lucas and his children, planning together things that had to be done — more than once the thought had crossed her mind, *Why, we're behaving like a married couple.* She had put it out of her head instantly, and now as he stood awaiting a reply, she knew she could only be honest with him

"Yes, Lucas, I have thought of you like that."

Lucas stepped forward and reached out his arms, and she knew he was going to kiss her, but she put her hands on his chest and said firmly, "You can come calling on me, Reverend Bennington."

She saw the surprise flare in his eyes, and she added, "This is not the time nor the place, and you know it."

"You're right," Lucas said at once. "But no other woman has ever stirred me as you have. I've come to think of you lately, Hannah, with fear."

"With fear? Fear of what?"

"That I might lose you."

Faint color stained Hannah's cheeks, and she held him with a glance that was half possessive. At that moment something whirled rashly between them, and she knew that it was time indeed for her to leave.

"I expect to be courted in a most circumspect manner, Reverend," she said, and suddenly her eyes danced. "Perhaps you could learn to come and stand beneath my window and play love songs on a guitar."

"I doubt if I'll do that, but I will come, Hannah."

"You'll have to convince the elders that your intentions are honorable."

He took her hand then, and again she felt the strength of this man. "They *are* honorable, for I've come to care for you."

These were words Hannah had wanted to hear for a long time and had not realized it. Now as she stood there, her hand in his, she felt something come together in her heart and in her mind and in her life. She had felt like a bell waiting to be struck, and now she felt like a woman complete as never before.

Rees walked along the side of the *Callie,* running his hands along the planking. He turned to Thad, who had accompanied him to the ship, and said, "Were you surprised when Hannah came home?"

"No, but I was surprised when Reverend Bennington came calling on her."

"Why were you surprised?" Rees asked. "She's an attractive woman."

Thad pulled his coat around him. The March breeze was cold and whipped the water into a froth as it rolled up on the beach. "I know that, but it just comes as a surprise. You never think about a preacher being romantic." He grinned and added, "But I've got to admit that he's as much in love as a man ought to be."

"They'll have a good marriage if he ever asks her."

"I think they're going to work that out."

"It was a dangerous thing, an attractive woman and an attractive man staying together in the same house."

"Oh, come on, you know neither of them would ever do anything wrong."

"There is foolish you are, Thad. David was a man after God's own heart, but he fell because of a woman."

Thad gave Rees a quick look. "Well," he said, shrugging, "it's over now."

"While we're talking of it, I'll have to warn you about Callie."

Suddenly Thad gazed directly at Rees. "What is that supposed to mean?"

"You're both living in the same house, and I want no familiarities."

Thad shook his head, saying in despair, "You're getting to be a blue-nosed Puritan. You have nothing to worry about."

"I want it clearly understood. There'll be nothing between the two of you."

"Of course not. Listen, Rees, I came out here to talk to you about this ship."

"Yes? What about her?"

"Well, you're doing so well with her. You've taken three prizes now."

"That's right. I'm thinking about building a larger ship. One that could go faster and have more guns. We had to pass up two ships because they had cannons, merchant ships though they were."

Thad's eyes lit with enthusiasm. "I want in on it. You and me and Matthew. We could do a lot against the British."

"You won't be going back to the army?"

"I think I can do more for General Washington and the cause this way."

"All right. If that's what you'd like, Thad, we can always use a good man."

The two talked over the arrangements. Thad had some money put back, and he spoke with enthusiasm of building a larger craft.

When Thad finally went back to the house, the first person he met was Callie. He took her hands and said, "Guess what? We're going to be partners, Rees and I."

Callie at once said, "Oh, that's wonderful, Thad!"

"But he warned me that you and I could not have any romancing."

"Well, of course. Why did he say that?"

"I think he's jealous of you."

"No, never that."

"I think he is. Well," — he leaned forward and kissed her on the cheek — "there's one kiss he won't get. Oh, Callie, I think it's going to be fine!"

Callie laughed. "You're just like a boy with a new toy."

"I know, but it's going to be wonderful!"

# Chapter Twenty-Six

NO MAN EVER ROSE IN THE BRITISH NAVY TO THE RANK OF ADMIRAL without learning how to play the game of politics, and Admiral Thomas Graves well understood that being a good sailor was not enough to ensure one's success in the Royal Navy. Now as he sat in the cabin of his flagship, the *Apollo,* he knew he must handle his visitor with great care. Reaching out, he let his fingers rest on the letter from Lord George Germaine, which in veiled language commanded him to give Sir Edward Masters any possible assistance that lay in his power. The letter was couched in the flowery terms so typical of Germaine, the minister of war, but it was a shadowed warning as far as Admiral Graves was concerned.

"Well, Sir Edward, I'm glad to see you. What can I do for you?"

"You can stop those accursed Americans from seizing my ships!" Masters was a tall, broad-shouldered man of fifty with salt-and-pepper hair and a pair of frosty blue eyes. He was wearing a dark green suit of fine wool with an overcoat that came below his knees. It was worn open to reveal a dark green waistcoat buttoned from top to bottom, and the ruffles of a white silk shirt showed at the neck and wrists. It was the dress of a wealthy man, and Sir Edward Masters was that indeed. He was also a power in British politics, holding a seat in the House of Lords, and it was reputed that he had the ear not only of the king but of Germaine, which was even more significant.

"I did hear that you had lost a ship, Sir Edward. I regret to hear it."

"Lost *a* ship? I've lost *four* ships captured by those bloody pirates!"

Carefully Admiral Graves said, "We have a large coastline to patrol, and you understand it's very difficult."

"I understand I've lost four ships, and I understand that George Germaine has promised me that I will lose no more of them. And," Masters said loudly, "I understand that it is your responsibility to see that the minister's wishes are carried out."

If Graves had intended to smooth this over with words and promises, he gave up that idea instantly. Sitting up straighter, he said, "It will be difficult, but I will see that as many of your ships as possible have an armed escort."

Masters shook his head, his face florid with suppressed rage. He loved money, and to lose four ships had touched him where he hurt most easily. "The last three were taken by something like a rowboat."

"Yes, I believe the rebels refer to them as spider catchers."

"To have a ship taken by a craft like that . . . But I can't arm all my vessels. It's your responsibility, Admiral. I trust you take this seriously."

"Yes, I certainly do. If you will give me a little time, I have a plan that I think may rid the waters of these so-called spider catchers."

"The boat that stole the last two, according to the report of one of my officers, was called the *Callie*. An abominable name! I am especially interested in seeing that crew hang."

"I will be equally anxious, Sir Edward. You may depend on it."

"Very well. I will expect to hear from you shortly. Good day, sir."

"Good day, Sir Edward." Graves watched as the burly man left his cabin. Then he turned to stare out the stern windows, which gave him a view of New York. He thought how pitiful the city looked when compared with London. Nothing but a collection of stubby houses sending up thin tendrils of smoke, a few commercial buildings, and a harbor filled with ships, most of them British warships. He stood still for a long time, his brain working quickly, and finally the plan he had begun to toy with seemed to fall into position. He turned and walked to the door. When he opened it, he said to the marine stationed there, "Pass the word for the first lieutenant."

"Aye sir."

Graves sat down at his desk, and when a rangy lieutenant walked in and saluted, he said, "Towers, we're going to have to put a stop to these small craft that are capturing merchant ships."

"That may be difficult, sir."

"I have a plan and I'm putting you in charge of the operation. It might mean a promotion for you if you're successful. Certainly a mention in the dispatches."

Towers' eyes danced and he said, "It will be a pleasure and a duty, sir. What is your plan?"

"Sit down and I'll tell you."

"Thad, I wish you'd go outside and find some work to do." Callie gave an exasperated look toward Thad as he sat in a chair tilted back against the wall. He had come into the kitchen over an hour ago, and she had gotten almost nothing done since. Now she stood before him with her cheeks flushed, and Thad took her in with a steady gaze. Ever since he returned from the army, he had hung around the house, and when she had rebuked him for not spending more time at his gun shop, he had simply replied, "Well, Matthew takes care of that. I'm the weary veteran. I have to take care of myself."

Now he said, "My feelings are hurt when you talk like that, Callie. I have very tender feelings, you know."

Callie sniffed. "They're about as tender as the anvil in Billy's blacksmith shop."

Thad let his chair down, put one elbow on the table, and placed his chin in his palm. "I'm sorry, but I always find it's more pleasant to look at a pretty woman than to repair an old, rusty musket. Always been that way. I don't understand it." When he saw her grow rosy, he noticed that she was becoming quite a woman. She wasn't smiling at him exactly, but the thought of a smile hinted at the corners of her mouth. Thad had shrugged off Rees's suggestion that he might try to make love to this girl, but he had become more aware of her every day since coming home. Now he looked with approval on Callie. Her face seemed to be a mirror that changed often. She had a self-sufficiency and was usually on guard, but lately that seemed to have changed, and he flattered himself that he was part of the reason for it. He had discovered that there was a gentleness beneath the external behavior, and he had come to admire Callie, not as a half-grown girl but as a woman, with a woman's beauty and inner charm.

Getting up out of his chair, Thad moved around the table and stood close beside her. "What are you fixing there?" he asked.

"Raspberry flummery."

"That sounds good. Is it hard to make?"

"Why do you care? You're not going to be fixing any."

"I might. My wife might like it. I might have to be very careful to make her happy."

"I feel sorry for a woman who has to put up with you."

Callie finished washing the raspberries, and she put them into a pan filled with water and set it on the stove, Thad standing close to her the whole time, carrying on a running conversation. While the raspberries were cooking, she measured out a cup of sugar, a half teaspoon of salt, and six tablespoons of cornstarch into a bowl and stirred them with a fork. She added the sugar mixture to the cooked berries, stirred them, and then suddenly felt his hands on her waist. Quickly she turned. "Thad —"

"Now, Callie, don't get upset with me. I just think that from time to time good friends should show each other a little appreciation — in a physical way."

Callie suddenly laughed. "You get your grubby hands off me, Thad Thomas! I know your ways."

"No you don't," Thad said, making his face as sober as possible. "You don't know how I've suffered. Women just don't understand me."

Callie enjoyed his teasing. "I'll just bet you've suffered! Did that fat witch down at the White Eagle Tavern make you suffer while you were chasing around after her?"

"She's not really fat. Just pleasingly plump. But I don't count her. I'm interested in real women — like you."

He pulled her closer, and Callie allowed herself to be embraced. "I'm going to tell Rees on you. He warned you about fooling with me."

"Who says I'm fooling?" Thad protested. He had started out in a teasing manner but suddenly he was enticed by the pout on her lips. He leaned forward and kissed her, and she did not fight him.

"Now, you've mauled me enough. Go outside and find something to do."

"Don't you have any romance in your soul?"

"Not for you, Thad Thomas. You go out and chase those tavern wenches."

"I gave that up. That was in my younger days."

Callie laughed. "That was last Tuesday, that's when it was."

Suddenly the door opened and Matthew came in. He stopped abruptly, seeing Thad holding Callie in his arms, and said, "Thad, you'd better stay away from Callie. You know what Rees said."

Thad frowned but Callie moved away. "That's right. What are you out of breath for, Matthew?"

"It's a ship! We got word that she's coming down the coast. Not too big. Fat and wallowing. Probably loaded with great stuff. We've got to take her! Where's Rees?"

"He went to Charlestown to set a leg," Thad said. His eyes were bright and he asked, "What about that ship?"

"Why, it'll be nothing for us, judging by what Captain Moon said. She'll be passing right by the cove where we hid the *Callie*. All we have to do is go out and fire a couple of shots and we'll have her."

"You can't go without Rees," Callie said quickly.

"We'll have to," Thad said. "He may not be back for hours. That ship will be gone by then." He looked at Matthew and said, "How long did Captain Moon figure we'd have?"

"He said she ought to be along in an hour, maybe less. He was real excited about it, Thad."

Thad nodded. "All right," he said authoritatively, "we'll do it."

Suddenly Callie said, "Let me go with you."

"Not a chance," Matthew said at once.

"Please, Thad. I won't be any trouble and according to Matthew, it'll be easy."

Thad shook his head firmly, but Callie came to him and put her hand on his chest and looked up with a pleading expression. "Please, Thad, let me go. I'll be so nice to you if you will."

"You will?"

"Yes, I will. Can I go?"

Thad laughed suddenly. "You are a sight, Callie Summers. Come on. Get dressed in something other than that pretty dress."

"You can't let her go!" Matthew exclaimed. "You know what Rees said."

"This is different," Thad said with a shrug. "From what you say, it'll be like eating a piece of cake." He gave Matthew no chance to argue. Turning to Callie, he said, "You have four minutes to change."

Callie dashed off but Matthew was worried. "What if something happens, Thad?"

"What's going to happen? You've taken four prizes. Nothing happened with any of them, and this one sounds the easiest of all."

Matthew shook his head. "I don't like it."

"You don't have to. Now, tell me more about the ship."

Callie crouched in the center of the ship, pulling one of the oars. Across from her Billy Gaston was pulling his. He had been shocked to learn that she had been permitted to go, and now he turned to her and shook his head. "You don't need to be here, Callie."

"Well, I am here and nothing's going to happen."

"That's right," Thad said. He was steering the *Callie* as it made its way toward the transport moving sluggishly ahead of them. The wind caught their sails, giving the spider catcher extra speed and causing the craft to close the distance smoothly. "Look up there. Only three men on deck and no guns at all."

The men on the *Callie* well knew the drill, and one of them trimmed the lateen sail so the *Callie* drew even with the transport. There were now four men on the deck of the bigger ship, all sailors, staring at her, and Matthew aimed the cannon and set it off. It exploded with a roar and the shot plunged directly ahead of the other ship.

"That's the way, Matthew," Thad said, laughing. Then he stood up and said, "All right, you fellows, take in sails. You're the property of the Continental Navy of the United States."

Thad had no sooner spoken than suddenly armed men appeared. They had evidently been crouching down, and Matthew yelled, "Look out! They have a cannon behind that rail!"

Everyone in the boat saw two parts of the rail suddenly disappear and the blunt noses of small cannons suddenly appear.

"It's a trap!" Thad yelled. He threw his weight against the rudder and said, "Put her over! Put her over!" The *Callie* wheeled, making a sudden turn, but even as she did, the blast of the enemy cannons rent the air. The *Callie*'s occupants heard the hiss of one missile as it traveled over their heads and struck the water a few yards beyond them. Thad was screaming, "Row! Row for all you're worth!"

He need not have screamed, for everyone at the oars saw their danger. The cannons roared again, and this time a geyser of water erupted so close that it threw water over Callie and the others in the boat. She was pulling on her oar as hard as she could, her heart thumping.

"I knew you shouldn't have come!" Matthew cried. He turned to shout, "If you'll turn us broadside, I can get a shot at her, Thad."

"We can't match them. Look at those musket men. They were waiting for us."

Musket balls began to strike the *Callie*, and a man directly in front of Callie suddenly gave an unhealthy cough, stood up, and fell over. Blood was pumping from his throat and his feet were kicking. Callie stared with horror as his blood mingled with the water in the bottom of the boat.

"Keep rowing!" Thad cried. Matthew left the front of the boat, picked up the fallen man's musket, and began firing, quickly reloading between shots. He was a good marksman but the distance was growing. Musket balls were hitting the water all about the *Callie*, but they were almost into the cove.

"They can't get us once we reach shallow water," Thad yelled.

His words put new heart into the rowers, and as they passed between the two points that held the shallow cove, suddenly Callie felt hope. She was facing the British ship and could see the puffs that the cannons made.

Matthew was still firing the musket. Suddenly the mast cracked and fell over.

The sail collapsed, covering some of the rowers, and Thad yelled, "Get that canvas out of the way! We'll have to row the rest of the way in!"

By the time the sail was cut away and moved, Callie saw that the enemy ship had lowered a small boat. Thad shouted, "We've got to get away. They're sending a party after us!"

Callie turned to see that another of the sailors had been hit. He was struggling to row with one arm while blood flowed down the other. She pulled with all her might, but the small craft pursuing them was growing close. She could see the smoke from the muskets as they fired away.

The *Callie* seemed to move very slowly, and the musket balls struck with a deadly regularity. Callie used every ounce of her strength, but the enemy boat was manned with strong sailors, and they were very close now.

Suddenly Matthew yelled, "All right, we're here! We made it!"

Thad said, "Grab those muskets. We may have to make a stand."

Callie felt the bow of the *Callie* crunch against the rocks on the shore and at once stood up. As soon as she did, however, she was driven backward. She did not lose consciousness, but she lay flat on her back, and when she looked down, she saw blood welling out high in her chest.

"Callie!" Thad yelled. He jumped over a seat and crouched over her, his eyes fixed on the swelling stain of crimson. "Everybody out!" he yelled as he picked Callie up. Matthew and the others began leaping out of the boat into the shallow water. Billy Gaston said, "Give her to me!"

Callie was losing consciousness now. She saw Billy Gaston's face and felt she was being lifted into the air. Then she heard Matthew say, "Thad, she's been shot in the heart!"

A great wave of darkness seemed to envelope Callie. She felt herself sinking into it, and then the pain exploded in her chest and she knew no more.

# Part

# -5-

# Chapter Twenty-Seven

"AND CALLIE WENT WITH THEM? YOU CAN'T MEAN THAT, HANNAH!"

Rees had stepped inside the kitchen expecting to find Callie there but had been greeted by Hannah, who had told him in a flustered fashion that Callie had gone on a raid with Thad and Matthew. "I tried to get her to stay here but she wouldn't listen to me."

"You should have made her stay here, Hannah!"

"How could I do that? She's a grown woman."

Anger raced through Rees and he doubled up his fists unconsciously. "And Thad encouraged her, I suppose. Did you kick him for that, Hannah?"

"No, I didn't."

"I should have been here!" Rees said bitterly. He began to pace the floor, then suddenly turned and said, "Well, when did they leave? What sort of ship was it?" He listened as Hannah related what little knowledge she had, and then he snorted with disgust. "Wait, you, until I get my hands on Thad!" He whirled abruptly and walked out of the house.

Hannah watched him through the window and saw him pacing back and forth. His face was set with anger and she shook her head. "He's right," she whispered. "It was a foolish thing to do."

For nearly an hour Rees paced. Once he almost mounted his horse to go down to the beach, but there was no telling when the ship would come back or indeed if they would come back to that particular spot, for there were other coves they sometimes used. Heavily he went back inside the house and at Hannah's urging ate a little. Finally he rose from the table and sat in a chair that faced the window. He was very tired, and despite his anxiety he dozed off into a fitful sleep. The sound of Hannah's voice awakened him. "Rees, they're coming!"

Rees came out of his chair and stared out the window. He saw Matthew and Thad sitting in the front seat of a spring wagon. Billy Gaston rode alongside the wagon on a chestnut gelding, but there was no sign of Callie. "Where's Callie?" he demanded. Without waiting for an answer from Hannah, he stepped outside the door. He called out, "Where's Callie?" And then further words were cut off as he saw that both men were stricken. Matthew's face was pale and Thad gave Rees a haggard look. Matthew pulled the team up and Thad jumped off.

"It's Callie," Thad said hoarsely. "She's been shot."

A coldness seemed to flow over Rees then, and when Thad turned to the bed of the wagon, he saw the form of Callie. She was wearing some of Matthew's old clothes, and Rees saw that the front of the shirt she wore was wet with bloodstains. His heart seemed to close up, but he tried as best he could to shove his feelings away. "How long ago was she shot?"

"It's been nearly two hours," Thad whispered.

"We tried to stop the bleeding as much as we could. I thought she was going to die," Matthew said.

"Let's get her into the house."

Ten minutes later Rees was standing by the table, over which Hannah had placed a clean sheet. He and Thad had carried the limp form in while Matthew ran to the other room to get an end table for Rees's instruments. Now Rees stood looking down into Callie's pale face. Quickly he opened the shirt and exposed the wound area.

"Is it bad, Rees?" Hannah whispered.

"She's been shot in the chest. Of course it's bad." Anger burned in him, and his eyes, as they fixed themselves on Thad, were hot. But he forced himself to put that aside for the moment. "I'm going to have to operate," he said. He studied the wound more carefully, aware that Billy Gaston had come into the room. Hannah stood across from Rees, her hands clasped tightly together. "Can you help her, Rees?"

"That ball will have to come out." He picked up his bag, grabbed an instrument, and began probing the wound. When he found the ball, he shook his head, his lips pressed together. "It struck the third rib," he said. "It's awkwardly lodged. It's going to be hard to get it out of there."

"What can I do, Rees?" Hannah asked.

"You'll have to help me with the surgery. When I make an incision, there'll be a lot of blood, and you'll have to stanch the flow. Can you stand it, Hannah?"

"I can do it, but God will have to help me."

Thad asked, "Is there anything I can do?"

Rees turned and looked at Thad and Matthew and Billy. "You three will have to hold her down in case she regains consciousness. She's got to be kept absolutely still, and I've got to be fast. She's already lost too much blood. Let me get my things ready."

He quickly arranged his instruments on the end table and then checked Callie's pulse. "Her pulse is weak. I'm afraid for her," he said.

"Get the ball out, can't you, Rees?" Matthew pleaded. "Why did we ever let her go?"

"That's a good question," Rees said bitterly. "Both of you are fools!" He would have said more, but he shook his head, knowing it was useless. "All right. Billy, you come up here by me. You've got to hold her shoulders there no matter what she does. The pain may awaken her. You mustn't let her move."

Billy swallowed hard but came forward. His blacksmith's muscles rose under his shirt as he put his hands on Callie's shoulders.

"Like this, you mean?"

"Just like that." Rees positioned Thad and Matthew to hold Callie's lower limbs, and then he turned to the instruments. "We've got to do it right now. That wound could get infected and she could develop a fever. I'm afraid the ball carried in some of the cloth. I've got to get that out, too."

Suddenly Hannah said, "Look. She's waking up."

Rees turned quickly and saw Callie's eyes flutter. He moved until he was looking right down at her. "Can you hear me, Callie?"

He saw Callie's eyes focus, and then she whispered, "Yes, Rees."

"Callie, you've been shot and I've got to get the ball out. It's going to be very painful. I'm sorry, but there's nothing I can do about it."

Callie was barely conscious, but suddenly as she understood, her lips softened and she whispered, "I'm glad you're here to take care of me."

Rees put his hand on her forehead and smoothed her hair back, saying, "I hate to cause you pain, but it'll just have to be." Then he steeled himself. "All right, you three, hold her down. Don't let her move any more than you can help." Picking up the scalpel, he bowed his head, and his helpers all heard him say, "Lord God, if you ever gave me skill, give it to me now."

Thad Thomas considered himself a rather tough individual, and if anyone had asked him before the surgery, he would have said he was not afraid of the sight of blood, his own or anyone else's. But when Rees deliberately opened up the flesh with one swift movement and the blood began to ooze out, he felt himself growing light-headed. And then later when Rees had to use a bone saw, the grinding sound made the bile rise in his throat. He knew he should have turned away, but he kept his eyes fixed on the operation. He heard the metallic clinking of instruments, and once he almost cried out when Rees had to use what seemed like terrible force to move a rib. Thad looked up to see that Matthew's face was as pale and sweaty as his own, and Billy's was no better.

Finally Rees had gone after the ball, using a strange-looking instrument with little jaws and a long neck. After an interminable time Thad heard him gasp. "There! I've got it!" Thad looked up and saw within the grasp of the bloody pliers a flattened ball. "Thank God, it didn't break in two, as they sometimes do. Now I've got to get the cloth out."

Thad held on although he was sick in the pit of his stomach and afraid. Callie had passed out at some point and now lay absolutely still, but he knew she had been in terrible agony during the first part of the operation.

Finally the stitching began, and when it was over, Rees said, "You can let her go now." Thad straightened and fled the room. He burst out the door and stood trembling, and then he made his way to a flower bed and threw up. He came back, feeling weak, to find

Matthew standing outside. "I saw her heart, Matthew!" Thad whispered. "I saw it beating!"

"I . . . I saw it, too." The two men stood there leaning against the house, seemingly drained of every bit of strength.

Inside Rees was finishing up. When he was done, he simply stood there looking down on Callie's pale face, his hand covering the white bandage.

"Will she . . . will she live, Rees?" Hannah asked.

"It's in God's hands. Just pray that she doesn't get an infection." He looked up and whispered, "I didn't know how much I loved this girl until now."

"Neither did I. She's a precious thing."

Rees stroked the blond hair of the girl who lay so still. "Yes, a very precious thing. . . ."

Arriving in front of the Gifford house, Rees stepped to the ground and secured the reins of his gelding to the hitching post. He paused long enough to run his hand over the horse's smooth neck and murmur, "You're a good fellow." He laughed as the gelding turned and looked at him with large and liquid eyes. "I'll give you an extra bit of feed when we get home," he promised.

As he walked up the steps and banged the brass knocker, he felt the weariness pulling him down, almost like the force of gravity. He had gone more or less without sleep for two nights, having assisted a fellow physician, Dr. Kavendish, with three difficult operations. One of them had been completely unsuccessful. The patient, a young woman, had died in Rees's hands, and facing the distraught husband and weeping children with the news was harder than anything he cared to remember.

The door swung open and a small, rounded black servant smiled at him. "Why, Dr. Kenyon, come in."

"Thank you, Martha. Is Miss Elaine at home?"

"Yes, she is, sir. You wait right here in the parlor and I'll get her for you."

As Rees moved to the best parlor, he was aware as always of the ornate decorations and expensive furniture. The hardness of his youth had not conditioned him for opulence, and he walked over to stare up at a painting—a new one, at least for him. The artist had caught the essence of a fox hunt, with horses jumping over stone fences, one of them falling, trapping the rider underneath. The dogs were in full chase, their mouths open, their ears blown back by their exercises. The painting was so real that Rees could almost hear the baying of the hounds and the sound of the horses' hooves as they thundered over the ground. He suddenly remembered somewhere hearing fox hunting defined as "the unspeakable in pursuit of the inedible." The definition amused him, and he had a sudden distaste for such sport, if that's what it was.

The sound of footsteps turned Rees around, and he brightened as Elaine came into the room. She was wearing a coral-colored gown with a delicate pattern of flowers woven in. It was tied at the waist with a green ribbon, and as always it had been specially cut to emphasize her figure. "I didn't expect you so early, Rees," she said, and coming over, she gave him her hand. He took it and kissed it, feeling somewhat ridiculous. Hand kissing was not something he particularly admired. He had done it once and it had pleased her, so it had become one of their courting rituals.

"I've been in Charleston for two days," Rees said. "Some difficult cases over there."

"You look tired. Come and sit down."

"Well, I can't stay long. I'm beat out."

"Let me have the servant fix you some tea."

Rees leaned back and she busied herself with the ritual of teatime. She had a way of throwing herself into ceremonies. She liked them and sometimes grew impatient with Rees when he found them tedious. He never had cared much for ceremony, but he had learned that to Elaine they were very important.

As they spoke over the tea, the sound of the large grandfather clock announced the time with a sonorous patience. The regularity of the sound made Rees sleepy, and he found he was not listening with attention to what Elaine was saying. He straightened, busied himself with fixing another cup of the tea, but when he picked up on her conversation, he was somewhat taken aback. "What did you just say, Elaine?"

"Weren't you listening to me? I said Father and I are thinking of moving."

"Moving? But you're all settled in this fine house. Where would you go?"

Elaine shrugged, saying, "We're tired of Boston. I would suppose you would be, too."

"No, I'm not."

"Well, you don't remember it as it was before this awful revolution. Everything is different now."

Rees was trying to adjust to this revelation. He had somehow assumed that someday his courtship of Elaine would grow more serious, and far off in the distance there possibly would be an engagement. Beyond this he had not gone, but now she had upset his thinking. "But where would you go?"

"We've thought of New York but it would be no different there. Father says he can transfer his business to England." Elaine smiled and said, "That would be like home for you, wouldn't it?"

"Not really. Wales is the place I think of as home."

Elaine looked at him with surprise. "But England is so much more convenient and civilized than America. You could have a wonderful practice right in London, as you did before."

Memories of Grace suddenly returned, as they often did when England was mentioned. Rees did not want to go back there, but he could not go into this with Elaine. "I don't think I would care for that."

Elaine was silent for a moment and kept her eyes fixed on him. "Well, what are your plans, Rees? I never hear you talk about the future."

"I suppose I've been too busy with the present."

"But we need to think about what is to come. Surely you've made some plans."

"I suppose I'll do all I can for the cause by taking British ships."

Elaine grew cool at once and he knew his answer did not please her. "I want you to think about coming to England."

Somehow Rees understood that his relationship with Elaine Gifford had reached a moment of decision. It was as if he had been walking down a road he had never traveled, and suddenly the road forked — one side leading to the right, the other to the left. He stared at her and confusion kept him silent for a moment. "I don't think I could ever live in England, and I hope you won't."

Elaine said no more but her manner had become increasingly remote. Rees, feeling her displeasure, got up after five minutes and said, "I must get home."

"Thank you for coming, Rees." Elaine rose from her chair but she did not hold her hand out. She was watching him in a peculiar manner, and he could not fathom it. He had the feeling that they'd had a quarrel and he'd fallen into it unwittingly.

"I'll see you, perhaps, tomorrow," he said.

"Perhaps."

Elaine showed Rees to the door and as soon as it closed, walked slowly down the hallway. She paused at the stairs, intending to go up to her room, but then she moved swiftly and went farther down the hall. Her father's study was at the end and when she walked in, she found him sitting in his favorite chair, reading a book. "Hello," he said. "Was that Rees I heard?"

"Yes. He just left."

"Well, why didn't you have him stay for dinner?"

"He's tired — and I didn't feel like it tonight."

Robert Gifford at once became more alert. Putting down his book, he asked quietly, "Did you two have a quarrel?"

"No, nothing like that, but we don't agree." She shook her head, her lips drawn together in a tight line. "I tried to talk to him about the future, but all he wants to do is go out in that stupid boat of his. His practice is going downhill because of that foolishness."

"Did you mention that we might be moving?"

"Yes, I did."

"What did he say?"

Elaine gave her father a long look. The two understood each other very well. "He'll never leave this place."

Robert had not spoken directly to his daughter about her relationship with Rees, but now he felt the time had come. "They're going to lose this war, you know, and when they do, everyone who's had an active part in it is going to be in trouble. I'm afraid Rees won't have much of a life when that happens."

Elaine seemed to be struggling with her thoughts, but as Robert watched her, he sensed that she had come to a decision. He quickly said, "You know, I've been dickering over that estate in Sussex."

"Oh, Father, that's such a beautiful place!"

"It is, isn't it?" Getting up from his chair, Gifford went to his daughter and took her hands. "We could have a fine time there," he said quietly. "I might even go into politics. I have important friends there among the nobility." He laughed and said, "I might even get knighted myself, if I pay enough for it. How would you like that — Lady Elaine?"

Elaine's eyes suddenly grew bright. "Tell me more about it, Father." She pulled him over to the couch and listened avidly as he spoke in glowing terms of the estate, and Robert Gifford felt that somehow things were going to work out with his daughter — the way he envisioned it.

# Chapter Twenty-Eight

THE DARKNESS HAD BEEN BLACKER THAN ANY MIDNIGHT CALLIE HAD ever known. Sometimes she had felt as if she were suspended in a block of solid ice, too cold even to shiver, while at other times she felt as though a terrible heat were wrapped around her.

Finally the sound of a voice came to Callie, and she realized that she was lying on her back, but she was sure of nothing else. She had never been so confused, but then she recognized that the voice was Rees's. She opened her eyes and saw nothing but the ceiling. Turning her head toward the sound of Rees's voice, she saw him sitting there, reading aloud. As she studied him, she thought, *He looks so tired.*

She whispered, "Rees — " She saw him drop his book, a startled look on his face, then move quickly to stand over her. She felt his hand against her cheek. It felt cool and she whispered, "What happened? Where am I, Rees?"

"Don't you remember anything?"

Callie closed her eyes for a moment and then opened them. "I remember hurting. I was shot, wasn't I?"

"Yes, and I had to take the ball out." He brushed her hair back with his hand. "You were a brave girl," he said.

"I feel so . . . so weak!"

"Well, you are weak, but you're going to get well quickly. Could you eat something?"

"I'm thirsty."

Rees at once went and poured water into a tumbler. Coming back to the bed, he half lifted her with his arm, holding her in a sitting position. Pain twisted her lips but she made no sound. "Just take it in sips, Callie."

Nothing had ever tasted as good to Callie as that water! She found it impossible to sip it and gulped thirstily.

"That's too fast. You're going to choke. You can have all you want — but a little at a time."

Callie lay back against his arm, feeling safe and secure. He fed her the water slowly and finally said, "Now, you lie back down. Hannah has some broth on the fire. You need to start eating."

"All right, Rees."

Rees smiled at her. "You gave me quite a scare," he said. He leaned forward and kissed her on the forehead. "I can't afford to be without my Callie."

The words sank into Callie and she watched as he left the room hurriedly. She looked down and, lifting her gown, saw the white bandage on her chest. When Rees came back, she said, "I nearly died, didn't I?"

Rees was carrying a steaming bowl of soup. Placing it on the nightstand, he pulled up the chair. "Yes, you did," he said. "You're going to have to sit up." He arranged her pillows, and after he helped her into an upright position, he sat, picked up the bowl, and blew on a spoonful of broth. "Open your mouth," he said.

Callie swallowed the broth, which was delicious. "That's so good."

"You can have all you can hold." He offered her another spoonful, saying, "It's just like feeding a little bird."

Callie ate all she could, and when he laid her back down, she whispered, "Hold my hand, Rees."

Rees took her hand in both of his, completely swallowing it.

"Tell me what's been happening," she said. "Talk to me."

Rees smiled. "You must be getting better, wanting all the gossip. Well, I almost took a pistol to Thad for letting you go out. I don't think he'll try that again!"

"It wasn't his fault. I made him do it."

"It *was* his fault. He was totally irresponsible."

Callie listened awhile as he spoke, then finally she began to grow sleepy. "Have you seen Elaine again, Rees?"

When Rees did not answer, she opened her eyes and saw that he was chewing his lower lip. She wondered at this, and then he leaned forward and kissed her hand. "You just concentrate on getting well."

Callie smiled and felt herself drifting off. "Stay with me, Rees," she whispered.

"I will, Callie. Don't worry. Sleep you now."

Callie moved around the kitchen carefully. It had been three weeks since she was injured, and she was feeling better. The door opened and she turned to find Thad coming in, bearing a fistful of wildflowers. "Are those for me?"

"You don't think I'd be bringing flowers to my own sister, do you? Here."

"Let me put them in a vase."

Callie found a vase on top of the shelf, put the flowers in it, added water, and then put them on the windowsill. "They're very pretty. Nobody ever gave me flowers before."

"Well, somebody ought to." Thad came over to stand beside her. "How are you feeling today?"

"Better than ever. I'm all well."

"Rees says you're not. He says for you to do no heavy work."

"I'm going to get fat and lazy."

Thad pinched her arm. "No, you're not fat, but you're going to be. Maybe I'll cook supper for you tonight."

"Hannah will do that."

"Not tonight. She's going to a meeting with that preacher who's courting her." A thought struck him and he smiled. "How do you suppose a preacher courts a woman, Callie?"

"Why, just like any other man, I suppose."

"I don't think so. I just think they sit around and read the Bible to each other. Why, I bet he's never even kissed her."

"He's a fool if he hasn't. She's so pretty."

"Well, I'm glad to hear you say that." Thad suddenly leaned over and kissed Callie on the lips. He moved so quickly, she could not resist.

She frowned. "You stop that, Thad."

"I just couldn't help it. You shouldn't be so pretty. Maybe you could get vaccinated against it."

"You're impossible, Thad!" Callie laughed. He made her sit down and then sat across the table from her. He had been terribly worried about her, she knew that, and now that his fear of Rees's anger was passing, he had come every day, sometimes twice. She enjoyed his visits, for he was a witty man and she enjoyed his mild teasing.

"You know, Callie, I think I'm falling in love with you. I must be."

"Don't be foolish. You're not falling in love with me!"

"Yes, I think I am," Thad said, his eyes dancing. He put his hand on his chest and said, "I feel my heart beating very fast."

"How many girls have you said that to?"

"I didn't mean it when I said it to them."

Callie laughed. "A woman would have to be a fool to believe you, Thad."

Suddenly Thad stopped smiling. He took her hand and his eyes were serious. "Maybe I'm not fooling. Maybe I do mean it."

Callie blinked with surprise. She saw that indeed he was serious, but she shook her head. "Don't fall in love with me."

"Why not?"

"Just because. Now, be off with you."

Thad laughed and shrugged. "I have to keep my hand in romancing young women."

"Go practice on Mary Heatherstone. She'll make you a good wife."

"Mary Heatherstone! Why, she's as ugly as a can of worms."

"She's a fine young woman and her family has lots of money."

"Maybe I could have two wives. You and Mary Heatherstone. I could enjoy her money and I could enjoy your good looks."

"That's all I want to hear from you. So leave right now!"

Laughing, Thad rose and came over and put his arm around her in a friendly gesture. "I'm so glad you're better, Callie. I was worried sick."

"I know you were."

"And it was all my fault." When Callie tried to protest, he shook his head. "No, let me bear the guilt. It was my fault. I should have had better sense. Callie, when Rees was taking that ball out, I thought I was the one who was going to die! It was God's own mercy he was here!"

"Yes. I know that."

Thad squeezed her then and said, "I'll see you later. You be sweet — like me." He left the room, and as always she felt a warm feeling toward Thad Thomas. It was nothing like love, but she enjoyed his company.

Saturday afternoon brought Rees to examine her. He insisted on changing the dressing, and when he studied the wound, he said, "You're going to have a scar."

"No one will see it." Callie felt odd standing before him with her dress pulled down to expose the wound, but after all he was her doctor.

"Your husband will."

"He won't mind."

"No, he won't. Well there." He finished the bandaging, and when she had pulled her clothing into place, he smiled. "I have a surprise for you."

"What is it?"

"I'll tell you tomorrow."

"No, tell me now! I don't like to wait for surprises."

"All right. The new ship is going to be finished soon. Next week I'll take you out to inspect her."

"Rees, will you do something else for me?"

"I probably will. What is it?"

"Will you take me to church tomorrow?"

Rees had been smiling but now he grew very serious. "Why, of course I will. I'm glad you want to go."

Callie hesitated. "I've been feeling very strange since I was shot. I really almost died, didn't I?"

"Yes, you did, Callie. It was very close."

"I've never thought much about things like that, but I know you have." She hesitated, then lifted her eyes to his. "I'm afraid to die, Rees."

"Well, you have time to get ready. I hope it's a long way off, but we never know about that."

"I know. That's why I want to start going to church. Maybe I can find my way."

Rees took her hand. He held it for a moment, then smiled. "I'll help you," he said simply. "Will you wear the red dress?"

"No! I gave it away, remember? Besides, I've learned better than that, I think."

"That was a hard time for you, Callie." He picked up his bag and said, "I'll be here in plenty of time. We'll go together."

Callie enjoyed the singing, especially Rees's. He had such a fine, powerful voice and he sang the hymns effortlessly. She was proud to sit beside him. Callie was wearing a honey-colored dress made of light woolen material, and around her shoulders she wore the fine lace she had brought with her from England. Now as she touched it, she remembered her life back there, but she reassured herself by glancing at Rees, who sat on her right, and at Hannah, who was on her left.

The singing had moved Callie greatly, but when Lucas stood to speak, suddenly she knew that God was in the room — at least he was inside her somehow. She had never felt this way before, and noticed the unsteadiness of her hands. She clasped them together over the Bible she held in her lap.

"I'm going to ask you to use your imaginations," Bennington said. "Imagine that you are Lazarus. We will read now from the eleventh chapter of John's gospel, which begins, 'Now a certain man was sick, named Lazarus, of Bethany, the town of Mary and her sister Martha.'" He read the entire chapter, the words seeming somehow to burn into Callie's heart.

Finally he began to preach. "I asked you to imagine that you are Lazarus. You have a friend called Jesus, and you have seen this man raise the dead, perhaps. You certainly heard of his raising the widow's son at Nain, and now you are dying. What would you do? Why, you would send for Jesus. That's what I would do if I had a friend like that and I were dying.

"But the hours pass and then the days, and you feel yourself slipping away. What would you do then? Lazarus knew that Jesus loved him, but he didn't come."

Bennington suddenly looked out over the congregation, and Callie felt his eyes on her. She knew he was gazing directly at her. "When you face death, there is only one who can save you, and that one is Jesus."

These words too burned into Callie's heart, and she listened intently as Lucas began to speak of how Jesus deliberately stayed away.

"In verses fourteen and fifteen Jesus says, 'Lazarus is dead. And I am glad for your sakes that I was not there.' Why would Jesus be glad that Lazarus had died? For only one reason. He has said before that this sickness was for the glory of God. And I intend to speak to you this morning on that very subject. When we face hardship, even when we face death, is there something of the glory of God in it? There can be if you will bow down before the One who loves you more than anyone else does."

Callie found that she could not move or speak. When Bennington spoke of Jesus, it was with a warm tone, as if he were speaking of a personal friend, and she knew somehow that she had been brought to this place to hear exactly this sermon.

Finally Bennington closed his message. "Jesus said, 'I am the resurrection and the life.' There are different interpretations of that. One is of course that there is a day sometime in the future—perhaps far off, perhaps not—when the dead will hear the voice of Jesus and come out of the grave. But some of you are dead in sin, and Jesus wants to call you out of that sin and death, just as he called Lazarus out of that physical tomb. What will you say to him who calls you? For Jesus this morning is saying to you, as he said to Lazarus, 'Come forth.'"

At that moment, deep in her spirit Callie Summers somehow knew that God was speaking to her, and she knew he was saying, *Come forth, Callie.* She sat there trembling, unable to speak. When the benediction was spoken, she got up silently, saying nothing until they were outside the church.

"Are you all right, Callie?" Rees asked.

"I . . . don't know."

Rees stared down at her. "What's wrong? Are you ill?"

"No. I just need to think."

"All right. I'll take you home."

Callie spent the rest of the day in her room. She knew something had happened to her as she sat in the church, but she did not know what it was. Eventually she heard a tap on the door. When she opened it, she found Rees standing there, concern on his face. "I was worried about you, Callie. Can I come in?"

"Come in, Rees." He entered the room and she sat down on a chair, motioning toward another one. Then she moistened her lips and said, "Something happened this morning in church during the sermon. I don't know how to explain it, but I know God was speaking to me. I've never had anything like that happen to me before."

Rees at once leaned forward. "I knew that something was going on in your heart, but it's a good thing, Callie."

"But what am I to do? I don't know anything, Rees."

"God isn't looking for geniuses. He's looking for willing, open hearts. I think this is your hour, Callie. Would you mind if we prayed together?" She nodded and he said gently, "Let me pray for you. And then I want you to ask Jesus to come into your heart. Will you do that?"

Callie took a deep breath, then tears came to her eyes. "Yes, I'll do that, Rees, if you say so."

Rees bowed his head and Callie bowed hers. Rees took her hand and held it. He prayed very simply for a while, thanking God for Callie, and as he did, she knew that she cared for this man who had come to play such a big part in her life. Eventually she began to pray herself. It was awkward and she stumbled over the words. She prayed silently at first but finally she could not keep it in. She began to weep and sob and cried out, "Oh, Jesus, I want to come forth as that dead man did! I need you so much!"

The two prayed for some time, then Callie fell silent. She lifted her eyes and saw that Rees was watching her. "I feel . . . different, Rees."

"How is that, Callie?"

"I feel so peaceful. What's happened to me?"

"I think you've simply let Jesus do what he's always longed to do — come into your heart."

"Am I saved, then, Rees?"

"That peace you feel, it's what you've been looking for all of your life."

Suddenly Callie knew this was true, and a great joy came to her. He was still holding her hand, and she grasped it with both of hers and squeezed hard. "That's true," she whispered. "It's true, Rees! What do I do now?"

"Whatever Jesus says," he said, smiling. "Come, we must go tell Hannah."

In the weeks that followed, Callie knew a joy she had never known before. She spent an enormous amount of time with Hannah, who explained the Scriptures to her. She found herself with a hunger to know more, and when Reverend Bennington came to call on Hannah, she told him what had happened to her, and he advised her to be baptized. She agreed to that at once.

As the days passed, Callie found herself closer to Rees than she had ever been. He did not miss a day coming to see her, and only once was she disturbed during that period. Rees had come and Hannah had gone out to meet the post. She brought in a letter, saying, "It's for you, Rees."

Rees had taken the letter and said, "Excuse me." Callie watched as he read it, and studied his face. It was a short letter and he looked up and said, "It's from Elaine." He said no more but put the letter away. It darkened the day for Callie, for somehow she felt that this woman was bad for Rees. However, she said nothing.

Rees was thoughtful for a time and silent, but finally he seemed to pull himself together. "Get your coat on," he told Callie. "We're going out to see the ship."

"Oh, Rees, I've so wanted to see it!"

"Well, it's cold out there. You'll have to bundle up."

Indeed, it was cold. September had come, and as Rees drove the carriage down to where the ship was being built, the wind was bitter. "I'm worried about General Washington and his army," he told Callie.

"I'm worried about Billy." Billy Gaston had joined Washington's forces, and Callie had found that she missed him considerably. "I hope he's all right."

"Well, they've had some hard battles." He described the Battle of Brandywine, which Washington had fought and lost. "Washington lost again at Germantown, but the army is still holding together."

"Where are they now, Rees?"

"They're wintering at a place called Valley Forge, somewhere in Pennsylvania. They're in pretty poor condition. Congress won't send the proper supplies."

"Why not?" Callie asked indignantly.

"I don't know. They say they have no money."

"I hate to think about men being hungry in this weather."

"So do I. Look, there she is."

Rees pulled the carriage to a stop and Callie cried out, "Why, she's almost finished!"

"Yes. That's the surprise."

Many men seemed to be crawling all over the ship. "There are so many workers."

"I used the profits from some of the prizes we took with the *Callie*. I wanted her done in a hurry."

"She's so much bigger!"

"Yes. She's a sloop. She'll go faster and carry several mounted guns. There will be no oars. Actually, I'm thinking she'll be the fastest thing on the water."

Rees got out of the carriage and helped Callie down. They went around speaking to the workmen, and Callie saw that Rees was very proud. She had to see every bit of the new ship. When finally he insisted they go home because of the bitter weather, she settled down into the carriage. He covered her with a blanket and then spoke to the horse. Callie looked back at the ship and asked, "When will she be finished?"

"Another two weeks."

"What will you name her, Rees?"

Rees turned and smiled broadly. *"Callie II,"* he said.

Warmth came to Callie then. "There is soft you are."

"Watch it! You're beginning to talk like I do. I'll make a Welshwoman out of you if you don't take care."

She leaned over and took his arm. "Thank you, Rees."

"For what?"

"For everything you've done for me. Where would I be if it weren't for you? You saved me from everything."

Rees looked down at her. Her face was turned toward him and he caught the fragrance of her hair. It suddenly revived old memories, and he thought about how her sweetness and her strong spirit had become so evident, especially in these last few days. He wanted to put his arms around her and tell her how attractive she was. Her lips were red and expressive, and now they held a soft curve of pleasure. As she watched him, he was not sure of what she felt. But he knew one thing: she never tired a man. The thought that passed through his mind he spoke aloud. "A man would never find you boring."

"Do you think not, Rees?"

"No. Not ever." He suddenly put his arm around her and said, "You're not much like the girl I met at the inn in England."

"No. Things change. We've both changed, Rees."

"Have we?"

"Yes."

Rees did not know exactly what she meant. He felt she was trying to tell him something, but he could not grasp it. "Come now. Let's get us home, and I'll let you pamper me a bit."

Callie felt the strength of his arm and murmured, "All right, Rees. Let's go home."

# Chapter Twenty-Nine

A SHARP, PINCHING COLD LAY OVER BOSTON, AND AS REES PULLED his buggy to a stop before the Thomas house, he paused for a moment and gazed around at the scene. A heavy snow had fallen the night before and now mantled the earth, making it pristine and beautiful. The trees stood stiffly, reaching for something they could not contrive, and the world to him seemed to be a dead ball rushing through dead space. Smoke rose from the chimney and was caught by a whirling wind that sighed like some discontented animal. The sunlight touched the snow, giving it a crystal appearance, making it glitter in spots like white diamonds.

Rees got out and walked up to the house, longing for the spring and the sunshine and the greenness of earth. Stepping up onto the porch, he hesitated and watched as the sunlight flashed against the windowpanes of the house. The smells of winter were faint and not like the rich fullness of spring and summer, which he loved. A mood was on him that he could not define, and as he knocked on the door, he wished for a change — but he did not know what sort of change he sought. Something was absent from his life but he could not pin it down. The missing element was vague and nebulous, and he felt like a fool for being discontented. So many people he knew were in such poor condition, and he had his health, his strength, a profession. Impatient with himself, he rapped sharply on the door, and when Hannah opened it, he smiled and said, "I'm a little late, Hannah. Is Callie ready?"

Hannah looked up at him and something crossed her face. "Why, Rees," she said, "we thought you'd been called out on a case."

"I was, but I'm here now."

"Callie and Thad left early."

The breeze ruffled Rees's black hair, and his mouth twisted suddenly. He ceased to smile and stared at her with a rather harsh expression. "All right," he said but then added, "She knew I was coming."

Hannah quickly said, "Let me get my coat and bonnet. You can take me to church."

Rees waited until she emerged from the house, tying her bonnet beneath her chin. He walked with her toward the buggy, handed her in, and then climbed in and spoke to the horse, which moved forward at once. A silence was upon the land, and they did not break it until finally Hannah said, "I'm so proud of the way Callie has taken to the study of the Scriptures. She's as hungry for the things of God as any young woman I ever saw."

Her words seemed to cheer Rees and he nodded at once. "You're right about that. She has a quick mind and a lively curiosity." He smiled and glanced at her. "She asked me the day before yesterday where Cain got his wife."

"What did you tell her?"

A private and ridiculous thought took him, and she saw the effect of it dancing in his eyes. "I told her I didn't know, but if she suited Cain, she suited me."

Hannah laughed aloud and touched his arm. "That's as good a theological explanation as I've ever heard. I know you're proud of her and happy for her, Rees."

"Of course I am."

The moodiness seemed to have departed from Rees, but when they were halfway to church, Hannah mentioned Thad's interest in Callie, and it seemed to return. "It would be good if Thad and Callie fell in love and got married," she commented.

Rees's answer was long in coming, and he sat there a limber man with dark eyes half hidden by the droop of the lids. There was a looseness about him, and his features were sharp. Something from his past had put shadows in his eyes and at times laid a silence on his tongue, as it did now. Finally he said without emphasis, "I don't think that would be a good idea, Hannah."

Hannah turned and stared at Rees. For a moment something like anger flared in her eyes, but she waited for a time and then shrugged. "You would never think any man was good enough for Callie."

A silence fell between the two then, and they spoke only briefly until they pulled up in front of the church. The whiteness of the ground was broken by the dark shapes of saddle horses, buggies, and wagons. From inside the sound of singing issued, and as Rees helped Hannah to the ground, he murmured, "I always hated to be late to church."

"It doesn't matter."

The two of them walked up the steps and moved inside. The sound of singing filled the auditorium, and Rees saw at once that Callie was seated between Matthew and Thad. Hannah whispered, "There they are. Let's go sit beside them."

"All right."

They made their way down the aisle, keeping their coats on. There was no fire in the church, and people's faces were pinched white with the bitter cold. Hannah and Rees found their place beside the others, and Hannah noticed that Rees's singing seemed perfunctory. Usually his voice was the strongest of all and would soar above the others, but he was caught in some sort of dark thinking and did not lift his voice.

Rees found himself hard put to listen to the sermon. He admired Lucas Bennington, and the thought was pleasant to him that Hannah and the preacher would someday be married. To Rees they seemed perfectly matched. However, Rees's thoughts wandered as they rarely did under a good message. He found himself unable to concentrate. Finally, at the end of the sermon, he did come fully aware. He was preparing to hear the benediction and leave when he heard Bennington say, "Before the benediction I have an announcement to make."

Suddenly Rees felt his arm grasped by Hannah. He turned to her quickly. Her lips were half parted, and behind the composed expression she usually wore, a little-girl eagerness vaguely stirred and displayed itself. Her face was expressive, more than he had ever seen it, and the joy that Lucas's words gave her graphically registered in her eyes.

"It gives me a great deal of pleasure to announce that Miss Hannah Thomas has agreed to be my wife. I count myself a blessed man indeed." Lucas was smiling and ignoring the hum of voices that rose in the church. "All of you," he said, "will be telling me what a lovely wife I will have — and none of you will be telling Miss Thomas what a lovely husband she will have! But there will be an announcement about the date in the near future."

After the benediction Rees at once turned and smiled down at Hannah. "Congratulations. Are you happy with you, then?"

"Oh yes."

"He's a fine man." Rees had no chance to say more, for Hannah was besieged with well-wishers. Rees himself had not gone more than three steps down the aisle when a young man stepped before him. He was as tall as Rees himself and had a pair of steady gray eyes. Rees knew him slightly as a young lawyer but could not remember his name.

"I'm Joshua Johnson, Dr. Kenyon."

"Yes. Good to see you."

"This is not a propitious place, but I want to ask your permission to call on Miss Callie."

"Why, of course — if that's what she wishes."

"Thank you, sir."

Rees made his way through the crowd and as he stepped outside, he was greeted by Tom Jenkins, whose father was a patient of his.

"Doctor, could I have a word with you?" Jenkins asked.

"Yes, of course, Tom."

Jenkins was a compact man, well built. He had red hair and dark blue eyes and asked at once, "I'd like to come calling on Miss Callie, Doctor."

"Calling on Callie?"

"Yes sir, if you don't mind."

"Well, I suppose it'll be all right, Tom."

If Jenkins noted the reluctance with which Rees gave his permission, he did not show it. He smiled and nodded and then turned away.

Rees had no option but to wait, for he was committed to taking Hannah home. He was in no mood for talking, but several people approached him and he felt obliged to be pleasant.

Finally Callie came out, accompanied by Thad. "I'm glad to see you, Rees," Callie said at once. "I thought you had been called out and wouldn't be able to come to church."

"I was a little late."

Thad laughed. "That's the penalty of being a doctor. If you were a trifling gunsmith like me, you'd never get called out."

Rees hesitated, then said, "Joshua Johnson asked if he could call on you."

"What'd you tell him?" Callie asked.

"I told him it was up to you."

Something in his manner disturbed Callie. She said, "If you don't want him to call on me, just say so."

A tension sparked between the two, and Rees said stiffly, "Tom Jenkins wants to come calling, too. I suppose we'll have to make a schedule for all your gentlemen callers."

Callie stared at him. She could not speak for a moment, and then finally she said quietly, "I'll do as you say, Rees."

Rees felt he had spoiled the morning for Callie. She'd had such happiness when she walked up. He could see it in her eyes, but now there was a sadness in her, and he knew he had grieved her. With a stiff, desperate expression on her face, she turned away without saying another word.

Thad at once said, "Rees, what's wrong with you?"

"Nothing's wrong with me."

Thad shook his head and said, "You're like a dog in a manger. You don't want her for yourself, and you don't want anybody else to have her."

"That's not true, Thad," Rees responded quickly. He could say no more, for Thad turned his back and walked off. Rees watched as he put his hand under Callie's arm and the two of them walked away toward their buggy.

"Am I a snake with fangs, then?" he muttered, totally dissatisfied with himself. "There's a beast I am to speak like that to her!"

"Don't pay any attention to Rees, Callie." Thad slapped the reins against the mare and urged her to a faster speed. "He didn't have any business talking to you like that."

Callie had been silent on the way from the church. Sitting beside Thad, she had thought about how joyful she had been in church. She had enjoyed the sermon and had been so thrilled when the announcement was made of Hannah and Lucas's engagement. She had been happy, too, when she had gone up to Rees, but his words and his attitude had crushed her. She said finally, "I think he was just tired."

"You always make excuses for everybody — except me," Thad said.

"You can make your own excuses, Thad."

"You know what's wrong with him, don't you?"

"No. I don't."

"Why, he's jealous." Thad turned quickly and saw a slight change in her face. He noted the quickening, the loosening of the small expression as it came and went. Thad Thomas had come to admire the range of Callie's spirit. Now he saw hurt stain her eyes, and something had gone out of her smile that he had always admired. He put his hand on hers. She had folded them and held them clenched in her lap. "Don't let him hurt you. Don't let any man hurt you," he said quietly.

"How can I help but be hurt?"

"Well, you have to be hard at times, Callie."

"No, I don't want to be like that. I've been that way all my life, Thad. I grew up hard and there was something in myself I hated. Only now have I begun to know what gentleness and softness is. And I learned some of it from Rees. He's a good man but he's sort of mixed up, I think. I know what it is — why he acts like he does."

"Why, Callie?"

"He's never gotten over the woman he loved so much. Her name was Grace."

"I never heard him speak of her," Thad said.

"He doesn't very often but when he does, you can see in his eyes that memories of her are still walking around inside him."

"What happened?"

"She died. But she's not dead to him. He'll never forget her."

"Well, it's hard to lose someone you love." Thad said no more, and as Callie turned away from him, she felt a great sense of loss. She had been so happy since putting her faith in Christ and knew she always would be, but Rees had wounded her, and she knew that the wall between them was still there, and it hurt her deeply.

Thad had been pleased at the dinner they'd had to mark the completion of the new ship. Callie had seemed happy, and Matthew and Rees as well. Now Thad stood beside Rees in the bow of the *Callie*. No one called it *Callie II*, as was painted on the side; they were all used to the original name. Casting a quick look at Rees, Thad was tempted to say something about the scene at church, but he repressed it. *None of my business,* he thought. *What's between a man and a woman is private. They'll have to work it out themselves.* Instead he said aloud, "She's a sweet-sailing ship, isn't she, Rees?"

Rees's smile came then, a white streak against his tanned features. "As sweet as ever I saw. There is proud I am." He looked up at the full sails and felt the humming of the wind as it drove the sloop ahead. "She's a fine ship."

"A little different from the first *Callie*."

"Yes, but I'll always remember that little spider catcher."

Thad's brow clouded. "I'm afraid I'll always remember losing her."

"Not your fault. It was a clever thing some British officer thought up."

The two walked around the ship as it skimmed across the water, both of them pleased with her speed. Matthew was there inspecting and admiring the guns, which were mounted on each side of the vessel.

"We could tackle a frigate with this," he said with excitement, his eyes dancing.

"I doubt we'd want to do that," Rees said, laughing. "But we could run away from one if she caught us."

Rees was glad to be at sea. They had heard a rumor that a British ship was headed their way, but they had not found it. Now as he moved along the deck, he felt pride in the vessel, more than he ever had in any ship he had helped build. In truth, she was a miniature warship. The *Callie II* was built for speed, and Rees knew with certainty that she could outrun any ship the British had.

His thoughts were interrupted when the lookout said, "Sail off the port bow!"

Instantly everyone began to move to a position where they could see. Rees threw up the brass telescope and studied it. "It may be one of our schooners. Put her about and we'll investigate."

As they drew closer, the ship proved to be the enemy. Rees's voice crackled with excitement. "She's a British transport and not a warship! Battle stations, all hands!"

Instantly the deck was a beehive of activity. The *Callie II* mounted four eight-pounders on both port and starboard, and the ship was so quick that it was possible to fire one broadside, heel the vessel around, and fire another while the first guns were being reloaded.

"Do you think she'll put up a fight?" Thad asked.

"She's a fool if she does. We could sink her in a wink."

Indeed, Rees's words were prophetic, for when a shot was placed across her bow, at once the transport furled her sails and came to a halt.

Thad was in charge of the boarding party, and when the two ships were tied together, Rees stayed on board while Thad went over the side, accompanied by ten of the sailors.

Rees directed the rest of the crew to stay ready to fire in case something went wrong.

Nothing did, however, and Thad appeared to cry out, "She has a full load!"

"Start bringing some of it onto the *Callie*," Rees commanded. "We'll want to take part of it at once to General Washington's troops."

The transfer of the goods had satisfied Rees. Evidently, the transport was bound for New York with supplies for the British army. There were fine, warm, thick blankets, food supplies of all sorts, and even crates filled with medical supplies, which pleased Rees.

The *Callie II* had taken on as much as she could carry, when suddenly Matthew's voice rang out. "Rees, there's a ship! I think it's a British warship!"

Instantly Rees ran to the rail, threw up his glass. One look was enough. "It's a frigate!" he yelled. "Set all sails!"

Thad groaned. "We have to leave this prize."

"Better to lose the prize than to lose the *Callie*."

The crew was well trained and cast off all lines to the transport. The sails filled almost instantly, and the *Callie II* shot off under the stiff breeze. Rees took position in the stern and watched carefully. Thad and Matthew came to stand beside him. "All sails are set," Matthew said. "She's really flying."

Rees gave a sigh of relief and collapsed the telescope. "We're running away and leaving her," he said, smiling.

Thad was still disturbed. "We could have had that whole ship for a prize, but we lost it all."

"There'll be other days," Rees said, shrugging. "Now, let's outrun this frigate and then we'll go home."

Rees stood looking at the wagon, which was heavily loaded with blankets and food. "I'll take this wagon in," he told Thad. "We'll have to find a way to get the rest of these supplies to General Washington."

"All right. I'll go buy some wagons."

"That's good, Thad. I'll see you later."

Rees mounted the seat, and the horses pulled against the collars. The wagon was loaded so heavily that they moved out rather slowly, but Rees was content.

His mind was active as he urged the team onward, thinking of how to get the supplies they had captured to Washington. Rees knew a glow of satisfaction as he glanced at the contents of the wagon. "Right, you," he said, speaking to the piles of supplies. "We'll see you get to the right place."

As Rees pulled up in front of the house, he saw Hannah come running out. He leaped off the wagon and said, "What's wrong, Hannah?"

"We've had a hard word, Rees," Hannah said. "It's Billy Gaston." Gaston had joined the Continental army weeks before and there had been no word of him. "He's been wounded and may not live."

"How do you know that?" Rees demanded.

"Jake Trumble was soldiering with him. He got wounded himself but was able to travel. He came here to tell us about Billy."

"Is the army still in Valley Forge?"

"Yes."

"Well, we have some supplies. Maybe they'll help."

"I haven't told you everything, Rees," Hannah said. She seemed rather breathless and she shook her head. "It's Callie. When she heard about Billy, she threw some blankets and food and what medicine she could find of yours into a buggy and started off."

"Started for Valley Forge in the dead of winter! Hannah, she shouldn't have gone!"

"I tried my best to stop her. She's so stubborn, Rees. You know how she is."

"How long has she been gone?"

"She left about ten o'clock this morning."

"Well, she couldn't have traveled far. I'll have to catch up with her."

"Will you bring her back?"

Rees thought hard for a moment. "We need to go help Billy if we can, and those other poor fellows too. I'll catch up with her and I'll send her back, but I'll go on to Valley Forge."

"Rees, you'll never be able to do it."

"What do you mean?"

"I mean she's set on going. She feels that . . . well, she feels responsible for Billy."

"Why, she didn't shoot him!"

"No, but you know Billy fancied himself in love with Callie. He joined the army as a reaction, I think."

"Well, that was foolish."

"Men do foolish things when they're in love, Rees. Didn't you know that?"

Rees could not answer. A subtle look of determination came into his face. "I'm leaving as soon as I can hitch up a fresh team. It's a long way."

"What will you do about Callie?"

"I'll try to get her to come back, but if she doesn't, you'll know I couldn't do it."

"Rees, don't be hard on her when you find her."

Rees stared at Hannah. "Hard on her? Why would you think that, woman?"

"You're as stubborn as she is. She wants to do this for Billy. Let her do it."

"All right," Rees said. "We'll go together. Now, give me all the food you can that I can take with me. I won't have time to stop much."

# Chapter Thirty

THE ROAD OVER WHICH CALLIE TRAVELED WAS FROZEN SO HARD that the wheels of the buggy slid from side to side, causing her to grab the seat. The ruts were deep, and she had to clamp her teeth together to keep from biting her tongue as the wheels dropped into them. The day had been long, but now the night had closed down thick and solid and mysterious. The sky was an enamel black, and already a sickle moon lay low in the sky, turned butter yellow by the atmosphere. The stars sharply glistened and the wind moaned, softly driving granules of snow across the frozen land. The air was frigid, and from time to time Callie pulled a hand out of her thick gloves, breathed on it, and then put the glove on again and tried to warm the other hand.

She was weary, but when she heard the sound of horses behind her, she leaned out and looked backward. At once she knew a relief of spirit and cried out, "Rees!" She pulled the horse up and was so stiff by the long ride that she staggered when she leaped out of the buggy. She started for Rees, who had already stopped the wagon and jumped out. He came toward her and without preamble grabbed her shoulders. "What in the world do you think you're doing, Callie Summers!" His dark blue eyes were smoldering and anger mixed with relief marked his features. "You scared the life out of me."

"I . . . I'm sorry, Rees. I didn't know when you'd be back and I'm so worried about Billy."

"It was a fool thing to do."

"I'm so sorry, Rees. I didn't mean to worry you."

Rees squeezed her shoulders and then said gustily, "Say nothing against you I was, but I haven't been so worried in a long time."

Callie heard the relief surging in his voice and put her hand on his chest. The darkness painted shadows in his eyes and touched his solid face with a brand of loneliness. He was looking at her in an odd fashion; then a half smile pulled his lips into a long, tough line. It was a wistful expression that seemed to absorb everything, and although she could not read his thoughts, she saw the concern in his eyes. Then he smiled fully and one deep line broke out from the corner of each eye, something she had noticed before. "Well now," he murmured, and his voice had grown soft. "It's too late to go on for the night. We'll have to camp out. It will be bitter cold."

"I've been looking for a house to stay the night."

"I brought some canvas. We'll make a tent of sorts out of it."

"I'll gather some wood and we can at least make ourselves a fire."

They pulled the wagon and the buggy off the road and Callie began to gather firewood. When she came back, he had pulled out a large roll of canvas and draped it over the wagon so it touched the ground on all four sides. He lifted up a corner and looked in and said, "We'll have blankets enough so we won't freeze."

"That will be fine, Rees. When I get the fire started, we'll cook something."

By the time the fire was blazing against the blackness of the night, the two had pulled out the makings of a meal. Hannah had thrown in a saucepan, and they boiled coffee in it, then roasted the large cut of mutton she had cut up and put on sticks.

Sitting close to Rees in front of the fire, Callie listened as he told the story of how the *Callie II* had taken the prize and then been forced to outrun a frigate.

"I wish I could have been there. It sounds exciting."

"You're not likely to be going on any more raids, girl, so don't be trying to work me."

Callie knew the finality in Rees's voice and murmured, "All right. If you say so."

Suddenly Rees laughed, making a ringing sound in the silence of the night. "I'm always suspicious when you do that."

"When I do what?"

"When you pretend to be a good and obedient girl."

Callie gave him a smile and the two finished the meal. "It's awfully cold out here," Rees said. "You'd better get under the wagon. I'll sleep by the fire."

"You can't stay out here, Rees. You'll freeze."

"I can't sleep under there with you. It wouldn't look right."

Callie stared at him. "Look right to who? That owl flying around hooting? Don't be silly!"

Rising to her feet, Callie went at once to the wagon and pulled out blankets destined for Valley Forge. Throwing the cover back from the rear of the wagon, she crawled underneath and quickly formed two beds. "Come along," she said.

She rolled into her blankets and then Rees came inside. When he dropped the canvas, it was utterly dark. "It's blacker than the inside of a black cat," Rees complained. Callie felt him fumbling with the blankets, and when he had pulled them about him and settled down, he gave a hearty sigh and then fell silent.

Callie thought she was so tired that she would fall asleep instantly, but she found that sleep eluded her. She knew Rees was also awake, for he kept shifting his position. Finally she said, "Rees, are you asleep?"

"Yes."

Callie giggled. "You're not either. Tell me again about capturing that transport."

She heard him shift again. "The *Callie* is going to be a great prize-taker," he said. He spoke for some time of the new ship, and finally he said, "You'll never know how I worried about you, Callie — when you were shot."

"Did you, Rees?" Callie lay still and then said, "That's sweet of you."

She shifted to her side so she could face him, and she knew he was facing her. A fear came to her for a moment, for they were together in a way that was almost totally intimate. He said, "Callie, are you angry with me because I wasn't too enthusiastic about your suitors?"

"No, not at all."

"I don't want to be mean ever to you."

Callie reached out and touched him. "You could never be that." She felt his breath cut short and then knew how it was with him. He could not hide his desires from her. He was a man, and in a situation like this any man would be tempted. She lay absolutely still and then strangely enough was not shocked when he dropped his hand over her back and pulled her to him. She was caught by the loneliness and isolation of their setting, and when he pulled her forward and held her tightly, she did not rebuke him, and her arm suddenly went around his neck. She received his kiss, which was gentle at first, but then his desires revealed themselves in the strength of his arms and the demand of his lips. The thrill of something timeless brushed against her and frightened her in a way. There was a triumph deep inside her that she had the power to stir him, but she was shocked at the wave of emotion that went through her.

And then for no reason that she could know, as he held her in his arms, his mouth on hers, something came to her. She did not know why but she pulled back and found that she was silently crying. She clung to him, laying her face against his. She knew he must be feeling her tears, and he lay absolutely still. Finally she heard him whisper, "I'm sorry, Callie."

"Sorry? Why are you sorry?"

"I . . . didn't mean to take advantage."

Callie knew then that in this man there was a goodness she had sought in others and not found. She was helpless against him, and he was not using his strength to force her. She felt his arms release and she drew back, but she put her hand on his cheek and whispered, "Thank you, Rees."

His answer came quickly. "Why are you thanking me?"

"Because . . . because you're good. You could have been like other men but you're not. I've never met another man as gentle as you." Suddenly she knew that she was fragile and weak, and her own desire had made her so. She whispered then, "Good night, Rees," and turned over.

She felt him settle down and then finally he said, "Good night, Callie."

Neither Callie nor Rees spoke of the moment of intimacy, but as they made their way through the harsh weather, headed for Valley

Forge, each was aware that something had changed. Callie had found it difficult to meet Rees's eyes the morning after the incident. He had been outside when she awakened, with a fire already started and breakfast cooking. When she scrambled out from beneath the wagon, he had greeted her with a strange constraint, and she wondered if she had cheapened herself.

They had traveled hard, stopping at houses each night. It was difficult, and usually impossible, to explain an unmarried man and woman, but somehow that didn't seem to matter.

As they came to the end of their journey, with the sun exactly overhead and the bitter cold still probing beneath their thick clothes, Rees said, "I think we must have arrived." He had pulled his wagon alongside her small buggy, and the horses, as if sensing the end of a long trip, lifted their heads and nickered.

"It doesn't look like an army camp," Callie said quietly.

"No, it doesn't." Rees had pictured in his mind rows of sturdy tents with men dressed in neat uniforms, but what they were looking at was a group of scarecrows. Their faces were blue with the cold, and their eyes looked enormous as they stared at the newcomers. And the clothing! Not a good coat or pair of boots among the lot. Parts of their bodies showed through huge rents — one man even exposed a portion of bare, blue buttocks where his pants had worn away. Most of them looked deformed, elephantine, with their feet wrapped in blankets.

"Halt! Stop them horses!"

Rees pulled up at once and studied the tall man in the ragged uniform who had stepped in front of the team. The soldier came around and said, "Well, what's your business?"

"We brought some medical supplies, Sergeant, and a little food for the wounded."

"For the wounded, eh? Well, I wish you had twenty wagons full! Come along. I'll take you to the hospital."

"Do you know a man named Billy Gaston?"

"Shore, I know Billy. You family of his?"

"Just friends."

The sergeant moved ahead and Rees nodded to Callie. The two guided their horses to the top of a knoll, where they pulled up in front of a shack built of logs. The building was long and narrow, and smoke was puffing out of a clay and waddled chimney. The sergeant waited until they both dismounted. "I'll have to put some guards near them wagons. The men would steal anything. Not that I blame 'em."

The sergeant stepped inside and motioned for them to follow. The interior was lit with candles, and daylight showed through cracks in the logs. A man with a long, gray apron splattered with blood came to peer at them. "Who's this, Sergeant?"

"Folks who say they brought some supplies." The sergeant turned to Rees and Callie. "This here is Dr. Reeves."

"Supplies? What kind of supplies?" Dr. Reeves asked sharply.

"Some food and blankets and medical supplies," Rees answered. "I'm Dr. Rees Kenyon from Boston, and this is Miss Callie Summers."

"Sergeant, start bringing those supplies in."

"Yes sir, Doctor."

"You're a physician?" Dr. Reeves asked Rees.

"Yes sir."

"Good! I need all the help I can get."

"Well, we're very interested in Billy Gaston," Rees said. "He's a good friend of ours."

"Oh, Gaston! Why yes, I'll take you to him right away."

"How is he, Dr. Reeves?" Callie asked.

Reeves stared at the young woman as though he wondered about her presence here. "He's *bad*, that's how he is. They're all bad! I don't have anything to work with. Thank God you brought something."

He turned and walked down the long corridor, and Rees and Callie followed. Men were lying on the ground, some in shredded blankets, some with nothing at all. The cold was bitter and most of the men seemed asleep. But some of them moved restlessly and there was a continual groaning. The stench was so overwhelming that Callie found it hard to breathe.

Stopping beside a man who was lying on his back, Dr. Reeves said, "Billy, you have some visitors."

Callie at once moved forward and shock ran through her. Billy, who had been a burly man of flesh, now appeared to be little more than a skeleton. His eyes were sunk in his head and were dull and lifeless. "Billy," she said, "it's me, Callie."

"Callie? Is it you, Callie?" The voice was raspy and faint.

She bent down and pushed his hair back from his forehead. "Yes, and Dr. Kenyon is here. We've come to take care of you, Billy."

Billy Gaston looked at her strangely and silently. Finally he managed a thin smile. "I reckon I need somebody, Miss Callie. I . . . I'm right glad you've come."

Callie took his hand and Rees knelt beside the lank form, saying, "We're going to take care of you. Callie wouldn't have it any other way, so here we are."

Billy's eyes seemed to light up at that. "I never thought anybody would come to this place."

"Well, we're here now," Callie said strongly, "and we're going to do our best for you."

Dr. Reeves was almost pathetically grateful for the supplies Rees and Callie had brought. He guarded them like a miser. Rees helped him with the wounded for two days. Callie spent most of that time sitting beside Billy, fixing him nourishing soup and cleaning him up. He improved almost magically and Callie was encouraged.

"Most of these fellows would get well if they had good care," Billy said to her. "But doesn't anybody care about us? Doesn't Congress care?"

Callie had no answer for this, but she did walk up and down the rows, doing what she could. It was amazing what a kind word from a woman would do to a man who was sick and filthy and starving.

On the second day after their arrival, a visitor came. Callie was sitting beside Billy, keeping him entertained with small talk, when she heard voices. Billy raised himself and whispered, "That's General Washington."

Callie stood at once. The big man coming toward her seemed to fill the corridor. Behind him Rees and Dr. Reeves followed, and when the general stopped before her, she could not speak.

"Miss Summers, we meet again."

"Yes, General Washington," Callie said. She was almost breathless, and when he put out his hand, it seemed to swallow hers.

"I have to express my thanks to you. You'll never know how

much it means to the men when somebody shows concern, as you and Dr. Kenyon have."

"I . . . I can't do much. I'm not a doctor."

"If everyone were as concerned as you, things would be different." Washington was a big man, and although his face was now drawn, there was a kindness in his eyes. A strength emanated from him, and for the first time Callie understood why men would follow him through the snow with bare, bleeding feet. She did not know how to explain it, nor would she ever, but in that moment she knew that this man was the strength of the American Revolution.

Washington turned to Rees and said, "Dr. Kenyon, you tell me that you have more supplies?"

"Yes. We've just captured a transport ship and we loaded the *Callie* with supplies."

"The *Callie?* That's the name of the ship?" Washington turned to Callie and smiled. "Named after you, I presume."

"Yes sir."

"You could do your country no better service than to go as quickly as you can and get those supplies here to the camp. We desperately need them, as you can see."

"I had thought of staying here to help with the wounded, General Washington."

"You can serve them much better by bringing food and medicine and more blankets. I can't promise you payment for them, but I can promise you the gratitude of one old soldier."

Callie felt a lump in her throat at the humility of this man. She knew Congress had ignored his requests and that he had spent his own money many times to keep the army in the field, and now he was having to ask for favors. A fierce determination rose in her. "Dr. Kenyon, we can do that. We can buy wagons and bring all the supplies we can lay our hands on."

"I wish the Congress were as understanding," Dr. Reeves said rather bitterly. "They've done nothing for our men."

Washington would never hear any criticism of Congress. He quickly said, "Spring will be here soon and I've got to get an army ready to fight. If you can help us with supplies, you'll be doing as much as any soldier in the line, Dr. Kenyon and Miss Summers."

"We'll leave at once, Your Excellency," Rees said.

Washington wished them good-bye, and when he left, Rees said, "We'd better get going. I can see now where our job is."

Callie nodded. "We've got to take Billy back with us in the wagon." She turned and knelt beside Billy. "You ready to go home, Billy?"

"As ready as a man can be!"

The trip home was slower, for they had to consider the wounded man. Many times it was easier to travel beside the road than in it, thus avoiding the deep, frozen ruts. They moved as quickly as they could and Billy stood the trip well. Each night when they camped out, they made a bed for him in the wagon and covered it with canvas. The good food and care had already begun to take effect, for which Callie and Rees were grateful.

On the last night before reaching home, Callie fixed a good stew, and Billy ate three bowls of it and at once became sleepy. Callie and Rees tucked him in and closed the canopy of canvas over the wagon; then the two of them sat around the fire.

"It's so clear tonight," Callie said, poking a stick into the fire and watching the yellow sparks spiral upward like a whirlwind. "They seem to mingle with the stars up there."

"I think the stars are a little farther," Rees said.

"What did you think of General Washington?"

"I never saw anyone like him. No wonder the men love him."

"They do, don't they? He's held the whole revolution together, the whole country. I'd do anything for him." Callie poked the fire again with her stick, then looked up. "I think what he said is right. We need to go back and find other English ships, take them, and then buy up some wagons and start a steady supply line."

Rees laughed softly, his eyes on her. "You're getting to be quite a patriot."

"Aren't you?" Callie asked at once.

"Yes, I am. I love this country. I want to stay here always, the rest of my life." He got up, moved around the fire, and filled two cups with coffee from the blackened saucepan. When he came back, he handed her one and then sat beside her. An owl flew over, a ghostly figure, and they both watched it until it disappeared into the darkness. Rees finished his coffee, put the cup down, then turned to her. "I wanted to ask you something."

"Yes, Rees?"

"Which of the men who want to come calling do you like the best?"

"Oh, I like Tom Jenkins as well as any."

"He's a fine man."

Rees fell silent, and when he did not speak, Callie finally grew restive. "Can I ask you something, Rees? Something real personal."

"Why, of course you can."

"I want to ask you about the woman you loved — Grace."

Her words brought Rees's head up and he turned to face her. "Grace? You want to know about her?"

"She meant a great deal to you."

"Yes. I loved her a lot."

"Do you still love her?"

"In a way I guess I do. I guess I always will. I'll never forget her. Of course, time blurs things and I forget a lot. Sometimes I forget what she looked like. I don't even have a painting of her."

Callie was quiet, and then finally she said, "I guess you'll be marrying Elaine Gifford one day."

"What makes you think that?"

"Well, you've been in love with her for a long time."

"You're wrong there, Callie. She's an attractive woman but we'll never marry. As a matter of fact, I got a letter from her. You remember? It said she was moving to England with her father. It was a good-bye letter."

Callie expelled her breath and said, "Well, thank God for that."

Rees looked at her quickly and saw a change come over her face. A warmth began to illuminate her eyes.

"Why are you thanking God for that? Didn't you like her?"

"I wanted to strangle her!"

"Callie, you didn't!"

"Yes, I did. She wasn't the woman to make you happy."

He took her hand and held it silently. The wind was making a keening noise. "How long have you been thinking like this?"

"A long time," Callie said.

Rees tightened his grip. "I've been telling you that it's all right for Tom Jenkins to come around, but I don't want him to do that."

"You don't want him calling on me?" Callie straightened, her eyes fixed on him. "You don't want me, and you don't want any other man to have me. Is that it?"

Rees blurted without thinking, "Who says I don't want you?"

"*I* say it!"

And even at that instant, as if a curtain had been lifted between them, Rees Kenyon knew the truth. He wondered at his own folly at not having recognized it sooner. He took her in, the fine features highlighted by the flickering fire, her lips lying together in a fullness that was provocative. Her breasts lifted and softly fell with her breathing, and her presence was an urgent thing pulling him toward her. The glow of her eyes came from a deep place, part of her spirit.

"Of course I want you."

Tears formed in Callie's eyes and she could not speak for a moment. "You don't show it, Rees Kenyon! Running around after that woman! You . . . you never treated me like a woman."

And then Rees knew what he wanted. "Is that what you want? To be treated like a woman?"

"Yes!"

Rees kissed her hand and held it as if it were a precious thing. Her eyes were fixed on him, and he put his free hand on her cheek. It was cold and smooth and he held it there for a long time. "Lovelier than Job's daughters you are, Callie Summers." He pulled her toward him and kissed her. It was a gentle kiss, for he knew at this moment that she needed gentleness. He was aware that she was crying, and when he drew back, the tears overflowed. He pulled out a handkerchief and whispered, "Please don't cry!"

"Oh, Rees, I've loved you such an awful long time, and you've never showed me that you cared!"

"Well, I will." He kissed her again and said, "Am I doing this right?"

"Well, not as well as Tom Jenkins — "

Rees grabbed her and squeezed her until she gasped, "Rees, you're crushing me!"

"You need a thrashing, woman! Now, do I kiss better than Tom?"

"Oh, much better!"

Rees released her then but kept his grasp tight as he held her in the circle of his arms.

"How long have you loved me, Rees?"

"That's the wrong question."

"What's the right question?"

"How long *will* I love you."

Happiness was revealed in Callie's lips, which were turned upward now in a smile, and in her eyes, which were glowing. She put her arms around his neck and raised her face within inches of his. "All right. How long will you love me?"

Rees shook his head. "I don't know. How long do you think you can keep me interested?"

And then Callie laughed — a rich, full laughter that came from deep within. "I think I can keep you home, Rees Kenyon." She kissed him, then put her head against his chest.

Rees held her tightly and whispered, "Yes, I think you can. I'll never leave you, Callie!"

Read an excerpt from Gilbert Morris's
*God's Handmaiden*

# Chapter One

A soft but persistent touch on her lips brought Gervase Howard out of sleep instantly. Opening her eyes, she saw Mr. Bob staring at her. Smiling, she stroked the head of the huge cat.

"Good morning, Mr. Bob. How are you this morning?"

The cat at once began to purr, the rumbles deep in his chest humming as if generated by a miniature engine. He rose at once, arched his back, and yawned mightily. Placing his front paws on Gervase's chest, he began kneading her powerfully, eyes half shut with pleasure. The purring reached a crescendo, and although the claws of the cat were painful, Gervase did not object.

"You've been fighting again, Mr. Bob. Why do you have to do that?"

Mr. Bob was a dark-gray tabby with a large blunt head marked with a dark *M* and scarred from many battles. The only white spot on him was at the tip of his tail, and when he held it up straight, it always reminded Gervase of a candle.

For a time Gervase lay there, shutting out everything except the cat. She stroked Mr. Bob as he continued to knead her chest; then finally she pulled him down, rolling over so she could face him. He had big golden eyes, round as shillings, and he watched her carefully, still purring.

"You're all I have left, Mr. Bob."

The whispered words frightened Gervase, and her vivid imagination suddenly began to function despite her attempts to will the world away. Ever since the funeral, she had tried to blot out the details of her future, but now, graphically and powerfully, she could see her mother's face as it had looked in the wooden coffin — pale, worn, completely different from the way she had appeared in life. Gervase closed her eyes but the image seemed to magnify itself. She clutched Mr. Bob tightly and forced herself to think of her mother as she liked to remember her best. A series of images flashed in front of her — her mother smiling and laughing, her blue-green eyes dancing. Gervase remembered a time when she had come to her mother hurt and frightened — she could not even recall why now — and her mother had simply picked her up and spun around until Gervase was dizzy. Then she had pulled Gervase onto her lap and held her tightly, whispering comfort.

That poignant memory triggered others like it, for Gervase's mother had always known how to give comfort to her only daughter. Sometimes she had quoted Scripture, always with a fervency and a faith that Gervase had never seen in anyone else. At other times she had sung happy songs to Gervase, sometimes popular songs but more often hymns they sang together in the Methodist chapel they attended every Sunday. Often she would tell Gervase fantastic stories filled with wonder and hope. Somehow she had always been able to drive away Gervase's fears and anxieties.

The memories were jolted and driven away as Mr. Bob began to protest. He stiffened his legs and squirmed, saying, "Yow!" — which meant, as Gervase well knew, "It's time to turn me loose."

She released her grip and the big cat sat up and began washing his face. Then he gave himself a complete bath. Enviously Gervase thought, *I wish I had no more worries than you have, Mr. Bob.* But she did not dwell on this.

Throwing back the worn coverlet, she stepped out of the bed and stood for a moment, dreading the day. Then she dressed hurriedly, putting on her one good dress — the one she had worn to the funeral — and moved to the oak washstand. Slowly she washed her face and then, looking into the small mirror, brushed her hair. As always, for a moment she stared at herself, disliking what she saw, for she felt plain and homely. She had a thin face dominated by large blue-green eyes she had inherited from her mother. Her hair was light blond and came down well below her shoulders. There was a slight curl in it, and she quickly bound it up so it made a bun on the back of her head.

She looked down at herself, frowning, for at the age of fifteen she was very thin indeed. She knew other girls her age who had already blossomed into womanly contours. Another memory of her mother, whispering to her, *"You're going to be a beautiful young girl. Right now you are like one of the colts you see out in the pasture — all legs and awkward. But that will pass."*

Gervase quickly turned away and moved into the other room. Her only hope for beauty was that her mother had been a well-shaped woman with winsome features. *If I could only be as pretty as Mum!*

She halted abruptly and stared at the calendar her mother had made: a single sheet of paper with the weeks set out in pencil. Gervase touched it, sadness welling up as she remembered her mother urging her to draw birds at the top for decoration. She ran her fingers over the year, 1851, and the scrolled word *May.* She stopped at the number 5 and her throat grew thick — for she had circled the number when she came home from her mother's funeral.

Turning to avoid the calendar, she blinked back the tears and looked around the room. This was the only home she had ever known, and she was saddened further at the thought that this was the last day she would spend in it. There were only the two rooms, the bedroom and this one, the larger, which served for all other purposes. Two windows at one end of the room let in the feeble sunlight that illuminated it. She stared at the walls she had helped her mother paper. The wall covering had been salvaged from the dump — evidently, a wealthy patron had had too much. It featured small bluebirds and thrushes singing their hearts out. She had a painful memory of the day they had pasted the paper on, and she immediately moved toward the woodstove which served for both heat and cooking. The rest of the furniture included a pine table and four chairs — none of which matched — a settee, and beside it a lamp. A bookcase made of boxes was now empty, for Gervase had given away most of the books, keeping only a few. She had spent the week since the funeral getting rid of things, giving some of them away, selling some for what she could get, and now the room looked bare and alien — not at all like the warm, cheerful place in which she had grown up.

Deliberately pushing these thoughts from her mind, Gervase built a fire. She was very efficient at this and soon it was blazing. She had given away all the groceries to Mrs. Warden, who had a houseful of youngsters, retaining only enough for this final breakfast. She fried the last of the bacon and the one thin slice of ham, but when she sat and tried to eat, the food seemed to stick in her throat. When she picked up the last of the bread she had saved, the thought came to her, *This was the last loaf of bread Mum ever made.* The thought so distressed her that she quickly put the bread down and wiped her lips.

Mr. Bob came to press against her leg, and she broke the rest of the ham into small fragments and set it down. She watched as he wolfed the morsels down eagerly, then looked up and said, "Yow!" — which meant, "More, please!" Gervase snatched him and pressed her face against his fur, whispering,

"That's . . . that's all there is, Mr. Bob, but I'm sure we'll have plenty for you in our new place."

The thought of a new place disturbed Gervase and she got up at once. Picking up the bread, she went out the back door and began dividing the bread and tossing the crumbs on the ground. Quickly birds began to gather, mostly sparrows that were so tame now, they came almost close enough to take the bread out of her hand. It was a daily ritual for her, and had been so for so long that she could not remember when it first began. The birds chirped and made cheerful noises, scuffling in the dust and battling over the crumbs. "You don't have to fight. There's plenty today."

As she broke off bits of bread and tossed them on the ground, she lifted her head. This was the sight most familiar to her: a long line of identical houses jammed together so closely that one could scarcely squeeze between them. They ran in a curving circle down a hill, and all had clotheslines out back, most of them containing garments swaying in the breeze like lazy ghosts. Children were out now in a few of the yards, and she could hear their voices as they shouted and laughed.

It was a poor enough section of the small village. Almost all the inhabitants of the poorly painted houses worked in the garment mill. Smoke was rising in ragged gray streams from the chimneys of the dwellings, scoring the sky, which seemed clear of clouds for the first time this May.

There was nothing beautiful about the scene, yet Gervase Howard almost cried out as she realized that this would be the last day she would see it.

⤳

"Gervase? There you are, darlin'!"

Agnes Warden noted that Gervase was wiping furtively at her eyes, and felt a quick pang of pity. Gervase's mother had been Agnes's closest friend, and the heavyset woman was sad as she approached and stood before the young girl. Shifting her two-week-old baby girl to a more comfortable position, she said, "We're going to miss you so much, Gervase — especially Betsy here."

Gervase took the baby, cuddled her and touched her cheek, watching the bubbles that rose from the red lips. "I'll miss you, too, Miss Agnes, and . . . and the children." Misery was written across her face. "Oh, I wish I could stay here!"

Mrs. Warden made a comforting noise as she hugged her. "You'll be much better off with your uncle and aunt, luv. Everybody needs family, and it's a fine place where they live, ain't it?"

"I guess so. I don't know them, Miss Agnes."

The woman wanted to say something to comfort the young girl but nothing came. She had always loved Charlotte Howard and this daughter of hers, and the death had hit her hard indeed. Death was common enough in this place but it was never easy.

"I miss Mama, Miss Agnes!"

"Why, of course you do! You wouldn't be a good girl if you didn't — but the Lord took her to himself, dearie, and he's given you a home. You'll have your uncle and aunt to love you, and you'll make many friends."

Gervase handed the infant back. "The vicar is supposed to come and pick me up very soon, so I'll say goodbye now." She threw her arms around the woman, whispering, "Goodbye, Miss Agnes." Then she kissed the baby. "Goodbye, Betsy. Be a good girl." Agnes watched sadly as Gervase turned and walked blindly away.

For a long moment Agnes stared after the slight form of the young girl; then she turned and walked slowly back toward her own house. She was greeted by Bertha Willington, a tall, thin woman who lived in the house next to hers.

"How's she taking it, dearie?" Bertha asked.

"She's bleeding in her 'eart, she is, but there's nothing else for it."

"Wot about the aunt, the one she's a-going to? Is she a good 'un?"

"Oh, I never met her, and Gervase only met her once, years ago. But Charlotte said as 'ow she was a good woman."

"They wasn't too close, was they?"

"No. They lived too far apart, but she's quick, Gervase is. She'll make a place for 'erself."

"But I'll miss the both of them."

"So will I. She's a dear child!"

~⁓~

"Whoa, Geraldine, stop now! Do you hear me?"

The Reverend Gerald Howells tugged at the reins and brought the brown mare to a stop. She shook her head rebelliously and would have gone on, but Howells jerked the lines again, saying, "That's enough, now! You're too blasted ambitious!"

Reverend Howells sat very still in the small buggy, considering the task that lay before him. It had been a hard thing, the funeral of Charlotte Howard, as it always was when a child was left an orphan. Howells had developed a great affection for Mrs. Howard, for she was a faithful member of the church. She had little money to spare, but anytime there was work to be done or a case of need, she was always ready to give what help she could. The funeral had been better attended than he expected. He was surprised to discover how many friends Charlotte Howard had made in her brief lifetime. Her husband had died not long after they were married, and now there was only the child Gervase. It was to this problem that the minister now gave his thoughts.

Howells was not an impulsive man by any means. He liked his sermons well planned, as he liked everything else. It disturbed him when routines were broken, and often before a difficult interview he would go over what he planned to say. Now his lips moved as he reviewed the speech he had been working on. The mare's ears twitched, though she was accustomed to her master's soliloquies.

"Now, my dear Gervase, this has been very hard for you," Howells whispered. "You and your mother were so close — and with no father, even closer. I know your grief has been almost unbearable. But you must put that behind you, child, and I thank God that you have an uncle and an aunt who are willing to take you in. From all reports, they are respectable and good people indeed. Their invitation was most warm and you will have a good home. You will be lonely but that's only natural. Now you must look forward. Treasure your mother's dear memory, but she would want you to be happy in your new place."

For a moment Howells sat wondering how his speech would be received by the child, but he could do no better. Securing the reins, he stepped off the buggy and gave the mare a pat. "There, Geraldine, you behave yourself." Then he moved toward the house. He was a long, limber man and a busy one. This task of seeing Gervase safely embarked was the chore he had most on his mind this day.

When Howells knocked on the door, it opened almost at once, and he smiled and took off his hat. "Good morning, Gervase."

"Good morning, Vicar."

"I came a little early so I might help you take care of any chores remaining."

"Everything is ready. I'm all packed. Come in, please."

As the vicar stepped inside, he glanced around the room. It was a poor enough place, as were all the houses on the Row, but everything was clean and neat. He nodded. "The new tenants will appreciate moving into a home this tidy." He waited for the girl to respond, but he saw that her face was tense, and she seemed unable to speak. "Well now," he said as cheerfully as he could, "we may as well go a little early. Let me help you with your things."

"The box is in the bedroom, sir."

Howells went into the room and picked up the box, surprised at its weight. As he carried it out, he asked, "What do you have in here, Gervase?"

"All the things of my mother's that I could keep. Some of her books and a few pictures and some of my things that I had when I was a little girl."

"That's very good. You sold everything else, I suppose?"

"I gave a lot of it away."

"That's a good child." Howells went outside and loaded the heavy box into the buggy, then returned. Gervase was holding a rather large bag of some sort. "What is that, Gervase?"

"These are my clothes."

"And this?" Howells motioned to a wicker basket.

"That's Mr. Bob."

"Mr. Bob?"

"Yes sir, my cat."

Howells appeared disturbed. "You're taking your cat with you? I'm not sure that's wise."

Instantly Gervase drew up, her whole body taut. "Oh, sir, I have to take Mr. Bob with me! I've had him since he was a kitten."

"Yes, child, but —"

"I've got to have him, sir! I won't go without him!" Gervase blinked rapidly several times and her voice was unsteady. "I found him when he was just a little kitten, four years ago. He would've died if it hadn't been for me. I fed him with drops of milk and I can't leave him here, sir!"

Reverend Howells suddenly felt a great compassion for this girl. "Well, I'm sure your uncle and aunt will understand."

"I hope so," Gervase whispered, and then she looked the minister straight in the eye. "I won't stay if they won't let me keep Mr. Bob."

Howells was taken somewhat aback by this defiant statement. He knew that the child was afraid, as any youngster would be under the circumstances, but there was a purpose in her he had not seen before. He cleared his throat. "Well, I will write them a letter and ask them to let you keep Mr. Bob."

"Oh, thank you, Reverend!"

"There, there. Don't let that be a bother to you." Howells reached into his pocket and pulled out a small cloth purse. "This is a gift from some of the members of our congregation." He extended the purse and when Gervase took it, he nodded. "You might need a little extra."

"I wish I could thank them, sir. Will you thank them for me?"

"Of course I will." Howells hesitated, his rehearsed speech on the tip of his tongue, but somehow he felt it would not do. He cleared his throat and said briskly, "Well, are we ready to go?"

"Would you carry this, and I'll bring Mr. Bob?"

"Of course."

Gervase handed over the sack containing her clothes and picked up the wicker basket. From inside came a plaintive meow and Gervase said, "It's all right, Mr. Bob." She walked outside and the minister accompanied her. He put the bag in the back of the buggy and asked, "Do you want me to put your cat beside us?"

"Yes, please."

The minister took the wicker basket and his eyes widened. "He is a heavy cat!"

"He weighs over a stone."

"How did you figure that? You don't have scales, do you?"

"No, but we got flour in one-pound bags and I found stones that weighed the same. I put a board down and put him on one end and put the stones on the other until it balanced. He weighs sixteen pounds."

"A fine animal, and I'm sure he will be a comfort to you." The two got in the buggy and Howells picked up the reins. "All right, Geraldine, now you can go." He slapped the lines on the back of the mare, who started out at a lively pace.

As the buggy moved forward, Howells glanced at the girl, noting that her thin face was pale. She looked straight ahead for a time until they reached the top of the hill, and then she turned around. He had a full view of her face then. It was a good face, with a child's immature features. Her lips trembled but she said nothing. Finally she turned forward again, and he said cheerfully, "Now then. Have you ever ridden in a coach before?"

"No sir. I never have."

"Well, it will be an experience for you. I think you'll like it!"

As the wheels of the coach dropped into a pothole, all the passengers were jarred and thrown to the left. The coach had been practically empty when Gervase got on, but it had picked up passengers as they went along. It was the middle of May and hot and dusty so that perspiration ran down the faces of all the passengers. The coach seats had straight backs and no padding, making them uncomfortable. All morning long the coach had lurched over the rough road, picking up passengers and putting out a few, and eventually Gervase found herself sitting between a young man with a disagreeable countenance and a very large, rather silent man. She was holding Mr. Bob's basket in her lap, and from time to time he would meow and she would open the lid enough to slide her hand in and caress his head.

"Coaches is for people, not for mangy cats," the young man said harshly. He had a dirty face and his clothes were rough. He was evidently a working man, rather short and skinny. His teeth were bad and his breath was terrible. "I can't stand mangy cats!"

Gervase said nothing, for she was afraid. The other passengers seemed indifferent but the young man kept complaining.

Finally the big man sitting on the other side of Gervase turned. He was well dressed and wore a gold ring with a green stone on his right forefinger. "You have your cat there, do you, miss?"

Gervase quickly glanced at him and saw that he was smiling at her.

"Yes sir, I do."

"I've always liked cats myself. Look, now — you move over and take my seat by the window. Here, I'll hold your cat while you do that."

Gervase did not know what to do, but his smile encouraged her. She stood up and the big man moved to the center of the seat, holding the wicker basket high. "There you are," he said, giving it back to her after she sat again. "Now you can take him out of that box for a while and let him breathe some fresh air."

"This ain't no cat coach," the young man growled. "It's fer people."

The big man turned and leaned over, his weight crushing the smaller man. "You shut your mouth about this young lady's cat or I'll throw you through the window!"

The young man looked up, ready to argue, but something he saw in the big man's face caused him to reconsider. "None of my affair," he muttered sulkily and turned to stare out the window.

"Right enough," the big man said. He turned to Gervase. "Now, take your cat out and let him look around. He's been in that box all morning."

"Will it be all right?"

"I say it will be."

Gervase opened the lid and took Mr. Bob out. He stretched and sat in her lap and made no attempt to get away.

"Well, he's a right good one, ain't he now?" the big man said. He reached over and stroked the cat's head and asked, "What's his name?"

"His name is Mr. Bob."

"Well, Mr. Bob, let's me and you make friends. We got a way to go before we get to London. . . ."

# Edge of Honor

_Gilbert Morris_

Quentin Larribee is a surgeon—one of the best. But in the confusion of one of the Civil War's last, desperate skirmishes, the hands devoted to healing bring death to William Breckenridge, an enemy soldier in the act of surrendering. Now the deed haunts Quentin.

A bright future lies before him, with marriage to the lovely Irene Chambers and eventual ownership of her father's prosperous medical practice. But it cannot ease Quentin's troubled conscience. Honor compels him to see to the welfare of the dead man's family. Quentin moves from New York City to the little town of Helena, Arkansas, where he attempts to save the wife of Breckenridge and her children from financial ruin.

_Edge of Honor_ is an unforgettable novel of redemption and honor, where good is found in the unlikeliest places and God's unseen hand weaves a masterful tapestry of human hearts and lives.

Softcover: 978-0-310-28796-4

## The Ultimate Journey.
## The Impossible Decision.

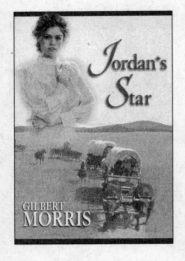

# Jordan's Star

### *Gilbert Morris*

Bound for the Oregon frontier, Jordan Bryce and her new husband, Colin, a dashing ex-mariner, face danger from both man and nature: a deadly buffalo stampede . . . tragedy at a river crossing . . . hostile Indians . . . and hatred within their wagon train, escalating from bitter words to the point of bloodshed. All that separates the Bryce's party from disaster is seasoned leadership, the skillful guidance of Ty Sublette, and the hand of God.

For Jordan, the journey west is more than a trip into an untamed land. It is a passage from a teenage girl's romantic fantasies to the wisdom and character of womanhood. But nothing can prepare Jordan for the testing that awaits her beyond the journey's end. There, in the face of staggering circumstances, she will face an impossible decision . . . as two good men—one wounded by past grief, the other branded by his own impetuousness—struggle with the demands of faith and honor on behalf of the woman they love.

Softcover: 978-0-310-22754-0

*Pick up a copy today at your favorite bookstore!*

**ZONDERVAN**®
.com

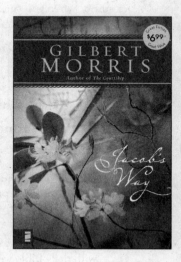